Enticements

N.J. WALTERS

D1157446

ELLORA'S CAVE
ROMANTICA® PUBLISHING

What the critics are saying...

∾

Capturing Carly

5 Cupids "This is a definite winner with two characters to love, a plot that is erotic, emotional and captivating and like a glorious cherry on top this book is just so well written."
~ *Cupid's Library Reviews*

5 Angels "The chemistry between Nathan and Carly held me captive from the first page with its playful streak and then glued to my seat with the intensely hot display of passion."
~ *Fallen Angel Reviews*

"The author continues to shine with this latest installment! It is filled with an intense eroticism and two vibrant characters that the reader will fall in love with." ~ *The Road to Romance Reviews*

"A book that touches our deepest feelings and totally brings us into the middle of the story. I love the depth of emotion and passion so easily evoked by the author."
~ *Romance Reviews Today*

4.5 Stars "Ms. Walters has given this reader spine tingling chills and heart pounding delight while reading of this romance between such a loveable couple." ~ *Ecataromance Reviews*

4/5 Stars "From a little bondage, to a whole lot of passionate loving, these sex scenes scream with ecstasy. Sex aside, the love between Carly and Nathan is tactile while their relationship is both believable and desirable." ~ *Just Erotic Romance Reviews*

CRAVING CANDY
Winner of the 2008 Eppie Award in the Erotic Contemporary/Suspense/Mystery Category!

Joyfully Recommended "Craving Candy is poignant, sexy as all get out, and I am completely in love with Lucas. It is the perfect story for Lucas and N. J. Walters has another winner on her hands." ~ *Joyfully Reviewed*

"N. J. Walters is an exciting writer who from the first page totally involves you in a story and holds your interest until the last word. [...] Its hot and exciting writing is sure to titillate and enthrall you." ~ *Romance Reviews Today Erotic*

5 Angels "The instantaneous chemistry is as sweet as the treats Lucas cooks up. [...] N.J. Walters did a tremendous job creating a story worth reading and reinforcing why she is a favorite author of mine." ~ *Fallen Angel Reviews*

5 Hearts "Ms. Walters delivered with CRAVING CANDY another terrific keeper. She has a talent to write very steamy and emotional stories that keep her readers absolutely captivated and to bring her characters to life." ~ *Love Romances and More Reviews*

4 ½ Hearts "I couldn't put the book down and when my Palm Pilot died from a low battery I scrambled to my computer to finish this story. This is the fourth in Ms. Walters's Awakening Desires series and let me tell you. [...] Desires were awakened!" ~ *The Romance Studio Reviews*

An Ellora's Cave Romantica Publication

www.ellorascave.com

Enticements

ISBN 9781419957840
ALL RIGHTS RESERVED.
Capturing Carly Copyright © 2005 N.J. Walters
Craving Candy Copyright © 2006 N.J. Walters
Edited by Pamela Cohen and Mary Altman.
Cover art by Syneca.

This book printed in the U.S.A. by Jasmine-Jade Enterprises, LLC.

Trade paperback Publication June 2008

ENTICEMENTS

ജ

CAPTURING CARLY

CRAVING CANDY

CAPTURING CARLY

℘

Dedication

❧

A huge thank you to Pamela, whose enthusiasm for Nathan inspired me to give him a book of his own. And as always, thanks to my husband for allowing me to talk through all my problems and ideas. This book would never have happened without you both.

Chapter One

ഗ

"You'd better run." Nathan Connors growled as he pulled the vehicle to a halt in front of Carly's house. He wasn't sure if she'd heard him, but she had already jumped out of the truck and was running up the walkway. Her laughter trailed behind her, making him smile. That's what she did for him. She made him smile, made him feel complete.

Grabbing his keys out of the ignition, he hurried after her. She already had her keys out and was unlocking the front door. God, she made him hot just standing there.

Carly Ames was five feet and three inches of pure temptation. Rounded in all the right places, her plain black skirt and white blouse hid a body that was made for sin. His mouth watered at the thought of tasting the sweet pink nipples that tipped her rather impressive breasts. He loved the way they hardened at his slightest touch. Her hips were wide, her ass a handful, and she made him hotter than a teenage boy with his first girl.

Glancing over her shoulder, she shot him a grin as she shoved the door open with her hand. When she saw him right behind her, it quickly widened into a genuine smile that was reflected in her blue eyes, which shone with happiness. She had light brown hair that was cut short for convenience as well as style, but it suited her round face and her small, tip-tilted nose to perfection.

She looked like an angel, but Nathan knew that beneath her angelic exterior lay a fiery temper and a wicked sense of humor. His cock was already hard and straining against the front of his jeans. It seemed that no matter how many times he fucked her, he still wanted her.

Putting all her weight into it, she leaned against the door, trying to close it behind her. He caught it with the flat of his hand and easily shoved it open. Carly jumped back and the door crashed into the wall behind it before bouncing back. Nathan stepped inside and kicked it shut with his boot, shutting the world outside. She licked her lips as she gazed up at him.

Keeping his eyes locked on her, he followed her tongue as it glided across her plump, full lips. He wanted to taste them and suck on them until she moaned. He'd never met a woman who turned him on as quickly or easily as Carly.

But it was more than that. Quite simply, she fascinated him. She was one of the most intelligent women he'd ever met, but it was balanced with a commonsense attitude that made her a force to be reckoned with. All of that was tempered with genuine kindness and compassion. She was one of a kind. And she was his.

The last few weeks had been incredibly explosive. But he supposed that that was only natural. He'd lusted after her for years, but had kept her at arm's length, certain that his taste in sex would probably shock her to death. Not only that, she was his sister's best friend and a smart man knew that there were unwritten rules about dating your sister's best friend.

But everything had changed a few weeks ago.

He'd had been looking for his sister, Erin, one night and had gone to Carly's house expecting to find her there. Instead, he'd found Carly home alone naked, except for a flimsy blue robe that had enticed more than it had covered.

One thing had led to another and they'd finally succumbed to the hot flood of passion that flowed between them. They'd gotten engaged that same night. There was no way he was letting her slip away from him now that he finally had her.

Her chest was rising and falling rapidly as she backed away from him. Whether it was because of her run from the truck or from anticipation, he didn't know. With every breath she took, her breasts moved up and down. Her nipples were puckered into hard nubs, pushing against the front of her shirt.

"Take off your blouse."

Shooting him a saucy grin, she raised her hand to the top button and slipped it out of the hole. Slowly, she lowered her hand and traced her finger around the next white plastic circle. The little vixen was teasing him.

His hand shot out and snagged the front of her blouse. Her eyes widened as he tugged her closer. Gripping the sides of the garment, he ripped it open. Buttons popped and fell to the floor, rolling in every direction.

Her laugh was low and sexy as she raised her hands to his chest and her nimble fingers stroked the front of his T-shirt, massaging the muscles beneath it. "Was I too slow?" She gave him a sultry smile as she batted her long dark lashes at him.

Instead of answering, he shoved the torn blouse down over her shoulders. She removed her hands from his chest, allowing him to slip the garment off. He let it fall on the floor and went straight to work on her bra. Unhooking the back closure he slipped it down over her arms, but not off. When the lacy bra was dangling around her wrists, he quickly wrapped it around her wrists binding them together.

"Nathan?" He could hear the question in her voice.

"You know better than to disobey me." He traced a callused finger over one of her puckered nipples and she shivered. "Now you have to pay up."

Her eyes were wide blue pools of desire as she stared up at him. "What…what price?"

"Whatever I want." Backing her against the wall, he gripped her bound hands in one of his and slowly raised them over her head, hooking them around the back of her neck. Stepping back, he admired her half-naked body. "Beautiful." With her hands behind her neck and her elbows wide, her breasts were thrust forward. Their pink nipples were too tempting to ignore.

Lowering his head, he slowly kissed and nuzzled the pale mounds, taking care to give equal time to each one. Carly made little mewling sounds and pushed her breasts closer to his face. Flicking out his tongue, he rasped one of the swollen buds, savoring its texture before taking it into his mouth and sucking softly on it.

"Nathan." Her breathy moan made his cock swell even more. Reaching down, he unbuttoned his jeans and undid the zipper. He shoved his underwear out of the way, allowing his cock to spring free.

"Soon, honey, soon," he crooned as he shifted to her other puckered nipple, giving it the attention it demanded.

While he feasted on her breasts, he skimmed his hands down her sides and around to the small of her back. The rasp of her zipper was loud in the small foyer as he lowered it. Nathan shoved the skirt downward and Carly gave her hips a shimmy, helping it slip from her body.

Burying his face between her breasts, he breathed in her sweet scent of vanilla and arousal before kneeling in front of her. His lips kissed the smooth, creamy expanse of her stomach, gradually moving lower. When he stuck his tongue in her belly button, she sucked in her breath. Her tummy began to shake and he raised his head, cocking an eyebrow at her.

She tried to suppress her laughter, but it escaped her. "I can't help it," she managed to gasp out between giggles. "I'm ticklish."

Growling, he nipped at the band of her panties with his teeth. As he slowly tugged the garment lower, her laughter faded and she moaned instead. Nathan licked and kissed her inner thigh as he used his hands to push her underwear all the way down her legs. Carly lifted one foot at a time and he tugged off the underwear, pulling off her shoes at the same time. She was left wearing nothing but her thigh-high stockings.

"Spread your legs." Her legs parted immediately and he buried his face in her sweet pussy. She was already wet and ready for him, but he wanted her even hotter.

He tongued the slick folds of her sex, avoiding the hard nub at the apex. She pushed her hips forward, trying desperately to get him to touch her clit with his tongue. "Tell me what you want."

There was no hesitation. "I want you to lick my clit. I want to feel you inside me."

Nathan paused and gripped her hips tight in his hands and absorbed her words like a caress. His entire being was demanding that he take her now. He could feel his testicles drawing up tight to his body in anticipation. His cock flexed and liquid arousal seeped from the tip. But not yet. First, he wanted to pleasure Carly.

Spreading the lips of her sex wide with one of his hands, he finally drew his tongue over the swollen nub of flesh. She shoved her hips closer as he continued to lick at her clit. Slipping two fingers inside her pussy, he buried them deep before sliding them back out. They were coated with her cream.

Savage pleasure filled him. She wanted him as much as he wanted her.

He continued to work his fingers in and out of her slick pussy as he covered her clit with his lips and sucked. Her entire body jerked and heaved as she undulated against him.

"Don't stop." Her breathy cries filled the air as she cried out once more, coming against his face and his fingers.

He reveled in the gush of liquid that flowed down his hand. Her inner muscles clamped down tight on his fingers, trying to draw them deep. But he withdrew them and lapped at her cream, enjoying the evidence of her orgasm.

Lazily, he nuzzled and sucked her pussy until he felt her slump against him. Coming to his feet, he grabbed the ends of his T-shirt and hauled it over his head before unhooking her hands from around her neck and slipping them around his neck. Her head came up and she gifted him with a satisfied smile.

Gathering her close, he kissed her forehead, her cheek and her nose, before taking her luscious lips. They were soft and parted eagerly for him, so he took her mouth, claiming it as his.

Using his tongue, he tasted every part of her mouth before enticing her tongue to play with his. Then he withdrew. Triumph filled him when her tongue followed his. He sucked it into his mouth, toying with it.

Every throb of his cock was painful now. He could feel a bead of sweat rolling down his back and disappearing in the waistband of his jeans. Carly's tight nipples rasped against his chest and he could feel her heart pounding against his. Her fingers gripped the hair on the back of his head, tugging his mouth closer to her.

Gripping her hips in his hands, he picked her up and wedged his body between her legs, spreading them wider. She wrapped her legs around him and tilted her pelvis up, trying to take his erection inside her. Supporting her with one arm, he shoved his jeans and underwear further down, grinding his erection hard against her silky mound.

Gripping his cock in his hand, he teased her pussy with the swollen head. Pleasure shot through his body as he traced the folds of her sex, moistening his erection with her cream. At this point, he didn't know who he was teasing more, him or her.

Pushing the head of his cock just inside her swollen slit, he savored the feeling of her wet inner muscles gripping him tight, drawing him deeper. One slow inch at a time, he entered her.

Carly pulled her mouth from his and tilted her head back against the wall as she dug her heels into his back. Burying his face in the curve of her neck, he pushed himself home.

Neither of them moved. The sensation of being held in her hot depths was almost enough to make him come. He concentrated on taking deep breaths until he finally managed to regain some control. Then he began to thrust.

Keeping her back braced against the wall, he slowly pulled back until just the head of his cock was still inside her pussy. Driving hard, he buried himself to the hilt. Over and over, he slammed his hips against hers. His balls slapped against her with every stroke, adding to the pleasure that was building inside him.

Her pussy expanded and contracted around him. She gripped him so tightly, he could feel her fingernails in his scalp. Both of them were panting hard now, gasping for breath, as he kept up the driving rhythm. Gripping the sensitive flesh at the base of her throat with his teeth, he nipped hard as he thrust into her one last time.

His cock jerked and his entire body heaved as he came inside her hot, silky depths. She cried out and arched herself against him, her entire body drawn tight as a bow. Giving one big shudder, she came.

He could feel the hot gush of her orgasm around his cock. Unable to stop himself, he pulled himself almost out and shoved his cock back in again. Carly cried out and then sagged forward into his arms.

Sinking slowly to his knees, he wrapped her tight in his arms and inhaled the raw smell of sex as he savored the feel of her lush body next to his. Every breath she took ruffled the hairs on his neck. As she snuggled closer, the hard nubs of her breasts pushed against him. As he stroked his hands up and down her back, caressing her soft skin, his mind drifted.

It was necessary for him to be in charge of his woman's sexual pleasure in order to be satisfied himself. He'd expected an independent woman like Carly to be appalled by his sexual wants and needs. It had surprise both of them when, she'd not only accepted his sexual demands, she'd embraced them. The woman was his perfect match in every way, and once he'd claimed her, it was for keeps.

He knew that she was still a little uncomfortable at times, acquiescing to him sexually. And that made him uneasy. He'd kept the last few weeks fairly light and undemanding, giving her time to get used to him and what he wanted from her. This was the most he'd asked of her since their first explosive night together. And it had been perfect.

Carly stirred restlessly in his arms. Reluctantly, he lowered her arms from around his neck and unwound her bra from her hands. He kissed both of her wrists before lowering her arms to her sides.

Giving him a sleepy smile, she snuggled closer, resting her head on his shoulder. "That was amazing."

His arms closed tighter around her as he cradled her smaller, softer body against his large, hard frame. "You're amazing." Kissing her temple, he reluctantly lifted her off him. Her pussy made a sucking sound, trying to keep his cock in her moist depths. Nathan resisted the temptation to thrust again. Barely.

Standing, he hitched up his jeans and underwear around his hips before tugging her to her feet. Scooping her into his arms, he carried her down the hall to her bedroom. There was still over a month until their wedding. More than enough time for Carly and him to solidify their sexual relationship.

Chapter Two

ဢ

Nathan smiled and shook his head as he watched his sister being carried off by her new husband. He didn't blame Abel for dragging her away from the wedding and off to their wedding night. Erin looked happier than he'd ever seen her as she waved over Abel's shoulder.

The wedding was starting to wind down now that the bride and groom were leaving. He was glad that the whole event had gone off without a hitch and had made his sister happy. He just wished it were his wedding night. His and Carly's. It couldn't come a minute too soon for him.

Nathan walked up behind Carly as she buried her nose in the roses of his sister's wedding bouquet. It had been ten long days since he'd taken her in the foyer of her house. He wrapped his arms around her and pulled her back against his chest. "I can't wait much longer." His days were filled with frustration, as he and Carly could barely seem to get two minutes together lately.

"I know," she leaned back against his chest and sighed. "I've just been so busy, especially with two of my staff down with the flu."

"And I've been working double shifts. Some of the guys at work are down with the same damned thing." Nathan tugged Carly back into the shadows and kissed the back of her neck.

"Hmm," she agreed as she tilted her neck to one side to give him better access.

"I don't think I can take three more weeks of waiting," Nathan grated out between clenched teeth. His cock was so hard against the front of his pants he thought he might explode. He tortured himself further by rubbing it against her rounded backside.

Moaning, she pushed her ass back against him. His hands started to slide up toward her breasts. "Carly." A woman's voice broke the sensual spell between them. Nathan groaned and buried his face in her hair.

Nathan kept Carly in front of him as her mother walked toward them. Nathan liked her parents. Jenny and Carl Ames were good people. But right now, he wished them to the devil. They'd come home a week ago to spend the month with their daughter and help her get ready for her wedding. Since then he and Carly hadn't managed to get two minutes alone, even for a quickie.

Carly shot him a pleading look, begging him to understand. He bent down and nipped at her ear lobe. "Soon," he promised. "I won't wait much longer."

He nodded to her mother before stalking off in the other direction. He needed to be alone for a while. With his cock rock-hard, making a huge bulge in the front of his dress pants, he wasn't fit for polite company.

The sound of Erin's laughter caught his attention. He turned just in time to catch a last glimpse of her being whisked away. His sister looked happy with her new husband's arms wrapped tight around her. Hell, Abel looked happy too. And why wouldn't he, Abel Garrett knew he'd be spending the night with his woman. At that moment, Nathan envied his new brother-in-law.

* * * * *

Carly did her best to ignore the blatant stares of the men sitting at one of the window booths in her diner. Seasonal workers, here to help the farmers with the fall harvest, they were strangers and a bit more friendly than she'd like.

Pushing a lock of hair out of her eyes, she looked away and started another pot of coffee. They might lack manners, but they were still paying customers. She only wished they would keep their eyes on her face instead of her chest. To bad she hadn't thought to put on an apron on over her crisp white blouse and black skirt.

As she worked, she made mental lists of everything she had to do before the wedding. Carly could hardly believe how quickly the time was slipping away.

Frowning, she realized that she and Nathan had barely laid eyes on each other since Erin's wedding. Carly mentally tallied up the days. Nine days ago. That explosive encounter in her front entryway was the last time they'd been alone together, and that was beginning to seem almost like a dream.

Sighing, she consoled herself that in less than two weeks they'd be married and have all the time in the world to spend together. Butterflies fluttered in her stomach at the thought. Anticipation and fear mingled together, making her hands shake.

Lord, she was a mess. There was nothing more she wanted in the world than to be with Nathan. But, at the same time, the thought scared her. She'd always known that Nathan was very much an alpha male. He had an innate confidence and a take-charge personality that made him a great cop. Tough, but fair, he was very protective of those he considered under his care.

But she'd seen a whole other side of him since the first night they'd spent together. Nathan was an incredible lover. Just the thought of him was enough to make her cream her panties. His body was hard and strong and he was a very generous lover. The only thing he wanted was complete control in the bedroom.

She shook her head at her wayward thoughts. Never in her wildest fantasies had she ever imagined allowing any man to have complete control of her sexual pleasure. But with Nathan she had done just that. And furthermore, she'd loved every minute of it. And that scared her just the tiniest bit.

She chewed on her bottom lip as she grabbed the fresh-brewed pot of coffee and worked her way around the diner, filling empty cups. Nathan was even more intense than she'd ever guessed. It was as if he kept a part of himself leashed all the time, only giving the world a glimpse of the man he truly was.

Shaking off her melancholy mood, she cautiously approached the front booth. The four men were just finishing up their lunch. Plastering a polite smile on her face, she quickly refilled their empty coffee cups. But she wasn't quite quick enough.

She had to lean in over the table to reach two of the cups and she caught several of them trying to look down her blouse. *Morons.* Straightening back up, she glared at the worst offender. He looked to be in his mid-twenties and was good looking in his own way, but the cocky, smug look in his brown eyes made her want to smack him. And she wasn't a violent person.

"Do you want any dessert?"

Brown-eyes laughed as he stared at her breasts. "I like sweets, but what I'm looking for isn't on the menu."

Carly counted to ten, ignoring his thinly veiled innuendo. "We have apple, cherry and peach pie for dessert, as well as double chocolate fudge cake and chocolate chip cookies."

When the bell over the door rang, she automatically glanced over to see who was coming or going. This time a real smile covered her face as her best friend, Erin, walked through the door with Abel right behind her.

The feel of a hand on her bottom made her jump. Spinning around, she glared down at brown-eyes as he now held his hands up in mock surrender. "I couldn't resist such a sweet ass."

"My ass is not on the menu." She slapped their bill on the table. "Pay at the counter." Turning on her heel, she stalked away from the table, ignoring the male laughter that trailed after her.

She promptly forgot all about them as she walked into Erin's open arms and hugged her tight, careful to keep the coffeepot out of the way. They hadn't seen each other since Erin's wedding, so they had a lot of news to catch up on.

They were unlikely friends. Erin was tall and fit, with reddish hair, and she'd grown up on her family's farm. While Carly herself was a short, rounded brunette who'd lived in town and worked at her family's diner her entire life. But life was strange and the two of them had been best friends since grade school.

"You look so good." Pulling back, she stared up at her friend. Erin did look good. Fantastic, in fact. There was a glow of happiness that just radiated from her.

"Thanks. You, on the other hand, don't look so hot."

Carly shrugged off the other woman's concern, not wanting to get into anything. "I've just been working hard lately is all."

Erin continued to stare at her, concern filling her blue eyes. "Nathan doesn't look too great himself these days."

"Erin, honey, leave it alone." Abel wrapped his arm around his wife's waist and kissed the top of her head. Carly was thankful for the reprieve.

Smiling at him, she stood on her toes and kissed his cheek. He still had to lean down in order for her to be able to reach him. The man was huge. "Why don't you both sit down and I'll get you some coffee. We can catch up."

Abel caught her free hand before she could hurry behind the counter. "Trouble?" He jerked his head toward the booth where the four men were still drinking their coffee.

Carly shook her head. Then she shook it again, harder, as she caught the skeptical look in his eyes. He didn't quite believe her. "Really, it's okay. Just a little male posturing, but nothing I can't handle."

He said nothing, but he did let go of her hand. Ushering them both up to the counter, she hurried behind it. Pouring two fresh cups of coffee, she plunked them down on the counter in front of them. "So tell me everything."

Abel's booming laughter filled the diner and people's heads swiveled around as they looked to see what was so funny. Erin stared at her new husband, a blush crept up her cheeks and she began to giggle.

Carly could feel her own cheeks turning red. "Okay, so not everything." In spite of her embarrassment, she started to laugh. Their obvious happiness was infectious.

She served up two pieces of apple pie while she listened to Erin's news. Abel would stop chewing long enough to add his two cents worth occasionally, but mostly he just ate his pie and smiled at his wife.

"Less than two weeks until your wedding," Erin said with a huge grin on her face. "It's not long now."

"Don't remind me." The moment the words left her mouth, she wished she could call them back. Her friend's smile disappeared and the happiness faded from her eyes to be replaced by concern.

"Is there anything wrong?" Erin glanced at Abel and he stood immediately.

"I've got a few things to do, so I'll let you ladies talk." Leaning down, he kissed his wife's cheek.

She appreciated what they were trying to do, but Carly just didn't want to talk about her and Nathan right now. Filling up his cup again, she motioned him back to his seat. "Sit. There's nothing to talk about."

She offered up a smile, which must have looked pretty weak, because Erin was still giving her a funny look. "Really. I'm just a little frazzled right now." She must have been a bit more convincing this time because the worry slowly faded from Erin's eyes to be replaced by excitement once again.

"I'm here to help." Leaning over the counter, she grabbed Carly's hand. "Just tell me what you need me to do."

Carly stared at the hand wrapped around hers. It was a strong, sturdy hand, much like the woman it belonged to. She was very fortunate to have such a good friend, but she couldn't talk to her about Nathan. How could you tell your best friend that you were having doubts about your relationship with her brother? No, this was something that she had to work out on her own.

A motion by the front door caught her attention and she felt every nerve ending in her body come alive. Nathan. Damn, the man looked good striding across the room. His shoulders looked so wide under the crisp khaki of his uniform shirt. But it was the knowledge of what was under that shirt that was making her feel hot and uncomfortable. Her fingers tingled at the thought of running her fingers through the neat crisp mat of hair that covered that fine chest. She shifted as the ache between her thighs grew.

Ignoring both his sister and brother-in-law, Nathan reached over and snagged her hand out of Erin's grasp. "Hi, honey."

His voice washed over. It was low and intimate and filled with promise, and she all but melted into a puddle of need on the floor. She locked her knees to keep herself upright. "Hi."

Leaning over the counter, he planted a soft kiss on her lips before he sat down on one of the counter stools. Her fingers were still tangled with his.

"Well, don't mind us." Erin's amused comment broke the spell between them and Carly became very aware of her surroundings once again. Damn, the man made her forget all her good sense whenever he was around.

She tried to tug her hand away, but he just held it tighter. He kept his hold on her as he turned to his sister. "Hi, Erin. Hi, Abel." He arched a brow at his sister. "Good enough?"

Laughing, Erin leaned over and planted a quick kiss on his cheek. "It'll have to be."

Dr. Jenkins, the local veterinarian, waved toward the counter, catching Carly's attention and pointing at his coffee cup. He was a regular customer and she knew that his lunch break was almost over. "I'll be right back." Leaving the others to talk, she grabbed a fresh pot of coffee and hurried toward his table.

Unfortunately, she had to pass the booth with those four jerks again. She kept her head turned toward Dr. Jenkins, determined to ignore them. The hand squeezing her ass took her off guard. She should have expected it, but she couldn't quite believe he'd actually have the nerve to grope her yet again.

"What is wrong with you?" She swung around so fast some of the coffee sloshed out of the pot and over her hand. The hot liquid burned her skin and she quickly plunked the pot on the table and cradled her hand against her chest.

"Let me see." Nathan's calm voice came from right next to her. He didn't wait for her to offer her hand, but reached out and took it in his. She could feel the tension in him as he examined the red splotches covering the back of her hand.

"It's not too bad." She tugged her hand away from him.

Nathan had already turned away from her and the men in the booth were now the recipients of his laser stare. "I suggest that you pay your bill and get out." It might have sounded like a suggestion, but the tone of his voice left no doubt in anyone's mind that it was an order. One of the men glanced from Nathan's badge and then to the gun strapped to his side.

"I can take care of this," she bristled, trying to edge her way in front of Nathan. He easily blocked her and she was left trying to look around him. This was her diner and this was her problem.

"There's nothing to take care of. These men are finished here." He never took his eyes off the men as he spoke.

"Hey, we don't want any trouble." One of the other men slid out of the booth. The others quickly followed. They paid quickly and then left. Brown-eyes glared at her as he walked out the door.

Carly glared right back at him. She was so mad she could scream. It might seem like people were eating their meals and minding their own business, but she knew that not one of them had missed a word of the entire exchange.

"You should have let me handle that." Brown-eyes might be gone, but Nathan was still here and she had quite a few things she wanted to say to him.

He forestalled her when he carefully lifted her hand and kissed her burn. "We need to see about your hand."

"But, I want to talk about this." She couldn't let this go so easily.

"It's done, Carly."

And that was that as far as he was concerned. His words deflated her anger and left her feeling slightly sad and tired. He had no idea how important it was for her to handle these things for herself. To him, taking care of a situation like this was nothing. He'd probably never even give it another thought. But to her, it was a matter of pride and being strong enough to take care of herself.

Dr. Jenkins was getting up from his table, forcing her to forget what had just happened for now and focus on the room full of customers she had. Grabbing the coffeepot, she hurried over to his table. "I'm so sorry about your coffee."

His smile was as genuine as the look of concern that he gave her. "It's no problem. But you should put something on that hand."

"I will," she promised. "I can give you a cup of coffee to go, if you'd like. It's on the house."

"That will be fine." She walked over to the counter with him, rang up his order and then got him a coffee to take out with him. She also bagged a couple chocolate chip cookies for him, knowing they were his favorite.

Melinda bustled over to the front cash register. "Let me finish ringing up customers. You need to put something on that hand." She jerked her head to the end of the counter. "Besides, I think Nathan is getting impatient.

Sure enough, when she glanced in that direction, he was staring right at her. Erin was talking to him, but his eyes never left her as she walked toward them.

"You need to see to your hand."

"I know that," her reply was sharp, but she was completely out of sorts and tired of everyone telling her what she should do. "I can take care of myself and I have enough common sense to take care of a burn."

"I know that, honey. I'm just worried about you."

Erin glanced at her husband, both of them watching the byplay between her and Nathan. Carly knew her reaction was totally unreasonable, but she didn't care. Nathan hadn't done anything out of character. In fact, she'd have been surprised if he hadn't done something. He was a protector by nature.

Carly was beginning to wonder if she was strong enough to handle a man like Nathan and not lose herself totally to him. He was so naturally protective and caring, it would be easy to give up control outside the bedroom as well. And that just wouldn't do. She wanted a real marriage, an equal one. She wanted to be strong enough for him to lean on when he needed to.

She snorted under her breath. Yeah, like that would ever happen. She couldn't imagine a situation where Nathan would ask for help with anything. Still, she wanted him to feel that he could if he needed to. But now, she was beginning to have doubts herself.

It also didn't help that she was trying to plan a wedding and working extra shifts at the diner. She also wasn't sleeping well because she lay awake at night wanting to be with

Nathan. Sexual frustration didn't make for a good night's sleep.

She didn't know if she wanted to curse or to cry, or both. Mostly, she wanted to have some time for them to just talk and to be together.

Nathan lowered his voice as he leaned toward her. "I've got a couple hours off, do you want to go out and have some lunch?"

The gleam in his eye and his low, intimate tone suggested he had more in mind than just lunch, and that was fine with her. Glancing around the diner, she decided that Melinda could handle the thinning crowd. The lunch rush was over and the forty-plus-year-old waitress had worked here since Carly was a teenager. She could handle anything.

Anticipation curled low in her belly and she squeezed her thighs together to ease the ache. She didn't care where they went as long as they got to be together.

"I'd love to have lunch." The words were barely out of her mouth when the bell over the front door rang loudly. Swallowing back a groan of disappointment, Carly watched with growing dread as her mother strode briskly toward them.

"Are you ready to go, dear?" Jenny Ames had the look of a general about to go into battle. Both men got up from their stools and stood back out of the way.

"Ready for what?" With all the different emotions swirling around inside her, she could barely think.

Her mother frowned at her. "We're going to get the final fitting done on your dress this afternoon. Really, Carly, we scheduled this last week."

Her heart dropped as a vague memory of her agreeing to this flashed in her brain. Regret filled her as she faced Nathan. He looked anything but pleased, but what could she do? Shrugging her shoulders, she offered him a tight smile. "I'm really sorry. I forgot all about this."

Jenny patted Nathan on the arm. "You'll have lots of time together when you're married. Right now, we've got a ton of things to do if we want this wedding to go off on time." Turning back to Carly, she shooed her toward the back of the diner. "Go get your things and I'll let Melinda know that I'm stealing you away for a few hours."

She opened her mouth to speak, but closed it again. Shaking her head, she sent Nathan a silent apology. He took a deep breath and slowly let it out. "I better get going and get back to work." Without another word, he turned and stalked away. As she watched him go, the butterflies began to jump in her stomach once again.

"I'd love to go, if you wouldn't mind."

Jerking her gaze back toward Erin, Carly missed her last sight of Nathan. Sighing, she gathered her scattered wits together and smiled at her best friend. "You know I'd love for you to come with us."

"I'll leave you to it then." Abel leaned down and captured Erin's mouth with his. It was a long, intimate kiss that didn't help Carly feel any better.

Muttering her goodbye to Abel, she hurried back to her office to get her things. She detoured to the bathroom first and dug through the first-aid kit for some ointment to put on her burn. It really wasn't that bad, just a couple of red splotches. Still, it was better not to take chances, so she slathered on some of the cream.

That done, she put everything away underneath the bathroom sink and went to her office. With one hand over her stomach to try and settle it, she grabbed her sweater off a hook and snagged her purse, slinging it over her shoulder. Locking her office door behind her, she straightened her shoulders and prepared to enjoy herself. And she'd do it too, even if it killed her.

Chapter Three

ॐ

Nathan grunted as he hefted the ladder in his hands. It was a beautiful October morning, and for the first time in weeks, both he and Carly had the morning off.

Then what the hell was he doing hanging storm windows?

Unfortunately, he could answer his own question. Carly's parents.

Carly had called him yesterday almost incoherent with excitement. Her parents were going to spend an entire day at a friend's cabin. Oh yeah, he'd been one happy man last night.

He'd had plans. Big plans. And they'd all revolved around Carly being naked and spread across her bed, awaiting his pleasure. Her sex would be pink, hot and wet as she spread her thighs wide for him. And those luscious breasts that he loved so much would be tipped with hard rosy nubs, begging to be tasted.

After he'd teased the soft white mounds for a while, he'd have her cup her own breasts so he could admire her tight nipples while he tasted the sweet heat between her legs. He wanted to lap at the slick folds of her pussy before sinking into her heated slit.

Groaning, Nathan dropped his head against the side of the small shed. Propping the ladder against the wall, he reached down and adjusted the erection straining against the front of his jeans. It didn't help. There was no way to make himself any more comfortable. Nothing would help but fucking Carly.

And that wasn't going to happen.

He'd pulled his truck up in front of her house at eight o'clock sharp this morning. Awake since six, he watched the clock impatiently and waited until he was sure her parents had left for their day of fishing and fun with their friends. The surge of pleasure had been so great that when he'd started up the walkway he'd all but run to her front door. Carly had promised she'd be naked and waiting for him.

She'd even told him, quite graphically, what she wanted him to do to her. Oh yeah, he'd planned to taste and touch every inch of her delectable body until she was hot, sweaty and begging him to fuck her.

Rock-hard and ready, he knew he couldn't wait. He'd planned on a quickie to relieve their tension before he settled down to really enjoy himself.

The first inkling he had that his day wasn't going to go quite as he'd planned came when Carly met him at the front door. She was fully dressed and looked very unhappy.

Stopping dead in his tracks, he'd waited for her to speak. Every muscle in his body was clenched as he braced himself for the disappointment he knew was coming.

She opened her mouth to speak, stopped, swallowed hard and tried again. "They cancelled."

She sounded so sad and forlorn that he bounded up the steps and wrapped his arms around her. "Who cancelled?" Burying her face against his chest, she mumbled something but he couldn't understand her.

Cupping her face in his hands, he tilted her face up to his. Unable to resist, he licked her top lip. Sweet. She always tasted so damned sweet. Needing another taste, he covered her lips with his. Gently. Carefully. He skimmed her mouth with his, not deepening the connection, just enjoying the feel of her soft lips against his.

The door behind her swung open. "Morning, Nathan." Carly's father stood in the doorway with a big smile on his face. "Carly said you were coming by to help me with the storm windows. It's a shame that Milo and his wife had to cancel out today, but it's a great day for doing a little work around the house."

Nathan straightened and stared at Carl Ames, trying to clear the sensual haze from his brain and make sense of his words. Everything clicked into place at once, including Carly's words and her disappointment now made sense. It was all he could do not to tip back his head and swear at the world.

Instead, he swallowed back his displeasure and gave Carly a squeeze before releasing her. "Morning Carl. I'm glad to help."

Knowing there was nothing else he could do, he allowed himself to be ushered into the small kitchen where her mom was hard at work cooking pancakes and bacon for breakfast. Unable to sate his hunger for Carly's body, he fed his stomach instead.

After a huge breakfast and polite conversation, he found himself rummaging around the small backyard shed looking for a ladder. Taking a deep breath, he raised his head. Rolling his shoulders, he tried to rid himself of some of his tension.

It didn't help.

The last few weeks had been like one cosmic bad joke. It seemed impossible that two people who lived and worked in the same small town could see so little of each other. Almost from the moment, he and Carly had spent their first night together, it was as if the world had conspired to keep them apart. And he was getting damned tired of it.

He heard her coming toward the shed. The sound of her small feet padding across the grass was recognizable. Her perfume wafted in just ahead of her, mixing with the slightly stale and earthy smell of the shed. It was a clean scent, the smell of vanilla, soap and woman. It tickled his senses, making his cock twitch and swell even larger.

Cursing, Nathan took another deep breath before swinging around. She stood in the doorway, hesitating. Sighing, he opened his arms wide.

Launching herself at him, she wrapped her arms around his neck and dragged his head down to hers. "I'm so sorry," she said as she peppered his face with kisses.

Locking one arm around her waist, he lifted her off her feet. Reaching out, he gave the door a shove and it closed with a satisfying thud. A small window at the back of the shed was the only light. It was dark and intimate in the confines of the small room.

Turning, he pushed her back against the wall. His erection was now in the perfect position and he took full advantage of it, rubbing his cock against her jeans-covered mound.

Moaning, she wrapped her legs around his waist and ground her pelvis against his hard length. It felt so damned good, he thought he might come in his jeans. Gasping for breath, he anchored her tight to him. "Stop, baby. You have to stop."

"But I don't want to." Her tongue was busy teasing the outside of his earlobe.

"If you don't stop, I'm either going to haul off your jeans and fuck you or I'm going to come in my pants." His words were blunt, but he was a man on the ragged edge.

Carly stilled. He could feel her chest heaving against his and knew she was close to coming as well. Holding her easily with one arm, he slipped his other hand between them and cupped her breast through her cotton T-shirt. He could feel her heart pounding against his palm as he moved it over her chest.

"I'm sorry, Nathan. I tried to call you this morning, but by the time I could get to the phone alone, you were already gone." She pushed her breast deeper into his hand. "You must have left early."

"I couldn't wait any longer." Now he wished, he had. This was torture. "But why did you tell your dad I'd come to help with the windows."

"I panicked."

"You panicked?" He laughed in spite of the fact that he was in agony because his cock was so damned hard. "Now, I've got to spend my morning off, working." He'd had a much more pleasant job in mind this morning when he'd left home.

"I'm sorry." She looked so forlorn he couldn't bear it.

"It's not your fault." Her nipple was hard and straining against the fabric of her bra and top, so he pinched it lightly, wringing another moan of pleasure from her. "I don't mind doing the work. I just wish I'd gotten your call in time."

"Me too," she gasped, digging her fingers into his shoulders. "It sure amused the heck out of Jackson."

Nathan paused and knew he was due for some good-natured ribbing from his brother later. "Doesn't matter. He won't say anything to you about it."

"You sure?" She was moving again, her hips were making a slow circle over his cock.

"Yeah," he was surprised he could string two thoughts together with Carly moving sinuously against him. "I'm sure."

Jamming his hips against hers, he held her in place as he shoved her soft shirt up over her breasts, exposing the lace cups of her bra. Leaning down, he nuzzled the soft pale mounds and traced his tongue along the edge of the lace.

"Nathan." She buried her fingers in his hair and jerked him closer.

Laughing, he used his teeth and tongue to tug down one of the cups. Her lush breast spilled over the lace and Nathan latched onto the hard peak with his mouth. He licked at the tip with his tongue and sucked hard, drawing it into his mouth.

Carly was almost incoherent now. She clutched him tighter to her, scattering frantic kisses across the top of his head. Her hips were pumping up and down against his cock.

His balls ached they were so heavy. With every push of her soft mound against his hard shaft, they tightened even more, pulling closer to his body. His own arousal seeped from the head of his cock. Nathan knew he was going to come if he didn't stop.

But there was no way in hell he was going to disappoint the giving, beautiful woman in his arms.

Reaching a hand down between them, he tugged at the opening of her jeans. The zipper gave way when he pulled and he shoved his hand down the front. His fingers were soaked the moment he touched the slick folds of her pussy.

He felt like a king. Like a god. It was always like this with Carly. She responded to him so quickly and held nothing back. Her arousal was the biggest turn-on in the world.

And if she didn't come in the next thirty seconds, it was all over for him.

Not wanting to come in his jeans, he stroked over the hard nub of her clit, past the slick folds of her pussy, and slipped a finger right inside her waiting heat. At the same time he carefully bit down on her nipple.

Her entire body arched and she was strung as tight as a bowstring. Then she let out a small cry and came. Her inner muscles clamped down hard on his finger as he moved it in and out of her cunt. His tongue lapped at her swollen nipple even as his teeth held it taut. She jerked and heaved in his embrace, but he kept up a steady rhythm until he was sure she could take no more.

Even though the air in the shed was cool, he could feel a light sheen of sweat cover him. His body felt like it was on fire and there was no relief in sight. He knew he couldn't chance taking her here in the shed. It had been a big enough risk just to pleasure her with her parents only as far away as the house.

Part of him was attuned to the world outside the shed. His need to protect Carly overrode all other instincts. There was no way he was taking the chance of her parents catching them together like this. He didn't care, but he knew that Carly did. And that was all that mattered.

Carefully, he removed his hand from her jeans, murmuring reassuringly to her when she protested. Then he kissed her breast one last time before he eased the lace cup back over it and pulled her T-shirt back down.

She looked so damned beautiful with her face all flushed pink with pleasure and her hair all mussed. Her lips looked slightly swollen and were parted on a sigh.

Nathan smiled as he traced the folds of her lips with his tongue. But it quickly disappeared when her tongue darted out to duel with his. And when she started to move her hips again, he knew he had to stop.

Reaching behind, he unhooked her ankles and eased her legs back down until her feet were firmly on the floor. Holding her steady with one hand, he took a step backward. He needed the distance to regain his control.

The sleepy satisfaction was fading from her face, replaced by concern. Using his thumb, he smoothed the wrinkles from between her brows.

Her small hand cupped his beard-rough cheek and he nuzzled her palm. "What about you?"

"I'm fine," he lied. In truth, he felt like he might explode. But that was his problem.

"But that's not fair." Now she looked more peeved with him than anything.

"Honey, your parents are only a few yards away?"

"Omigod. I forgot." She looked appalled. "How could I?"

Nathan couldn't help it. He felt rather smug and satisfied that he could make her totally disregard her surroundings when he was pleasuring her. Carly was always so in control and put together, it aroused him to the point of madness how she let go of herself with him. It was addictive.

Carly pushed away from the wall and hurriedly tucked in her top and zipped and buttoned her jeans. Running her fingers though her hair, she hurried to the door and opened it a crack before peeking out. Her shoulder sagged with relief. "I don't see them."

Grabbing a loop on the back of her jeans, he tugged her backward. "Don't worry, I knew there was no one there. I'll take care of you, Carly."

An unexpected shudder racked her body at his words and the look she gave him was half-sad, half-tender. "I know."

Something was wrong all of a sudden, but he didn't know what had changed. Then he felt Carly's hands on his chest and that thought slipped away. She looked fine now as she smiled up at him. It was probably no more than a trick of the light that had made her seem sad.

"I'm sorry." Reaching down, she cupped his erection with her hand.

His hand manacled her wrist and tugged it away when all he really wanted to do was haul down his jeans and have her wrap her fingers around his cock. "Don't. Someone's coming."

Her eyes widened and she tugged the door open and poked her head out the door. "I'm just helping Nathan find the ladder. We'll be there in a second."

Carl's good-natured laughter rang as he assured Carly that there was no hurry. Nathan took the opportunity to adjust his swollen cock again before he reached out and grabbed the ladder.

"Will you be okay?" Her concern was like a balm on his heat-ravaged body. It helped. Not much, but enough to help him gain control.

"Yeah. But you go on first. I'll be there in a minute."

Carly nodded and slipped out the door. Stopping at the last second, she turned back. "Thank you, Nathan."

He nodded. Then she was gone and he stood there and listened to the sound of her footsteps fade into the distance. Standing there, he counted to one hundred before getting a better grip on the ladder and following her footprints around to the front of the house.

Chapter Four

∽

Nathan Connors' pale blue eyes glittered dangerously and he gritted his teeth, clinging to his temper by the thinnest of threads. He was a patient man by nature, but even he had limits.

People were milling around, chatting to one another and generally having a great time. His brother Jackson was there, as was his sister, Erin, and her husband, Abel.

Hell, a good portion of the town was here to celebrate his and Carly's upcoming wedding. An engagement party, she'd called it. They'd been engaged for weeks, he didn't know why they suddenly needed a party to celebrate it. But, if it made her happy, he was all for it. But she didn't look happy these days. He'd hardly seen her smile since the incident in the diner. He hoped she still wasn't worried about those men who'd hassled her. He'd handle them if they became a problem.

The sounds of people chatting and laughing wafted around him as he stood in a dark corner and watched her every move. As his eyes followed her, he could feel his cock stirring to life.

Withdrawing further into the shadows of the bar, Nathan discreetly adjusted the front of his jeans. Seemed to him that he was having to "adjust" himself a lot lately. A lot more than he liked.

Damn, she looked so pretty, working her way around the room, speaking to everyone. The smile on her face was genuine as she greeted everyone by name and had something friendly to say to each of them. She had a knack of making people feel at ease. Some people might think it was because of all the years she'd spent working as a waitress at the family diner she now ran. But Nathan knew that it was just an innate part of her personality.

On the night he'd finally made her his, he'd proposed marriage. Well, actually, he'd told her she was marrying him. But that was beside the point. She had agreed and he'd been in heaven.

Damn, he loved the girl. He'd even agreed to let her set a wedding date. He figured they'd get married in the garden like his sister and Abel had. Quick and simple. But the whole wedding thing kept growing. Carly was constantly busy with one thing and another and she was wearing herself out. He'd offered to help, but she kept insisting that she could handle everything.

He understood that a woman wanted her wedding day and the days leading up to it to be special. Hadn't he dressed up in a shirt, tie and jacket and pressed his best jeans and shined his boots for this shindig? He'd agreed to rent part of the local saloon, Lucky's Bar and Grill, for a private potluck dinner and dance to celebrate their engagement.

But enough was enough.

Ever since they'd spent their first night together it was if the world was conspiring to keep them apart. As a result, Nathan had spent the last several weeks tired and frustrated. He and Carly couldn't even manage enough time alone for a quickie, let alone any real quality time. Desperate times called for desperate measures.

And Nathan was way past desperate.

"You look like you're ready to throttle someone."

Sighing, he turned toward Jackson. His older brother was also wearing a shirt, tie and dress jacket and looked about as comfortable as Nathan felt.

Impatiently, he loosened his tie and opened the top two buttons of his shirt. Nathan wore his sheriff's deputy uniform to work every day, but that felt more natural and right somehow. Other than that, he wore jeans and T-shirts.

Dressing up fancy made him feel uncomfortable no matter what. He was glad that Carly didn't have a problem with him wearing his jeans to the dinner.

"I might yet." Nathan muttered as he tipped up his now warm bottle of beer and took a swallow.

Jackson slapped him on the back and laughed. "Only seven days to go until the big day, or rather, the big night."

"If I live that long." Nathan had been surprised when his brother hadn't said anything about his and Carly's ill-fated attempt to get together a few days ago. Well, that wasn't entirely true. Jackson had asked him if he wanted to hang the storm windows on the farmhouse. The idiot had been grinning from ear to ear when he'd asked.

Sighing, Nathan tried to shake off his dark mood. He had plans set in motion for this weekend. He only hoped that Carly was still willing to marry him after it was over.

"Smile. Your bride-to-be is frowning at you."

Sure enough, when he glanced her way, Carly was staring at him from across the room with a worried look on her face. He smiled at her, but it felt more like a grimace. She nibbled on her bottom lip and shot him a worried smile before her mother claimed her attention again.

"Carly is worn out trying to plan the damned wedding." Only he seemed to notice the faint circles under her eyes. And if he wasn't mistaken, she'd lost a few pounds lately. And that was a crime. He loved her lush curves and didn't want her to lose any of them. She'd been working much too hard and not taking care of herself lately, and he'd been too busy at work himself to be much help to her.

But that was all about to change. It was up to him to take care of her and make sure she got some much-needed rest and pampering.

He snorted. Yeah, he was an altruistic bastard all right. He needed time with Carly to recharge his own batteries. They were both running on empty these days.

"Here, hold this." He thrust the half-empty bottle into his brother's hands and sauntered across the room.

As Carly absently reached up and pushed a lock of hair out of her face, the diamond on her left hand glittered in the faint light. A savage pleasure filled Nathan every time he thought about the fact that she now wore his ring. He wanted to shout to the world that she belonged to him, but he restrained himself. Barely.

There was something about this woman that brought all his primal instincts to the fore. And the need to fuck her, to cover her with his body and brand her as his, burned in his belly. It had been weeks since he'd had her and lust was riding him hard.

The dress she was wearing really wasn't provocative in any way shape or form. It had buttons from the waist up to the neckline, not giving even a hint of cleavage. The sleeves came down to just above her elbows and the skirt of the dress fell to her knees. She'd worn the dress to church on several occasions.

She might as well been wearing nothing but a G-string as far as he was concerned. His struggled to control his body's responses as he sidled up behind Carly and wrapped his arm around her waist. His cock was rock-hard against the front of his jeans and he knew she could feel it nudging against her back.

Her conversation faltered for a moment, so he took up the slack and greeted the people around them. He allowed his hand to fall low on her stomach and almost growled with pleasure when she moved every so slightly, pushing her backside against him.

Nathan could feel the sweat on the back of his neck as it took every ounce of his control not to toss Carly to the floor and mount her in front of an audience. He had to have her. Now.

Keeping his hand on her stomach, he gradually edged her away from the crowd, pulling her further into the shadows. He pushed her hair behind her ear before bending down to whisper in it. Unable to resist, he flicked at the whorls with his tongue. His entire body clenched when she shivered in his arms.

"I've missed you, baby." Drawing small, tight circles, he began to move the hand that was still low on her belly.

Her lips parted on a sigh. "I've missed you too." She gave herself a subtle shake and tried to pull away from him. But he tightened his hold on her.

"I need you, Carly."

She bit her lip as she looked up at him, her eyes liquid with desire. Nathan rubbed his thumb across her bottom lip, pulling it away from her teeth and soothing the small sting. Her tongue snaked out and stroked his thumb.

Nathan bit back a groan at Carly's hungry response to his touch. He didn't think she had any idea of what she'd just done. Her sensuality was so natural and unrestrained with him. It was one of the things he loved about her.

"The wedding is only a week away." Her voice sounded slightly strained now.

"Seven days," he said. "Seven fucking days." It was out of his mouth before he could stop it and he could see the sudden hurt in her eyes. Releasing her, he rubbed his hand over his face and sighed. "I'm sorry, honey."

Slowly, she turned around to face him. He felt her slender arms go around his waist, hugging him tight as she leaned into his side. "It's okay." She fit so perfectly, he couldn't resist tucking her a little closer under his arm.

"No, it's not okay." Cupping her face in his hand, he tipped up her chin with his thumb. "I can't wait any longer, Carly."

Her eyes widened and she glanced nervously around the room. The party was going on around them and no one seemed to be paying them much attention. "Maybe later tonight."

He made a quick decision. "Now."

"That's impossible." She said the words slowly as if they were being reluctantly pulled from her.

"Not impossible, just difficult." Shifting Carly so that her back was against the wall and he was blocking her view of the room, he slipped his hands down to her behind and squeezed the globes of her ass in his hands. Damn, she felt good.

"You're not wearing any panties, are you?"

She shook her head as she stroked his chest. "Just thigh-high stockings and my dress."

Nathan almost swallowed his tongue. "No bra?" He couldn't believe that she was naked under her dress at their engagement party while she talked to all of these people, including her parents and his family, and acted perfectly normal.

"No." She gave him a shy smile at odds with her brazen actions and shrugged. "I thought that it would please you. And I guess I hoped…" Her voice trailed off.

"Hoped what?" Damn, his cock felt like it was going to explode.

"Hoped that we might find a few minutes to be alone later tonight before I went home." Her voice was muffled as she leaned against his chest. He could feel her breath through his shirt and wanted her lips pressing against his bare skin.

He gently pushed her away from him while he still had the strength. "Meet me in the men's room in two minutes."

"What?" she squeaked.

"You heard me. I want you. Now." He did up the button on his jacket to help cover the huge bulge in the front of his pants. "Don't make me wait."

Not looking back, he turned on his heel and strode across the room toward the men's room. He kept to the edges of the room and headed down the dimly lit hallway. His palm slapped on the door as he shoved it open.

A lone man stood washing his hands at the sink and turned his head toward Nathan as he slammed into the room. The man took one look at Nathan's angry glare, hurriedly dried his hands and left the bathroom.

Checking the stalls, Nathan made sure they were empty before going back to lean against one of the sinks. His fingers wrapped around the cold porcelain as he stared at himself in the mirror.

The face staring back at him was grim. He felt like a bastard for ordering Carly to meet him here just so he could fuck her. Taking a deep breath, he released it slowly. Unbuttoning his jacket, he rubbed the back of his neck and rolled his shoulders to try and release some of the tension he felt. He was damned lucky she hadn't slapped his face and told him to go to hell. He was half surprised that she hadn't.

He was further gone than he'd thought.

Yeah, the bathroom was clean, but it was still the men's room of a damned saloon. And Carly was a classy lady. Nathan shook his head and straightened his shoulders. He'd go back out there and make nice with their guests. He only had to make it through this evening, he reminded himself. For a moment, his need for her had driven all common sense from him and he'd forgotten his plans.

She didn't know it yet, but tonight she was his. That is, if she was still talking to him after his crude proposal.

The door squeaked as it was pushed open and he automatically glanced in the mirror to see who was coming in behind him. His hands froze on his tie that he'd been straightening as a pair of blue eyes peeked around the door.

"Is the coast clear?"

The minute he nodded, she scooted inside and leaned back against the door. She looked scared and turned-on all at once and Nathan felt his lust for her surging to the surface again. He turned toward her, hardly able to believe that she was here with him, but he wasn't about to waste the opportunity.

"Lock the door and come here." He waited as she fumbled with the lock and breathed a sigh of relief when it clicked into place. He held out his hand to her and waited.

Chapter Five

ဢ

Carly could hardly believe what she was about to do. But sometimes a woman had to take matters into her own hands. And this was definitely one of those times.

Poor Nathan had been so patient and understanding the last few weeks. Almost too patient. She'd missed being with him so much over the last few weeks, but having her parents stay with her was definitely putting a damper on her sex life.

She'd quickly grown addicted to Nathan's brand of lovemaking and found herself horny almost constantly. She needed some relief. But more than that, she needed to be close to Nathan. She missed the sex, but she missed the quiet times with him just as much.

When he'd ordered her to meet him in the men's room so he could fuck her, she'd felt her sex clench with desire. Her pussy was damp and ready and her juices had trickled down the inside of her leg. Her breasts were swollen, her nipples tight, and she wanted to rub them against his chest even as she rubbed her clit against his erection.

Her legs were shaky as she walked toward him and grasped his outstretched hand. His fingers curled around hers as he tugged her closer. Wrapping his strong arms around her, he hugged her tight to his chest and held her there for a moment.

Carly laid her head over his pounding heart, absorbing his heat. His erection was hard against the softness of her belly and she shuddered with desire. Nathan's arms tightened around her for a moment before he pulled back, holding her at arm's length.

"Are you sure?" His eyes were bleak and his mouth was tight. His face looked so harsh and hungry in the dim light of the men's room, she almost didn't recognize him.

She nodded, but he still didn't move. Swallowing hard, she opened her mouth to speak, but nothing but a croak came from her throat. Licking her lips, she tried again. "Yes."

Nathan stood her in front of one of the sinks and turned her around so that she was facing the mirror, her ass in front of him. "Place your hands on the sink."

He looked huge, looming behind her and she shuddered as desire and a slight tingle of fear trickled through her. But this was Nathan, a man she'd known all her life and one who she trusted like no other. It didn't matter that he was in a strange mood. She knew he would cut off his own hand before he'd ever do anything that would hurt her.

Lifting her hands, she laid them on the sides of the sink, curling her fingers around the cool porcelain. Behind her, Nathan heaved a huge sigh and she saw relief flash in his eyes before they turned hot with lust once again.

His arms wrapped around her and he rested his hands on top of her much smaller hands, caging her with his much larger frame. The heat was incredible as he leaned down to nuzzle the nape of her neck.

He nipped at the tender flesh, making her moan. All her doubts vanished, replaced by her need for this particular man. She rotated her hips and pushed her behind against the hard bulge of his jeans. Leaning forward slightly, she raised herself up on her toes, bringing her pussy in closer contact with his erection. With him angled over her the way he was, every movement of her hips brought his hardness closer to where she needed it.

"God have mercy," he muttered as his hands moved to the front of her dress and began to undo the row of buttons there. He didn't stop until he had every button undone and her dress open to her waist. Standing back, he eased the fabric down over her shoulders.

She started to pull away from the sink so she could remove her dress, but he stopped her. "Don't move." His harsh command echoed throughout the empty bathroom and she stiffened momentarily before gripping the sides of the sink once again.

"Perfect." His voice was a deep, satisfied purr in her ear as he eased the dress down until it was caught just above her elbows and kept her arms totally immobile. Her breasts were totally exposed, framed by the gaping fabric of the dress.

Carly shuddered at the wanton picture she made in the mirror. Her face was flushed with desire and her eyes were large and round with expectation. The lighting was dull, but her breasts looked pale and even larger than normal as they swelled under his hot stare. Shifting slightly, she clenched her thighs together, trying to find some relief from the throbbing of her sex. But Nathan wasn't even going to allow her that.

His jeans-clad knee pushed between her legs and nudged them apart. "None of that, sweetheart. I want you hot and wet and wanting." He traced his thumb around one of her swollen nipples, coming close, but never quite touching it.

She groaned and he laughed a low, sexy laugh that sent a shiver down her spine. "Spread those legs wide if you want me to touch your breasts." Now he had both thumbs slowly circling the edges of her areolas. "It's up to you. All you have to do is open yourself up wide for me."

Carly slid her feet apart until she could open her legs no wider. Her gaze never left Nathan's in the mirror and she saw the savage pleasure in his face as she complied. She closed her eyes and hissed as his thumbs gently scraped her swollen nipples.

It was too much. It wasn't near enough.

"Damn, you are so beautiful." Her eyes popped back open at the reverent tone of his voice. He was watching her in the mirror, his eyes on his hands as they continued to torment her breasts.

Carefully, he took both swollen tips between his thumb and forefingers and rolled her nipples between them, slowly increasing the pressure. "Yesss," she sighed.

"I'll bet your pussy is soaking wet for me." As if he had to find out for himself, one of his hands released her breast and slowly slid down her belly. He didn't stop, but kept going and slipped his hand between her legs, fingering her sex through the cloth of her dress.

Carly gasped and felt her pussy clench with desire. Nathan's fingers explored the damp folds and stroked the hard bud of her swollen clit. Her breath was coming quicker now and she knew that she was close to coming.

As if sensing that, he pulled his hand away. Carly almost stamped her foot in frustration. She struggled against the confines of the dress, wanting to free her arms.

Cupping both her breasts once again, he pulled her back against his hard body. "I want to be inside you when you come." He left a string of hot stinging kisses from her shoulder to her neck and then took the lobe of her ear in his mouth and bit gently.

Nathan's firm hold was the only thing keeping her upright. Her legs felt like jelly as he continued to touch her. He tugged at the small gold hoop in her ear before sweeping his tongue over the outer rim of her ear.

"Now." She didn't recognize her own voice. It was low and breathy, sexy.

"Fuck, yes." Stepping back, he flipped up the back of her skirt, leaving her bottom totally exposed.

She shivered as the cool air hit her heated flesh. His hands were large and hot as they cupped her bottom. She'd always thought her bottom was too large, but Nathan seemed to love it.

Suddenly, he dropped to his knees behind her. His lips were warm and moist on her bottom as he licked and bit its flesh. She squirmed and let out a squeal when his tongue traced a wet path down the dark cleft of her behind toward her pussy.

Nathan wrapped his hands around her thighs to keep her still while his clever tongue explored the soft, damp folds of her cleft. There was no part of her pussy he didn't taste or touch with his mouth.

And when his tongue stabbed into her throbbing slit, she almost came undone. Her entire body was poised on the edge of completion. Her inner muscles were flexing, desperately wanting to wrap around his cock and squeeze it tight. Her breathing had quickened and she was panting hard as she flexed her hips back toward him.

Nathan surged to his feet. The metallic sound of a zipper being tugged down had her panting in anticipation. Then she could feel the broad head of his penis pushing between her legs from behind, searching for entrance.

He swore as he guided his cock to her slit. The moment his tip was settled inside her, he drove himself to the hilt.

Carly cried out as a massive orgasm shook her. Her entire body was vibrating as her pussy clenched around him. She came hard and fast as Nathan's arms banded around her waist and held her steady until only the occasional aftershock made her shiver.

"That was incredible." He hadn't moved, but was still seated to the hilt inside her. He nibbled on her shoulder as he covered her breasts with his hands and began to massage them.

Amazingly, she felt her body springing to life once again. She had come, but she needed more. She wanted his cock pounding into her, making her come again. "Fuck me, Nathan." She clenched her inner muscles around him, and was pleased when he groaned.

His large body gave one massive shudder. When she caught his gaze in the mirror, she could see the determination in his eyes. Keeping one hand at her breast, he pulled the front of the dress up out of his way and shoved the other hand between her thighs. Then he started to thrust.

At first his strokes were long and slow, but gradually they picked up speed until his cock was pounding into her aching pussy. She could do nothing but surrender to the pleasure he was giving her.

The hand between her legs had parted the folds of her sex and with every thrust he allowed his finger to stroke across her aching clit. The hand at her breast was tugging her nipple with each surge his cock made into her.

Carly was almost out of her mind with ecstasy. Her fingers dug into the sink as she braced herself for his thrusts and she was panting so hard, she was afraid she might faint. "Nathan," she gasped out. She wasn't quite sure what she wanted him to do, but she knew she couldn't last much longer.

"Now, honey. Come for me now," he rasped out.

His next thrust was so powerful that her feet almost left the floor. She felt the hot spurt of his cum deep inside her as he came hard and fast. It set off an explosion within her and she could feel herself coming again. She tried not to cry out, but couldn't stop herself as her body tightened and clenched around his cock.

Nathan grabbed the edge of the sink with one hand and wrapped his other hand around her waist. His breath was hot and harsh in her ear as his head came to rest in the curve of her shoulder. She could feel his heart thumping against her back. Her own heart was racing madly and she took deep breaths to try and calm herself.

"Hey, anybody in there?" The pounding on the door made them both jump.

Nathan swore long and soft before answering. "What do you want, Jackson?"

"You better hurry back. People are starting to miss the two of you." Carly could hear the underlying teasing in Jackson's voice and wanted to disappear into the floor. She could feel her face heating with embarrassment.

"Yeah." Nathan took a deep breath. "Stall them."

The masculine chuckle had her struggling against Nathan, but he ignored it and just tightened his hold. "Will do," Jackson called out through the door.

Carly shivered as Nathan slid himself out of her. She'd been so involved in their lovemaking that, for a second, she'd forgotten where they were and that they could easily be discovered. And to be discovered by Jackson. She didn't think she'd be able to look her almost-brother-in-law in the face again anytime soon.

The sound of water running pulled her out of her reverie and back to reality. Nathan wet some paper towels and gently placed them on the sensitive flesh between her thighs. Carly flinched.

"Shh, let me get you cleaned up, honey." Carefully and thoroughly, he cleaned her sex and her upper thighs before lowering the skirt of her dress and smoothing it down over her behind.

As she pushed away from the sink, Nathan turned her toward him, his face solemn as he tugged the sleeves back up and buttoned the front of her dress. When he was done, he stood back and inspected her. "The light isn't that good in the bar, nobody should notice."

Sighing, she glanced at herself in the mirror. One look at the satisfied expression of the woman staring back at her told her that he was wrong. Her lips were swollen where she'd bitten them and her neck was blotchy where Nathan had nipped at her. At least she didn't have a hickey. She looked like a woman who'd been making love, but there was nothing she could do about it.

"I'm sorry, honey." He placed his fingers under her chin and tipped it up. Bending down, he brushed a light, chaste kiss across her lips. "I'll make it up to you."

It didn't seem fair to her that Nathan didn't even have a hair out of place. He'd zipped and buttoned his jeans and looked absolutely no worse the wear for their adventure. While she, on the other hand, looked mussed and rumpled. She ran a hand through her hair and sighed.

"Come on, we've got to get you back." Grabbing her hand, he pulled her behind him toward the door.

Her legs felt slightly wobbly, but she didn't complain. He listened at the door before unlocking it and opening it just a crack. When he was sure the coast was clear, he pulled the door open all the way and hurried her out of the men's room.

Heaving a sigh of relief, she tugged her hand free. "You go on ahead, I'm going in here for a few minutes." She pointed to the ladies' room.

Nathan nodded. "It's probably a good idea for us to go back in separately." Giving her hand one final squeeze, he turned and strode down the hallway and back toward the party.

Carly pushed into the ladies' room and came to a dead stop. Erin took one look at her and her eyes opened wide. She knew she looked bad, but she didn't think it was that bad.

"My brother obviously has no sense of timing." Opening her purse, Erin pulled out a comb. "Now let's see if we can't hide most of the damage." She let Erin tug her to the sink and leaned back against it, grateful for its support.

As Erin fussed over her, a small grin crossed her lips. "Well, was it worth it?"

Carly felt a slow smile spread across her own face. Her friend just looked at her and laughed. "No, don't answer that. There are just some things a girl doesn't need to know about her brother."

The laughter bubbled out of her and Carly began to shake. She felt totally spent all of a sudden and very tired. The last few weeks, she'd felt like her life was spinning out of control. She swallowed back the laughter when it threatened to turn to tears.

Erin looked concerned, but Carly gave her a watery smile and just shook her head. Luckily, she didn't say anything, didn't ask any questions. Instead, she continued to comb Carly's hair into some semblance of order.

She had done her best to convince herself that she was just tired, but now Carly was afraid that it was much, much more than just that.

The whole thing with Nathan had happened so quickly. One day they'd been nothing but friends, the next, they'd been engaged. Then there were all the wedding arrangements. Her life had been a runaway train for weeks now and showed no signs of stopping.

It was time for her to regain control.

Right then and there, she decided that she needed to take a few days off from work and get away from everything and everybody. She needed time to think. She loved Nathan, of that there was no doubt. But so much had changed so quickly, that she wasn't sure she'd come to grips with all the implications. And with her parents staying with her, she couldn't get one moment to herself.

Nathan was in such a hurry to marry her, but she wanted to be sure she was ready when she finally marched down the aisle. There was still so much that needed to be done for the wedding and then there was her business. The thought of leaving everything hanging for a few days made her stomach hurt.

Pressing her hand against her stomach, she took a deep breath before slowly releasing it. Her stomach calmed slightly as she mulled the idea over in her mind. It was the right thing to do. The only thing to do.

This was her life too, and she had to be sure that she was strong enough to handle a man as strong-willed as Nathan and not lose herself in the process.

"Are you sure you're okay?" Erin was tucking the comb back in her purse. Carly hadn't even noticed her finishing.

Looking in the mirror, she was pleased to note that she looked more like herself again. She took the compact that Erin handed her. "Yeah, I'm fine." She powdered her nose as she spoke. "I've just got a lot on my mind right now."

"So you've said." Erin folded her arms across her chest and was giving her a look that said she didn't believe a word that Carly was telling her.

Carly sighed. That was the problem with best friends, they always knew when you weren't telling them everything. She powdered her neck, hoping to hide the blotchy spots, clicked the compact closed and handed it back to Erin. "Thanks."

Taking the compact, she tucked it back in her purse. "You know you can always talk to me." Erin paused and fiddled with the strap of her purse before slipping it over her shoulder. "About anything." Reaching out, she grabbed Carly's hand and held it tight.

Carly squeezed the other woman's hand. "I know," she whispered before releasing it and giving herself one final check in the mirror.

"You look fine." Erin suddenly grinned at her. "No one will guess what you've been up to."

"Except you and Jackson," she muttered under her breath.

But her friend had heard her and started to laugh. "Don't tell me Jackson caught you?" When she nodded, Erin laughed even harder. "I'm sorry," her shoulders shook as she tried to stifle her laughter.

"You don't look very sorry." She tried to scowl, but her own sense of humor began to get the best of her and she began to giggle. "It's not funny."

"I know," Erin said as she wiped a tear from her eye. Then she looked right at Carly and burst into laughter again. "Yes it is. I can just imagine Nathan's face."

"But can you imagine mine?" That statement started Erin giggling once again. Carly shook her head and smiled, still unable to believe her own outrageous actions.

By the time they both had control of themselves again, Carly was feeling more like herself. She was ready to face her guests and the rest of the evening. She had a plan now and that helped her feel more in control of her life than she'd been in quite a while.

"Let's get back to the party." Her voice was stronger now as she gave her dress one final tug and headed for the door. She could feel Erin's eyes on her back, but her friend said nothing and fell into step behind her.

Chapter Six

✿

"What did you do to Carly?" His sister had cornered him at the bar and was glaring at him with her arms crossed over her chest. "Well, I know what you did to her." A sly grin crossed her face and then disappeared. "But did you say anything to upset her?"

Nathan grabbed her by the hand tugged her away from the small group of men gathered around the end of the bar. Glancing around to make sure they wouldn't be overheard, he scowled at her. "What do you mean? I didn't do anything to her."

His conscience pricked him even as he spoke and worry started gnawing at his gut. He'd done something to her all right. He'd fucked her in the men's room of a bar. He pushed that thought to the back of his mind and tried to concentrate on what his sister was saying. "Why? Did she say anything?"

"No, not really. It's just that…" Erin trailed off and shook her head. "I don't know, she had this almost lost look on her face. And she laughed and cried." She shrugged and sighed.

"But she's all right?" He started looking around the room and relaxed slightly when he saw Carly standing next to her parents. She glanced up and then away without smiling at him. Nathan could feel the tension building in him.

Erin pulled on his arm. "Nathan, you've really rushed her into this."

"Did she say that?"

"No, you big lughead. I'm saying that." His sister looked totally exasperated with him now. "All I'm saying is that she's probably going to be a little emotional right now and that you should try to be more understanding. She's under a lot of pressure running the business, planning a wedding, and having her parents staying with her for so long."

Nathan drew in a deep breath and slowly let it out. "I know you're right." He gave her a small grin. "Don't worry, everything will work out fine."

Erin stared at him for a long time before leaning in close and giving him a big hug. "I love you both and just want you two to be happy together."

"Me too." He whispered as he watched his sister rejoin her husband and Jackson on the other side of the room.

His instincts were screaming at him to grab Carly and hold her tight because, although they'd never been closer than they'd been when they made love in the men's room, at this moment, she'd never felt further away from him.

His hand tightened around the bottle of beer he had in his hand. He'd warned her before they'd gotten involved that he was a hard man to live with and she'd made her choice. Now it was up to him to convince her that she'd made the right one.

There was no backing away from his plan now, and in fact, he felt sure now that he'd made the right decisions. They needed some time alone together, away from the madness that their lives had become.

He'd captured Carly at last, after all those years of wanting her, and there was no way he was letting her slip away from him. Laying his beer on a nearby table, he stalked across the room to her side. He nodded at their friends and reluctantly resigned himself to a couple more hours of socializing.

His time was coming. He could wait.

Two hours later, Nathan heaved a sigh of relief as he led Carly to the center of the dance floor and pulled her into his arms. It was the band's last song for the evening and the party was finally winding down. Once this dance was over, they could leave.

Their bodies swayed to the slow music, her smaller frame tucked in close to his larger one. He could feel her breath on his chest as she hummed to the music.

"Did you have a good time?" He reached down and pushed an errant lock of hair out of her face when she looked up at him and smiled.

"Yes, I did." The hand she had on his shoulder slid down until it was centered over his heart. "Did you?"

He thought about it before answering her. "You know, I did."

She gave a small laugh. "You sound surprised."

He shrugged. "I didn't really expect to, but it was fun." He led her hand to his lips and placed a kiss in the center of her palm. "I like everyone knowing that you belong to me now."

She sighed and looked away. Her teeth chewed nervously at her bottom lip. Nathan returned her hand to his chest before rubbing her bottom lip with his thumb. "What's wrong, honey?"

"Nothing really." She gave him a smile that didn't quite reach her eyes.

"You've been distracted since earlier this evening." He continued to slide his thumb over her lush mouth. "If you're worried that anyone other than Jackson knows what went on, don't be. And trust me, he might tease me, but he'll never mention it to you. And he won't say anything to anyone else." Nathan paused as he thought about it. "Well, I guess Erin knows too, but she'll keep it to herself."

"It's not that exactly."

"Then what is it, exactly?" He could feel her growing more tense as he took her hand in his once again and continued to turn her around the dance floor.

"I'm just tired, I guess." She shrugged and glanced around the room at the still fairly large group of people remaining. "Everything is moving so fast I barely have time to breathe."

His entire body grew rigid as Erin's earlier words came back to haunt him. Unconsciously, he tightened his hold on Carly. It was only when she flinched slightly that he realized he was squeezing her fingers too tight. "Sorry."

"I'm thinking I need a few days away." She glanced up at him as if gauging his reaction.

Nathan could feel the grin spreading across his face. "It's funny you should say that. I've been thinking the exact same thing."

"Really?" The surprise on her face irritated him a little.

"Really. I can understand how you might be overwhelmed by everything." She gave him a soft smile and snuggled closer to him. See, he could be as sensitive and understanding as the next guy, damned if he couldn't.

"So you understand my wanting to get away by myself for a few days."

His good humor fled and he came to a sudden and complete stop in the middle of the dance floor. "Who said anything about you being by yourself?" His voice was soft, but there was an edge of anger to it.

He could see the growing confusion in her eyes. "But that's what we've been discussing."

"No, we've been talking about us going away for a few days."

She shook her head. "I really need some time for myself. You understand, don't you?"

He understood only too well and he wasn't going to give her time to have second thoughts about their wedding. "You can have some time to yourself while we're away. Together."

Carly scowled at him. "Sometimes you can be just so darned autocratic and annoying."

"Yeah, but you knew that when you agreed to marry me." He could feel his temper starting to slip.

"But that doesn't mean I have to like it." She pulled away from him and rubbed her hand across her forehead. "I'm getting a headache. We can talk more about this tomorrow."

"Carly, honey." He gathered her back in his arms. "You need a break and I'm going to make sure you get it. Don't worry this to death. It'll all work out."

"That's easy for you to say." Her words were muffled against his chest as he hugged her close to him. "Right now, I just want to go home. We'll talk more tomorrow."

"No, we won't." Nathan was trying to figure out the best way to break his plans to her.

She pulled out of his arms and frowned at him. "If you don't want to talk about it, fine, but I'm still planning on getting away for a few days as soon as I can make arrangements."

"I've already arranged everything. The diner is covered for the weekend and your parents will take care of the house."

"I don't understand."

Shrugging, he gave her what he hoped was a reassuring smile. "It's simple. I'm taking you away for the weekend."

"But I've got wedding plans to finalize and the diner is extra busy on Saturdays." Carly's brows knit in consternation and he smoothed out the wrinkles with his thumb. "I can't go away this weekend."

"Not this weekend. *Now*."

"Are you out of your mind? I don't even have a bag packed." She poked him in the chest with her finger to punctuate each of her words.

He grabbed her hand before she drilled a hole in his chest. "You don't need any clothes."

"That's so like a man to assume that." She huffed and with obvious effort reined in her temper. "Look," she began.

63

"Obviously, we're just going to have to disagree on this. Will you take me home now?"

"No." His words were a stark challenge between them.

"No." She looked incredulous.

He shook his head emphatically. "No. This is not open for discussion. You're coming with me. Now." Sighing, he rubbed his hand over his face and looked up at the ceiling, praying for divine intervention. When nothing happened, he slowly looked down at her. "You need a break. I'm providing it for you. What's so wrong with that?"

Her blue eyes softened. "There's nothing wrong with it. But I would have liked to be consulted."

Okay, he could do that. He nodded his understanding. "So I'll ask next time. But this time, you're going with me." The last four words seemed to echo in the room and it was only then that he realized that while they were talking, the song had ended.

Several people chuckled, but looked away when he shot them a black scowl. Carly glanced around with a half-apologetic, half-embarrassed look on her face. That only made his blood simmer. Who gave a damn what other people thought? This was between the two of them.

"Let's say our goodbyes to everyone and finish this discussion outside." She kept her voice low and restrained. He knew she was trying to placate him, but it was having the opposite effect.

He was through talking. It was time for action. "You can talk in the truck." Reaching out, he took her hand and strode off the dance floor.

"Nathan," she tugged on his hand as he pulled her along behind him. "Stop. I want to say goodbye to everyone."

He stopped and turned to the crowd. "Good night, folks. Thanks for coming." He swung his gaze back to her. "Satisfied?" Part of him knew he was being totally unreasonable, but he no longer cared. All he cared about was getting to spend some time alone with Carly, away from other people.

"No. I. Am. Not." She spaced each word carefully, displeasure dripping from every word.

"Well, too bad. That's as good as it gets." Without warning, he swooped down and scooped her up in his arms. Not looking back, he carried her across the room, ignoring the catcalls and encouragement from a group of men gathered around the bar.

She struggled in his arms, but he just held her tighter. "Settle down," he muttered as he shouldered his way out the door. Carly's parents had left earlier, but he could see Jackson standing next to Abel, the two of them laughing their fool heads off.

Erin, on the other hand, looked totally appalled as she hurried over to them. "What are you doing?"

"Leaving." He ignored Erin and kept walking.

It was too late to worry now. What was done was done. The moment they were outside, she groaned and buried her face against his shoulder.

"How will I ever face those people again?"

"It's not that big a deal, Carly."

She reared back in his arms and glared at him. "Not for you, maybe. You're a man and what you just did makes you manlier in their eyes. It just made me look like a silly female."

"That's just…" He was smart enough to shut up before he finished that statement, but she wouldn't leave it alone as he carried her across the parking lot toward his truck.

Her laugh was tinged with bitterness. "Silly?"

Nathan sighed. All he'd wanted to do was make things better for her, but things weren't working out quite the way he'd planned. "You're not silly. You're the smartest, strongest and most amazing woman I've ever known."

"Thank you, Nathan. But you have no idea how hard it is when you're short, stacked and have a young face, to get people to take you seriously. It's been a challenge my entire life."

He was shocked at her assessment of herself. "That's not true."

"It is. You're male, big, strong and a sheriff's deputy to boot. People respect you and take you seriously. Me, I've got to be careful about what I say and do or people treat me like a silly child who doesn't know her own mind."

Leaning against the passenger side of his truck, he lowered his arm until her feet were touching the ground. When he was sure she was steady, he cupped her face in his hands, making sure he had her full attention before he spoke. "It was never my intention to belittle you or embarrass you in any way. It's just that I see you working so hard and wearing yourself down. Everyone depends on you so much, and you give so much of yourself, but no one ever takes care of you. And that's my job."

He lowered his forehead to hers. "Honestly, honey, all I wanted was to give us a weekend away so that we could both have a break." He kissed her before pulling back enough to see her face in the dim spotlight that was shining from the end of the building.

"I need it as much as you do. I've missed you so much these last few weeks." He knew deep down that if she really didn't want to go away with him for the weekend that he'd take her home. But he wanted her to want to be with him. "Please."

"Oh, Nathan." It was her tone more than her words that told him he'd won.

He closed his eyes and swallowed back the emotion that threatened to overwhelm him. Opening his eyes once again, he tugged open the door of the truck and waited. She gave him a look he couldn't interpret, but he didn't worry when she climbed aboard and settled herself in the passenger seat.

Making sure the tail of her dress was tucked out of the way, he closed the door with a solid thunk. He walked around the vehicle and shucked both his jacket and tie, tossing both of them behind the seat, before climbing in on the driver's side. Jamming his keys into the ignition, he started the engine and backed out of his parking space.

When he reached the end of the parking lot, he turned left instead of right, heading away from the town.

Chapter Seven

The interior of the truck was dark and intimate as it rolled down the highway. Nathan gripped the steering wheel with both hands as he drove. Every now and then, he'd shoot her an inquiring look, but she wasn't ready to talk yet. Her head was still spinning with the events of the last half hour.

She could feel the heat on her cheeks as she imagined the sight of herself being half dragged and then carried from the bar in front of an audience. She couldn't forget the smirks on the faces of the men at the bar as Nathan carried her past them and out the door. They were the same men she'd had problems with at the diner. It wasn't surprising that they'd been there as Lucky's was one of the few bars in town, but that didn't mean she had to like it. Most of their friends might tease her about it, but they would all mean it in fun. As for those other men, well they didn't come into her diner very often, so she wouldn't worry about them. They'd be gone as soon as their jobs here were done for the season.

Her biggest concern right now was the man sitting next to her. He was so tense, his knuckles were white and his posture was rigid. His speech in the parking lot had surprised her. Obviously, Nathan was trying to give her some space away from the madness that was her life. He alone had seen what neither her friends or even her own mother had seen—that she needed some time away.

For that reason alone, she loved him even more. But what he didn't seem to understand was that she needed time to herself. He'd seemed almost hurt by the fact. She sighed and rubbed her throbbing temples with the pads of her fingers.

"Headache?" His right hand gripped the back of her neck and he began to rub some of the tension away.

"Oh, that feels good." She moved her head from side to side and could feel some of her tension slipping away. His long, strong fingers dug into the stiff muscles with just the right amount of pressure.

"Why don't you put your head in my lap, close your eyes and try and rest." His hand tightened around her neck as he urged her closer.

Sighing, she allowed him to pull her toward him, scooting down until her cheek was resting against the rough denim of his jeans. She tucked one hand under her face and wrapped the other one around his thigh.

Nathan's hand absently rubbed her hair as he continued to drive. "Sleep if you want to. I'll wake you when we get there."

"Where exactly are we going?" It occurred to her that she had no idea where he was taking her. Not that she was overly concerned, but she was curious.

"It's a surprise."

Glancing up, she could see the wicked grin on his face, illuminated slightly by the dim light from the dashboard. Shrugging, she closed her eyes. Taking a deep breath, she slowly let it out, beginning to finally unwind from the hectic evening. She'd find out when they got there. Another thought niggled at her brain as her mind wandered. "You did pack some clothes for me, didn't you?"

Nathan's chuckle was low and sexy in the close confines of the truck. "Don't worry about clothes."

"I'm not wearing this same dress all weekend, Nathan."

"No, you're certainly not." His hand slipped down from her hair and caressed the side of her neck before sliding down along her arm.

Carly shivered as goose bumps covered her arm. "So, you did pack me some clothes?" She didn't know why she kept

69

harping on the subject. She suspected it was a way of keeping her mind occupied and away from her larger worries.

He reached over to the dashboard and turned up the heat so that she could feel the blast of warm air hit her bare arms and legs. She was just starting to relax again when he finally answered her question. "No."

Sitting up quickly, she turned and scowled at him. "What do you mean, no?"

"You won't be needing any clothing this weekend."

His calm tone was making her crazy. "But that's absurd. What if I want to go out for a walk or go out to eat?"

"We're going to somewhere isolated and I plan to keep you naked all weekend. You can eat, sleep and walk around in your own skin."

Her toes curled in her shoes and her breasts began to tingle as they tightened with desire. She quivered at the thought of being naked for an entire weekend. It was incredibly exciting, erotic and scary, all at the same time.

"What else do you have planned?" She hardly recognized her own voice. It was more of a sensual purr than her normal no-nonsense tones.

"I've got lots of plans for you."

She shivered again, but this time it wasn't from the cold. Her nipples were puckered into hard nubs that rubbed against the fabric of her dress with every movement she made. Not for the first time this evening, she wished that she'd worn a bra and panties under her dress. Clamping her thighs together, she tried to ease some of the growing ache. She felt empty and needy with nothing more than a few spoken words. She had to get a grip on herself.

"What kinds of plans?" Two could play this game and it was time to assert herself.

Nathan glanced at her before turning his attention back to the darkened road. His eyes practically glowed with desire. "I plan to fuck you until you can't think straight." His fingers clenched and unclenched around the steering wheel. "In between, I plan to feed you well and let you rest."

Carly swallowed hard. He was serious. She glanced down at his lap and even though there was hardly any light in the truck cab, she could make out the large bulge in the front of his jeans. Nathan was fully aroused. Again. She licked her lips in anticipation.

He'd had her off-kilter and at a disadvantage all evening. It was now her turn to take control. With more nerve than she thought she possessed, she toed off her sensible pumps and knelt up on the seat facing him as she reached for the buttons of her dress. "Well if you plan to keep me naked all weekend, we might as well start now."

Nathan's head jerked around as he stared at her in disbelief. He swallowed hard as he quickly yanked his gaze back to the road. "Damn it, Carly. Don't tease me like that."

"Why not?" She opened the buttons one by one as she spoke. "You tease me."

"Yeah, but you're not driving at the time." His voice was thick and ended on almost a growl.

Anticipation flowed through her veins like molten lava. She could feel the trickle of fluid from between her thighs. Her clothing felt heavy and confining and she quickly slipped the top of the dress off her arms allowing it to fall to her waist.

She cupped her breasts in her hands, holding their weight for a moment before massaging the tight nipples with her palms. Her breathing was getting quicker and shallower. But even more arousing, was the sound of Nathan's breathing getting heavier and louder.

"Finish it." His words were harsh and loud, making her jump.

Not giving herself time to question the wisdom of her actions, she raised herself up on her knees and shimmied the dress down over her hips until it pooled around her knees. Gripping the back of the seat for support, she levered herself up until she was able to slip it under her knees and remove the dress totally. The seat creaked under her as she maneuvered awkwardly in the cramped area. Shaking out the fabric, she laid it across the back of the seat.

Totally naked, except for her stockings, she sat back on the leather seat with her knees slightly spread and her hands resting on the tops of her thighs. The leather was cool against her heated skin. Her breasts swayed with the movement of the truck, making them feel heavy. Her entire body felt languid and liquid with desire. She wanted to mount Nathan and fuck him, but knew that was impossible.

"Damn, but you're gorgeous."

His words washed over her like a caress. She knew that he had to keep his attention on the road, but she sure didn't. "How long will it take us to get where we're going?"

"About thirty minutes." His words were strained as he continued to concentrate on driving.

"That should be just enough time." She slipped along the leather seat until she was kneeling right next to him, her knees touching his thigh. The heat was rolling off him in waves and she could practically smell his arousal mixing with hers in the small confines of the vehicle.

"Enough time for what?"

"For this." Reaching out her hand, she cupped the large erection pushing at the front of his jeans, feeling quite satisfied when he groaned.

His hand clamped down over hers. "You're playing with fire."

She laughed, feeling more energized and alive than she'd felt in weeks. "I like your fire."

Nathan shoved her hand away and quickly unbuttoned his jeans. Very carefully, he eased down the zipper and shoved both the jeans and underwear out of the way. His cock sprang forward, large and needy.

Before she knew what he meant to do, he'd wrapped his large hand around her neck and pulled her face down to his lap. She nuzzled the dark, curly hair on his groin. "Impatient, are we?"

"You're damn right." His cock flexed and rubbed the side of her cheek. "You started this, you can darn well finish it."

Carly nibbled at the base of his cock before licking a long, wet path all the way to the top. The tip was already wet and she licked off the salty fluid before closing her lips around the head.

Reaching out with her hands, she cupped his swollen balls in one hand and wrapped her other one around the base of his erection. She felt him jerk and swear as she began to move her fingers on his aroused flesh.

She traced the swollen sacs at the base with her fingers, gently squeezing and massaging them. At the same time, she started to pump her fist slowly up and down his length. Once she'd established a rhythm, she lowered her mouth downward on his cock, taking it as deep in her throat as she could.

She could feel his liquid arousal seeping from the tip every time she pulled her mouth back and plunged again. His smell was intoxicating, a combination of soap and musk and man that had her squeezing her own thighs tight together. Her own juices were dripping down her thighs onto the leather of the seats. Whimpering, she angled her breast toward one of her arms, rubbing herself to help ease some of her own needs.

"Enough." Nathan gripped her hair in his hand and pulled her back. It stung slightly as she was reluctant to stop. But he kept up a steady pressure until his cock popped out of her mouth.

Denied that, she traced the dark vein running down the side with her tongue. The truck hit a sudden bump and she clutched at his leg for support. He groaned and gripped her tight, keeping her from sliding off the seat as the truck came to a sudden halt.

The inside of the truck went dark and still as Nathan cut the engine. The only light came from the half-moon riding high in the night sky and the silence was cut only by the sound of their heavy breathing. Then his hands were on her.

Gripping her waist, he pushed her back until he had enough room to slide out from behind the wheel to the middle of the bench seat. Once he was free, he swung her around, pulling her right leg over his thighs so that she was facing him. Her knees slid slightly on the leather seat as she straddled him. Positioning himself at her wet opening, he pulled her down on top of him, driving his cock deep.

Arching back, she clutched at his wide shoulders for support. Before she could even catch her breath, he leaned forward and clamped his mouth over one of her engorged nipples, sucking hard.

Her whimper of desire turned into a cry of delight as his thumb and forefinger captured her other swollen nipple and lightly pinched it. She could feel the pulsing of his cock deep inside her and it filled her with a desperate need to move.

Spreading her knees wide on either side of him and supporting herself by gripping his shoulders, she raised herself slightly and then came back down. Hard. Nathan banded one arm around her back and urged her up again.

She continued to thrust herself up and down on Nathan's cock while he helped to support her with his arm. His other hand left her breast and slid down over her tummy and between her thighs. The moment his finger touched her clit she could feel herself coming.

Tipping back her head, she absorbed every sensation. The rasp of his tongue on her nipple, the light flick of his finger on her clit and the heavy thrust of his cock as it filled her with each thrust. She gasped as her entire body tightened before it exploded. The muscles of her sex clamped down hard as she came.

Carly slumped forward and he caught her easily in his arms. His lips nipped at her collarbone before sliding up her neck toward her ear. "I'm not done with you yet." His words shook her and had her body responding almost immediately. It was only then that she realized that he hadn't come yet.

He lifted her off his cock, her body making a wet sucking sound as it tried to keep its grip on him. Nathan chuckled and laid her back on the seat. It was cool beneath her skin.

Kneeling between her thighs, he wrapped a hand around each of her ankles. He lifted her left leg and placed a kiss on the inside of her thigh before draping it across the back of the seat. He shifted her right leg until he could prop her ankle up on the dashboard.

She was spread wide, open and vulnerable for him. When the light suddenly hit her eyes, she closed them and turned her head away. "Turn off the cab light."

"No, I want to see you." He turned her head back toward him and dropped a kiss on either eyelid. "And, I want you to see yourself. Open your eyes."

Carly blinked several times before her eyes became accustomed to the dim light. Nathan loomed over her, his cock angry-looking and red, bobbing in front of him. She licked her lips and could still taste him there.

"Look at yourself." His harsh command had her eyes dropping to her own body.

Her nipples were swollen and red, her legs sprawled wide and the hair between her thighs glistened with her cum. She felt totally exposed, totally debauched, and she loved it. She loved the way he looked at her, as if she was the most desirable woman in the world. It made her feel powerful and very aroused. And she wanted him again.

Digging her ankles into the dashboard and the top of the seat, she arched her hips toward him. "Nathan," she pleaded.

"Do you want me, baby?"

"Yes." Oh, yes, she wanted him. Now. Badly.

"Ask me, Carly." His eyes glittered as he leaned over her, plucking at her nipples with his fingers. He rubbed his swollen cock against her needy slit, but didn't enter her.

"Nathan." She frantically pumped her hips, trying to get him inside her.

"Ask me," he growled.

"Fuck me, Nathan. Now." The words weren't even out of her mouth when he braced one hand against the door of the truck, gripped her waist with the other, and plunged deep. That was all it took. Her body contracted around his as he pulled back and slammed into her again and again.

"I can't wait any longer," he gasped out between thrusts. He buried himself one final time and shook as he emptied himself into her.

She wrapped her arms around his shoulders, gripping the material of his shirt in her fingers, as her inner muscles continued to spasm around his cock. When he finally collapsed on top of her she held him tight, her fingers digging into his back.

Now that it was over, she could feel her legs starting to cramp and groaned as she lowered first the one that was on the back of the seat and then the one that was propped on the dashboard. Her thighs felt like jelly as her legs flopped back to the seat.

Nathan heaved a sigh and reluctantly sat back, pulling his cock gingerly from her body. She groaned, but didn't move. Quite frankly, she no longer had the energy. She could hear him rustling around and then he was easing her into a sitting position. She grumbled in protest, but he kissed her softly on the lips and she sighed instead.

She opened her eyes when she felt something being draped around her body. Nathan's shirt was still warm from his body heat and she gratefully thrust her arms into its warmth.

Nathan did up several buttons before looking at her with a gentle smile on his face. "Thank you." He kissed the tip of her nose and she smiled back at him. He looked more relaxed than she'd seen him in a long time.

"You're welcome." She tried to stifle a yawn, but couldn't stop it. He just chuckled and then the light went out in the truck. The roar of the engine cut the silence and then he put the truck in gear and carefully eased back onto the road.

It was only then that she took note of where they were. Narrowing her eyes to help them adjust, she watched the land as the headlights cut the darkness. They'd barely pulled off the main highway for goodness sakes. Anyone could have come by and seen them.

Carly shook her head. He made her forget herself completely. She was supposed to be a responsible member of the community, but instead, he has her acting like a teenager out parking with her boyfriend. The image made her smile. Nathan had been a lot of firsts for her and this was just another one.

She swallowed a giggle at the thought of them being discovered by a passing patrol car. How would he explain that to his fellow deputies? Another yawn took her by surprise as exhaustion started to weigh her down.

"Come here." He urged her down to his thigh once again. This time, she snuggled in close and allowed her eyes to drift shut. The satisfaction of their lovemaking, the tiredness of the last few weeks, and the gentle movement of the truck hit her all at once and she felt herself drift off to sleep.

Chapter Eight

ഔ

Nathan glanced down at the woman lying with her head in his lap for the tenth time in about as many minutes. She hadn't moved since they'd hit the highway again. He shook his head in wonder. She continually surprised him. Who'd have thought that she'd strip naked in his moving truck and give him a blowjob?

Who'd have thought he'd respond like some hot teenager and pull off the road for a quick fuck? This woman turned him on faster than any other woman he'd ever known and he knew that no matter how many times he had her, he'd never get enough of her.

She suited him on every level—physically, emotionally and intellectually.

Easing his foot off the gas, he slowed the vehicle, turning off the main highway and onto a dirt road. The truck rocked back and forth on the rugged terrain, but Carly didn't stir. She was totally exhausted.

He felt his jaw tightening and forced himself to relax. Getting her away for a few days was the right thing to do. She needed someone to take care of her, pamper her a little. That job belonged to him now and he was looking forward to it. He planned to look after all of her needs.

Wrapping his right arm around her shoulder, he held her steady as the truck bounced along the rutted road. Within another minute, a small log cabin came into view and he pulled up in front of it.

Leaving the truck lights on, Nathan eased Carly's head off his lap and climbed out of the cab. She mumbled under her breath, but quickly settled back to sleep. Leaving her there, he went to the back of the truck and hauled out a box of supplies.

Balancing it with one arm, he dug in his pocket for the key to the cabin. There were three steps up to the porch that wrapped around the small building and Nathan had the key in his hand by the time he reached the door. Unlocking the door, he pushed it open and hurried inside.

He'd been here once before with his buddy, Jim Wallace, for a fishing weekend. It was quiet and restful and, best of all, no one would bother them here. No one but Jim knew where they were and he would keep it a secret unless it was an emergency.

Using the light from the truck headlights as a guide, Nathan made his way across the room and laid the box on the small kitchen counter. Running his hand along the wall, he found a small switch and flicked it on. The light from the overhead lamp was dim and bathed the room in a soft light, but it was more than enough for him to see.

He made two more trips to the truck, unloading all the things he'd packed for the weekend. Jim had assured him that the place was clean, but lacked amenities. Nathan only hoped he'd packed everything he needed to make this a memorable weekend for Carly.

Checking to make sure that she was still sleeping soundly, he went back into the cabin. There was a small bedroom off the main room that contained a bed and a chest of drawers. Nathan opened one of the boxes he'd brought and took out a set of clean sheets and quickly made up the bed. He covered the sheets with a fluffy comforter and turned back the covers.

Satisfied that the room was ready for her, he headed back out to the truck for Carly. Turning off the truck, he pocketed the keys before turning to the woman sleeping soundly on the seat in front of him. She was curled up with her knees drawn up to her chest as if she were cold. Nathan frowned. She was still wrapped in his shirt and he'd left the heat on in the truck, but now he wasn't sure that was enough. Her legs were bare, except for her thin stockings, and as he watched her, she shivered slightly.

The fact that he wasn't wearing a shirt didn't bother him at all. He felt quite warm and comfortable in the night air. But then, he was male and much larger than she was. She had such a dynamic personality, he sometimes forgot how much physically smaller she was than he, how much more delicate.

Swearing under his breath, he eased her up into a seated position before scooping her into his arms. The last thing he wanted was for her to catch a cold. Using his hip, he closed the truck door and carried her toward the cabin.

"Nathan." Her sleepy voice broke the silence of the night. He could feel her breath on his neck as she snuggled closer to the warmth of his bare chest.

His arms closed tighter around her. "Go back to sleep honey, I've got you."

As simple as that, she sighed and he could feel her go limp against him. Nathan swallowed the lump at the back of his throat as emotion welled up inside him at her absolute trust in him.

He was reluctant to place her in the bed when he got her to the room, not wanting to relinquish his hold on her. But when he noticed the goose bumps on her legs, he quickly placed her on the bed and tucked the covers around her. Digging around in the small chest of drawers, he uncovered another blanket and draped it over her.

Carly sighed and rooted around for a moment before settling back to sleep. He didn't know how long he stood there watching her sleep. This small, sleeping woman meant more to him than anyone else in the world and he knew that he wouldn't relax until they were finally married and she officially belonged to him.

He knew his thinking was old-fashioned and outdated, but he couldn't help how he felt. Something about Carly brought out every primitive instinct he possessed. Heck, if he'd had his way, he'd have married her the day after he proposed to her.

He rolled his shoulders, trying to shake off the tension that had been riding him for weeks. She was here with him now and that was all that mattered. Forcing himself to move, he strode back to the main room and finished unpacking the groceries.

When he was satisfied that everything was as it should be, he turned out the light and waited for his eyes to adjust to the darkness before making his way back to the bedroom.

She hadn't moved from her original position and was still curled into a little mound beneath the covers. Nathan hauled off his boots and socks, shucked his jeans and underwear, and crawled into bed.

The mattress dipped as he climbed under the covers and she rolled toward him. He gathered her into his arms and smiled as she nuzzled her face against his chest. When she found a position she liked, she sighed and he could feel her body melting into his.

Lying there in the dark and quiet of the night with Carly nestled in his arms, Nathan felt all the tension slip away from his body. Damn, he was tired. It had been a heck of a few weeks for both of them.

Her even breathing was the only sound in the room. Its slow, steady rhythm lulled him, as he closed his eyes and allowed himself to drift off to sleep.

Something was tickling her nose. Carly turned her head, noting that her pillow felt harder than usual. Gradually, she became aware of the hard, male body lying next to her and the steady rise and fall of Nathan's chest beneath her cheek. In her sleep, she'd wrapped herself around him, resting her face on his muscled chest and throwing one of her legs across his thighs.

One of his strong arms was wrapped around her shoulders, cradling her tight to his body. The other one cupped her hip, encouraging her to keep her leg draped across him. It was a comfortable position and she lay there content to loll in his arms.

Her thoughts drifted back to the night before. Had it only been last night that they'd made love in the men's room at Lucky's Bar and Grill? Then there was the episode in the truck on the way here, wherever "here" was. Carly didn't know where Nathan had brought her, but she didn't care.

Just the thought of being away from the madness of her life for a couple of days made her feel as giddy as a kid playing hooky from school. A sleepy smile crossed her face as she tried to imagine two whole days without work or responsibilities.

Nathan's actions last night, coupled with them being away for a few days was sure to raise a lot of eyebrows. They'd certainly given the local gossips more than enough to talk about.

Her smile slipped at the thought, but she quickly thrust it from her mind. She'd deal with that when she got home. With any luck, the gossips would be onto something else. For now, she wanted to do nothing more than bask in the peace and quiet.

Nathan's chest rose and fell in a deep, steady rhythm. She knew that he'd been working just as hard as she had these last few weeks, if not harder. Not only had he been pulling double shifts at the sheriff's department, but also he'd been helping out with the fall apple harvest at the family farm.

Now that she was awake, she was beginning to feel hot and sticky. She was still wearing her thigh-high stockings and Nathan's shirt, which had ridden up to her waist. The feel of his hand on her bare skin made her blood start pumping. As if he knew what she was thinking, his fingers tightened on her hip before relaxing once again.

Taking a deep breath, she released it slowly. She could feel the moisture pooling between her thighs. Honestly, the man was turning her into a sex fiend. She'd never had this kind of reaction to any other man in her life. But there was something about Nathan that she found irresistible. Not only was he intelligent, kind, caring and giving, but he had a body to die for.

Tall and strong with a classic six-pack abs and buns of steel, the man looked good coming and going. Nathan was prime, grade-A male. His brown hair was straight and fell to just below his collar and framed a ruggedly handsome face. His lips were immensely kissable and his blue eyes were irresistible.

Knowing she had to get out of bed before she jumped his bones, she started the slow process of trying to ease out of his arms. Normally, she wouldn't hesitate to wake him, but she'd seen the dark circles under his eyes yesterday and the strain behind his smile. He needed his sleep.

She barely even remembered arriving last night. Nathan had driven them here and she had a vague memory of being carried into bed and carefully tucked under the covers. All she knew for sure was that she hadn't felt this good in weeks. Well, except for the fact that she was in desperate need of coffee, a bath and some breakfast.

An inch at a time, she slowly eased out of his arms and rolled off the bed, careful not to disturb him. Standing by the side of the bed, she looked down at him. Even asleep, he exuded a vitality that drew her. The covers had fallen to his waist and he moved restlessly, his hand reaching out in search of her. She froze, afraid that he would wake. But finally, he threw one arm over his head and sighed deeply before settling back into a deep sleep.

The muscles in his arm bulged even as it lay at rest, and Carly found herself mesmerized by the sight of him lying there on the bed. The blankets were bunched around his hips, allowing her an unrestricted view of his broad chest. He had a light dusting of hair in the center, which narrowed to a thin line that ran down his stomach before disappearing beneath the blankets. Even the tuft of hair under his armpit looked soft and sexy.

Giving herself a little shake, she clutched his shirt tight around her as she tiptoed out of the room. She didn't realize she was holding her breath until she gently eased the door shut behind her.

Now that she was sure that Nathan was still sleeping, she was curious to see where he'd brought her. A small bathroom was tucked away in a nook across from the bedroom, but she noted with satisfaction that it contained a bathtub, which she definitely planned to make use of. Continuing her exploration, she padded across the one large room that made up the bulk of the place. The wood floor was cold against her stocking-clad feet and she curled her toes against the chill.

The kitchen and living area shared the space. Carly headed straight for the kitchen and the coffeemaker sitting on the small countertop.

There was an empty box sitting on top of the wooden kitchen table, so she poked around the cupboards and tiny refrigerator until she discovered a can of coffee. When she had a pot of coffee brewing, she went back to exploring.

From the view out the small kitchen window, she could see nothing but woods. The sun was already high in the sky. Glancing at her wristwatch, she was shocked to see that it was half past ten in the morning. For a woman who was used to being out the door by five-thirty every workday morning, this was sleeping really late for her.

The living area of the cabin was sparse, but comfortable, the rugged log walls and wood floor giving it a homey feel. The sofa and chair were large and obviously well worn, but they looked extremely comfy arranged around a stone fireplace. A rag rug and a coffee table rounded out the room.

As her eyes continued to roam, she noted a back door. She could see more of the outdoors from the window next to the table, and it was too inviting to resist. Pouring a cup of coffee, she dug out some sugar and added two heaping spoonfuls, before stirring it and taking her first sip of the day. She almost moaned, it tasted so good.

Her stomach grumbled, but she ignored it. The view tugged at her senses, drawing her toward it. Cradling her mug in her hands, she padded quietly across the floor and tugged open the back door. The air was warm, but there was a slight nip to it, as if to remind her that it was October. Birds were singing in the trees and she could hear the gurgle of a river not too far in the distance.

Wandering out onto the back porch, she allowed the peace to envelop her. Laying her mug on the railing, she raised her hands over her head and stretched the kinks out of her body. She winced slightly at the soreness in her legs and between her thighs, but knew that a hot bath would help soak away the worst of it.

She was grateful that the small cabin had a bathtub. In fact, it was an old-fashioned clawfoot tub. It wasn't very big, but it was deep and she was really looking forward to sinking into it after breakfast.

Picking up her mug, she sat down at the top of the stairs that led down from the porch. A ray of sunshine warmed the spot and the bulk of the house sheltered her from the slight, cool wind that was dancing among the leaves.

She could see a worn path and assumed that it headed toward the river she could hear gurgling just beyond the trees. Stretching her legs out in front of her she saw the snags and runs in her poor stockings.

Taking another sip of coffee, she plunked the mug down next to her and then pulled up the tail of Nathan's shirt. First one leg and then the other, she rolled the stockings off and laid them to one side. They were only fit for the garbage now.

Wiggling her toes, she enjoyed the sensation of the cool air flowing across her skin. She still felt sticky and mussed and knew that a bath would have to come before breakfast. But not yet. Right now, she was too busy enjoying doing absolutely nothing.

Contentment filled her as she sat and watched the antics of the birds as they flew from tree to tree while she sipped her coffee. When her coffee was gone, she laid her mug aside. Tipping her head back, she closed her eyes and just absorbed the sunshine. She sighed, longing for another cup of coffee, but too lazy to move.

"That was quite the sigh." She felt Nathan's large body settle behind hers, his denim-clad legs surrounding hers and his bare arms wrapping around her waist.

"I thought you'd sleep longer." His presence hadn't startled her at all, but had felt totally natural. She leaned her head back against his chest, absorbing his heat and his strength.

"I missed you." His voice was a deep rumble in his chest as he leaned down and kissed the curve of her neck.

"Hmm." She shifted her head to one side, silently encouraging him.

"You look content." He sat back, but continued to hold her in his arms.

Tilting back her head, she looked up at him. "I feel content."

"So, you're not mad at me for bringing you here?"

"No," she paused as she thought about it. "Not for bringing me here. Maybe for the way you went about it, though."

Nathan laughed. "That's something at least."

Her stomach chose that exact moment to grumble loudly. She pressed her hand over it, but couldn't stop the sound.

"You haven't eaten yet?" His large hand nudged her out of the way and he began to rub small circles over her stomach.

Suddenly, she wasn't thinking about food at all. The heat from his hand penetrated the thin fabric of her shirt and she was very aware of him seated behind her wearing nothing but his jeans. She could see his feet and they were bare like hers. He hadn't even pulled on a shirt, but still he was incredibly warm.

Seated in front of him, she could feel his cock stirring and poking her in the back. She licked her lips. "No, I've only had coffee."

"Good." Nathan stood up, pulling her with him. Leaning down, he kissed the tip of her nose and then her mouth. His lips grazed hers, but he didn't try to deepen the kiss.

"Good?" She was trying to make sense of the conversation, but it was hard when she kept getting distracted by his kisses.

"Yes, good. I'm going to put you in a hot bath." Turning, he guided her back into the cabin. "And then I'm going to feed you breakfast."

Carly almost groaned at the thought of a long, hot soak in the tub, but his other proclamation was just as interesting. "You're going to cook me breakfast?"

His blue eyes danced with mischief. "I promise you that I'm going to feed you breakfast."

That was what she'd said, wasn't it? He was up to something, but she promptly forgot all her questions when he led her into the small bathroom. He'd obviously been busy before he'd come out back to join her.

Fragrant steam filled the room as it rose from the tub and mounds of bubbles floated on the top of the water. She sniffed the air. "Vanilla?"

"I knew it was what you used at home." Testing the water with his hand, he nodded with satisfaction.

Carly was stunned by his thoughtfulness. She hadn't even imagined that he would notice such a thing. As well, several large, fluffy bath towels sat on a small wooden stool and a thick washcloth and a bar of vanilla-scented soap rested on a small shelf that sat just above the tub.

Nathan tugged her onto the small bathmat and began to unbutton the shirt that she wore. Her hands covered his, stopping them from continuing. He raised a questioning brow to her.

She swallowed hard. No one had ever done anything like this for her in her entire life. "Thank you." Her words, though heartfelt, sounded totally inadequate.

He shrugged it off. "You're welcome." He pushed her hands aside and continued until all the buttons were undone. Tugging the shirt off her shoulders, he let it fall to the floor. "I told you I wanted to take care of you this weekend."

Lifting her hand, he placed a kiss in the center of her palm before helping her climb into the tub. The moment her body hit the hot, soothing water she let out a sigh of relief. "This feels incredible."

Nathan smiled, but said nothing as he picked up the soiled shirt and left the room. Closing her eyes, she lay back against the rim of the tub, allowing the heat and the fragrance to soak all the aches and stress from her body.

He didn't make a sound, but she immediately knew when Nathan entered the room again. She could sense his presence and opened her eyes. They widened as he extended his hand to her. She reached out, ignoring the bubbles that covered her arm and took the tall glass flute that he offered.

"Orange juice?" It seemed awfully fancy for orange juice.

"Taste it." He took a sip from the other glass he had in his hand.

Raising the glass to her lips, she took a sip, allowing the cold liquid to slide down her throat. It bubbled in her mouth as the flavored filled it. "Champagne and orange juice?"

"Good, isn't it?" He propped himself against the wall, seeming content just to watch her.

"Very," she replied before taking another sip. It was unnerving to have him stare at her while she was bathing. It was more intimate than she'd expected it to be.

His eyes watched her lips as she drank from the flute then fell lower, to where her breasts disappeared into the mound of fragrant bubbles. Beneath the water, she could feel her nipples hardening. It suddenly got harder to breathe and her chest rose and fell rapidly as she tried to catch her breath. She shifted her legs restlessly in the tub.

He gave her a knowing look before saluting her with his glass. "Relax for a while. I'll be back after I see to breakfast."

Turning, he walked away without looking back, leaving her half aroused and half amused by his actions. Get her all hot and bothered and then leave. Her body thrummed with arousal, but she forced herself to take another drink before sliding down further into the water. Taking one deep breath after another, she tried to relax.

Chapter Nine

ജ

Carly had almost drifted off to sleep by the time Nathan returned. She'd heard him rustling around the kitchen and gradually the smell of bacon frying had permeated the air, making her mouth water and her stomach rumble. Once again, she was reminded that she'd missed her usual breakfast and it was now almost lunchtime.

The water had cooled some, but it was still warm and fragrant. She was contemplating dragging herself out of the tub when a rustling sound caught her attention and she opened her eyes. Nathan was watching her, his eyes hot with lust.

"Time to get out." He held out his hand and waited until she grasped it. Using her hold on him for leverage, she pulled herself up out of the tub, stepped over the side and onto the bathmat that lay on the floor.

She reached for a towel, but Nathan grabbed it first. Shaking out the large, fluffy towel he wrapped it around her and hugged her tight. She loved the feel of his muscled arms wrapped around her, holding her close to his heart. Arousal began to pulse low in her belly and a shiver skated down her spine. The moment he felt it, he pulled back and began to briskly dry the water from her skin.

He started at her neck, working his way down her torso and over her belly before going back and toweling off her arms. He was very thorough, leaving no part of her untouched. Going down on one knee in front of her, he dried first one leg and then the other, his hands firmly stroking her thighs and calves. She grabbed his shoulders for support as he lifted her foot and wiped it dry before doing the same to her other one.

Carly looked around for a robe or something she could slip into, but there was nothing in sight. She opened her mouth to ask him if he could loan her a shirt but nothing came out of her but a gasp.

The towel lay discarded on the floor at her feet and Nathan was now kneeling between her feet. The pads of his fingers felt rough against her sensitive skin as he gently caressed a path up the inside of her thighs before pushing back the slick folds of her labia. He leaned closer and she could feel his warm breath on her sex.

"Nathan." Her voice was breathless as she gripped his hair, tugging him even closer.

"Umm." She could feel the vibration of his response right to her core as his tongue slipped up one side and then down the other.

Thrusting her hips forward, she encouraged his exploration, but he stopped and sat back on his heels. "Don't stop." The words were out of her mouth before she could stop them. The sexy devil just smiled at her as he slipped his hands behind her and kneaded her ass in his large palms.

"Open your legs wide and spread the lips of your pussy wide with your fingers." His fingers traced the cleft of her behind, sending a shiver up her spine. "I want to lick every part of you." Leaning forward, he lapped at her sex with his tongue. "To taste you." Raising his head to look at her, he licked his lips. "I want to eat you up." His eyes were so hot as they devoured her, she thought she might catch on fire.

Oh, lord. She wanted that too. Her hands slipped between her legs and she spread her sex wide even as she was widening her stance. Carly looked down at her body. Her nipples were puckered into hard nubs and she could see the pink lips of her labia and her swollen clit just begging for his touch.

"That's what I like to see." Nathan gently scraped her clit with his thumb. "Your pussy, hot and wet and wanting me."

"Yes," she hissed.

Holding her ass tight with his hands, he leaned forward and buried his face between her thighs. Moaning, she thrust her hips toward his face and he laughed as he lapped at her flesh. His tongue stroked the outside of her slit before slipping inside.

She closed her eyes as she felt her inner muscles clench tight. It felt so incredibly good as his tongue slid in and out of her body. He withdrew his tongue and inserted a finger instead. It was long and thick, but not enough. She gasped as he slipped a second finger in to join the first.

Her hips bucked toward him as he stroked his fingers within her. His clever tongue was now flicking at her clit. She could feel the tension thrumming throughout her body, knowing she'd come any second. Her breathing was shallow, her chest heaving up and down with each gasp of air she sucked into her lungs. Her inner muscles clenched hard. She was so close.

She pumped her hips toward his clever mouth and fingers. Only a few more strokes. On the next swing of her hips, she met...nothing. "No," she cried. He couldn't leave her empty and aching.

One minute she was on the brink of ecstasy, the next she was standing there poised on the edge with Nathan sitting back on his heels watching her. She couldn't believe he'd leave her hanging like this.

"Don't stop now." She tangled her fingers in his hair, trying desperately to pull him back to her.

He leaned closer, blowing on her wet pussy. "Oh god," she moaned as his warm breath feathered across her sensitive flesh. This was torture. Then he kissed a path up her tummy and along her torso, stopping to nibble at her breasts as he rose to his feet. She stamped her foot in frustration.

Wrapping his hand around the back of her neck, he yanked her close and kissed her. It was hot and carnal as he drove his tongue into her mouth, claiming it as his. He stroked her tongue, teasing it with his before enticing it into his mouth where he could suck on it. There was no part of her mouth he left unexplored.

The man certainly knew how to kiss, she thought as she rose on her toes and grabbed his shoulders for support. But again he left her wanting more. Frustrated. Tearing his mouth from hers, he took a step back. His chest was heaving and a fine sheen of sweat covered his bare torso. "Enough. Food first."

"Why?" She was hot and horny, and if the huge bulge in the front of his jeans was an indication, so was he.

The corner of his mouth crooked up in a half smile. "It's all about anticipation. The hotter you get, the harder you'll come."

He took her arm and tugged her behind him. She tried to pull away, but it was useless, his hand was wrapped around her wrist like a manacle. "Hey, I'm naked here."

Coming to a sudden halt, he turned and his eyes raked over her body. "I know." Before she could respond, he was moving again, continuing to tow her toward the kitchen table. "Up you go." He gestured to a small pillow that was sitting in the middle of the table.

"Nathan, I am not sitting naked on the top of the breakfast table." She shivered, but it wasn't with cold. He'd started a fire in the stone fireplace while she'd lolled in the tub and the flames were crackling merrily, giving the room a warm, cozy feel. It was a slight fear of what he might demand of her sexually, tinged with anticipation that had her quaking.

Releasing her, he stood back and crossed his arms over his chest. The muscles rippled and bulged, distracting her for a moment. But his next words certainly got her attention.

"You promised."

She frowned at him. "I did no such thing."

He was already nodding at her. "Yes you did. You agreed that I would be in charge in the bedroom. And baby, for this weekend, this entire cabin is one big bedroom."

"That's not fair."

He shrugged, seemingly unconcerned. "Fair or not, it's a fact." He motioned toward the pillow again. "You knew what you were getting yourself into when you agreed to marry me. It's your choice."

She almost stomped back to the bedroom and slammed the door in his gorgeous face. The nerve of the man to get her all worked up in the bathroom, leave her hot and bothered, and then demand that she obey his sexual whims. She started to move, stopping suddenly when a slight look of panic flickered in his face. It was only there for a split second and if she hadn't been watching him closely she would have missed it.

Taking her time, she studied his face as she replayed his words in her mind. His face was stoic, showing no emotion whatsoever. It was what she called his "cop face". He looked hard and totally unconcerned about her decision. But the muscles in his arms were tight and his knuckles were almost white because his hands were fisted so tight. A muscle under his left eye twitched slightly.

He was testing her.

The realization struck her so hard she felt it like a physical blow. He still doubted her commitment to him and if she was capable of fulfilling his sexual needs. That's what these demands were all about. He was acting this way, all cold and demanding, to see if she would stay with him or if she'd run like a frightened little girl. Her head began to throb as she tried to work it all out.

Never mind that she had her own doubts as to whether she could handle a man like Nathan and not lose her own sense of independence. The funny thing was that her second thoughts weren't really about their sexual compatibility, although she did worry sometimes that she wouldn't be able to give him all that he needed. It was mainly life outside the bedroom that was causing her some anxiety.

"Carly." His hand stilled hers on her temple and she realized that she must have been rubbing her head. Leaning down, he kissed her forehead while his fingers massaged the sides of her face. Taking a deep breath, he slowly released it. "It's okay if you don't want to."

She sensed his disappointment, as well as his concern for her, and it was those two things that spurred her to action. It was time to put away any doubts and lingering embarrassment and embrace her sexuality. That meant coming to grips with the fact that she got turned on when Nathan dominated their sexual play. She trusted him never to ask her to do anything that would be degrading or distasteful to her. That last thought made her next move easy. Making a quick decision, she stepped back from him. His hands hovered in the air for a second before dropping back to his sides.

Turning away, she stepped up onto a chair, bent her legs and knelt on the table. She positioned herself on top of the pillow before settling her behind on it. The satiny material felt slick and cool against her bottom. Resting her hands on her thighs, she sat there and waited.

"Spread your legs wider." His voice was slightly hoarse, but she complied instantly. "Now, put your hands behind your head."

Looking straight at him, she licked her lips as she slid her hands up over her legs and across her torso. Taking her time, she cupped her breasts in her hands and teased her nipples before raising her hands to the back of her neck.

Nathan shuddered and reached between his legs to adjust his straining cock. He walked slowly around the table. She could feel his eyes on her like a physical touch as he hovered around her, never touching.

Coming around to the front, he put one hand on each of her knees and widened them slightly. Then he pushed the small pillow back so that only her ass rested on it. Her pussy was wide open and exposed to the air. Stepping back, he looked at her. "Perfect."

Leaving her there, he went to the kitchen counter, picked up a huge platter loaded with food, and brought it back, placing it at the head of the table. Her legs, spread as they were, surrounded his plate.

She could feel her nipples tightening as he watched her. More than anything she wanted to move, but forced herself to be still. She could feel the liquid seeping from her pussy and rolling down her inner thighs to drip onto the table.

Nathan picked up a slice of toast and raised it to her mouth. She bit off a piece and chewed carefully before swallowing. He popped the rest of the slice into his mouth and ate it as he watched her.

When he reached out for the saltshaker, he slipped his hand between her spread thighs and stroked her heated flesh. She moaned and shuddered. He removed his hand, picked up the shaker and salted his eggs.

"It's all about anticipation," he murmured as he fed her a forkful of eggs.

She made a huge production of licking her lips. If it was anticipation he wanted, she'd darn well give it to him. His eyes narrowed as she tipped back her head and swallowed. "Anticipation is good."

Picking up a slice of orange, he bit it in half. The juice sprayed and filled the air with a citrus scent. Slowly, he raised it to her lips. But just when she would have taken it into her mouth, he pulled it away.

"Not yet," he murmured as he rubbed the half-eaten slice over her bottom lip before sliding it over her top one.

Some of the juice trickled down her lip and over her chin. She tried to catch some of it with her tongue, and the tart flavor exploded in her mouth. Never had an orange tasted this good.

Laughing, Nathan squeezed the orange section, sending juice down over her throat and dripping over one of her breasts. Looking down, she could feel a drop pearling on the end of her nipple. It hovered, preparing to drop.

Nathan leaned up out of his chair and flicked the tip of her breast with his tongue, capturing the drop of juice before it could fall. Sitting back, he licked his lips. "Delicious."

Biting her lip to keep from moaning, she squirmed on the table. Her pussy felt so hot and wet and she wanted to close her thighs tight to try and ease the throbbing ache.

As she watched, he deliberately picked up another orange slice. Holding the fruit between his fingers, he made a production of biting off a piece. He rolled it around on his tongue before carefully chewing it and swallowing it. She wanted to lunge at him and bite the strong column of his neck as she impaled herself on his length.

Her hips arched toward him. Smiling, he moved his hand between her thighs. She swallowed back a cry as the cool pulpy flesh of the fruit was brushed across her heated folds, up one side, across her clit, and down the other.

She thrust her hips forward, but he ignored her silent plea. Raising the orange piece to his mouth, he licked it before popping it into his mouth and eating it. "Tasty." He licked his lips and picked up a piece of bacon.

This time, she couldn't hold back the moan of need that welled up inside her. He was torturing her. Half of the slice of bacon went in his mouth before he offered her the rest. She automatically opened her mouth, chewing it before she swallowed.

He sat back, rested his elbows on the arms of the chair and steepled his fingers together. "I think you're ready for more."

Chapter Ten

ജ

Her mouth went dry and she swallowed hard, chewing uncertainly on her bottom lip. He watched her like a hawk, his eyes never leaving her face. Again, he waited for her decision. Giving him a single, quick nod, she held her breath and waited.

A tiny smile of satisfaction crossed his face as he reached into his back pocket and pulled out a piece of black cloth. The silky fabric slid easily through his hands. "Do you know what this is?"

She shook her head, almost afraid to try and speak. She wasn't sure she could. Her lungs felt like they were bursting and she realized she was still holding her breath. Sucking in needed air, she stared at his hands. Breathing was almost too hard at the moment, talking was beyond her.

Nathan wove the silk between his fingers before slowly sliding it out. "This is a blindfold." She blinked at him and concentrated on taking one breath at a time. Her entire body was one large pulsing ache.

He came to his feet as quick as a cat and sauntered around the table, still playing with the blindfold with his fingers. She wanted to turn when he walked behind her. What was he doing? In spite of her determination not to move, her hands slipped from behind her neck and, as uncertainty filled her, she hugged herself tight.

His feet barely made any sound on the wood floor, but she heard the brush of his jeans against the table as he moved back into her field of vision. Ever so slowly, he looped the length of black silk around her neck and leaned toward her. His lips were gentle, so very gentle as he kissed her.

"Don't be afraid," he whispered as one kiss became two. Her lips parted easily as he slipped his tongue inside her mouth. Unwrapping her hands from around her waist, she slid them up his torso, loving the way the muscle rippled beneath her fingers.

Carefully, as if he was afraid to startle her, he withdrew. Their moist lips seemed to cling together before reluctantly parting. Carly licked her lips and tasted Nathan. Her hands tried to hold on to him, but he slipped away.

The corners of his eyes crinkled as he stood in front of her and smiled. Then he reached into his other back pocket and pulled out a pair of leather cuffs. "I've tied your hands before, so you know you like it." He didn't even ask her, but simply held the cuffs in front of her.

Her heart was pounding against her chest as she held out her right hand to him. Competently and quickly, he cuffed it. The leather felt snug around her wrist, not tight, but she knew it was there. The other cuff was empty, dangling in the air. Her left hand shook slightly as she handed it to him.

She watched his hands as he affixed the restraint around her wrist. When both cuffs were on, she stared at her bound wrists. They were the only thing she was wearing. It was different from the other times they'd done it. The last time he'd used her bra to bind her hands. Somehow that hadn't made her as nervous as this did. But in spite of her nerves, she was incredibly turned on.

Her pussy was clenching rhythmically now and she thought she might come just sitting there on the top of the table with her hands cuffed in the smooth, supple leather. Her breasts felt incredibly heavy, her nipples tight and achy. She felt fragile, but powerful at the same time, knowing that Nathan watched her.

She could hear him beside her, his breathing harsh in the quiet room. Raising her eyes, she stared at him. Her eyes widened at the stark look of lust and need on his face. Slowly, she lifted her bound hands in front of her, and as he watched, she hooked them behind her neck.

Nathan tilted his head back and closed his eyes. The strong column of his throat rippled as he swallowed hard. His hands were by his sides, clenching and opening rhythmically as if he was grasping for control. It made her feel more secure to realize he was as much a prisoner of their desire as she was.

Lowering his head, he opened his eyes and the heat in them almost melted her heart. Love and tenderness shone from his incredible blue eyes, mixed with the hot burning need that was still there.

He grazed his knuckles against her swollen nipples. The pleasure shot straight to her core and she moaned as she felt her cream slip from her body and down to the table. She was going to come. There was no way to stop it.

And it seemed that he didn't want her to stop. As one hand continued to pleasure her breasts, he inserted the other one between her legs and slipped two of his fingers as far up her core as they would go.

Screaming, she came. Her entire body spasmed as the pleasure rocketed through her. Gasping, she shoved her hips toward his hand. Sobs came from her throat as he continued to stroke her, spinning her orgasm out so long she feared she might pass out.

But his touches became lighter, more comforting, until he finally withdrew his hand and raised it to her face. She hadn't even known she was crying until he wiped away the tears with his thumbs. "Shhh," he hushed her. "You look so beautiful when you come." His lips grazed her cheeks, her forehead and her lips, calming her.

Heaving a huge sigh, she finally looked at him. His soft smile made her smile back at him. "It gets better." His words washed over her and her calm fled. Surely he was finished. That thought was barely complete when she felt the length of silk being slowly tugged from around her neck.

Holding it so it was covering both her swollen nipples, he slowly pulled it back and forth. The friction was exquisite and Carly could once again feel the arousal jumping to life inside her.

"You were made for me, Carly." He resumed walking around the table. "You respond so perfectly and immediately to everything I do." She felt the silk on her back and it sent a shiver along her naked flesh. "It's incredibly arousing."

She gasped as the silk covered her eyes and her vision disappeared behind the blindfold. "You make me so damn hard all the time." The whisper in her ear made her jump slightly. "I want to fuck you constantly." The fabric tightened around her head as he tied it. "Now and always."

"Yes." His words were like a balm to her soul. She could read between the lines. He was letting her know that she had power over him as well.

With her vision gone, her other senses heightened. He trailed his fingers down over her spine before kissing his way back up. She could smell him, an arousing scent of musk and soap, as he nipped at her nape.

The table creaked as he climbed onto the table behind her, and his jeans-clad legs wrapped around her naked thighs. His fingers rested lightly on her waist and she could feel their roughness on her skin. They were hardworking hands, slightly callused and hard. A man's hands. Her man's hands.

Leaning back against his chest, she felt safe and secure. His cock was hard and huge against her back and she loved that she could do this to him. He moved his hands then and inched his way up her torso toward her breast. She didn't know whether to laugh or cry it felt so incredibly good with just his fingers touching her.

He was barely touching her skin as he circled his hands around her breasts. She shifted her shoulders back, pushing her breasts toward his hands. But they weren't there. She didn't know where they were, couldn't see them. More than anything she wanted to feel them on her, see them on her. Even though blackness filled her vision, she imagined his large, strong hands on her body. Dark flesh on pale. The image was so real in her mind that she could almost feel it.

Then the waiting was over. Nathan cupped both her breasts and rubbed the tips with his thumbs. Burying his face in her shoulder, he took a ragged breath. Her own breathing was unsteady as she ached for completion yet again.

Swearing suddenly, he pulled back. She could feel him still behind her, hear him there, even though he was no longer touching her. The table creaked again and a light breeze brushed her skin, telling her that he was no longer behind her.

Listening hard, she tried to locate him. It was easier than she suspected. She could hear him move, hear his heavy breathing. She recognized the sound of the chair being moved back into place.

She caught a whiff of bread and butter just before she felt it against her lips. "Open up, honey." Nibbling off a piece, she chewed it and waited to see what he would do next.

The scent of her arousal filled the air around her. The sound of their breathing, the crackling of the fire, and the scrape of the fork on the plate were the only sounds in the room. Carly barely tasted any of the food he offered her.

All of her attention was focused on her sexual needs. She moved her hips, subtly trying to relieve the ache between her legs. She didn't know how much longer she'd be able to sit here when all she wanted to do was jump Nathan's bones.

Wood scraped across wood. He unhooked her hands from the back of her head and drew them forward. They were a little bit numb from being in that position for so long. He undid the cuffs and tossed them aside. She thought she heard them land on the floor as he sat back down in his chair, which creaked under his weigh. Even though she was still blindfolded, she could feel his eyes on her. She rubbed her hands against her thighs, but said nothing, sensing his sudden agitation.

"Fuck." She flinched at his harsh tone and the sound of dishes crashing to the floor as they were swept from the table. His hard hands gripped her shoulders, dragging her down into his lap. His mouth fused with hers.

She could hardly breathe as Nathan devoured her. His hand was hard on the back of her head, holding her steady as his other arm banded around her back, binding her to him. Framing his face with her fingers, she held on tight and gave back as good as she got.

Tearing his lips from her mouth, he peppered her face and neck with hot, biting kisses. "I've got to have you now." Reaching between them, she could feel him tearing at the opening of his jeans.

She struggled to help him, but he pushed her hands aside and tugged down the zipper. His cock sprang free, large and hungry, and right into her waiting hand. She wrapped her fingers around it and pumped it hard.

Groaning, he lifted her with one arm and stood. Her hands flew to his shoulders for support as her bottom hit the table with a thump. Then he was fitting his cock between her legs and thrusting deep.

Lying back on the table, she reached for him, locking her legs around his hips and crossing her ankles over the small of his back. She had him now and she wasn't letting him go.

Burying his face between her breasts, Nathan slipped his hands under her shoulders, his fingers tightening around them as he began to thrust. Hard. There was no finesse as he slammed himself into her again and again. She could feel his balls slapping her sex with each stroke.

"Harder," she gasped as she clamped her legs tighter around him and levered herself off the table to meet his every thrust.

Rearing back, he drove deep. His hips pumped hard and quick and it was only his tight grip on her that kept her from sliding right across the table. She could feel the stinging bite of his fingers digging into her shoulders, the slickness of the hard planes of his chest as it slid over her breasts, and the thickness of his cock as it squeezed in and out of her, stretching her pussy.

She was frantic now. Wanting to come. Needing to come. A long, low wail escaped her as he pounded her pussy hard and deep. Then finally she got release. Her entire body seemed to contract at once and she exploded. She squeezed her eyes shut behind the blindfold, as pleasure rushed through her and felt it in every cell of her body. Her pussy continued to contract around him as he continued to pound into her.

She heard him yell and felt his cock pulsing deep in her core as he came. He thrust several more times before burying his head in her shoulder, his entire body shaking as he emptied himself. He slumped across her and she automatically wrapped her arms around his back, holding him to her.

Time passed slowly, but eventually, her body cried out for rest. She was cramped in this position and a small cry escaped her as she slipped her legs from around his flanks. They dangled off the edge of the table. Next she relaxed her arms and they flopped down on the hard wood beside her. Never in her life had she been this exhausted or replete.

The fire continued to crackle and from the kitchen she could hear a steady drip from the sink. Her own breathing finally returned to normal and the pounding of her heart slowed. She could still feel Nathan's heart beating hard against his chest as he grunted and pushed away from her.

The blindfold slipped from her eyes, the silky fabric sliding easily as Nathan lifted it off her head and threw it to one side. She blinked as the light hit her eyes. It wasn't bright, but it seemed that way after the darkness.

A bead of sweat rolled down the side of his face and she reached up and wiped it away. He caught her hand in his and raised it to his lips, placing a kiss in the center. When he released her hand, her fingers curled tight around the warmth left from his lips.

Neither of them spoke as he gritted his teeth and pulled out of her. She flinched slightly, but didn't have the strength to move. Nathan hitched his pants over his hips before scooping her up into his arms.

Carrying her to the bedroom, he tucked her into the bed, then shucked his jeans and climbed in beside her. Hauling the covers over them both, he wrapped his arms around her so that her bottom was tucked up against his front. She snuggled into the pillow and wiggled around until she was comfortable. He cupped her breast with one hand and placed his other hand under her head.

Sighing, she felt sleep drag her down. His lips nibbled at her ear and as she drifted off she thought she heard him whisper, "I love you." But she was asleep before she could reply.

Chapter Eleven

৪৩

It was dark when he finally woke. Carly was lying on her back with her legs and arms sprawled wide. For a small woman, she sure took up a heck of a lot of the bed. He smiled as he propped himself up on his elbow so he could see her better.

Sleeping, she looked like an angel. Her long lashes feathered against her cheeks, her nose tilted up slightly and her flawless skin was tinged a healthy pink. What pleased him most was that the dark shadows under her eyes were fading.

Her chest rose and fell and she made a slight snoring noise as she slept. He knew she'd deny it, but she did snore, even if it was a tiny, almost dainty, sound.

Reaching out, he brushed a lock of hair from her forehead and leaned down to kiss her. She was sleeping so soundly, she didn't even stir.

He eased his legs out from under the covers and pushed himself up until he was sitting on the side of the bed. Glancing at his wrist, he squinted to try and see the numbers. It was almost eight o'clock. They'd slept the entire afternoon away.

Nathan rolled his shoulders and raised his arms over his head to stretch. He had to admit, he felt physically better than he had in weeks. His stomach growled, reminding him that it had been a long time since brunch and he hadn't eaten very much of that. Just the thought of his last meal had his entire body hardening and his cock stirring to life once again.

He looked down at himself and shook his head. It was crazy that just the thought of Carly made him hard. Snagging his jeans off the floor, he got up from the bed and hauled them on. He zipped them, but didn't bother to button them.

Scratching his belly, he padded to the door. Glancing back at the bed, Carly still hadn't moved so he quietly shut the door behind him.

A slight beam from the moon lit the cabin enough for him to make his way to the kitchen. Flicking on the light, he squinted until his eyes adjusted. The kitchen was a mess. All the pans he'd used to cook breakfast were piled on the stove.

Groaning, he looked at the floor and found the remains of his plate and breakfast scattered across the hardwood. Sighing, he mentally thanked the coffee gods for automatic shut-off and dumped out the cold brew left over from earlier. Once he had a new pot set to dripping, he dug around in the small utility closet and dug out a broom and dustpan.

In no time, he had the broken glass and crumbs of food swept up and disposed of. Running hot water in the sink, he dumped in the pans and remaining dishes and wiped down the table. Quickly, he scrubbed everything and left it to drain in the tray by the sink. Wiping his hands, he snagged a clean mug and poured himself a cup of the fresh brewed coffee.

Leaving only a small light on in the kitchen, he wandered back toward the living area, stopping at the table long enough to snag the small pillow. Raising it to his face, he inhaled the scent of Carly's arousal. His body, which had relaxed while he was doing the mundane chores, stirred once again. "Damn," he muttered as he threw himself down on the sofa in front of the fireplace.

The fire had long since burned down to a few pieces of charred wood and embers behind the protective screen. Nathan stared at the red-hot coals and brooded. He didn't know what the hell was wrong with him. He'd planned to do everything in his power to convince Carly she'd made the right decision in agreeing to marry him. Instead, he was acting like a bastard and doing his best to drive her away.

He took a sip of coffee and contemplated his actions. A piece of wood dropped and a few sparks sprang up, their dramatic show short lived. He knew that once he had a wedding ring on her finger, she would be totally committed to making their marriage work. That's why he wished they were already married.

On the other hand, he didn't want her marrying him and then having second thoughts. Just the thought of Carly regretting their marriage turned his stomach sour. No, he wanted her to know exactly what she was getting herself into before she said, "I do".

He plunked his mug down on the table and buried his face in his hands for a moment before scrubbing them over his face and running them through his hair. He'd gone too damn far in the other direction.

In the last twenty-four hours, he'd practically ordered her to have sex with him in the men's room of a damned bar, kidnapped her, had sex with her in the front seat of his truck…okay, that was her idea, but still.

He continued to list his questionable actions. And today, he'd pushed her hard to see if she would obey his sexual commands. Usually, he'd have confined it to the bedroom, but he'd pushed her outside those confines just to see what she would do.

If he was honest with himself, he wouldn't have blamed her if she'd up and left him after he'd ordered her to stay naked, climb on the kitchen table and then allow him to cuff and blindfold her. But deep in his gut, he'd been thrilled and had been deeply satisfied when she'd done what he'd asked of her. She was his.

Sitting back, he tipped his head back on the edge of the sofa. His cock was stirring and pushing against the zipper so he undid it and let it spring free. Just the idea that she was lying naked and tousled in the bedroom, his for the taking, made him hard.

He knew he had unique sexual tastes, but he'd never realized just how damned primitive he could get until he'd become involved with Carly. He felt like a conqueror with his slave. He wanted her primed and ready for him at all times.

Yeah, like that was going to happen. Shaking his head at his own foolish thoughts. Carly was a totally independent woman with a business and house of her own. She didn't need him to survive.

He stilled. That was his problem right there in a nutshell. She didn't need him. The only reason she had for wanting to be with him was because she wanted to. He had nothing to offer her except himself and his love. And after his actions this weekend, he was wondering if she'd now think that that was enough.

The memory of her all pink and flushed from her bath rose again in his brain. Unable to resist, he picked up the pillow once again and breathed in her unique scent. His cock grew harder and longer, the bulbous head twitching.

Sighing, he wrapped his hand around his cock and moved it slowly up and down. He wanted Carly again, but he wasn't going to wake her. She needed her sleep and he was darned well going to try and act like a gentleman this once.

"Oh, my." The quiet whisper had his head jerking around. He'd been so wrapped up in his own thoughts he hadn't heard her creeping up behind him.

He didn't move his hand from his erection as she edged closer. She was still totally, gloriously naked. Her body gleamed in the dim light. Every hollow and curve was visible and her breasts jiggled slightly with every breath she took. She had amazing breasts.

A pearl of liquid seeped from the tip of his penis and Nathan spread it over the head with his thumb. "I thought you were still sleeping." He kept up the steady pumping of his fist.

"No." She licked her lips as her gaze went from his face to his lap where he was jerking himself off. "No. I woke up after you left. It was cold in bed without you."

Like a woman in a trance she came to stand in front of him and slowly went to her knees at his feet. She reached out to touch his cock, but he stopped her, grabbing her hand with his. "You don't have to, honey. I can take care of this myself." He'd been demanding enough this weekend.

Her blue eyes were wide as she stared up at him with that angel's face. "But I want to."

A shudder went though his entire body at her words. No doubt about it, this small woman could bring him to his knees. Except it was her on her knees in front of him.

She tugged her hand out of his and pushed his hands away. They fell to his side, useless as she wrapped both her hands around his length. Her small fingers massaged his cock as they moved up and down from base to tip.

"Carly." Her name spilled from his lips. A prayer and a plea.

Coming up on her knees, she leaned forward and took the head of his cock into her mouth. He gritted his teeth and swore as her tongue swirled around the top before licking at the sides.

Her hands stayed as busy as her pretty little mouth. She cupped his balls with one hand, massaging them gently. With her other hand, she gripped the base of his cock tight and pumped up and down in a slow, steady rhythm.

"I want to fuck your mouth." Tangling his fingers in her hair, he began to guide her mouth up and down over his cock. His good intentions flew out the window as her moist, hot mouth fitted itself over his straining length.

Every time he pushed her mouth down on him, she took him deeper until he could feel himself touching the back of her throat. She made little sounds of pleasure that vibrated around his shaft, driving him closer to the edge.

He wanted to stop. He didn't want to stop. Suddenly it was out of his hands. Her hand squeezed his cock tight as her mouth took him deep and sucked hard.

Gripping her head to hold her in place, his hips jerked as he came in her mouth. She continued to suck and swallowed his cum, not stopping until he was drained dry. Nathan continued to buck as a litany of swear words fell from his lips before he finally slumped back against the sofa cushions.

Carly continued to suck at his cock and lick at his balls as her fingers combed through his pubic hair. It took every ounce of energy in him, but he carefully untangled his fingers from her hair and smoothed it back out of her face.

She was every man's wet dream, sitting there naked at his feet, still sucking on him after giving him the most amazing blowjob of his life. She tilted her head up and looked at him then and gave him a soft, satisfied smile.

Damn, but he was the luckiest man alive. She'd actually enjoyed herself. It was written all over her face. She might look like an angel, but she was a temptress at heart.

"Come here." Urging her up, he helped her to her feet and then pulled her down into his arms. She curled herself around him like a sleepy kitten and snuggled up close to him.

He didn't quite know what to say. Somehow "thank you" didn't seem adequate enough. "That was amazing." He ran his hand over her from thigh to shoulder, just wanting to feel her skin under his fingers.

She nodded, nuzzling his chest as she burrowed closer. Nathan continued to stroke her. That was another thing he loved about her. She was restful to be around. She didn't feel the need to fill the silence with unnecessary chatter.

Goose bumps rose on her flesh as he stroked it and it belatedly occurred to him that she must be cold. The cabin was cooler now that the fire was burned down and she was totally naked.

"Carly, honey, let me get up." When she didn't answer, he realized she'd dozed off again. Standing with her cradled in his arms, he laid her on the sofa. A blanket lay folded across the matching chair, so he grabbed it and shook it out before draping it over her.

He quietly walked over to the fireplace, and crouched down in front of it. Pulling the screen from in front of it, he stoked the embers and carefully added more fuel until the fire was crackling cheerfully once again. When he had the screen set in place once again, he turned back to the sofa. Carly had the blanket pulled up to her nose.

Padding back to the sofa, he looked down at her. She seemed peaceful and relaxed and the longer he watched her, the more those same feelings seemed to permeate his entire being. Taking his time, he tucked the blanket tightly around her.

His stomach growled again. He'd let her sleep while he was making supper. She needed a good, hearty meal and another good night's rest.

He couldn't see her from where he worked at the kitchen counter, but that didn't matter. Just the fact that she was in the same room with him gave him a contented feeling as he washed some potatoes and threw them in the oven to bake. Taking his time, he dumped a pre-made garden salad from a bag into a bowl and laid out some frozen rolls to bake. Hauling the steaks out of the refrigerator, he laid them in a large pan on the top of the stove.

While he was waiting for the potatoes to bake, he rummaged around in the fridge and pulled out a beer. Opening it, he took a deep swallow and wandered back in the living room and settled into the chair next to the sofa. As the minutes ticked by, he alternately stared in the fire and watched Carly sleep.

When he thought it was time, he went back to the kitchen and popped the rolls in the oven and fired up the stove to cook the steaks. He could hear her stirring by the time he was taking everything up.

She was just sitting up and wiping the sleep from her eyes when he laid the two plates loaded with food onto the coffee table. "Wow. This looks great." Her stomach gave a huge growl and she laughed. "Smells even better."

"You need to eat to keep up your strength." He handed her a plate and went back to the kitchen for cutlery and a glass of red wine for Carly. She looked uncertainly at the blanket wrapped around her as he handed her the glass of wine, so he tucked the ends around her. "I don't want you to get cold."

"Thank you." Her smile warmed his entire body and he watched as she eagerly dug into her supper. "This is wonderful," she told him as she chewed a piece of her steak.

Absurdly pleased, Nathan grabbed his own plate, settled down next to her and started to eat.

Chapter Twelve

෨

Carly could hardly believe that the weekend was over so quickly. All she'd done was eat and sleep. Well, that wasn't quite all. She could feel the heat of a blush on her cheeks and hoped it didn't show too much.

The sex had been totally amazing. Nathan was amazing. The weekend had started out rocky, but everything had changed Saturday night when she'd awakened in time for a very late supper. After they'd finished eating, they'd curled up on the couch and talked and dozed late into the night.

The conversation had consisted mostly of mundane things like what was going on at work for both of them and what they had on their schedules for the week ahead. Talk had then turned to family and other ordinary topics. And sometimes there was no need for talk at all. Both of them had been content to lie in each other's arms and just watch the fire dancing in the fireplace.

She'd drifted awake early Sunday morning to find herself flat on her back with him already inside her. Their lovemaking had been slow and gentle, as he'd rocked them to completion. Afterwards, they'd curled up in a blanket on the back porch of the cabin and eaten a huge breakfast before reluctantly packing up to leave.

She couldn't quite put her finger on what the difference was. Nathan was quieter, more relaxed, less determined. Settling back in her seat, she watched him drive out of the corner of her eye. He was a much different man from the one who'd brought her to the cabin Friday night.

"What?" He glanced at her before turning his attention back to the road. "I can hear the wheels of your mind spinning."

She should have known that he would feel her staring at him, even if it was covertly. "I don't know." Shrugging, she gave a little laugh. "I guess I was wishing that this weekend didn't have to end."

"It's not really ending, Carly. This time next week we'll be married. It's just the beginning." He didn't look at her while he spoke, but his jaw tightened ever so slightly.

Smoothing the wrinkles on her dress with her hands, she sighed and let her hands fall back to the seat. "And you could have brought me a change of clothing." Avoiding the questions that plagued her wasn't going to help, but truthfully, she wished the wedding was over and it was next weekend, so she could stop thinking about it.

His large hand reached out and covered hers as it lay on the leather seat between them. "Everything will be all right."

She nodded, but said nothing more. He kept his hand wrapped tightly around hers for the rest of the ride home.

Her stomach was starting to churn as they drew closer to home. She really didn't want to deal with all her responsibilities right now, but she would. She'd run her own business for years now and had employees and customers depending on her. But right now, all she wanted to do was get away from all the pressures for a little while and just have some quiet time to think.

Taking a deep breath, she placed a hand on her stomach and willed it to settle. There was no time for nerves, she had too many things to take care of, both with her business and with the wedding plans.

Nathan pulled up in front of her small bungalow, put the truck in park and turned off the ignition. The silence was almost deafening. "Well, I better get going." She tugged her hand free and reached for the door handle.

"Carly." His voice was rough as his hands reached for her, yanking her into his arms. Then he was kissing her as if there would never be another chance to do so.

She could taste the desperation in their kiss and wondered if it was coming from him or her. Her fingers threaded through his hair, clutching him tight. She didn't want to let him go.

His lips slanted over hers and his tongue tasted and probed her mouth as if searching for something. She didn't know what he wanted, but whatever it was, she wanted to give it to him.

Pushing all thoughts and doubts from her mind, she kissed him back. She poured all her love for him into this one kiss that went on and on.

Nathan's arms were banded so tight around her that she could hardly breathe, but she didn't care. She wanted to crawl into his arms and stay there until it was time for the wedding.

A truck went by, the driver blowing the horn as he passed. She could hear the sound of male catcalls in the distance. Reality had intruded.

Pulling away, she scrambled out of the truck and up the front walkway of her home, desperate to get inside to all that was familiar. Safe.

Footsteps pounded behind her. A large hand clamped over her shoulder, spinning her around. His face was hard, his jaw tight. "I won't let you run from me. From us." With an obvious effort, he shook himself and tried to smile. "Everything will be fine."

"Will it?" She didn't know why she needed his assurance, but she did.

"It will." His blue eyes bored into her. "I'll take care of everything."

Carly closed her eyes to block out the sight of him. That's what she was afraid of. She loved this man so much, but he was so commanding and compelling. It was his nature to take care of everything. But he needed a woman who could be strong beside him, not disappear and become part of him. She wanted to be that woman, but deep in her heart, she feared she might not be strong enough.

She felt his lips on her forehead. His sigh ruffled her hair. "I've got to get going, but I'll drop by the diner for lunch tomorrow."

He didn't give her time to answer. He just turned and walked back to his truck, his boots echoing on the walkway. She felt chained to the spot, unable to move until his truck was out of sight.

Squaring her shoulders, she marched into her house and went straight to her phone. The house was quiet and she was grateful that her parents weren't there. Her fingers dialed the number by rote and her hands choked the receiver until she heard the familiar voice on the other end.

She was so overwhelmed with emotion, she could hardly speak. "I need your help."

"Anything."

Carly had known that would be the answer, but she also realized that this time was different. "You can't tell Nathan."

There was silence on the other end for a moment. "Okay."

The butterflies in her stomach began to settle. "I need a place to stay for a few days." She began to make a mental list of everything she had to do before she could leave. "I need to think."

"Oh, Carly." The sympathy in the other voice was almost her undoing. Tears pricked her eyes and she blinked them back.

"I'm okay. I just need some time to think." She desperately wanted her friend to understand. "Alone."

"Come on out to the farm. No one needs to know you're here."

"Thank you." She didn't know what else to say. It was a lot to ask of her friend, especially since Nathan was her brother.

"Everything will be all right." Erin's words echoed her brother's.

Carly gave a small laugh that held no humor. "That's what everyone keeps telling me."

Sighing contentedly, Carly sat on the porch steps with her hands wrapped around a mug of hot coffee and enjoyed the sunrise. The air was cool, but she was wearing a jacket and the coffee helped warm her insides.

She found herself wishing that Nathan was here to enjoy it with her. The memory of the way he'd sat behind her, warming her, as she'd sat on the back steps of the cabin made her smile.

It was early Tuesday morning and she'd been tucked away at Erin's since late Sunday afternoon. After ending her phone call with Erin, she'd hurriedly changed her clothes and packed a bag. A few more quick phone calls had ensured her that the diner would survive without her for a few more days.

Her mother had surprised her the most. Her parents had come home just as she was putting her suitcase in the car. They hadn't asked any questions when she'd told them she was going away for a few days. Instead, her mother had assured Carly that she would take over the running of the diner while she was gone.

Carly had protested at first, but her mother had put a quick end to that, asking "Who do you think ran the place for years?" The look of determination on her mother's face made her realize that she had nothing to be concerned about.

So, she'd said goodbye to her parents. Her father had looked worried, but had refrained from saying anything, keeping his thoughts to himself. Carly had noticed the way he'd looked to her mother and the subtle shake of her mother's head.

Her parents spoke in the shorthand language of gestures that most couples who were married a long time used. She envied them their closeness and knew her mother would explain everything to her father later.

Abel was standing on the back porch waiting for her when she'd pulled up at the farm. When she hesitated, he'd walked over to the car and opened her door. As she climbed out, he reached into the backseat and grabbed her suitcase. She'd seen the questions in his eyes, but he'd said nothing as he opened the back door for her and motioned her inside.

He was a solid presence behind her as she walked up the stairs and into one of the guestrooms. Placing her bag by the bed, he turned to leave. When he was almost to the door, he hesitated. He opened his mouth as if he wanted to say something to her, but closed it again, shaking his head.

"What?" She was curious to know what he thought of her being here.

Sighing, he rubbed the back of his neck with his hand. "It's none of my business," he began.

"But?" she prompted.

"But, I think you need to talk to Nathan. Just because he's a man, doesn't mean he doesn't need reassurance too." A ghost of a smile crossed Abel's face. "No man can ever claim to understand the mind of a woman, so don't expect him to know what you're thinking unless you tell him."

With those words of wisdom, he'd walked out of the room, leaving her alone with her own thoughts and his words echoing in her mind. Before she could really think, she'd heard Erin pounding up the stairs. Her friend had swept into the room, apologizing for not being there when Carly arrived because she'd run over to Jackson's to get some fresh apples to make a pie.

Erin kept up a stream of chatter, but had asked no questions, as she'd helped Carly settle into one of the guestrooms. "Come down for supper if you want any. But if you want to be alone, you can bring a plate back upstairs or just help yourself to whatever's in the refrigerator later."

Hesitating, Erin sighed and then turned to leave, but stopped just inside the door. The move was so reminiscent of Abel's it made Carly smile. "What?"

"I know that Nathan can be a bit intense at times and hard to live with."

Now that was an understatement if she'd ever heard one. Erin had no idea about the hidden depths that her brother possessed. But there were some things a sister didn't need to know, so Carly kept her thoughts to herself and waited for her friend to continue.

"Remember how he used to boss us around when we were kids? He's usually a laid-back kind of guy, but whenever you'd come out to the farm, he was always telling us what to do and trying to keep us out of trouble."

"Yeah, I do." They both smiled at the memories.

"But do you also remember how upset he was when we finally turned fifteen and started dating, and how he taught us how to handle ourselves in case the boys got out of hand?"

"Oh lord," she started to laugh. "I don't know who was more embarrassed, him or us. I remember that his instructions were quite explicit at times."

"Hey, be thankful he wasn't your brother. I never needed to use any of the things he taught us. Between him and Jackson, they scared off what few dates I did manage to get." Erin played with the end of her braid and sighed. "My point is that he might be difficult at times. He's got all these protective instincts that he tries to keep under control, but beneath it all is a good man who does love you." She smiled sheepishly. "And now that I've said my piece, I'll butt out."

Erin turned to go again, hesitated, and stalked back across the room. Wrapping her arms around Carly, she swept her up in a huge hug. The love and acceptance in that action brought tears to Carly's eyes as she returned the hug. Both women were swiping the tears from their eyes when Erin finally released her, turned, and left the room, closing the door softly behind her.

She'd taken Erin at her word and had stayed tucked away in her room until late that night. When she knew they had retired for the evening, she'd snuck down and helped herself to cold chicken and salad and a huge slab of apple pie. It was cowardly, but she hadn't wanted to face either Abel or Erin across the supper table. As kind and understanding as they both had been, it was still just too awkward.

She was grateful to them both for giving her space. They'd left her alone for the most part, except to make sure she was eating and had everything she needed. She didn't think she'd ever be able to repay their kindness and understanding.

So here she was, a day and a half later, and her thoughts were still going around and around. The one thing she knew for sure was that she loved Nathan and wanted to marry him. It was up to her to find the inner strength to be an equal partner with him.

It wasn't Nathan that she doubted, but herself. And for a woman who prided herself on her independence and self-reliance, that was a hard admission to make.

The sound of a vehicle coming up the deserted road made her turn her head toward it. As she watched, a familiar truck came into view and pulled up in back of the house. It was only then that Carly admitted to herself that she'd been waiting for him to show up here since Sunday night.

Carefully, she laid her half-empty coffee cup aside. She didn't move from where she was sitting on the steps, but watched and waited.

He parked the truck, turned off the ignition and just sat there staring at her through the windshield. She couldn't tell what he was thinking. His face was a blank mask, showing no emotions.

Finally, he broke their gaze and climbed out of the vehicle. Slowly, he walked toward her, the slight breezed teasing the ends of his hair. Her heart began to pound the closer he got to her.

Nathan just kept coming straight for her, his gait unhurried. Stopping at the bottom of the stairs, he put his hands on his lean hips and examined her from head to toe. The sweep of his eyes over her was like a caress and she gripped her hands tight in her lap to keep from reaching out to him.

The tension between them was palpable and then it suddenly passed. Heaving a sigh, he eased himself down next to her on the step. Neither of them spoke. They just sat like that for a few minutes. She hadn't realized how much she'd missed him until she'd seen his face. Right now, she was content just to have him next to her.

"I went to the diner for lunch yesterday." His voice was steady and she could sense no accusation in his tone, only an unasked question.

"I know. My mom told me."

"Jenny wouldn't tell me where you were."

Carly finally turned and looked him straight in the face. He was watching her, his gaze solemn. "I didn't tell her or dad where I was going." She chewed on her lip, unable to be anything but honest with him. "Although, she probably knew where I was."

Nathan nodded.

"How did you find me?"

He cocked an eyebrow. "Carly, honey, I'm a cop. It wasn't that hard to figure out." Reaching out, he covered her hands with one of his. "Erin is your best friend."

It was her turn to nod. How polite they were both being. She knew he was waiting for her to talk and knew he was patient enough to wait until she was ready. Releasing the tight grip she had on her hands, she tangled her fingers with his. His grip was warm and comforting.

She owed him an explanation and now was as good a time as any. "I love you, Nathan."

"But?" He'd heard the underlying question in her words.

"But I'm afraid I'm not strong enough to be equal in our relationship. You're so strong and sure of yourself. I'm afraid of being overwhelmed by you. Of losing my independence." She bit her lip and waited for the outburst of anger she thought would follow.

Nathan laughed. Carly frowned at him. She'd just poured out her heart to him and he was laughing at her. But the laughter didn't reach his eyes and it had a bitter edge to it.

"Oh, Carly." His eyes were sad as he cupped the side of her face tenderly. "You're the most independent and the strongest woman I've ever known. The fact of the matter is that you don't need me."

He held up his hand when she started to speak, and she subsided. He shook his head, and his eyes were bleak as he gazed down at her. "I realized that I was acting like an overbearing idiot around you because I was afraid I was losing you. All that did was fuel your fears and make them all the more real."

He released her hand, stood, and stepped back down onto the ground. She felt cold without the bulk of his body next to hers. "The fact is, I love you just the way you are. I want to be in charge of your sexual pleasure, giving you everything you need, pushing your sexual boundaries." He shrugged, unapologetically. "I need to be in control in the bedroom."

Stuffing his hands in the pockets of his coat, he rocked back on his heels. "But beyond the confines of our sex life, you're all a man could want as a woman, as a partner to go through life with."

She reached her hand out to him, but he stepped back. Her hand hovered in the air, as lost and alone as she felt. Slowly, she lowered it back to her lap.

"I want to marry you. I want the world to know that I'm your husband and that you're my woman. I want to shout to the world that you belong to me." He paused and took a deep breath as if bracing himself. "But only if you're sure."

Surely he wasn't calling off the wedding. Her heart pounded in her chest and she could feel the sweat on her forehead and her palms.

"I'll be waiting for you. But it's up to you." He spun on his heel and marched toward the truck. At the last second, he turned back to her. "You know what I am, who I am. But you don't really know yourself, do you?" With those words, he slammed into his truck and drove away.

She watched the dust settle as his words tumbled around in her brain. Nathan's view of her had shocked her. He was right. She really didn't know herself at all. Or rather, she'd let all the events of the last two months overwhelm her, making her forget who she was.

The sun had climbed up over the trees in the distance. It was the beginning of a new day. Carly felt a new confidence rising from deep inside her. It had taken Nathan to remind her of who and what she was.

Gripping her mug in her hand, she rose to her feet. It was time to be the woman she was and embrace all that meant. Just because she found it sexually arousing for Nathan to be in control in the bedroom, to yield to his sexual demands, didn't mean she was weak. All it meant was that she was a complex woman who was strong enough, and honest enough, to accept all parts of herself.

The door creaked behind her and she turned to find Erin standing in the doorway with a look of concern on her face. "Everything okay?"

Carly thought about it for a moment. "Yes," she answered and for the first time in weeks, she finally believed what she was saying. "Yes, I think it is." Nathan had given her quite a bit to think about.

Erin cast a longing glance down the empty road even though the truck was long out of view. "I'm glad." Her words were simply spoken with no accusation. Carly understood that she'd put her friend in an awkward position and appreciated her kindness and support all the more for it.

Closing the gap between them, she wrapped her arms around Erin, giving her a quick hug. Erin straightened and wiped a tear from the corner of her eye. "Now look what you've done." Both women stared at each other before bursting out laughing.

It felt good to laugh again. To smile again. She felt as if a weight she'd been carrying around for weeks had tumbled off her shoulders.

"How about some pancakes and bacon?" Erin held the door wide open. Delicious smells were wafting through the open door and they could hear the sound of Abel humming in the kitchen. It was good to have friends.

Her mind was already racing as she followed Erin inside, planning everything that she needed to accomplish in the next few days. "I'll be leaving after breakfast."

Chapter Thirteen

৵

It was lunchtime Wednesday and the diner was hopping. She and Melinda were both working flat-out serving customers. It was much busier than usual. Every table was full and even the seats running along the counter were almost all occupied. Only one stool was vacant at the far end of the counter. Nathan's usual seat.

Carly had hurried home yesterday morning, dumped her stuff and rushed to work, sure that she'd see him at lunchtime. But he hadn't shown and he hadn't called. She'd tried calling him several times last night, but Jackson answered every time. Nathan wasn't home and Jackson didn't know when he would be. Finally, she stopped calling, unable to bear the pity she was sure she heard in Jackson's voice.

She almost called him at work. But it wasn't an emergency. Yet.

If she didn't see him soon, she'd go looking for him. It was hard for her to wait for him to come to her, but he'd given her some time to herself and she owed him the same courtesy in return.

It was only over breakfast yesterday morning that Erin had finally confided that Nathan had called about an hour after she had arrived at the farm. He'd informed his sister that he knew Carly was there, but would let her have some time alone. He'd ended the conversation with the admonishment for his sister to "take care of Carly for me."

That was so like Nathan to be concerned for her wellbeing even when she was trying to get away from him.

Now, she had a larger than normal lunchtime crowd to deal with. She pushed a strand of hair out of her face and kept filling coffee cups and distributing lunch specials. There was an air of expectancy in the air.

Small town gossip.

Everyone knew that Nathan had literally taken her away for the weekend. They also knew that he'd shown up here for lunch on Monday and she hadn't been here. Now, she was back and Nathan was nowhere in sight.

Speculation was running rampant. Was the wedding still on? Had they had a fight? Had Nathan dumped her? Had she dumped him? Carly had actually heard that some jerks had started a betting pool on whether or not the wedding was going ahead.

She knew that it would blow over in a few days, but right now they were the town's biggest entertainment. She consoled herself with the fact that most people were honestly concerned about her and Nathan. The rest, she didn't worry about. They'd be caught up in someone else's scandals next week.

Plastering a smile on her face, she chatted to regular customers and people she knew as she continued to serve lunches and take orders. There were a few people she didn't recognize and some that she wished she didn't.

A table right in the center of the diner was occupied by a group of four men. They were the same men she'd had trouble with before, including the jerk who'd grabbed her ass the last time he was in. So far she'd managed to avoid them.

Unfortunately, they had also been at the bar Friday night and had seen the confrontation between her and Nathan, including the part where Nathan had scooped her up and carted her out of the place. And apparently two of them had also been aboard the truck that had honked and shouted at her and Nathan on Sunday afternoon when they'd been kissing in front of her house.

Right now, they were talking loud and making references to both events. It was obvious that they'd also heard the speculation that she and Nathan had called it quits.

127

Melinda caught her eye and raised an eyebrow. Carly knew she was asking what she should do about them. Giving a subtle shake of her head, she motioned for the other woman to just continue serving customers.

Gritting her teeth, she ignored them as best she could. Other customers were starting to shift uneasily and stare at the men as their banter got louder.

Enough was enough.

Stalking over to their table, she slapped their bills on the hard surface. "Pay the cashier on the way out." She'd never been so rude to any customer in all her days, but she wanted them out of her diner.

"But we're not finished yet." One of them grabbed her hand as she turned to leave, forcing her to stop. She turned back to the table, knowing that it would be the same guy who'd groped her butt before.

She stared down at him. He was a big man, tall and heavily muscled, with a full beard. Not quite as large as Nathan, but close. His hair was a dark brown that matched his eyes. Not bad looking, until you noticed the look in those eyes. They were cold and calculating as they watched her to see what she would do.

Carly glanced at his long fingers wrapped around her wrist and back at his face. "Can I get you anything else?" She kept her tone level, but firm.

They laughed as if she'd told them a joke. "Oh yeah, honey, I want plenty more from you."

She inwardly sighed. Why were some men such jerks? She held onto her temper. Barely. "You can have whatever is on the lunch menu." It was hard, but she kept the tone of her voice even, but firm.

Brown-eyes wasn't smiling any longer. A frown crossed his face as his buddies snickered at her reply. "There's no need to be unfriendly about it." He used his grip to tug her closer to the table. "You were real friendly with your man on Friday night and again on Sunday. But seems like he's not around anymore and a woman like you needs a man." He paused for effect as he stared at her breasts. "A man that knows how to keep his woman in line."

Carly knew she shouldn't say it, but he'd asked for it. She eyed him up and down, her bland expression never faltering on her face. "Is that right?"

"Oh, yeah."

"Well, you let me know the minute you find a real man because I sure don't see any around here." She could hear muted laughter from a nearby table and knew that everyone in the diner was now watching their exchange.

Anger replaced the lust in his eyes and he glared at her. "You've got a saucy mouth on you, woman."

Carly ignored his angry words and stared at his three friends who were starting to shift uneasily in their chairs. "I think it's time you all left."

"I think I'll talk to your boss. You're being a mite unfriendly to paying customers." His grip on her arm tightened and she knew she'd have bruises, but she refused to flinch. "Maybe if you're nicer, I won't get you fired."

"You think my boss would believe you?" She couldn't believe that this moron was trying to blackmail her. He did it so easily, it made her wonder just how many times before he'd done something like this to some unsuspecting waitress.

"It's our word against yours." His grip loosened slightly as he pulled her so close that she could feel his breath on her skin.

"You'd all back him up?" She asked the three other men, mild curiosity in her voice. They nodded. "Well boys, I guess I don't have any choice." The brown-eyed man started to smile, sure he'd won. Carly smiled back at him as she reached in front of him, picked up his water glass and dumped the contents over him.

Releasing his grip on her, he jumped out of his seat in a hurry, sputtering and swearing. "You little hellcat." The chair tipped over, falling to the floor as he stepped back and grabbed some napkins off the table, using them to swipe at the water dripping from his face.

Carly marched right up to him and poked him in the chest. "You've got one major problem. I. Am. The. Boss." She punctuated each word with a poke to his chest.

Anger and astonishment warred in his face. "You've got to be kidding. A little girl like you?"

"This is my diner. You and your friends are no longer welcome here. Pay for your lunch and leave or I'll call the cops."

He moved threateningly toward her. "The cops can't do nothing."

Carly crossed her arms over her chest and glared up at the angry man hovering over her. "Don't count on it."

His friends bound to their feet, suddenly in a hurry to leave. "Let's go, Frank. It's not worth the hassle." One of them gripped his arm, trying to pull him away from the table.

The man called Frank didn't move. His fists were clenched at his sides and, for a second, Carly really thought he might take a swing at her. She braced herself, ready to move.

The diner was deadly quiet and then several chairs scraped back from tables and she knew that several male patrons had stood, ready to come to her assistance if she needed it. That was the good thing about living in a small town. Neighbors helped each other.

She never took her eyes off him as he flexed his fingers at his side. "Frank," one of his buddies said again. "Let's go, man."

"This isn't finished."

"Yes, it is." Her voice was low and steady even though her heart was pounding with adrenaline. "You and your friends aren't welcome here any longer. You've abused our hospitality."

He suddenly seemed to realize that the diner was completely still and quiet. Like a man coming out of a daze, he jerked his head from side to side, taking in the tension that filled the room. Every eye was on him. He shrugged and gave a forced laugh. "Who cares? The food is lousy and the service is worse."

Jerking his jacket off the back of his chair, he slung it over his shoulder. He ran an insolent gaze over her body and shook his head as if finding her lacking. "No wonder you couldn't hold onto your man."

"Oh, he's still mine and I'm still his."

"Yeah, right." He sneered as he turned toward the door. And froze.

Nathan was framed in the doorway of the diner. Taking off his sunglasses, he folded them carefully and placed them in the shirt pocket of his deputy's uniform. The movement made his muscles ripple. He looked extremely large and intimidating as he eyed each of the men in turn before coming to rest on the unfortunate Frank.

Carly almost felt sorry for him. Almost.

"Problem?" With his legs slightly spread and his arms crossed lightly over his chest, Nathan's stance should have looked relaxed. His voice was mild, even pleasant. But Carly wasn't fooled for a second. The air practically crackled with the force of his anger.

Frank sputtered out his reply. "There's no problem here."

Nathan's laser blue eyes bore into Frank. "I wasn't talking to you."

Frank swallowed hard, suddenly seeming to realize just how dangerous the man in front of him was. Badge or no badge.

"Everything is fine, Nathan. These gentlemen were just going to pay for their lunch and leave." That seemed to break the spell holding everyone in place. One of Frank's friends quickly went to the register and handed Melinda enough cash to cover all their meals.

The four of them hurried toward the door, but Nathan hadn't moved. He stood there like a mountain, blocking their departure. He looked over at her and raised his eyebrow questioningly. She could practically hear him asking her what she wanted him to do.

She knew that Nathan would like nothing better than to take the lot of them out back and teach them some manners. It was his self-control and the uniform he wore that kept him from doing that. But he would haul them into the station if that was what she wanted.

She gave her head a small shake and rolled her eyes. Nathan stepped back from the door and let the men file out one at a time. Warmth filled her as she realized that she and Nathan could communicate with just a gesture or two. Just like her parents. Just like a couple who'd been together a long time.

Not only that. He'd trusted her to deal with the situation and accepted her judgment. She felt positively giddy with delight.

But it wasn't quite over. Nathan stuck his arm out, stopping Frank as he tried to leave. Leaning close, Nathan whispered something to the other man. Frank paled and jerked his head back, bolting from the diner the moment Nathan lowered his arm.

Carly smothered a sigh. She should have known that he wouldn't be able to ignore his protective instincts. And truthfully, she didn't want him to. They were part of what made him who he was. A loving, caring, possessive and dominant man who would protect those he loved.

Nathan watched until all four men disappeared down the sidewalk. The second they were out of sight, he turned and stalked across the room. He looked dangerous and determined. A shiver rushed down her spine at the expression in his eyes. Hot and filled with lust. She recognized it well.

His eyes roamed over her body as he got closer, as if to reassure himself that she was all right. Stopping in front of her, he reached out his hard, callused hands and gently cupped her cheeks. "Well?"

She could feel his hot breath on her face and knew what he was asking her. "You were right."

"And?" His voice, laced with male satisfaction, made her laugh.

"And, you were right." She cupped his face in her hands, loving the slightly scruffy feel to his cheeks. "I am woman enough to handle you, Nathan Connors."

One corner of his mouth kicked up in a grin. "You sure about that, Miss Ames?"

The time for talking was over. It was time for action. Letting her fingers slide up into his hair, she tugged him down to her as she raised herself up on her toes. Just before her lips met his, she whispered, "Oh, yeah."

She tasted his lips, starved for the taste of him after so many days without him. He stood there and let her have her way with him.

For about ten seconds.

He cupped the back of her head with one of his large palms and angled it so he could get a better fit. She pulled him closer.

Carly was vaguely aware of her feet leaving the floor, but she didn't care. Nothing mattered but Nathan and being back in his arms. They were meant to be together. They complemented each other in every way — physically, emotionally and intellectually.

That didn't mean that they both wouldn't have to do some adjusting to make their marriage work. She knew it went against all Nathan's instincts to just let those men walk out of here. But relationships were meant to be give and take. That didn't mean that they weren't equal. That thought burst across her brain and then she couldn't think at all. There was nothing but pleasure as Nathan kissed her.

Time ceased to exist as his tongue plundered her mouth. She resisted when he tried to pull away, tugging on his hair to bring him back. "Carly, honey, let go." His satisfied chuckle joined the rest of the laughter.

Reality intruded on her sensual haze. She, the boss, was kissing Nathan in the middle of the diner with everyone watching. Burying her face in his shoulder, she waited for the usual unease or embarrassment to fill her, but it didn't come.

Nathan kept his arms around her as he let her feet touch the floor again. Gripping the front of his shirt for support, she looked up at him. His hair was tousled and his lips were moist. She knew that she must look the same as he did.

He looked satisfied and proud. She tried her best to keep a stern look on her face, but failed. He looked so damned pleased with himself.

This was necessary for him. She understood that. After letting her handle the situation with the men in the diner, he had needed to reassert his claim to her. If only to reassure himself that she belonged to him. Give and take.

Pulling away, she straightened her blouse and apron, ran a hand through her hair, and turned to face their audience. "Well, what are you all staring at?" She couldn't stop the huge smile that blossomed across her face.

The customers laughed good-naturedly and most of them returned to their meals. She noticed a group of women in the corner fanning themselves with their menus as they stared at Nathan. Carly didn't mind. They couldn't help looking. But if they ever touched him, she'd tear their hair out.

Good lord, Nathan was rubbing off on her. She was becoming as possessive of him as he was of her. She grabbed some empty dishes off a table and began to stack them.

Some of the regulars just couldn't resist a few teasing comments. "So the wedding is back on?" Old Mister Gower shouted from the booth in the corner.

"It was never off." The smile Nathan gave her as she shouted her reply almost brought her to her knees. The man was too sexy to be legal. He should at least come with a warning label. She stiffened her knees as she tried to ignore his lethal grin.

Moisture pooled between her thighs and her sex throbbed with need. She was glad she was wearing an apron because she knew her nipples were hard and pebbled against the cups of her bra. When she motioned Nathan toward his usual seat at the end of the counter, the movement made the fabric of her lace bra move ever so slightly. But it was enough to send a shot of pure desire rippling between her thighs.

She resisted the urge to clamp her legs together as she walked behind the counter with a pile of dishes clutched tight in her hand. Laying them on the counter, she plunked a fresh cup in front of Nathan and filled it with coffee.

"What did you say to Frank?" She'd told herself she wasn't going to ask, but curiosity had gotten the better of her.

"Not much. I just gave him a friendly warning and suggested that he and his friends might want to eat elsewhere."

She raised an eyebrow at him, but he said nothing else and she realized that that was all he was going to tell her. As far as he was concerned, it was over. Sighing, she tried to calm her jittery nerves and get back to work. "Do you want lunch?"

"I'm hungry." His words made her tremble. There was little doubt in her mind what he was hungry for. She'd felt the bulge growing in the front of his pants when they'd kissed.

She licked her dry lips and cleared her throat. "What can I get you?" All she wanted to do was throw him down and jump on top of him. Maybe it was the adrenaline rush from her confrontation. Maybe it was the fact that she finally felt sure about herself and their relationship. Whatever it was, she wanted him. And she wanted him now.

People were starting to leave now that the show was over. The lunchtime crowd was quickly finishing up and Melinda was ringing up a steady stream of customers at the cash register.

Carly took in the entire room in one glance. Several tables were dawdling over coffee and a couple of men at the counter were eating dessert. Melinda could easily handle things without her.

"If you're not busy, you could look at that problem with my computer before you go back to work."

Nathan choked on the mouthful of coffee that he'd just taken. He carefully laid his cup aside and wiped his face with a paper napkin.

She rested her arms on the counter and leaned closer to him. "If you want to, that is. I know you're hungry. I should just get you something from the kitchen." As she started to pull away from the counter, her arm was gripped in a vise.

Nathan's eyes were blazing with desire. "I can take care of your little problem now. I've got time."

Now it was her turn to sputter. Little problem, indeed.

Keeping her arm in his grip, he came around the end of the counter and hustled her down the short hallway toward her office.

Chapter Fourteen

❦

Nathan practically dragged Carly behind him as his long legs ate up the distance to her office. He was so damned hard, he thought his cock might explode. Adrenaline, anger and lust all surged through his body, needing a release.

His self-control had been pushed to the very limits by the scene in the diner. As an officer of the law, he'd wanted to charge the men for at least disturbing the peace. As a man, he'd wanted to take the one called Frank out back and beat him to a pulp for daring to lay his hand on Carly.

She was his. His woman. His to protect.

The hardest thing he'd ever done in his life was to let her handle the situation. The mixed emotions swirling inside him were almost impossible to control. Part of him was proud of the way she'd dealt with the situation. She was a hell of a woman and could certainly take care of herself. The more primitive part of himself didn't want her to have to handle these kinds of problems. He wanted to take care of them for her. Take care of her.

The volatile cocktail swimming in his blood needed to be released. And he knew one sure way to do it.

He could hear her breathing getting heavier as he tugged her behind him. She'd pushed him with her sexy innuendoes and her sensual smile. Now she'd have to deliver.

The flat of his hand slammed the door to her office open. The minute they were both inside, he kicked the door closed and pressed her back against it. Her eyes were wide and her face was flushed a pretty pink. As he watched, her tongue darted out to lick her lips. She had amazing lips. Plump, lush and ripe for the tasting.

His own chest was expanding and contracting like a bellows, so he took a deep breath and held it for a moment before releasing it. Damn, he needed to try and gain some control.

She chose that moment to slide her hands up his chest, her small fingers kneading his muscles through his shirt. It felt so damned good to have her hands on him that his control deserted him.

Tangling his fingers in her hair to hold her still, he tipped her face up to him. His tongue snaked out to sample her lips. She tasted of peppermint and a flavor that was uniquely Carly, inviting and addictive.

Her lips parted for him and he slipped his tongue inside, continuing to devour her mouth. Shifting closer to her, he ground his arousal against her soft belly. She moaned and squirmed closer to him.

Pulling himself away from her luscious lips, he took a step back from her. "Undo your blouse and open your bra." His voice was hoarse with desire. "I want to see your breasts."

Her fingers trembled as she slipped her apron off and dropped it to the floor. One button at a time, she unbuttoned her crisp white blouse. As it parted, he could see her lacy blue bra and her smooth, white stomach. His cock twitched and pressed hard against the zipper of his pants.

Her hands went to the front closure of her bra and hesitated.

"Do it." He crossed his arms across his chest and waited.

The front of the bra parted, exposing her large, round breasts. Carly pushed the lacy cups back, letting him see her puckered rosy nipples.

"Beautiful," he murmured as he backed away and leaned against the edge of her desk. "Touch yourself for me."

She looked at him, slightly uncertain.

"Cup your breasts with your hands and pinch your nipples with your fingers." His hands itched to touch her, but he wanted her to touch herself. He wanted to watch her pleasure herself. He'd fuck her when she was hot and primed for him. "But strip off the rest of your clothes first. I want you naked."

Pushing away from the door, she slipped her blouse and bra off, letting them drop to her feet. She toed off her shoes and then reached for the opening of her skirt. A quick shimmy of her hips and that was gone. She was left standing in her matching blue lace underwear and a pair of thigh-high stockings.

"Leave the stockings." His voice was thick with desire. Damn, but he loved the fact that she wore those sexy stockings.

Sauntering closer to him, she hooked her fingers in the waistband of her panties and skimmed them over her hips. When they fell to her feet, she stepped out of them and kicked them away with her foot.

He could feel his skin tightening as his arousal grew. "Touch yourself, baby." His own hands went to the utility belt strapped around his waist. While he watched her, he removed it and laid it across the desk, making sure his radio and gun were out of the way.

Her hands cupped her breasts and her head tipped back as she squeezed her distended nipples between her thumbs and forefingers. Her legs were slightly parted and he could smell her arousal.

Unbuttoning his pants, he slid the zipper down carefully and pushed his underwear out of the way. His cock sprang free, hard and ready. Wrapping his hand around it, he slowly pumped it up and down as he watched her.

"Put your hands between your legs and spread your lips wide. I want to see your pretty, pink folds, all slick and wet for me."

She was standing right in front of him, her breasts quivering with every breath she took. Her nipples were hard peaks that he wanted to taste, but not quite yet. He wanted to see her pussy first. He wanted her to show it to him.

Her thumbs rolled over the hard nubs of her breasts one last time before she slowly skimmed her hands down over her sides. Taking her time, she circled her belly button with her fingers, the movement almost hypnotic as her hips began to undulate. His mouth went dry as he watched her.

One hand sifted through the soft hair at the apex of her thighs and continued to stroke down the inside of her thigh. His cock pulsed in his hand, matching the pounding of his heart. Damn, she was a sight to behold.

A light sheen of sweat covered her skin as she slid both hands between her legs, cupping her sex. Her fingers glistened with her arousal as she tugged back the slippery soft lips and opened herself to his perusal.

"Is your pussy hot, baby?" Gripping the top of his erection with one hand, he used his thumb to spread the pearly liquid seeping from the tip over the head. Reaching out, he flicked one of her puckered nipples with his forefinger. She flinched and then pushed her breast toward his hand. He pulled it just out of her reach.

She moaned and her hips arched toward him. "Answer me, Carly. If you want me to fuck you, you have to answer me."

"Yes, I'm hot." Her voice was little more than a whisper.

He trailed a finger between her breasts, down her stomach and through her downy pubic hair before slipping it into her moist sex. He swirled his finger around her cunt, probing and stroking. Pulling it out, he brought it to his mouth and licked it. Carly shivered.

"Yeah, you're hot." Settling himself against the desk, he gripped her bottom and tugged her closer. "Climb up. Put your knees on the desk and mount me."

Gripping his shoulders for support, she put one knee on her desk and pulled herself up. Settling her other knee on the smooth wood so that she was straddling him, she rubbed her sex against the tip of his arousal.

Nathan cupped her ass in his hands and bit back a groan. Anchoring her with his hands, he maneuvered her until the head of his cock was touching her opening. Slowly, he pulled her down on top of him, one inch at a time.

Burying his head between her breasts, he nuzzled her smooth skin. His tongue traced the edges of her areola before he lapped at her nipple. A shiver racked her body and she moaned, tugging him closer. The movement caused him to slip even deeper inside her.

Groaning, he captured the peak of her breast between his teeth and allowed his tongue to tease it. His fingers dug into her ass, keeping her close to him, not letting her move.

His testicles were tight against his body. He didn't have much time left and he wanted to move. Needed to thrust into her.

Standing, he kept one arm under her behind and wrapped the other around her shoulders. Bringing her legs up behind him, she locked her ankles together at the small of his back.

He could feel the inner muscles of her pussy clutching at him as it contracted. She was right on the edge. Shoving her back against the wall, he ground his pelvis into hers.

"Nathan. Nathan. Nathan." Over and over, she chanted.

The sound of his name falling from her lips made him burn to give her what she wanted. Bracing her against the wall, he gripped her hips in his hands and began to thrust. Hard and heavy, he pumped his cock into her.

She squirmed and arched her hips into his thrusts. He drove into her faster and deeper. With each stroke, her body sucked his cock deep inside. He could feel it stretching her cunt to its limits as it wrapped around him like a silk fist.

Carly buried her face in his neck, licking and nipping at his skin. He gripped her tighter and kept fucking her. The tightness of his testicles increased. He gritted his teeth and slipped one of his fingers into the cleft of her ass, stroking the puckered opening, probing at it.

She gave a small scream and then her body convulsed. The second her inner muscles clutched his cock like a vise, he came. He flexed his hips as he emptied himself into her. Her pussy continued to squeeze him as he came.

Shuddering, he dropped his head against the wall and leaned into it for support. Her legs slipped from around him, dropping to the floor as she sagged against him. Not releasing his hold on her, he lowered them both to the floor.

He knelt there with her locked in his arms. His treasure. His woman.

Unfortunately, he knew he had to move. His lunch break was almost over. He was damned lucky that his radio hadn't squawked to life at a crucial moment.

Carefully, he lifted her off him and laid her on the floor. She didn't even open her eyes as he quickly tucked in his shirt and zipped his pants. He was no worse the wear, but he couldn't say the same thing for her.

Totally naked, Carly lay sprawled across the office floor. Her legs were slightly parted and her nipples were red and swollen. Damn, she looked good enough to eat. He only wished he had time. Soon, he promised himself. Soon, he'd take his time and taste every inch of her delectable body.

But for now, he had to get her up and back to work before she was missed. Squatting beside her, he cupped her pussy with his hand. Her eyes flew open when he stroked his finger over her clit. Gasping, she arched her hips against his hand.

"There's no time, honey." Even as he said the words, he traced the wet folds before flicking her clit again. "We've both got to get back to work."

Her eyes widened and she shot up to a seated position. She swayed slightly and he grabbed her, supporting her until she was steady.

"Omigod." Her eyes shot to the door as if she expected to see someone standing there. Scrambling across the floor, she grabbed her panties and shoved them on. Standing, she tugged them over her hips and grabbed her skirt. The minute she had it buttoned, she reached for her bra.

Nathan grabbed her from behind, enfolding her in his arms. He kissed the back of her neck and nipped at her ear lobe. "Thanks for lunch," he whispered wickedly in her ear.

He could feel her body trembling against his and as much as he wanted to spend the afternoon pleasuring her, he knew he had to get back to work. Reluctantly, he let her go. Snagging his belt from the top of her desk, he strapped it on as he watched her pull on her bra and then her blouse. Her fingers shook slightly as she did up all her buttons.

When she was fully dressed, she turned to him, her eyes large and solemn. "Thank you."

He nodded. He knew she was thanking him not only for letting her handle the situation in her diner, but also for encouraging her to find her own way back to him.

Straightening the collar of her blouse, he tried to lighten her mood. "I think you better sneak into the ladies' room before you go back to work." Leaning close, he sniffed her neck. "You smell like sex. And you're wrinkled too."

She swatted his hand away from her clothes. "That's not fair. You don't even have a hair out of place."

Nathan grinned. "I like you like this." He traced a finger over the front of her top, stroking the nipple that poked at the fabric. "I wish I could stay, but we've both got to work."

Carly shook herself and stepped away from him, pushing a hand through her hair. "You better go first. I'll go back to work in a few minutes."

Nathan wanted to kiss her one last time, but knew he couldn't risk it. He stopped at the door and looked back at her. She was slumped against the desk, but she had the glow of a well-pleasured woman. He was pleased.

The door closed behind him with a thud and he quickly made his way through the almost empty diner and out the front door. He didn't stop to talk, but waved to the waitress as he left.

He walked quickly to his car. If he hurried, he'd have time to run through the drive-through of the local fast-food joint. His stomach gave a large growl. He was starving.

Carly leaned against her desk and listened to Nathan's footsteps recede in the distance. No matter how many times they made love, each time was explosive. She shivered to think what their wedding night would be like.

The muscles in her legs were weak, and she felt hot and sticky. Her underwear was wet with the combination of hers and Nathan's cum. Grabbing her apron off the floor, she wobbled her way to the door and eased it open. Peeking out into the hall, she made a beeline for the bathroom when she saw the coast was clear.

Breathing a sigh of relief when she reached the safety of the bathroom, she locked the door and turned to the mirror to repair some of the damage to herself and her clothing.

Rumpled. There was no other word to describe her, except maybe satisfied.

The woman staring back at her from the mirror looked flushed. Her cheeks were pink, partly from exertion and partly from being abraded by the stubble on Nathan's chin. Her eyes were slumberous and her lips were swollen. There was no mistaking the look of a woman who'd been sexually fulfilled.

Laying the apron aside, she flicked on the cold water tap, scooped the frigid water up in her hands and splashed it on her face. When her fingers were almost numb from the cold, she stopped and blindly reached out a hand and grabbed some paper towels. She blotted her face dry as she looked at herself in the mirror. Better, but not great.

There was nothing to be done with her hair except run her fingers through it. It didn't look perfect, but it wasn't too bad. She was just thankful she had a simple cut because she didn't have a brush or a comb on her.

She checked to make sure all her buttons were secured and everything was tucked in properly before she wet a paper towel with some warm water. Skimming up her skirt, she tugged her panties out of the way, and washed away the evidence of their lovemaking as best as she could. She grabbed a fresh towel and patted herself dry before she shimmied her skirt back down. Gathering all the used paper towels together, she dumped them into the garbage can. Slipping her apron over her head, she tugged it into place and reached behind to do up the ties.

Taking a deep breath, she took one last look at herself. She looked more like herself, efficient and pulled together. Pink still tinged her cheeks, but it wasn't too noticeable. The only thing she couldn't hide was the huge grin on her face.

She shook her head at her own reflection and left the bathroom. It was time to get back to work. She had a lot to do between now and Saturday. Energy and confidence filled her as she strode back into the diner and began to clear tables.

A sense of wellbeing filled her. She felt good. Better, in fact, than she had in weeks More like herself, except stronger somehow. Humming under her breath, she dug into her work with a vengeance.

A shiver went down her spine as thoughts of Nathan crossed her mind. Now that they'd completely accepted each other, she had no idea what was in store for her wedding night. But whatever it was, she was ready for it.

Chapter Fifteen

જી

Carly sat back in her chair later that evening and rolled her shoulders as she glanced at her watch. It was just past nine o'clock and the supper hour had long ago passed her by. But it was worth it. Her desk was finally clear and a stack of envelopes with bill payments sat in a neat pile waiting to be mailed. Her financial journals were up to date, her schedules set for the next few weeks, and all her orders were ready to be called in to suppliers first thing in the morning.

Most people had no idea how much paperwork was involved in running a small business. There were government forms to be filled out, taxes to be paid, salaries, suppliers, and a hundred other chores to be seen to on a daily, weekly, monthly and yearly basis. Everything from the toilet paper in the bathroom to the daily special served was her responsibility. And she loved it.

It had never occurred to her to do anything else with her life. She'd practically grown up in the diner. For as far back as she could remember, the school bus would drop her off outside the diner at the end of the school day and she'd spend her afternoons doing her homework at one of the tables or helping her mother by clearing tables or sweeping the floors.

By the time she was ten, she was helping out in the kitchen and ringing up sales and, at age fourteen, started waiting tables. Working alongside her mother, she'd learned everything there was to know about running a successful diner. Good hearty food, reasonable prices, a clean place and friendly staff were the keys.

There were days that she wished that her job wasn't seven days a week, but for the most part it worked out well. The diner was open until six in the evenings, Monday through Thursday, but they stayed open until eight on the other three nights. They primarily catered to a breakfast and lunch crowd, but on the weekends some folks liked a quiet, home-cooked meal without having to cook it themselves, so they stayed open later to accommodate them.

When you considered that they opened at six in the morning, that made for a lot of long days. But Carly switched the schedules around often so that all of her staff, herself included, had every second weekend off. She was lucky that the people she had working for her were all loyal, hardworking folks. Many of them, like Melinda, had worked for her family for years. It was more family than anything and they all worked together and adjusted their schedules when there was a need.

She was pleased to have all that work out of the way, considering the wedding was only a few days away, but she was exhausted. It seemed like days since she and Nathan had almost set her office on fire, instead of only a few hours ago. She would have much preferred to go home early and soak in a hot tub of water, but this work couldn't be put off any longer. Besides which, her parents had gone out to spend the evening with friends and Nathan was working late himself, so nobody had been expecting her to be anywhere or do anything.

Laughing, she shook her head at herself. Most women would take that as a cue to spend the evening home alone in the tub with a glass of wine and a good book. But Carly knew herself well and knew that she'd sleep better once all this paperwork was done.

Pushing away from her desk, she stood and stretched. Some of her muscles complained about the workout she'd given them earlier today. But that was a small price to pay for the satisfaction that she'd gotten. It was hours later and she still felt like her insides were humming.

Melinda had come in to say goodnight and let her know that she and the rest of the staff were leaving. That was two hours ago and the diner had been quiet ever since. Shutting down her computer, she tugged on her sweater and got her purse out of the bottom drawer of her desk. Taking her time, she glanced around her office one last time to make sure everything was in order before turning out the light and locking the door behind her.

It was habit, more than anything else, that had her strolling to the front of the diner. As she'd known it would be, all the tables were cleaned and set for the breakfast crowd. The floors had been swept and mopped and the countertops gleamed in the shine of the security lights. Satisfied, she walked back down the hall, peeking into the kitchen as she passed. Order reigned in there as well. Everything was immaculate and ready for the morning.

Contentment filled her as she wandered toward the back entrance, digging her keys out of her purse as she went. She loved this place when it was quiet and everything was in its place, but there was nothing quite like it when the diner was hopping, filled with the sounds of happy chatter and the smell of great food.

She hesitated when she opened the back door and it was dark. In the distance she could hear a dog barking in the crisp evening air. Looking up, she squinted at the light fixture, but couldn't quite see it. She stared out into the alley and listened, but heard nothing. The muted sounds of traffic flowing up and down the road in front of the diner reassured her.

"There's nothing to worry about. It's just a blown light bulb," she assured herself. There was really no point in going back through the diner and out through the front door. Her car was parked out in the alley, so she'd have to cross the darkened area anyway. This way was quicker.

Still, she stood just inside the door and scanned the area for any movement. Everything seemed normal and her car was only about thirty feet from the back door. Stepping out, she pulled the back door shut behind her and locked it. She made a mental note to have that light bulb changed first thing in the morning.

Hoisting her purse higher on her shoulder, she started toward her car. Her steps were quicker than usual and she freely admitted to being slightly spooked by the darkness. She clutched her keys in her hand and could feel their rough edges digging into her palm.

A scraping sound behind her had her whirling around. "Who's there?"

"I don't know why you're always so unfriendly." The words were slightly slurred but whoever it was he was moving closer to her. She didn't recognize the voice, so she started to back up, every step taking her closer to her car.

"Who are you?"

"Not so brave when your boyfriend's not around, are you?" The laughter was low and mean.

She swallowed down her panic as recognition shot through her. It was Frank from the diner. Stay calm, she told herself. Stay focused and keep him talking. "What do you want?"

"Plenty." The scraping of boots on the pavement got closer and she could now see his large outline in the dark. "You owe me big-time."

"I don't owe you anything." Her mind was frantically sorting out her options. Running was the best. Her car was locked and it would take too long to open the door. The mouth of the alley was closer, but she needed to be closer to make a break for it. Trying not to be too obvious about it, she kept on backing toward the light at the end of the alley.

"Oh, but you do. You embarrassed me in front of my friends and all those people. That wasn't very nice of you."

A shiver went down her spine at the sinister tone in his voice. There would be no reasoning with this man. From the slight slur in his voice she could tell he'd been drinking. And there was no doubt that he was angry. That was a very dangerous combination.

There was a time to stand and fight, and a time to run. This was definitely a time to run. Whirling, she rushed toward the entrance. His boots thudded behind her, getting closer. She pushed herself harder, running toward the light and safety. She might have made it, but as she glanced over her shoulder, her foot caught in something and then she was falling.

Reacting quickly, she threw out her hands to catch herself. Her hands skidding along the pavement and her knees hit the ground hard. Her purse went flying. Ignoring the sudden pain shooting through her, she pushed herself up and kept going. But that slight stumble had been enough.

A large hand clamped down on her shoulder and whirled her around. She opened her mouth to scream, but found her air cut off as he slammed his mouth down on hers. Panic filled her. She couldn't breath. The stench of stale cigarette smoke and beer filled her nostrils. Clawing at his face with her hands, she raked her nails down his cheeks, splitting the skin.

He howled as her keys and nails gouged his face, tearing the flesh and leaving long furrows behind. She'd forgotten she'd still had them in her hand. They were a weapon she could use again him.

Frank retaliated immediately, backhanding her across the face. The pain shocked her as she fell backward, landing on the pavement so hard that the breath was knocked out of her. She could hear the clatter of her keys as they were knocked out of her hand and skittered into the darkness. A coppery taste filled her mouth, part blood and part fear. She knew that her lip was split.

"That wasn't very nice at all." She scrabbled backward as he stalked toward her, menace in every step.

She had to get out of this alley. *Think, Carly. Think. You know what to do.* She could almost hear Nathan's voice in her head calmly giving her directions, just like he used to do when she and Erin were kids.

As she skittered backward, her hand closed around a palm-sized rock. *Anything is a potential weapon.* Wrapping her fingers around it, she held it tight as she staggered to her feet. If he wanted a fight, he'd damn well get one.

"We're gonna have some fun, you and me. I've been dreaming about your tits for weeks now." Carly swallowed back the bile that surged up from her stomach. Breathing deeply through her nose, she tried to calm herself. Her legs and arms trembled with terror the closer he got to her. He was almost on her now, but she held her ground. She needed him close if this was going to work.

His big hand reached out and grabbed her. As he tugged her toward him, she erupted into action. Swinging her hand out, she hit the side of his face as hard as she could. The crunch of rock against bone echoed in the alley. Automatically, Carly shoved her knee toward his groin.

Swearing, Frank staggered and doubled over, dropping to his knees.

Not hesitating, she staggered toward the road. Her heart slammed against her chest and her lungs worked hard for breath as she ran as fast as she could. She could hear him cursing and the sound of his boots scraping along the pavement made her push herself harder.

She wouldn't let him catch her.

Putting on a final push, she burst through the front of the alley and straight out into the road. A horn sounded and tires screeched. Lights blinded her. Throwing up her arm to protect her eyes, she stood frozen to the spot.

A door slammed and footsteps hurried toward her. Frank, her mind screamed. She couldn't let him get her. Determination filled her as she clutched the rock in her hand and swung out at her assailant.

Strong arms wrapped around her from behind. She raised her leg and kicked backward. Satisfaction filled her when she heard him swear. But he didn't let her go. He was so big and so strong, she didn't think she could get away this time.

Then she noticed the whispers. The words were soft and comforting in her ear. It occurred to her that his hold was gentle and firm, not hurting. As she took a deep breath a familiar scent filled her nostrils and her struggles ceased. "Nathan."

"I've got you, baby." He crooned in her ear. "What the hell happened?"

"Frank," she managed to gasp out. "Alley."

Before she could say anything else, he scooped her off her feet. Within seconds, she was in the front seat of Nathan's truck and he was on his radio calling for backup. "Don't unlock the door for anyone but me," he told her just before he closed the door.

She didn't want him to leave her, but knew he had to. He might be off duty, but this was his job. She sat there shivering watching through the window as the scene unfolded in front of her.

Nathan stalked toward the alley, pure menace in every step. Just before he reached it, Frank staggered out and took a swing at him, clipping the side of his head. Nathan didn't hesitate. Hauling back his arm, he nailed the other man in the jaw. Frank fell like a stone to the sidewalk. Reaching down, Nathan hauled him up again.

Ignoring, what he'd told her, Carly unlocked her door and slid from the truck. She reached the two men just as Nathan pulled back his arm again. He hesitated and she could tell he was fighting every instinct he possessed. As much as she wanted to see Frank get what was coming to him, she knew that this wasn't the way to do it. Nathan would regret it after the fact. He was sworn to uphold the law, although sometimes that was a very hard thing to do.

"Nathan," she spoke softly, not wanting to startle him.

A shiver racked his body as she gently said his name. "He hurt you." Still holding onto Frank, he turned and looked at her. His eyes were bleak and filled with such pain that it brought tears to her eyes.

Those three words said it all. This stranger had hurt someone he loved and she knew that as far as Nathan was concerned that meant he had to pay. His protective instincts and his honor demanded it. But not like this. Carly knew her man too well to allow him to be hurt over this.

"But it's over and now I need you."

She could see his hands tighten on Frank before he finally let the other man drop back to the sidewalk. Frank groaned as Nathan rolled him onto his stomach. It was only then that she became aware of the crowd that had gathered around them. People were muttering and pointing at Frank and then looking at her. Wrapping her arms around her waist, she shrank back against the side of the truck. Her knees gave out and she slumped down onto the ground, leaning against the passenger door.

Sirens blared and moments later two police cars pulled up. Officers jumped out and took control of the situation. Cuffing Frank, they put him in the backseat of one of the police vehicles while they talked to Nathan. Two other officers were questioning the crowd.

She flinched when someone touched her shoulder. She recognized the officer who was trying to wrap a blanket around her but she just couldn't think of his name. "My purse and keys," she managed to get out, but he knew what she meant.

"We'll find them and take them to the station for you." Nodding her thanks, she huddled closer to the truck, put her head down and pulled the blanket closer.

When someone crouched down in front of her a short time later, she knew it was Nathan. Carefully, he parted the blanket and reached for her hands. "You can let go now." She looked down at her lap and realized the rock was still clutched tight in her hand. She'd held it so tight that her fingers were cramped, and she needed his help to unclench them.

The rock fell to the ground beside them. Nathan held her hand in his and she clung to it, absorbing his strength. "Are you up to giving a statement?" Cupping her face with his other hand, he tipped it up so he could see her.

She really wanted to go home, but she wanted this over with. Nodding, she gathered her strength to try and stand.

"I'm so sorry you were hurt." His heartfelt words made her pause. "I should have been here."

She could feel his anguish and knew he would feel guilty about this if she didn't put a stop to it right now. "You saved me."

His thumb traced a cut on her lip. "But not until after you were hurt."

"No, you don't understand." Coming up onto her knees, she cupped his face in her hands. The blanket fell to the pavement behind her. "It was because of you. Because of the things you taught me when Erin and I were teenagers. Because I could hear your voice in my head practically ordering me to save myself." He held himself still now, clinging to her every word. "Because of those things, I was able to get away."

"You're a strong woman, Carly. You didn't panic. You saved yourself."

"Yes, I did." She leaned into his chest, needing his arms around her. "But I did it with your help. And in the end, you were there when I needed you." His embrace was gentle, as if he was afraid to hold her too tight. "Why were you passing by here so late? It's out of your way."

"I got off work earlier than I expected and figured if you were still at the diner, we might catch a few minutes alone."

"I'm glad you came."

"Me too." She could hear the pain in his voice and knew it would take him a while to get over this. It was up to her to help him. They could get through anything. Together.

"Will you bring her down to the station?"

Nathan looked up at one of the responding officers. "Yeah. We'll be right behind you. I want to run her by the hospital first and get her checked out."

"No problem. Come in when you're finished." He pointed to the police car that was pulling away. "Our friend isn't going anywhere." When someone called out to him, the officer turned and left them alone again.

"I don't need to go to the hospital," she began, but stopped when Nathan scowled at her.

"That is not open for discussion." Standing, he bent down and lifted her into his arms and held her tight as he opened the passenger door. "You should have stayed in the truck like I told you to." His words were harsh, but his touch tender as he deposited her on the seat. "What if he hadn't been hurt as badly as he was? What if he'd had a weapon?" Carefully, he wrapped the seatbelt around her and buckled it.

She let him scold her, knowing he needed to get it out of his system. Reaching out her hand, she touched his head, sifting her fingers though his hair. He froze with his hands still on the seatbelt buckle. "I'm fine. He didn't get a chance to really hurt me."

Nathan shuddered and gave a single nod before pulling away. "You're everything to me." He leaned down and kissed her softly, making sure he didn't hurt her cut lip.

Reaching down, he plucked the blanket off the ground, shook it out, and draped it over her. He made sure the ends were tucked around her legs before he closed the door. Walking around the front of the truck, he climbed in and started the engine, but sat there unmoving.

Reaching across the seat, he held out his hand. She placed her much smaller hand in his, allowing his stronger one to cradle hers. He lifted it to his lips and kissed her left hand just below the diamond ring he'd given her. Wrapping her fingers around his, she gave them a squeeze.

Slowly, he lowered her hand and laid it back in her lap. Taking a deep breath, he let it out slowly before put the truck in gear and headed toward the hospital.

Chapter Sixteen

એ

Nathan Connors' pale blue eyes glittered dangerously and he gritted his teeth, clinging to his temper by the thinnest of threads. He was a patient man by nature, but even he had limits.

He had a moment of déjà vu and chuckled as he remembered that the exact same thought had run through his mind only a week ago.

The scene was similar. People were all dressed up in their fancy clothes, milling around and chatting to one another. His brother Jackson was looking slightly uncomfortable in his tuxedo, but his sister Erin was looking really pretty in her silky green dress. Her husband, Abel, stood behind her, his arms wrapped around her waist so she couldn't get away from him.

Nathan knew exactly how he felt. He wanted to do the same thing with Carly, but he'd had to let her go. For now. But that didn't mean he couldn't watch her.

Ever since the incident the other night, he hated to have her out of his sight even for a few minutes. It didn't seem to matter that logically he knew she was safe. He wanted her near enough so that he could protect her. The sounds of the celebration floated by him where he stood in the shadow of a tree and watched her every move.

He could feel his cock flexing and growing as he watched her walk across the garden. Swearing softly, he looked away until he had his body under control again. Carly Connors was pure temptation in a long, lacy gown of white. The top part of the dress sparkled with beads and showcased her breasts to perfection. Long sleeves covered her arms and the full skirt fell in a straight line to her ankles, a short train of fabric sweeping out behind her.

A coronet of white roses circled her head and a short veil covered her light brown hair. Her face shone with happiness and her blue eyes sparkled in the late afternoon sunshine. She'd never looked more like an angel.

He couldn't wait to get her naked.

Underneath that angelic smile, lay the heart and body of a temptress. And she now belonged to him. He felt himself relaxing for the first time in weeks.

It was over now. The waiting and the wondering. Carly had accepted him in front of God and all their friends this afternoon when she said, "I do", in their garden ceremony. There was a slight nip in the air, but the sun was still shining, even though it was beginning to sink in the distance.

She knew exactly who he was and she had accepted him. The good and the bad. His chest swelled with pride as he watched her. She was a hell of a woman. He watched as she flitted from group to group, making everyone feel welcome and special. It was her gift.

"Congratulations." A huge hand slapped him on the back and he felt himself stumble forward slightly.

He straightened and glared at his brother. "Thanks."

Jackson just laughed. "You've got to stop standing here glaring at everyone. Your bride is starting to get concerned."

His gaze immediately went to Carly and, sure enough, there was a small frown on her face as she watched him. He smiled at her, but she just shook her head at him and blew him a kiss. He wasn't quite sure, but he thought she mouthed the word, "Soon."

Reaching up, he loosened his tie before taking a swallow from the warm bottle of beer he'd been carrying around for the better part of an hour.

"I wish you both all the happiness in the world." Jackson's words washed over him and the enormity of the afternoon finally struck home.

He was married to the woman of his dreams. Swallowing hard, he turned to his brother. Eyes exactly like his own stared back at him. Jackson looked happy and sad at the same time.

It occurred to him then that, in the space of a few months, both he and Erin had left their family home. He'd taken the last of his stuff to Carly's house yesterday morning. Jackson was now living in the large farmhouse behind them all by himself. Yeah, both he and Erin lived close by. Heck, Erin only lived in the next farm down the road. But it wasn't the same.

Wrapping his arms around Jackson, he gave him a quick hug and then stepped back. "Thanks. But don't think you're getting rid of me. Carly and I will be out here so often you'll think we live here."

He just nodded, but said nothing. They both knew that it was different and nothing anyone said would change that. It was strange that Jackson, the oldest of them all, would be the last single one among them. But then, Jackson worked so damned hard on the farm that he didn't have time to socialize.

He felt her presence before he saw her. Carly slipped her arm around his waist and smiled at Jackson. "Thank you for letting us have the wedding in the garden." She gazed around the yard, which was still beautiful, even though it was late October.

"My pleasure." Jackson's voice was gruff, but Nathan knew that he'd been pleased by their decision to have the wedding here at the farm.

Carly's father came up to them and thrust his camera at Jackson. "Will you take a picture of the three of us?" He didn't wait for an answer, but was already moving to stand between the bride and groom. "Do you know how to operate it? I've got it set so you just have to point and shoot."

Jackson looked down at the camera in his hands. "I'll manage." Hoisting the camera to face level, he quickly snapped several pictures before offering the camera back to Mr. Ames.

"We're ready to sit down to supper now." Carly pointed at the large tent that had been set up. Tables filled with fancy silverware and china were arranged around a head table. Patio lights had been strung inside and votive candles glowed from the top of each table. People were laughing and chatting as they went inside and found their places.

"Shall we?" Nathan bent his arm and she placed her small hand on the dark sleeve of his tuxedo jacket. The heat practically seared his arm. He could wait a few hours longer. Barely.

Taking Carly into his arms, he swirled her around the makeshift dance floor. It had taken almost two hours to eat their supper, cut the cake and sit through a half-dozen speeches. But surprisingly enough, he'd enjoyed himself. All their friends and family were genuinely happy for them and he was reminded once again why he liked living in this small town.

But now, he finally had an excuse to put his arms around his new wife and hold her tight. A soft sigh slipped from her lips as he guided her to the rhythm of the slow music.

"Tired?" He dropped a soft kiss on her temple, breathing in the scent of the roses that crowned her head.

"Yes, but it's a good tired. I can't believe that it's over after all the hard work and last-minute rushing around." She leaned her head against his chest.

"I knew you were doing too much." Nathan scowled over her head. "You should have rested more like the doctor told you." After what had happened with Frank, it had taken all Nathan's control not to kidnap her again and keep her somewhere safe until the wedding.

Her laugh was partially muffled against his jacket, and he felt it more than he heard it. She patted his chest with her small hand. "I'm all right, Nathan. And it was worth it. The wedding was perfect."

His frown gave way to a soft, tender smile. If she was happy, that was all that mattered. He knew that this kind of stuff was important to most women and he was glad that it had been everything she'd wanted in a wedding day.

He'd gotten his ring on her finger and, as far as he was concerned, that was the only thing that truly mattered. All the other stuff was extra.

She leaned her small frame against his and he pulled her closer, tightening his hold on her. He'd had plans for their wedding night. Big plans. But if she was really tired...he sighed and resigned himself to a celibate night.

Damn, but being a sensitive guy was going to be the death of him.

"Do you think it would be rude of us to leave soon?"

Now he was worried. If Carly wanted to leave her own wedding celebration early, then she must be even more exhausted than he thought. The song came to an end and everyone clapped for them as he guided her from the floor. Keeping her tucked underneath his arm, he kept moving until they were away from the crowd that was now taking to the dance floor.

"If you want to leave, we'll leave." Placing his finger under her chin, he tipped her face up to his. His breath caught in his throat at the look on her face. Her eyes were half closed and a small smile played at the corners of her lush mouth. But it wasn't exhaustion that filled her blue eyes, it was arousal.

Nathan's cock sprang to life as anticipation surged through his body. Maybe he wouldn't have to adjust his plans after all. "You look exhausted, honey. We should leave now."

Not giving her time to respond, he tugged her toward the entrance of the tent. People noticed them and began to laugh.

Catcalls soon followed. Carly faltered, but he scooped her right up into his arms, never breaking stride. She buried her face in his shoulder. He could feel her shaking. Was she crying? He slowed as he reached the flap that led to the outside.

Lifting her head, she peeked up at him. A tear fell from the corner of her eye. His heart almost stopped. But then her smile almost blinded him with its brilliance. She was laughing so hard that she was crying.

"Honestly, Nathan," she managed to get out in between giggles. "You always seem to be carrying me away."

The feelings of lust and love that filled him were so overwhelming that he almost staggered with her in his arms. Anticipation began to grow and he was suddenly glad that the train of her dress was covering the front of his pants because anticipation wasn't the only thing that was growing.

He turned back toward their guests, and shifted Carly higher in his arms, making her squeal with laughter. "Thanks for coming, folks. See you all in a few days."

Jackson laughed as he pulled the flap to the tent back further. Nathan grinned at him as he ducked through the opening and carried Carly from the tent. Erin was coming from the house and she gave them a startled look before she too began to laugh, waving at them as they passed her.

Nathan didn't care. He was too damned happy.

Hurrying across the lawn, he headed for his truck. Carly wasn't making it easy. The second they were out of the tent, she began kissing his neck and nibbling on his ear.

"You're gonna pay for that," he warned.

"I certainly hope so." Her sensual purr was almost more than he could take. He wondered what the wedding guests would think if he dumped his new wife on the bed of his truck and fucked her.

The truck seemed like it was miles away and Nathan was so hot by the time he got them there, that he was afraid he might not have a choice. He managed to get the door open and stuffed Carly into her seat before slamming the door. Stalking around the front of the truck, he ripped his door open and threw himself behind the steering wheel.

Reaching out, he hauled her into his arms and captured her mouth with his. The little mewling sounds she made drove him crazy. He gripped her head with one hand and with the other, he palmed one of her breasts. The beads dug into his hand. He wanted to tear her dress off. Wanted nothing between them.

Those magnificent rose-tipped breasts were his to play with and he wanted all night to do so. As he pulled away from her, he was pleased to note that her eyes were glassy with desire and her breath was coming in huge gasps.

"I'm hanging by a thread here," he growled. "Sit there quietly or I'll fuck you in the truck. That will really give our guests something to talk about." She nodded, her eyes getting wider.

He started the engine and took a deep breath before putting it in gear and pulling away from his home. He had a new home now, with Carly, and he couldn't wait to get her there.

Reaching between his legs, he grunted as he adjusted his cock. The pressure was damned near killing him. A rustling of silk had him glancing at Carly. She'd subsided in her seat and had put on her seatbelt. She looked small and slightly forlorn and he felt like a jerk for destroying her happy mood.

"Did your parents get moved into their hotel?"

Carly started slightly when he spoke. "Yes. They did that just before we left home this afternoon."

He was thankful to her parents for that. They understood that a married couple needed to be alone and had decided to take a hotel room for the night and let him and Carly have their first night in their new home alone. Good thing, too. Otherwise, he'd have taken her to a hotel. No way he was spending his first night with Carly with her parents right next door.

Her folks were heading back to Florida first thing in the morning. It occurred to him then that he hadn't even given her time to say goodbye before he'd rushed her away from the reception.

"Did you get a chance to say goodbye to your folks?"

A fleeting smile appeared on her lips before disappearing again. "Yes, I did. Dad figured there might not be time later."

Nathan made a mental note to thank her father at a later date. Reaching his hand out, he tangled her fingers with his. She sighed and relaxed back against the seat.

The drive to her house passed in silence, both of them lost in their own thoughts. Well, he supposed it was their house now. He didn't really like that idea and was already planning to convince her to move to another house. One that he bought for her.

He wouldn't tell her that though, because she'd accuse him of being a Neanderthal. Which he was, but he didn't care. He wanted to provide a home for his woman. The way to get around her objections was to remind her that they'd need a bigger place for kids and maybe a dog. She'd like that.

Breathing a sigh of relief when the house came into view, Nathan glanced over at Carly. She was chewing on her bottom lip as she looked out the window. He couldn't tell what she was thinking.

Parking the truck, he jumped out of the front seat and hurried around to the passenger side. She had the door open, but was waiting for him. Scooping her into his arms, he carried her up the front walkway.

"The key is in my right jacket pocket. Will you dig it out for me?" He didn't want to let her out of his arms.

She withdrew the key from his pocket and quickly unlocked the door. Nathan carried her over the threshold and kicked the door shut behind him. It closed with a thud. The finality of his actions and the silence of the house settled on them both.

He walked quickly down the hallway and carried her straight to her bedroom before slowly letting her legs slide from his arm. Keeping his other arm around her, he glanced around the room to assure himself that it hadn't changed.

It was a lush and sensual hideaway with its heavy, dark cherry tone furniture, which included a four-poster bed with a thick burgundy spread. Pillows in a rainbow of jewel tones were tossed across the bed and a plush burgundy rug lay atop the hardwood floor. He had fond memories of this room. It was the first place he'd ever made love to Carly.

Carly moved restlessly in his embrace and he reluctantly let her go. She licked her lips and looked away from him.

She was nervous. Somehow it had never occurred to him that she would be nervous. But why wouldn't she be? It was their first night as a married couple. It was official and it was binding. They were joined for life.

Carefully, he plucked the pins from the flower coronet that perched on her head. Tossing them on the bedside table, he removed the circle of flowers and laid it aside. Her hair was tousled, so he smoothed it back with his hand. Her eyes softened as she looked up at him. This was what he wanted. He wanted that softness and sensuality that was such an innate part of her. He wanted her heat and her lust and her love. He wanted it all.

"You look beautiful in that dress."

A slight blush tinged her cheeks. "Thank you." Her soft reply went straight to his groin, reminding him that he was already skating the edge.

"But you'll look even better out of it. Go and get changed, honey. I'll be waiting here when you get back."

She turned her back to him, but didn't move. Instead, she shifted closer to him. "Unzip me?"

Gripping the small tab between his fingers, he slowly lowered the zipper. The fabric parted, exposing the long, soft line of her back. The zipper ended just above her ass and he traced his finger back up the line of her spine to her neck.

Unable to resist, he slipped his hands in on either side of the opening and reached around until he was cupping the lace of her bra. Her nipples were hard pebbles against the lace and he rolled them between his thumbs and forefingers.

She moaned and pushed her breasts harder into his hands. "I plan to suck your rosy nipples until you come. But first, you have to get changed." And he had a couple of things to take care of while she was gone.

Reluctantly, he released her breasts and eased his hands out of her dress. When she didn't move, he gave her a small push and she moved like a sleepwalker toward the bathroom to change.

"I'll be waiting." The second she was out of sight, he loosened his tie and went to work.

Chapter Seventeen

ဢ

"I'll be waiting." His words followed her out of the room and raised goose bumps on both her arms. Her panties were soaked with her arousal and her breasts ached. She didn't know what he had in store for her tonight, but she couldn't wait to find out.

She practically floated down the hallway and into the bathroom. Her wedding had been everything she'd ever imagined and wanted. Mostly because she had married the man of her dreams.

Nathan was all she'd ever wanted in a man. He was loyal, fair-minded, hardworking and protective of those he loved. It didn't hurt that he had a body to die for and an unending sexual appetite. Her inner muscles clenched at the mere thought of him and she could feel another gush of liquid flow from between her thighs.

With his long, muscled legs and wide chest, he'd looked amazing in his tuxedo. He wasn't handsome in the traditional sense of the word. His face was compelling, strong and incredibly sensual. The man radiated confidence and sex appeal.

Bending forward, she allowed her dress to slide off her arms in a shower of silk. Carefully, she stepped out of it and hung it carefully on the hanger behind the bathroom door. Kicking off her shoes, she flexed her feet, grateful to have the heels off after so many hours.

The relief was incredible when she undid her bra and slipped it off. Her breasts felt even heavier than usual and her nipples were drawn incredibly tight. Carly didn't hesitate, but skimmed out of her panties and tossed them in the hamper.

Standing naked, except for her stockings, in front of the bathroom mirror, she looked at herself. She looked wanton and very sensual. It surprised her slightly because, before she and Nathan had gotten together, she hadn't thought of herself in that way.

But she liked sex. Especially with Nathan. Until she'd been with him, she hadn't known that it was possible for a modern, independent woman to enjoy deferring to a man in the bedroom. But with Nathan it was not only right. It was perfect.

In fact, it heightened her responses. There was something about surrendering to his sexual whims that made her feel sexy and desirable. She was so close to coming now, she knew it wouldn't take much for her to explode.

Turning away, she propped one foot on the side of the bathtub and rolled off her stocking. Then she did the same with the other one. Totally naked now, she snatched up her long, blue silky bathrobe and wrapped it around herself.

Once she was ready, she took one last deep breath. This was Nathan. Everything would be fine.

Her feet made no sound on the carpet runner as she padded back down the hall. Pausing in the doorway, she watched him move about the room. He'd been busy while she was gone.

He'd removed his jacket, shirt and tie and tossed them over the chair in the corner. His shoes and socks lay on the floor next to it. Wearing only his pants, he stood with his back to her. Muscles moved and rippled with every movement he made. Her fingers longed to stroke him.

She must have made a sound, either that or he sensed her presence, because he turned at that moment. Avoiding his heated stare, she looked around the room. Candles gleamed from the top of the dresser, giving the room a cozy glow. A bottle of champagne was opened on one of the bedside tables, but there was only one glass. The bed hadn't been turned back yet.

When she'd run out of things to look at, she finally brought her gaze back to his. "Come here." He didn't move from where he stood, but waited for her to obey him.

This Nathan was the lover who wanted his every sexual demand met without question. By marrying him, she'd agreed to let him be in charge of her sexual pleasure. To allow him to be in control in the bedroom. Her stomach fluttered even as her feet moved forward.

She stopped when she was in front of him and waited.

"How are you feeling?" His hand grazed the side of her face where a very faint bruise remained from where Frank had hit her.

"I'm fine." Poor Nathan had been treating her like he was afraid she was going to break. And physically, she was fine. The tiny cut on the outside of her lip had healed almost overnight and she'd hardly bruised at all. The worst had been the scrapes on her hands and knees where she'd fallen and a few sore muscles. Nothing a few hot baths and a day of rest hadn't cured.

But emotionally, well, she'd be a long time getting over the attack. Images from that evening popped into her head at the strangest moments and her heart would pound and she'd break out into a cold sweat. Frank Stiles, it was strange to know his full name, had shaken her sense of personal safety. It would be awhile before she got over that, if she ever truly did. But she was confident enough in herself to know that, given time, she'd be just fine.

He was still locked up and awaited his first appearance in court to determine which charges would be laid against him. But that was next week. Tonight was her wedding night and she planned to enjoy it to the fullest.

But first she had to convince Nathan that she was perfectly fit for whatever he had planned for tonight. Smiling up at him, she ran her hands up his chest and gripped his shoulders. Coming up on her toes, she moved her mouth closer to his. "I'm perfectly healthy and more than willing."

He leaned his head down closer to hers. "You're sure?"

They were so close now. Her lips were almost touching his. "Yes." Anything to get him to kiss her. His mouth barely skimmed hers before he took a step back. Rocking back on her heels, she arched her eyebrow and stared at him.

"Take off your robe."

The belt opened beneath her fingers and she slipped the robe off, letting it fall at her feet. His eyes followed the fabric as it slid from her body. As she stood there, he reached out a hand, allowing his finger to trace the contours of her face, the line of her neck, and her collarbone. Letting his hand slip a little lower, he circled the outer edges of first one nipple, then the other.

She tried to arch into his hand, but he moved it just out of reach. "Be still."

Steadying her body, she held herself still as he once again began to outline her aroused nipples. Her breathing was rapid by the time his finger swirled lower and dipped in her belly button. She moaned when his fingers finally dipped between her thighs.

Stroking the slick folds of her sex, he coated his fingers with her cream before withdrawing them and holding them to her lips. "Taste."

Parting her lips, she waited for him to slide his fingers into his mouth. But he didn't move them. His hand remained poised in front of her. She realized that he wanted her to take them into her mouth.

Leaning forward, she lapped at his fingers, running her tongue up and down their length before sliding them inside. Her own musky arousal mixed with the salty tang of his flesh on her tongue. She wanted more. Sucking his fingers deep, she licked between his fingers.

"You're wet, but not nearly wet enough." He pulled his fingers almost out before thrusting them back inside. "I want you so damned hot that you'll do anything I want to get me to fuck you long and hard."

Her entire body shook as his words sank in. His fingers filled her mouth and her teeth gently scraped them as he withdrew them. She closed her eyes, imagining that it was his cock thrusting past her lips. Liquid slipped down her inner thighs. If she got any hotter she'd come just standing there.

Swearing, he turned away, yanking off his pants and underwear in one quick motion. Dumping them both on the chair, he stalked to the end of the bed. Naked and aroused, he looked huge as he stood there and held out his hand to her. His erection jutted out in front of him, blue veins pulsing on the sides and the head, red and slick.

Licking her dry lips, she walked toward him.

His eyes glittered with lust as she approached him. "Up in the bed and spread your arms and legs."

She crawled up onto the bed and rolled onto her back. Lying in the center, she positioned herself as he'd told her to.

"Wider."

She slid her arms and legs as far as she could, stretching to reach the corners of the bed. Nathan stood at the bottom of the bed, a satisfied look on his face. Reaching out, he grabbed something that had been tucked in by one of the posts. She almost balked when she felt the first cuff close around her ankle. It was then she realized that each post of the bed had a cuff attached to it.

He gave her time to object as he cuffed first one ankle and then the other. Walking to the head of the bed, he lifted her hand and kissed her palm before laying it back down and snapping the velvet lined cuff shut. He sauntered around to the other side of the bed and affixed the last cuff to her wrist.

She tested her bonds, tugging lightly. They didn't hurt and she wasn't uncomfortable, but her stomach was jumping with nerves, a combination of unease and desire. She knew that Nathan would never do anything to hurt her, but it still felt strange to lie bound to the bed awaiting his sexual pleasure. Strange, but incredibly arousing.

Arching her back, she rolled her hips toward him. She might be bound, but she wasn't helpless by any means. His eyes were glued to her pussy and she knew he could see their gleaming lips perfectly.

"I want you, Nathan." She undulated her hips again as she spoke and watched, pleased, as he shuddered.

"Not yet. First I need to gain some control." He knelt up on the bed and swung his leg over her, straddling her torso. "And you're gonna help me."

He slipped his hand behind her neck and lifted it while he shoved a pillow beneath her head. "Open your mouth."

Carly opened her mouth, wanting to taste him, to touch him in any way possible. Adjusting his position, he guided the tip of his erection to her lips. It was already wet when the head slipped into her mouth. He tasted potent, male, powerful.

His fingers cupped the side of her head as he slowly began to slide in and out of her mouth. Using her tongue, she lapped at the sides of his cock with every thrust. She allowed her teeth to gently scrape the top and bottom of his shaft as he withdrew and was rewarded when he groaned.

Satisfaction filled her. She might be cuffed to the bed, but at this second, she was in control. As he pushed his cock further into her mouth, she took him as deep as she could, lapping and sucking at his swollen flesh.

His motions got more frantic as he jerked his hips back and forth. She accepted every thrust, accepting him, encouraging him. She wanted him to come.

Her pussy was pulsing in time with each thrust of his cock as if he was actually plunging in and out of it. She felt her own inner muscles contract and she moaned with pleasure.

The vibrations rocked Nathan and he held her head tight as he came in her mouth.

She gagged once, when his cum first shot down her throat. But she recovered immediately and continued to suck him dry as she swallowed. Nathan leaned against the headboard, his chest heaving. Sweat covered his torso, making his incredible chest and abs gleam. Without thinking, she reached out to touch him and her wrist came up solid against the restraint.

She wanted to scream in frustration. Instead, she sucked his cock, hard.

"Damn it, Carly." Gingerly, he pulled himself out of her mouth.

"I want to touch you." Tipping her head up as far as it would go, she licked at the head of his penis.

Nathan laughed as he rolled off her torso. "Not yet." Sitting on the side of the bed, he reached out and poured a glass of champagne.

Taking a sip, he tried to catch his breath. He felt totally drained, but strangely energized. She looked absolutely beautiful lying across the bed, her slender pale limbs spread wide, awaiting his pleasure. Every breath she took made her breasts jiggle slightly. He didn't think that she even realized that her hips continued to rock slightly, seeking his cock.

It was better than he'd even imagined it would be. Now that they were married, there was a level of commitment and trust that was even deeper than before. The fact that she was not only willing to do whatever he asked of her, but seemed to enjoy it, was a gift beyond price. It was like nothing he'd ever experienced.

He'd been more than willing to forego any lovemaking tonight or to be extremely gentle with her. It might have killed him after watching her in that formfitting dress all evening.

But he would have done it without thinking twice. Nothing was more important to him than her health and her happiness.

After her ordeal, he hadn't been sure what to expect. The corner of his mouth kicked up. He should have known better. Carly was such a strong woman, he knew she wouldn't let the events of the other night control her. If anything, she seemed even more determined that tonight be everything they both wanted it to be. And he was more than willing to accommodate her.

She continued to amaze him with her enthusiasm and her willingness to do whatever pleased him. Her soft mouth had pleasured him and sucked him dry. Now it was his turn.

"You want some champagne?" He tipped the glass toward her lips as he slipped a hand beneath her neck to support it.

She sipped the golden liquid from the glass and licked her lips when he pulled it away. "That tastes wonderful."

He leaned forward and allowed his lips to skim hers. The combination of his cum, the champagne and Carly had his cock quivering to life once again. Amazing. Only Carly had this kind of effect on him.

"I'll bet it could taste even better." Tipping up the glass, he allowed golden droplets to fall in the valley between her breasts. He watched as it trickled down her stomach and pooled in her belly button.

Laying the glass aside, he dipped several of his fingers in it before turning back to her. His fingertips were rough against the tips of her breasts as he coated them in the liquid. He took his time, wanting to make sure every part of her nipple was covered in champagne.

"Oh god, Nathan." She tried to shove her breasts closer, but she couldn't move.

"I know what you want." Kneeling up on the bed beside her, he leaned closer to her breasts. Hovering over one of them, he blew gently. Her nipple hardened even more.

"Beautiful," he murmured as he took the entire nipple into his mouth and sucked it hard against the roof of his mouth.

She convulsed beneath him, her cry of release echoing around the room. He kept sucking, touching only her breast. He could feel her trying to close her legs and knew that her pussy still throbbed with need. An emptiness, aching to be filled.

But not yet.

The minute she sighed and relaxed, he began again. Her eyes widened slightly before she closed them tight. Her breath came out in a hiss between her clenched teeth as he lapped at one nipple and then the other. Using his tongue and teeth and fingers, he plucked and pulled and played with her breasts. Her nipples were no longer a rosy pink, but a swollen reddish hue.

Nuzzling the sensitive undersides, he kissed her torso, edging closer to her navel. His tongue lapped at the champagne that still filled the indent of her stomach. Carly cried out again, tugging at her bonds.

"Let me go. I want to touch you."

Situating himself between her open thighs, he parted the lips of her pussy with his fingers and gently blew on her heated flesh. "Not yet." He didn't think he'd ever seen her this aroused. She was soaked and swollen, ready for him to sink his cock into.

Reaching between his legs, he stroked his erection, which was rigid and ready to go again. Soon, he promised himself as he gripped his cock in his fist and gave it one hard pump before releasing it. But first, he wanted to give Carly a screaming orgasm she'd never forget.

Spreading the lips of her sex wide with one hand, he stroked the sensitive inner lips with the other. When her moans of pleasure filled the room, he reached out and snagged the glass off the nightstand. Tipping it back, he drank all but a few drops. Then, he tilted the glass forward and poured the rest on her clit. As he watched, it slipped down toward her slit and disappeared inside.

"Now that's champagne that I really have to try." Dropping the glass on the bedspread, he knelt between her thighs and rasped her clit with his tongue. It was swollen and peeking out from its hood.

Carly's cries became more frantic as he dipped a finger inside her cunt. The muscles clamped down hard on it even as he licked the opening. Her hips bucked toward him.

Sitting back, he licked his lips. He kept his finger steady inside her, not moving it. "Look at me."

Her hair was plastered to her head with sweat and her eyes were glazed with desire as she turned them toward him. "You taste so damned hot. Pussy and champagne." He ran his tongue around his lips.

She watched every movement, her blue eyes pleading. A low mewling sound came from her as her hips arched in need.

"Are you hot enough for me yet?" He slowly pushed another finger in to join the first one.

"Yes, oh yes."

"I don't think so." Watching her every reaction, he inserted another finger in her pussy, stretching her still wider. Her pupils dilated, her eyes becoming almost black. "How about now?"

"Nathan," she gasped.

Easing back his hand, he drove his fingers deep. "Come for me, Carly." She convulsed around his fingers. Hard. He kept up a steady movement, as she shook and came all over his hand.

Her entire body went lax as she sank into the mattress. Her breathing was harsh as she began to pull on the cuffs trapping her to the bed, struggling to release herself. A soft, tiny sob escaped from her mouth.

Reaching up, he undid the wrist cuffs and carefully lowered her arms back to her side. He thought that her muscles still might be a bit sore from the attack and didn't want her to hurt herself by pulling them.

Turning around on the bed, he quickly freed her ankles. As the last restraint fell back to the mattress, he felt her arms wrap around him.

Hauling her into his arms, he cradled her tight. Brushing back the hair that was plastered to her forehead, he dropped little kisses on her nose and cheeks. Rocking her in his arms, he soothed her.

She was muttering something under her breath, but he couldn't hear her. Bending down, he placed his ear closer to her mouth. "I love you, I love you," poured from her lips.

A wave of relief filled him. He had been afraid he'd pushed her too far. But he should have known better. Carly would have told him if he had. That was one of the things he loved about her. She wasn't afraid to speak her mind and challenge him. On anything.

He held her close to his heart and waited until he felt her totally relax in his arms. His cock was throbbing now and pushing against her side. There was no hiding the fact that he was aroused once again.

It was finally time to finish it. This time they'd reach satisfaction together. He lowered his arm and her head lolled back against it.

He stared in disbelief at first. Then a reluctant smile crossed his face. His angel was sound asleep. Between the events of the week, the long wedding day and the intense wedding night, she was worn out.

Shaking his head and swallowing a chuckle, he reached out and tugged the covers down. Easing her under the comforter, he tucked it around her. She just snuggled down in the bed and continued to sleep.

Nathan climbed out of bed and went to the bathroom. He checked the house before returning back to the bedroom. One by one, he blew out the candles until the only one remaining was the one on the nightstand.

She slept on peacefully and deeply. He plucked the discarded glass from the bed and placed it on the nightstand before blowing out the candle and slipping beneath the sheets.

She immediately rolled into his arms. He settled her head on his chest. With Carly wrapped safely in his arms, they both slept.

Epilogue

❧

She was totally aroused when she woke. Her eyes fluttered open to find Nathan propped up on elbows staring down into her face. His hard shaft was already inside her, filling her completely. It felt absolutely wonderful. She curled her toes into the mattress and sighed with contentment.

"Good morning, Mrs. Connors." He kissed her lightly on the lips as he flexed his hips, driving himself deeper.

Clutching his shoulders, she arched her hips up to meet his downward thrust. "Good morning, Mr. Connors."

"You fell asleep last night." He placed a string of kisses along her jaw and nibbled at her earlobe, making it hard for her to think.

She remembered having one of the most explosive orgasms of her entire life. She also remembered tugging at the restraints and crying because it had been so powerful. Nothing had been more important than being able to touch Nathan.

Frowning, she tried to piece the rest of last night together. He'd released her from the cuffs and locked her in his arms. She'd felt totally safe and loved. That was the last thing she could recall.

Using his thumb, he rubbed at the frown lines between her eyes. "Don't worry about it. We were both tired."

Running her hands down his back, she gripped his butt in her palms. The man had an amazing ass. "I'm not tired now." She used her grip on him to pull him closer. Wiggling her hips, she ground her clit against his pelvis. The man was hard everywhere. And it felt so incredibly good.

"I can see that." He grinned at her as he thrust harder.

She felt happy this morning. Almost lighthearted. Even Nathan looked different. Younger, not quite so intense. They did this for one another, she realized. They made each other happy.

Then she forgot everything as he plunged deeper with each stroke. There were no games this time. Just a man and a woman both reaching for release. Giving the other what they needed, while taking what they needed for themselves.

She lost herself in his intense blue eyes. Each thrust rocked her entire being. Every nerve of her body was alive. Every cell of her body wanted this man.

The feelings welled up inside her and spilled over. Unlike last night's release, which had hit her hard and fast, this one was long and almost gentle, but just as fulfilling and almost more satisfying.

She gave his butt a final squeeze before gripping his shoulders. Wrapping her legs around his waist, she met his every stroke.

He cried out her name as he emptied himself inside her and she held him locked tight to her. He was hers and she was his. They were meant to be.

She could feel his cum flooding her and she shivered. She felt almost like she was part of him at that moment. Nathan managed to shift most of his body to the side before he collapsed on top of her.

His face was buried in the pillow next to her and for the longest time he didn't move. Lying there, she stared at the ceiling and flexed her legs and her toes, desperately needing to stretch, but unable to do so with him lying across her.

"You're wiggling like a damned worm, woman." Raising his head, he gave her a bleary-eyed stare.

Carly giggled. He looked totally unkempt and debauched, a far cry from the polished, cool and composed man he usually was.

"Think it's funny, do you?" The corner of his mouth crooked up.

She nodded as her fingers inched out on the bed beside her.

Nathan grunted as he pulled out of her and sat back on his haunches. The move pulled the covers from her body. While he was busy staring at her breasts, she stretched her hand out. Almost there.

Catching the corner of a throw pillow in her fingers, she swung at him. He yelped as she scrambled up to a sitting position.

"Now you're gonna pay." He grabbed the pillow nearest her and began to pummel her.

Shrieking, she rolled to the side as she struck out again. She tried to move and got a pillow in the face. Laughing, she tried to hit him again, but his arms were longer than hers.

Dropping the pillow, he tackled her to the bed, rolling with her until he was on the bottom and she was on top. She noticed that he was very careful to keep his weight of her and his grip gentle as he'd rolled with her. He was always protecting her. Taking care of her. It was as natural to him as breathing and she loved him for it.

Clasping his arms in her hands, she raised them over his head as she sat on his chest. "Do you give up?"

His eyes darkened and all the laughter fled his face. Pulling one of his hands from her grip, he cupped her cheek. "I gave up the moment you told me you wanted me. The moment you accepted me the way I am. All of me."

"Oh, Nathan." She tried to move, but he held her still.

"I set out to capture you, using any means possible. But the truth is, you captured me first. And all you did was love me."

A tear rolled down her cheek and plopped onto his face. He wiped it off with a finger and brought it to his lips, licking the tear away. She'd never seen anything more beautiful.

"I love you, Carly. With all that I am." A smile quirked up on his face. "Good and bad."

Tracing his features with her fingers, she wanted to hold this moment in her heart forever. "I love you too. Good and bad. With all that I am."

Nathan pulled her down and kissed her long and hard. It was a long time before they had breakfast.

CRAVING CANDY

◌

Dedication

അ

This book is dedicated to my wonderful husband, whose support and encouragement still continues to grow after all these years.

Thanks to all the readers who have written to tell me how much they have loved this series and wanted to make sure I didn't plan to leave Lucas out.

And thank you to Mary. As always, I appreciate your hard work and your encouragement.

Chapter One

80

It was the screams that woke him.

He'd come home from working a double shift at the grocery store, totally exhausted, and had fallen into bed immediately. For once, the house had been blessedly silent. The money was starting to accumulate in his bank account and in less than a month he would be moving out of the cramped, cheap, squalid apartment he'd called home his entire life and into his own place. His life was about to begin.

And then the screaming had started.

He thought about pulling the pillow over his head and pretending he couldn't hear the male voice yelling obscenities in the other room, but he knew that was impossible. He'd never be able to rest until he knew his mom was okay.

Sighing, he rolled out of bed, clad only in his boxer shorts. The floor was cold against his feet, but he didn't take the time to pull on socks. Sounded like the old man was really on a bender tonight. He scrubbed his hand over his face, wishing he'd taken a shower and shaved before he'd fallen into bed earlier.

He paused at the door and listened. Maybe the old man would crash in his easy chair and drink himself into a stupor. That's what he did most nights. Only one more month of this crap, he consoled himself.

"You stupid bitch!" The sound of glass smashing was followed quickly by a woman's cry of pain.

Yanking the bedroom door open, he pounded down the hall just in time to see his mother crash against the wall, cowering in fear as her enraged husband loomed above her. She clutched her right hand to her chest and, from the way she held it, he suspected that it was sprained or broken. It wouldn't be the first time. Blood dripped from her nose as she turned her face away.

The world seemed to shift, almost as if it were in slow motion. This scene had played itself out over and over in this household for as long as he could remember. It was always the same. The old man would beat his mother or him until he got tired or some neighbor called the cops, complaining about the noise. The cops would come and his mother would tell the officers that nothing was wrong.

But tonight, he'd had enough. "Stop it!" He was across the room before he'd really thought about it and grabbed his father's arm just as he was about to strike his mother again. He was tall but scrawny. Certainly no match for his father, who was heavily muscled—a man in his prime.

He sensed his father's disbelief as the older man jerked around, and the fist that had been about to descend on his mother now swung in his direction. Rearing back, he barely avoided being hit and felt the whoosh of air against his cheek. As he stood there facing his father, a deep calm settled upon him. His mother sank down to the floor, whimpering in pain, but her eyes never left them as they squared off, father against son.

"Stay out of this, boy. It ain't your business." His father's voice was rough from too many years of smoking and hard drinking. A dull red suffused his face as he flexed his huge hands by his sides.

"Leave her be." He swallowed hard, his mouth dry as he dared to defy his father.

"You telling me what to do, boy?" Utter disbelief filled the older man's voice.

And why wouldn't it? The thought left a bitter taste in his mouth. He'd rarely stood up to his father and had always been beaten down when he had. But he'd just turned eighteen yesterday. He was a man now and a man protected those weaker than himself.

At least, a good man did.

He took a deep breath, knowing he was inviting a beating, but there was no turning back. It was as if his whole life had led him to this place in time, to this showdown with his father. "Yes, I am. I'm telling you to leave my mother alone."

He could see the bead of sweat as it dripped down his father's face. The old man looked more like fifty than thirty-eight. Hard living and just plain meanness had left their mark etched on his once-handsome face. He wore faded blue jeans, work boots and a white wifebeater, which showed off the tattoos that spanned the length of both massive arms from wrist to shoulder. His face was lined and worn, fixed in a perpetual sneer, and his cold, blue eyes glared at his only son. "This is between me and my wife. Stay the fuck out of it or get the hell out of my house."

"Shawn, please…"

As quick as a rattler, his father turned on his mother and kicked her in the ribs with his steel-toed boots. "You stay out of this. This is all your fault."

His mother's cry of pain awakened some sleeping beast within him. A red haze filled his vision as he let out a primal yell and launched himself at his father. They fell to the floor in a flurry of arms and legs, each trying to hit the other. With rage came strength and he rolled until his father was beneath him. Drawing back his arm, he punched his father in the face.

Blood spurted from his father's mouth, the crimson stream spraying across the white wifebeater. His father bucked beneath him, but he pushed him down and hit him again and again and again, releasing a lifetime of pain and anger against his father's face. The sickening, wet slap of flesh meeting flesh was lost beneath the rush of his own heartbeat, pounding in his ears.

His father ceased to struggle, lying limp against the faded blue linoleum that covered the living room floor. He could hear his mother crying and yelling, but it seemed to be coming from a great distance.

Finally, he stopped.

He stared down at his hands, hardly able to believe they were his own. Fisted, they were covered in blood. He reared back, half falling, half stumbling off his father's still body. His mother's weeping drew his attention and he turned to her.

Her blonde hair was matted with blood and her face was ghostly white as she stared at him. "What have you done?" She pushed herself up off the floor and staggered to her feet. Her red-rimmed eyes were wide as she glanced from her husband to her son. "Quick, honey, you've got to get dressed and get away before he comes to." She glanced at her husband as she skirted around his body, as if she expected him to jump up and start hitting her again. "He'll kill you if you don't get away. I've got some money you can have."

"Mom." He didn't know what else to say. All he wanted to do was bury his face in her lap and have her stroke his hair and tell him everything was going to be all right, like she used to do when he was little. But nothing was right and he was very afraid that it would never be right again.

"Shh, honey." Her gentle hands shook as she pushed his hair out of his eyes. "This is all my fault. I should have left him years ago. Should have taken you away from here." Resignation filled her timeworn face and, for a brief moment, he could see a flash of determination in her eyes. She tugged on his hand, making him stand. "It's not too late for you."

The old man groaned just as someone pounded on the front door. "Police. Open the door."

His mother tried to push him down the hallway, whispering at him to hurry to the bathroom and wash the blood off his hands and chest. He loved her more in that moment than he ever had in his entire life. He could see by the look in her eyes that she planned to take the blame for what he'd done and he couldn't allow that. A man took responsibility for his actions.

Leaning down, he cupped her battered face in her hands and gently kissed her forehead. "Everything will be okay." At least, he prayed it would be as he slowly walked to the front door and turned the locks.

The next few hours were a blur as he was arrested and charged with assault. It was strange, the things he remembered. The red lights flashing in the dark of the night, casting ghostly shadows on their worn brick building in the slums of the city they called home. The feel of the rain against his skin as he was placed in the backseat of the police car. The sight of his mother's face, filled with tears and grief. And later, the sound of the prison bars slamming shut behind him, the coldness of the cell and the faraway echo of voices. But it was the sense of desperation he remembered most. It permeated the very air and he sucked it into his lungs with every breath he took.

He kept telling himself over and over that everything would be fine. His mother came to visit often, but his father was out for vengeance. Playing the victim, the old man lied on the stand and smiled when they sentenced his son to five years in prison. They wanted to make an example of him for such a vicious assault against a parent. He was eighteen, an adult now, and would serve his term in prison.

His mother cried and screamed as his father all but dragged her from the courtroom. He knew the old man would hurt her, especially since he was no longer there to help protect her. He fought the guards, begging and pleading with them to help his mother. His father's smile was cruel as he waved goodbye to his son.

It was the last time he'd ever see her alive. A prison guard came by his cell less than a month later to tell him his mother was dead.

He covered his ears with his hands, but her screams echoed in his head. The agony vibrated in his very soul. It was the screams that woke him.

He bolted upright in bed, his lungs working like a bellows as he gasped for air. Sweat dripped from his body as he buried his face in his hands. His heart was pounding so hard against his chest that it hurt, and he concentrated on taking one deep breath after another, trying to calm the frantic beat.

The dream was a familiar one. He'd had it many times over the past twenty-three years. It usually occurred during times of stress or when he was exhausted from work. Tonight, he knew it was because he'd been pushing himself too hard lately.

Rolling out of bed, he planted his feet on the floor and stood. Naked, he strode to the bathroom off the master bedroom, trying to shake the remnants of his dream. He twisted on the taps, cupped his hands together and sluiced the cool water over his face. Turning off the taps, he rubbed his hands over his face and raised his head, peering into the mirror above the sink.

The skylight and the small window allowed enough light to filter in from the city streets so that he could easily see himself in the mirror. The lanky eighteen-year-old youth was gone. In his place was a large, muscular man whose grim face looked tough and mean in the dim light. Lucas Squires closed his eyes against the sight. Some days he hated to look at himself, for the face he saw peering back at him was eerily like his father's.

Swearing, he turned away and padded out of the bathroom, ignoring the bed as he passed through the bedroom and continued down the hallway. It was futile for him to try to go back to sleep. The adrenaline was still pumping through his veins, and time and experience had taught him that the best way to deal with it was with physical activity. Hot, sweaty sex or a workout were the two best options. And since he was currently without a female companion, a fast and hard fuck was definitely not in the cards.

Entering his workout room, he grabbed a towel he'd hung on the bar earlier and laid it across the weight bench. He didn't bother with lights. What little was filtering in through the window was more than adequate. Settling himself with his back on the bench, he braced his legs, hoisted the bar and began to lift. He could easily bench-press his weight of two hundred pounds and he counted off the repetitions. After he'd done three sets, he hefted the bar back into place and lay there on the bench, staring at the ceiling.

He really didn't want to work out tonight. What he really wanted was to lose himself in the softness of a woman's body. He wanted to hear her moans of pleasure as he stroked his hands over her smooth skin, longed to hear her cries of completion as he drove his cock into her hot, wet pussy over and over until they both came in a rush of heat.

It would be nice to have a special woman waiting for him each evening when he came home from work. He squashed that thought as quickly as it had formed. Years ago, he'd decided that he was better off alone. The incident with his father had taught him that the same violent tendencies that had existed in his father also lived inside him. The thought that he might be like his old man sickened him, and he wasn't taking any chances. There was no way he'd risk a woman's safety. The image of his mother's battered and bruised body still haunted him.

He'd had several long-term relationships with women who wanted a monogamous partner without all the ties and hassle of a "real" relationship. They'd all been intelligent, perfectly nice women who'd been focused on their careers and hadn't been looking for more in a man than a willing partner for sex. All of the relationships had eventually ended amicably as all three women had been ready to move on with their lives and he hadn't been willing to offer more. So he lived alone, and at forty-one, he was content with his life and proud of what he'd done with it.

But none of that changed the basic fact that he had a hard-on that wasn't going to dissipate any time soon. What he really wanted was a woman. His woman. Closing his eyes, he pictured her in his mind. She'd be curvy and soft with eyes the color of rich chocolate. She'd smile at him with her pouty cherry-pink lips as she flicked her cinnamon-colored curls over her milky-white shoulder. One corner of his mouth kicked up in a smile when he realized he was using food, specifically baking ingredients, to describe his perfect woman. But after all, they were his stock and trade.

His cock twitched and he reached down and wrapped his hand around it. Slowly, he moved it up and down the hard length, all the while imagining it was her touching his body.

Her hands would be small but eager as they grasped him, squeezing tight. She'd use her other hand to cup his scrotum and massage his balls. His breathing got deeper as he relaxed into the daydream.

Then she'd smile at him, a wicked smile that made her eyes gleam with mischief as she knelt in front of him. Lowering her head, she would lap at his cock with her tongue, swirling it around the tip. He could picture her pink lips sliding over the hard length as it disappeared into her mouth. Ever so slowly, she'd pull back, tracing her tongue over his pulsing erection.

Groaning, he pumped harder and faster as he imagined her hand working up and down his length as she continued to suck him off. Her breasts would be plump, tipped with large pink nipples, and they would sway with every movement she made. She'd moan and arch her sex against his leg, drenching it in her juices. Damn, but she'd taste fantastic too. He knew she would. A combination of sweetness and musk that would be addictive.

A bead of sweat rolled down his forehead and into his eye, but he ignored the sting. He was so close to coming. His balls drew up tight to his body as his hand continued its frantic rhythm. His cock seemed to swell even larger as he pumped harder, imagining her mouth sucking him deeper. Lucas' whole body jerked as semen gushed from the tip of his cock and he came onto his stomach. The daydream flickered away and his dream woman disappeared back into the mists of his imagination.

As he lay there panting for breath, his hand dropped away from his cock. Physically, he felt better, but there was an emptiness inside him that yearned to be filled. Liquid began to drip down his side and he swore. Sitting up quickly, he grabbed the towel out from under his body and used it to clean himself up.

Dawn was breaking as he pushed off the weight bench and headed back to the bathroom, dumping the towel in the laundry room as he passed. Sleep was definitely not going to happen now. He shoved a hand through his short hair, yawning so wide that he felt his jawbone crack. Pushing all thoughts of his restless night out of his mind, he focused on the coming day.

A shower was his first priority. Then it was back to work. He had a ton of baking to do this morning if he wanted to get everything done in time for the party that would launch Coffee Breaks in its new location. Work had always been his salvation and this time would be no different.

Chapter Two

ॐ

"Girl, you need to get laid."

Candy Logan burst into laughter at her best friend's pronouncement. Shaking her head and smiling, she turned her attention back to the papers strewn across her desk. She knew the address she was looking for was buried somewhere in there and she didn't have much time to find it.

"I'm serious, Candy. You need something else in your life besides work."

"You're supposed to call me Candace." The words were automatic, as much a reminder for herself as it was for her friend.

"I don't know why you want to change your name all of a sudden. What's wrong with Candy?"

Giving up hope of getting any peace and quiet until she'd placated her friend, Candy sat back in her chair and stared at the other woman. With her hands on her hips and a scowl on her face, Missy Sinclair was a formidable presence. At six feet tall, with dark ebony skin and piercing brown eyes, Missy was gorgeous enough to have been a fashion model. People literally stopped in their tracks when she walked by—or sauntered by, as the case may be. Missy never hurried anywhere unless absolutely necessary. She was also the best friend a girl could ever have and the two of them had been close since they started working at TK Publishing six years ago.

"People don't take a woman named Candy seriously." She'd heard every joke and innuendo in the book growing up. For some unfathomable reason, her mother had saddled her with a name that always made her the butt of jokes.

She pinched the bridge of her nose, ignoring the brewing headache as she tried to remember where she'd put that address. "And I want to make the most of this promotion." She'd been promoted to publicist, and this new project was the first she'd handled on her own for the company. Up until now, she'd been an assistant publicist—more a glorified secretary, actually. She was flying solo on this one and there was no way she wanted to screw it up. But nothing had been going the way she planned.

"Once people get to know you, they don't care about your name. You're damned good at your job." Missy pushed a lock of dark brown hair out of her face and sighed. "And I still think you need to get laid."

"That's your answer for everything, Missy. Sex." It was easy for her friend to suggest that, but then, she didn't have any trouble getting dates. Candy hadn't had a date since…well, she didn't even want to try to remember the last time she managed to have a date with a man who even remotely interested her. Too many of her friends had set her up on blind dates and she'd sworn off men altogether after the last fiasco.

"No, it's not." Missy gracefully lowered herself into the seat in front of Candy's desk and crossed her long, shapely legs. "Sometimes chocolate will do the trick." She grinned mischievously. "But this situation definitely calls for sex." She paused for effect before continuing. "When was the last time you even heated the sheets?"

"Just before Gary and I split over a year ago." She slapped her hand over her mouth, unable to believe she'd just blurted that out.

Missy didn't miss a beat. "See, I'm right. You really do need a night of hot, sweaty sex with some hunk. Practice safe sex and nobody gets hurt, but you'll certainly feel much more relaxed about things."

Candy chuckled in spite of herself. Missy always did know how to make her laugh and help her gain perspective on a problem. "I don't have time to relax. What am I going to do about Lucas Squires?" She switched topics easily, knowing Missy would drop the subject. For now. "He won't take my phone calls and I can't leave a message because he doesn't have an answering machine. What kind of person doesn't have an answering machine or some kind of message manager in this day and age?" She took a deep breath when she heard the frustration in her own voice.

"Obviously a person who wants to be left alone."

Candy scowled. "You're not helping. I know he wants to be left alone, but as a publicist for this company, I've got to get him to do some promotion for his new book. It's due out in two months and I haven't been able to set up any kind of advance publicity at all that involved the elusive Mr. Squires." This was her own very personal pet project and she desperately wanted it to succeed.

"It's not your fault that he's being reclusive."

She knew that Missy was right, but it didn't make her feel any better. "But I do feel responsible. I was the one who brought this project to the company in the first place."

It had all started innocently enough at a downtown Chicago art gallery. Candy had fallen in love with the work of local painter, Katie Benjamin, and had attended the showing. She'd been thrilled to meet the artist and even more thrilled a few months later when Katie had called and asked her out to lunch. Over dessert, the other woman had produced the rough draft for a cookbook and asked Candy's opinion.

She'd been enthralled by the idea of the book from the beginning.

Filled with original artwork from Katie—everything from simple line drawings to elaborate oil paintings—it was, quite simply, gorgeous. The text of the book consisted of recipes for all manner of desserts and treats as well as anecdotal stories about Coffee Breaks, a well-known local coffee shop. It was only after they'd talked for a while that Candy had come to realize that Katie had compiled the work, but the person behind the recipes was Lucas Squires, the owner of the shop.

Fired with enthusiasm, she'd convinced the editors at TK Publishing to take a chance on it. They loved the idea of combining the artwork of an up-and-coming artist with the recipes from a popular local coffee shop. They figured it would be a hit with locals and tourists alike and would have mass appeal as well. The recipes went from the simple to the complex, but there was something for everyone.

Now the book was close to release and management was pushing for advance promotion to coincide with the grand reopening of the new Coffee Breaks location. They wanted local television and media coverage, and she had yet to be able to track down Lucas Squires long enough to say one word to the man. It was frustrating, to say the least.

She was damned good at her job, but he was quickly becoming a mark on her otherwise unblemished record. And that, she could not allow. She knew she could do this job. After all, she'd done most of her old boss's work before finally being promoted after years of hard work. There was no way she was going to allow Lucas Squires to ruin everything she'd worked for. All she wanted was a few hours of his time over the next few months. That certainly wasn't unreasonable to expect considering the money her company had put behind this project.

"Earth to Candy." Missy waved her hand back and forth. "I recognize that look and it means you're up to something."

Candy jumped. She'd been so lost in her thoughts, she'd all but forgotten that her friend was still sitting there. "I don't know what you're talking about." She pasted an innocent look on her face, but Missy just laughed at her.

"I know you too well to be fooled by the 'I'm not doing anything' look."

Placing her hand over her heart, she shook her head sorrowfully. "I'm so misunderstood." Missy laughed but made no motion to leave, and Candy knew she wouldn't budge until she knew what was going on. "Okay." She leaned back in her own chair. "There's a party this afternoon, by invitation only, to celebrate the fact that the new location of Coffee Breaks will be ready to open its doors next week."

"And you know this because…" Missy's voice trailed off.

"Katie just happened to send me an invitation." She felt a large smile spread across her face. "And Mr. Elusive has to be at his own party, right? All I have to do is corner him and keep at him until he agrees to give me a few hours of promotion time."

"Very sneaky. I like that about you." Missy glanced at her watch, sighed and stood. "I've got to get back to work, but take it easy at the party. Maybe he's got a reason for avoiding you. Maybe he's just shy."

Candy nodded. "Maybe." In fact, she had a picture of the man in her head. She knew he was in his early forties and she figured he was short and probably balding. He also spent most of his time in a kitchen, so he was probably portly as well. She could relate to that as she was no lightweight herself, perpetually trying to shed that last ten pounds that would never go away and sat right on her hips and belly.

"I'll call you tonight for the scoop on the success or failure of your party crashing." Missy wiggled her fingers goodbye as she strolled out the door.

Turning back to her desk, Candy dug through the pile in her in-box. She was sure she'd tossed the invitation in there when she'd gotten it. Ah ha! She plucked the cream-colored envelope out from between two magazines and waved it in the air. Today, she would meet the infamous Lucas Squires. He'd soon find that he could run, but he couldn't hide from her.

Lucas stood in the shadows of the far corner and stared around the room. Pleasure filled him. He couldn't believe how much the building had changed since he had purchased it.

Even though it had been rundown and in need of major repairs, it had still cost him a pretty penny. But it was worth every cent, he thought as he took in the changes that weeks of hard work and sweat had wrought.

The main area of the coffee shop was warm and inviting. Hardwood floors gleamed underfoot—a pleasant surprise that they'd found when they'd ripped up the old linoleum. Wainscoting adorned the bottom half of the wall, while a rich French vanilla cream color topped the upper half. Wood tables and chairs were scattered strategically around the room, while five cozy booths lined the far wall. The sinking February sun was shining in through the series of small windows that ran across the front of the shop. All in all, Lucas was pleased with the work that had been done and in such a short time.

Right now the space was filled with people, many of them long-time customers or suppliers, as well as a smattering of friends and neighbors who'd all come today to celebrate the finish of the renovations. Chatter filled the air as people drifted from group to group, talking and laughing and eating. He'd already replenished the buffet table twice and this crowd showed no signs of letting up. Good thing he'd made plenty.

"So, what do you think?"

Lucas recognized the arm that slipped around his waist and he automatically draped his arm across her shoulders as he looked down at the woman standing beside him. Until recently, there had only been two people on the face of the planet that Lucas considered family, and Katie Wallace, former employee and the sister of his heart, was one of them. Not related by blood, they had long ago decided they were family. But in the past year, that small circle had expanded to three and now included her new husband as well.

"Lucas?" She was frowning at him now, so he gave her a quick squeeze of reassurance.

"It looks good."

She laughed, the sweet sound filling the room. "Honestly, could you tone down your enthusiasm?"

The corner of his mouth kicked up slightly as he glowered at her in mock anger. "All right," he conceded. "I love it." He gazed around the room again and his voice lowered. "I really love it."

It was the first home he'd ever owned. And that's what it was, really. He'd taken the main floor for the new shop, but the top floor of the modest three-story building belonged to him, and he was slowly renovating it to suit his own tastes and needs. The second floor had been gutted but still needed to be remodeled. He had plans to rent the entire floor either as office space or as two apartments. He hadn't quite decided yet.

"I'm glad. You deserve to be happy." She went up on her toes and kissed his cheek.

"Making time with my wife, Squires?" a male voice growled. Cain Benjamin was a huge man who stood well over six-and-a-half-feet tall. With a black patch covering his left eye and his long black hair flowing to his shoulders, he looked more like a pirate than a multimillionaire businessman.

Lucas just cocked his eyebrow at the large man who'd strolled over to stand beside them. "You treating her right?"

Katie laughed again and gave him another quick kiss before going over to slide into her husband's arms. "Honestly, anybody listening to you two would think you couldn't stand each other."

Lucas was glad that Katie had found a man who loved her as much as Cain obviously did. Their relationship hadn't been an easy one from the very beginning and for a while it didn't look like they'd make it. They'd had more than their share of problems to sort through, but the big guy had finally come to his senses, and not a moment too soon as far as Lucas was concerned. Now the two of them were happy together and Lucas had found himself with an unexpected friend.

The ironic part of the situation was that it was Cain's company that had bought the original building that had housed Coffee Breaks and had forced Lucas to look for another location. That had also caused problems for Cain and Katie when it had finally come out.

Lucas had thought about leaving Chicago altogether, but after much soul-searching he had decided to stay. After all, it was home. It had all ended for the best as far as Lucas was concerned. In fact, it was Cain who'd suggested this building to him.

"Congratulations, Lucas." Cain extended his hand and Lucas reached out and shook it. The two of them were friends now. Katie had been the reason they'd met, but they had forged their own bond of friendship over the last year.

"Thanks." The other man had helped him with much more than just finding the building. "For everything." Lucas meant to continue, but his mind suddenly went blank, all thoughts forgotten, as the woman from his dreams walked in through the front door of his shop.

He blinked, certain he was dreaming. But she was still there, chewing on her bottom lip as she peered around the room, obviously searching for someone. As she opened her coat, slid it off and handed it to the person in charge of the coat-check he'd set up for the evening, his cock stirred and every male instinct he possessed began screaming at him to claim her before another man did.

Her cheeks were flushed from the cold outside and her lips were rosy. He couldn't tell if the color of her lips was due to her lipstick or the fact that she was chewing nervously on them. Her hair was thick and curly, falling to just past her shoulders, and when she walked past the window, the fading sunlight made it glint. It was the color of a cinnamon stick. She was wearing a nondescript beige suit, which, in his opinion, was about two sizes too big for her. It hid her shape. But Lucas had always been a keen observer and this woman had some serious curves under that outfit. He'd bet on it.

201

As if from a distance, he heard Katie tell him that she and Cain were going to get something to eat. He must have made an appropriate response because they left him standing there as they wandered off toward the buffet table that had been set up on the main counter of the shop.

He tracked the mystery lady as she moved through the room. The heels on her boots were about four inches high and were ridiculously inappropriate for a slippery winter day as far as he was concerned. But man, they made her legs look good. The only redeeming feature about the hideous suit she wore was that the skirt fell about three inches above her knee. From what he could see, she had incredible legs.

He was starting to sweat now. He swore and took a deep breath as his cock pushed hard against the zipper of his jeans. A hard-on was definitely not appropriate for a crowded party, but what was a guy to do when a vision from his own fantasy walked through the front door?

She stopped to chat to someone and he growled with displeasure when she placed her hand on the other man's arm. He felt like stalking over and yanking her hand away.

What the hell was the matter with him? He turned away and took another deep breath. He had to get control of himself. Raking his hand through his hair, he gathered his composure before turning back to the room.

His stomach clenched when he didn't see her right away. Had she left? Quickly, he scanned the room and found her off to his right, looking slightly forlorn. Maybe he could help her find whoever she was looking for. After all, as host of this party, it was his responsibility to make sure his guests were taken care of.

Right, he snorted as he sauntered toward her, ignoring everyone who tried to catch his attention. His entire focus was on the woman in front of him.

Chapter Three

ର

Candy stared around the room in dismay. She couldn't believe that she'd missed Lucas Squires yet again. But the person she'd just talked to had told her that the object of her search had already come and gone. "Damn. Damn. Damn," she muttered under her breath.

This was definitely not going as planned. Besides which, her new boots hurt her feet and she was starving. It was just after five o'clock and she hadn't had time for lunch. Sighing, she thought about just hauling on her coat and going home to curl up with a pizza and about a gallon of vanilla ice cream. It had been that kind of a day.

"That's a big sigh. Is there anything I can help you with?"

Candy glanced toward the voice and had to look up. Oh my! For the first time in her life, all ability to speak left her. The man standing next to her cocked his eyebrow, obviously waiting for her reply. Well, he'd have to wait a little longer. There was no way she could talk. It was taking all her concentration just to breathe.

Never had she been so instantly attracted to a man in her life. He was much taller than she was, and she was wearing high-heeled boots. But then again, she wasn't very tall, so that wasn't surprising. Massive—that was the first word that came to mind to describe him. His shoulders looked to be about a yard wide and his thick biceps strained the sleeves of the short-sleeved T-shirt he was wearing. Her fingers itched to touch them just to see if they were as hard as they looked.

His blond hair was cut short, but there was just enough for her to run her fingers through. Her hands curled into fists at her sides as she fought the impulse to just reach out and stroke it. His face wasn't pretty. Instead it was compelling and tough, just like the rest of him. His nose looked as if it had been broken at least once, and his thin lips were set in a half-scowl as he continued to wait for her reply.

He was the kind of man you didn't want to meet in a dark alley, the kind of man that made other men nervous. But Candy wasn't the least bit afraid of him. For the first time in her life, she understood instant attraction. Everything feminine inside her was screaming out to jump this man's bones. Her breasts were aching and she was glad that she'd kept her suit jacket buttoned or he'd be able to see her pebbled nipples through her blouse. She fought the impulse to squirm as she creamed her panties just looking at this sexy stranger.

She could feel the heat creeping up her cheeks as Missy's earlier words rang in her head. Maybe she really did need to get laid. Sex with this man would be incredible. She didn't know how she knew that, she just did. And, oh God, she couldn't remember what he'd asked her.

Clearing her throat, she tried to appear nonchalant. "I'm sorry. What did you say?"

The corner of his mouth kicked up in a half-smile and her heart skipped a beat as she fought the urge to fan her face. This man was lethal. If she reacted this strongly to just the hint of a smile, she didn't even want to think about what she might do if he really smiled. He just oozed sex appeal.

"I asked if there was anything I could help you with." The low, sensual sound of his voice strummed over her like a lover's caress. Her entire body was tight and needy. She felt as if she'd spent the last half-hour engaging in intense foreplay and she was now close to coming.

"Ah," she stuttered. "No, but thank you. I was looking for someone, but he's no longer here. It's not important." She couldn't believe the nonsense she was babbling. *Not important*. It was supposed to be the most important thing in her life, but she no longer cared about the elusive Lucas Squires. Right now, all her focus was on the mystery man in front of her.

"His loss is my gain then. What's your name?"

"Candy." He'd slipped that question in so smoothly, she replied before she thought. "Forget I said that." She worried her bottom lip with her teeth.

"Why? It's a great name." He ran his laser-like, pale blue eyes up and down her body. "And it suits you."

Candy gaped at him, stunned. Was this man flirting with her? She glanced down at the lower half of his body. Immediately her gaze shot back up to his face, only to find him staring down at her with a knowing expression. That was an impressive hard-on pushing against the front of his jeans. She swallowed hard. There was no doubt that he was attracted to her and wasn't afraid for her to know it.

Oh God, what should she do? She could pretend she hadn't noticed, excuse herself and just go home to her pizza and ice cream. Or she could let go of her control, just this once, and enjoy a steamy, sexual encounter with a complete stranger. There really should be no choice. Candy wasn't the type of woman to indulge in a one-night stand, but the man standing in front of her was the kind of man who came along once in a woman's lifetime — if she were lucky.

Okay, no need to jump the gun. He hadn't even made a motion toward her. Maybe this was just her overactive imagination and her unruly hormones both running amok. She'd just play along and see where the situation led. And if it did happen to end in the two of them having wild sex, well then, that was okay. They were both two healthy, unattached adults.

She paused and glanced at his ring finger, which thankfully was bare. But she made a mental note to check that out for sure if she did decide to indulge with him. She was no poacher.

She thought about asking him his name, but decided against it. If she did choose to indulge her passion with him, it was definitely going to be a one-time thing. Better for both of them if they remained two strangers that passed in the night, as it were. Yes, she'd told him her first name, but he'd probably forget it in no time.

She consoled herself that if it did indeed happen, they'd probably never see each other again and they'd be nothing more than a pleasant memory to one another. Why her stomach turned over at the thought, she didn't know and there was no time to examine the feeling.

"Would you like to have a tour of the place?" He swept his hand out to encompass the coffee shop.

"Sure. If it's okay, I mean. I wouldn't want you to get in trouble with the owner or anything." Candy slammed her mouth shut. She couldn't seem to stop making an idiot of herself every time she opened it.

But luckily her handsome stranger didn't seem to notice. In fact, he seemed kind of amused. "No, it's fine." Wrapping his arm around her shoulders, he turned her and guided her toward the kitchen door. "Let me show you the kitchen."

The weight of his arm felt good around her. Not heavy, but protective. Her legs felt like jelly, making it hard to walk, but somehow she managed to get through the swinging doors. As the door swung shut behind them, the sound of the party faded away. Even though the light was on and a room full of people was right next to them, it felt incredibly intimate with just the two of them standing there.

She got the impression of a large, clean room, gleaming with stainless steel appliances and cooking utensils before she was swung around. Her back was against the cooking island that dominated the center of the kitchen. Gasping, she glanced up and swallowed hard. The lustful gleam in his eyes assured her that he not only wanted her, but he was more than ready to take her.

Candy licked her suddenly dry lips. His eyes followed their movement and he groaned. Had she been responsible for that? She did it again, just to be certain. Sure enough, he closed his eyes and a deep, rumbling sound rose from his chest. Well, she liked this. She'd never felt like a sexy siren before. Certainly none of the men she'd ever dated or been with had ever reacted quite like this before. It was heady stuff.

When he opened his eyes, they were so hot, she felt scorched by their intensity. He began to slowly lower his head toward her, leaving her no doubt that he was about to kiss her but giving her plenty of time to protest or change her mind.

Candy went up on her toes and met him halfway.

Lucas could hardly wrap his thoughts around the fact that he was alone with the woman who looked as if she'd stepped right out of his most erotic fantasies. She was nervous. He could tell by the way her eyes darted around the room and the fact that she kept chewing on her bottom lip. Damn, but he wanted to taste her mouth. *Candy*. His mystery lady had a name now, and somehow it suited her. She looked sweet and somehow innocent, with her big chocolate brown eyes staring up at him.

He had to taste her. Ever so slowly, he leaned down, giving her every opportunity to change her mind, all the while praying that she wouldn't. He fought the urge just to grab her and sweep her upstairs and into his bed. Flattening his hands on the countertop on either side of her, he effectively caged her in without touching her. His nostrils flared as he moved closer, and the sweet scent of peppermint drifted toward him, mixed with the smell of soap and aroused woman. He took a deep breath, imprinting her unique scent on his brain.

As if he'd ever forget it.

Then she stretched upward to meet him and he was lost. His lips skimmed hers ever so gently so as not to frighten her. Her mouth was soft and her lips parted as he stroked his tongue across them. Taking advantage of her invitation, he slipped his tongue inside her mouth and was immediately surrounded by her warmth. He groaned and slid his tongue into the recesses of her mouth, savoring the peppermint flavor. His cock was throbbing now as it pushed against the zipper of his jeans. It was almost painful, but it was a good kind of pain. The kind of pain that made a man feel vibrantly alive.

It was a feeling that had been missing from his life as of late.

Her tongue began a slow duel with his and he retreated from her. Sure enough, she followed him, her small tongue darting into his mouth. He sucked it deeper and she moaned low in her throat. The sound was much like a kitten's purr. He wondered what she'd sound like when he was buried deep inside her, fucking her hard, bringing her to climax.

Damn, he felt hot. His entire body was shaking with need and he could feel perspiration making his shirt stick to him. His fingers dug into the edge of the counter. He wanted to strip her naked, lift her onto the kitchen island and lose himself in her heat. Her pussy would taste sweet and she'd be so damned wet and ready for him. He groaned and broke away from her. Burying his face in the curve of her neck, he inhaled deeply as he tried to steady his breathing.

Her small hand grabbed the front of his T-shirt as she swayed toward him. Immediately, he wrapped his hands around her waist to support her. Her curves felt substantial beneath his questing fingers and he couldn't resist sliding his hands behind her and gripping her bottom, molding the soft globes with his palms. "You've got a great ass."

She froze for a second and then her gaze flew to his as she emitted a shaky laugh. *Way to go, Squires,* he berated himself. *You certainly know how to charm a lady.* But she seemed strangely pleased rather than offended.

"Ah…thank you." She shook her head and he was afraid she was going to tell him it was time for her to go. He wasn't quite ready for that to happen yet. So, before she had a chance to speak, he nuzzled the curve of her neck and left a trail of kisses behind him as he worked his way toward her earlobe.

Nipping the lobe between his teeth, he tugged slightly on the discreet gold hoop that adorned it. Everything about her turned him on, from her minimal jewelry to her oversized business attire and her ridiculous boots. The woman definitely had class written all over her.

Her breathing quickened and she shifted closer to him. He could feel her breasts pushing against his chest even through the material of her suit jacket, but it wasn't enough. Sliding one hand between them, he slipped the two buttons of the jacket open and pushed the lapels back, revealing the silky blouse beneath. He didn't pause, but kept his hand moving upward until his palm was between her breasts. She sucked in a deep breath, her heart pounding beneath his hand.

Lucas shoved one of his booted feet between hers, urging her closer with the hand still plastered to her backside. The skirt rode up slightly as his leg slid further between her thighs until her pussy was hard against his leg. He traced the whorls of her ear with his tongue. "I want you, Candy."

Leaving her straddling his thigh, he framed her face with his hands, tipping it up so that she was looking right at him. Her face was flushed and her lips parted as she gasped for breath. Her eyes were deep, dark and filled with desire. With her hair hanging down her shoulders in tousled curls, she looked like a woman in the throes of sexual release.

"I want to taste you, to touch you." He slid his fingers into her hair, tangling them in the cinnamon-colored locks. "I want to bury my cock in your pussy and fuck you long and hard. I want to hear your voice in my ear as you beg me to fuck you even harder." He leaned down until their lips were almost touching again. "And I want to hear your screams when you come."

"Ohmigod," she gasped.

He could feel her hips shift slightly, seeking better contact with his thigh and he almost howled with pleasure. She wanted him too. There was no doubt about that. But would she let him have her?

"Let me have you." His words echoed his thoughts as he untangled his fingers from her hair, sliding them down her back until he was gripping her ass once again. Pulling her closer, he lifted her higher on his thigh. Her whimper of need was music to his ears. "It'll be so damned good, Candy."

"Yes." She sprang to life suddenly, practically climbing him as she wrapped her arms around his neck and hooked her leg over his thigh.

Lucas lifted her right off the floor, groaning when she rubbed herself against the hard length of his erection. He was going to come in his jeans if he didn't get inside her soon. The sounds of the party just beyond them filtered through his muddled brain and he had sense enough to know he couldn't take her here.

Walking was pure torture as her heated mound moved over him with every step he took. Her hands were busy, too, and she was stroking his chest and shoulders as she leaned into him and placed hot little kisses on his neck.

He'd never make it to his office. Half stumbling, half walking, he managed to get them the few steps necessary to reach a large walk-in storage room. Kicking the door closed behind him, he shut the world outside.

Chapter Four

ॐ

The sound of the door slamming shut shook Candy out of her sensual daze. What was she doing? This man was a complete stranger and she'd just agreed to have sex with him. It was one thing to think about it, maybe even to fantasize about it, but it was another thing altogether to actually do it.

Their heavy breathing was the only sound in the room. The noise from the party had been shut outside the heavy door. She forced herself to unwind her legs from around his waist and lower them to the floor. She gasped and then moaned as she slid over the large bulge in his jeans.

He unhooked her purse, which was still miraculously slung over her shoulder, and eased it down her arm, dropping it onto the floor. A small window in the back emitted some meager light into the room, illuminating it slightly. Half in the shadows, he looked even larger and more intimidating, if that was possible.

As if he guessed her thoughts, he leaned down and nuzzled her neck with his lips. Unconsciously, she tilted her head to one side, wanting more of his touch. *God*, he was so good at that. He nipped at the sensitive skin where her neck and shoulder met, sending shivers down her spine and making her core pulse even harder. She shifted from one foot to another, but there was no relief to be had from the sexual frustration and need pounding though her veins.

"We can't do this." She didn't know how she found the strength to say the words, but she did. "I don't do this kind of thing."

"Of course, we can," he murmured as he flicked his tongue over her ear. "And I never thought that you did."

It took a moment for his words to make sense to her because she couldn't even remember what she'd said to him. She had to get a hold of herself. Putting her hands on his chest, she pushed and was mildly surprised when he immediately stepped back. She ignored the small flare of disappointment that he'd given up so easily. God, how perverse was that? Shaking her head, she struggled to regain her composure.

But before she could speak, he did, seducing her with words alone. "We won't do anything you don't want to." His eyes burned with desire as they drifted over her body. "I just want to taste you, to pleasure you."

The way his voice lowered on the last of his words caused a fresh gush of cream to dampen her panties. She closed her eyes to shut out the potent sight of him, but they jerked open again when she felt his touch on her body. His hands slipped inside her suit jacket, sliding over the silk of her blouse and coming to rest just under her breasts. She sucked in a deep breath as her nipples strained against the cups of her bra, begging for his touch. But he kept his hands resting just below her breasts, obviously waiting for her consent.

What harm would there be? the voice in the back of her head whispered. She ruthlessly tried to block out that voice even as every bit of her attention was focused on the large male hands almost cupping her breasts.

"You're not married or anything, are you?" She groaned as soon as the words left her mouth.

The appalled expression on his face actually reassured her. "No." He pulled his hands away from her body and she instantly felt the loss, suddenly cold where only seconds before she'd been deliciously hot. "Are you?"

Now it was her turn to be appalled. "Of course not." She bit her lip, realizing that she'd all but insulted the man. "I'm sorry. I'm just not any good at this."

His massive arms came around her and he hugged her gently. She rested her face against his shoulder and sighed.

"You're doing just fine, sugar." His erection poked her in the stomach, but he kept his grip on her shoulders light and undemanding.

She'd been called "sugar" many times in her life, but never before had she liked it. The way it rolled off his tongue, it was an endearment, not a taunt. The air was electric with the sexual desire that existed between them and, rightly or wrongly, Candy knew she wanted to sample it. She took a step back and he dropped his arms to his sides. Her eyes never left his face as she slipped her suit jacket off her shoulders and tossed it on top of her purse.

The heat in his eyes flared as he reached out and cupped her jaw in his large hand. "Only what you want." The look in his eyes was deadly serious and she felt that he needed her to believe that he meant what he said. She gave him one nervous nod before reaching for the buttons on her blouse. "Let me." His husky voice stroked her like a caress even as his hands pushed hers aside.

Candy watched as he tugged her blouse out of the waistband of her skirt. The slithering sound of the silk being drawn over the thicker fabric was incredibly arousing. She'd never had a man undress her before. Always with her other lovers, she'd undressed herself.

Starting from the bottom, he slowly slid each button from its hole. When it was open, he pushed it over her shoulders and let it drop to the floor behind her. His hands hovered over her lace-covered breasts for a moment before his thumbs brushed the turgid peaks pushing against the cups of her bra.

That one touch had her womb contracting tight and she couldn't stifle the gasp that escaped her. He met her gaze and smiled. That simple action transformed him totally. In that moment, Candy was lost. He looked like some fallen angel—tempting her, needing her, wanting her. And she wanted to give him whatever he needed.

Reaching between her breasts, he deftly opened the front closure and pushed back her bra, letting the straps slide down her arms. Her breasts sprang free from their confinement, feeling heavy and aching with need. He cupped their weight in his hands as he lowered his head. She thought she heard him whisper the word "perfect" just before his tongue stroked over one of the swollen tips.

She sifted her hands though his hair, as she'd wanted to do since the moment she first saw him. The short, silky strands slipped through her fingers. He groaned as he took her nipple into his mouth and suckled hard. Her fingers tightened, her nails digging into his scalp as she pulled his face tighter to her breast.

He stroked her other breast with his fingers, plucking at the swollen nipple, carefully rolling it between his thumb and forefinger. Candy lost herself in the incredible sensations that engulfed her. This felt better than any sex she'd ever had and he was only touching her breasts. The pulsing between her thighs increased as he pleasured her.

Suddenly he pulled back, breathing hard as he sucked air into his lungs. His hands wrapped around her waist as he walked her backward until her back touched the door. Kneeling on the floor in front of her, he gripped her ankles with his fingers and eased her legs apart. The action was constricted somewhat by the confining fabric of her skirt. Scooting closer to her, he stroked his hands over her boots, past her knees and under her skirt.

Candy sucked in a breath as his warm hands paused. He had discovered she was wearing thigh-high stockings and not pantyhose. "Oh, yeah," he growled as he continued to slide his hands upward, pushing the fabric of her skirt higher and higher until it was shoved around her waist. He tucked one end in the waistband to hold it out of his way. A stray beam of light from the outside streetlamp made his blond hair gleam as he moved his face closer to her panties. The sight of his dark hand touching the pale pink silk of her panties made her gasp.

His touch was so gentle, almost reverent, as he stroked the silky fabric, moving lower as he fingered the crotch of her panties. He raised his fingers to his nose and sniffed. "You smell hot, sugar."

Candy could feel the heat of a blush creeping up her cheeks and was glad that the room was mostly in shadows so he wouldn't see it. No man had ever said anything like that to her before and it was incredibly arousing, making her squirm.

He reached up, caught the delicate fabric in both his hands and yanked. The sound of silk rending was unusually loud. She could feel the cool air on her side and then her mound as he peeled the fabric aside. He slid the remains of her panties down her other leg and she automatically lifted her foot so he could pull it away. Raising the silky fabric to his face, he inhaled deeply before shoving it into his back pocket.

Candy was as appalled as she was aroused. He'd not only ripped her panties from her body, but it was obvious he wasn't planning on giving them back. But all that was forgotten as his hands stroked the skin on the inside of her thigh, moving closer to her core. She sucked in a deep breath, willing him to touch her. Needing to feel his hands where she ached the most. Strung on the tight thread of desire, she closed her eyes and waited for his touch.

Lucas felt his hands tremble as they slid up the inside of her soft, milky-white thighs. The strain of holding himself in check was beginning to make itself felt. Part of him wanted to haul her down to the floor, mount her and fuck her until neither of them could walk. But another part of him wanted to touch her gently and savor every inch of her body. Most of all, he didn't want to do anything to frighten her. He sensed his mystery lady was uncertain and could bolt at any second. He was determined to give her so much pleasure, she wouldn't even think of leaving.

The sight of his large, rough hands moving across her pale skin was incredibly arousing. He only wished that there was more light, rather than the dim beam shining through the window. But he'd take what he could get. There was no way he was going to disrupt the mood, not when she was waiting expectantly for him to touch her.

The room was silent except for the occasional muted blast of a horn from the street traffic just outside the building. So far from the party, they could only hear the occasional murmur from the crowd. Nothing else existed at the moment but the two of them here together. He traced the crease at the tops of her thighs with his thumbs and she shuddered. Her breathing was getting louder as she got more aroused.

Her hands gripped the top of his head and he stilled, afraid she was going to push him away. "Take off your shirt. I want to see you." Her hesitant request sent a shudder down his spine.

He sat back on his heels, reached his hands behind his shoulders, grabbed two handfuls of fabric and yanked his white T-shirt over his head, flinging it aside. She reached out and tentatively touched his shoulder. He gritted his teeth as his cock throbbed with need. Her small hand felt so damned good. He wanted to spend an entire night lying on his bed, having her run her exploring fingers over his body. But right now, she had to stop.

He captured her fingers as they slipped over the muscles in his arm. "Sugar, if you keep that up, I'm going to come in my pants." His blunt words startled her. He could tell by the way her hand jerked in his grasp and the way her breath hitched slightly. Glancing up, he half expected to see disgust on her face. Instead, a half-smile formed on her lips.

"Really?"

She seemed amazed and pleased by his statement, and he realized in that moment that she had no idea just how sexy she was. "Really," he replied as he brought her hand to his lips and kissed her palm. "You're so damned sexy, sugar, that if you keep touching me, I'm just not going to last." He traced the length of one of her fingers with his tongue. "And that would be a shame, because I haven't even tasted you yet."

He closed his lips over her finger, drawing it into his mouth. She shifted restlessly as he tongued the webbing at the base, and she moaned when he lightly scraped her flesh with his teeth as he withdrew. "And you're so sweet."

Releasing her hand, he shouldered his way back between her legs, intent now on touching her. Sifting his fingers through the curly hair on her mound, he smiled as the crisp hair wrapped around him. He kept going, skimming them over the slick folds of her pussy. Her juices coated his fingers immediately. Primal satisfaction filled him. There was no doubt that she wanted him.

"Omigod." Her whimpered oath made him smile. He was just getting started.

Using his thumbs, he spread the folds of her labia wide, once again inwardly cursing the lack of light. It was too dark for him to see her clearly, but he could smell her. Musky, mysterious and female, her scent drew him closer. He licked up one side of her and down the other, sampling her unique flavor.

Her fingers gripped his head, holding him tight to her. He welcomed the slight sting of her nails, as it helped him gain some control. He could feel the moisture seeping from the head of his cock and he knew he was close. Reaching down, he carefully unbuttoned and unzipped his pants. He wasn't wearing underwear, so his cock sprang free, the bulbous head wet with need.

Ignoring his own body's cry for completion, he focused all his concentration on Candy. He wouldn't take her until she'd come at least once. With his fingers, he teased and petted her hot flesh as he continued to stroke it with his tongue. Her cries and whimpers permeated the air around him as she rocked her hips back and forth, using her grip on his hair to pull him closer.

He traced the sensitive nubbin of flesh at the top of her pussy, flicking it lightly. Her cries grew louder and more frantic as she pumped her hips. Circling the entrance of her core with his finger, he pushed in deep. Her inner muscles clamped down hard around it, and he groaned as his balls drew up tight against his body in response.

He almost lost it when she whispered "No" as he withdrew his finger, arching her hips to try to keep him inside her. This time, he pushed two fingers to the hilt as he continued to tongue and suck her swollen clit. He began to finger-fuck her, slowly at first, but quickly gaining speed.

"I'm coming." He could barely make out her words over the pounding of his own heart and the gasping of his breath. But he did hear them and he pushed her harder and quicker.

A loud keening noise came from her lips just as her inner muscles began to contract. Lucas didn't stop. He kept up the long, firm strokes of his fingers even as he continued to pleasure her with his tongue. She spasmed long and hard, her cream flowing from her body to coat his hand. Damn, he couldn't wait to bury his cock in her sweet pussy. He only stopped when she tugged his head away from her and began to slide down the door.

"Stop," she gasped. "I can't take any more."

Tugging her down into his lap, he swore when her wet pussy pushed against his steely erection. She jerked slightly, but he wrapped his arms around her and held her close. She stilled for a moment, and then as if coming to some internal decision, she subsided against him, leaning into his body.

Cupping the back of her head with one of his hands, he used the other to stroke up and down her back, enjoying the feel of her skin beneath his palm. It was like some kind of exquisite torture to have her so close and to not be buried inside her heat. It would take so little. All he had to do was lift her slightly and slide her onto his cock. He swallowed back a groan of pain as his cock flexed. It was throbbing incessantly now, a never-ending ache.

Sitting back, she slowly raised her head and gave him a slow, sleepy smile before leaning forward and kissing him.

"Thank you," she whispered against his mouth as she traced his lips with her tongue. He followed her lead, letting her control the kiss. She was tentative at first, her movements slow and languid. But it wasn't long before he could feel the pulsing of her pussy against his cock. His sweet lady was getting aroused again.

He tore his mouth from hers. He was out of time. If he didn't take her now, he was going to come. "I want you, Candy," he gritted out between clenched teeth. He had no more control left. "I want to fuck you until we're both blind with pleasure."

She whimpered with need and he felt the slight nod of her head, but he wasn't leaving this to chance. He framed her face with his hands, tilting it upward so she was looking right at him. Her eyes were glazed with desire and her lips were swollen from his kisses. He almost said the hell with it and took her then and there, but he knew he'd regret it if he did. She might regret it too, and that was something he definitely didn't want.

"Are you sure this is what you want?" He couldn't believe he was giving her an out. Like a man strung on the rack, he waited for two long seconds which seemed to last an eternity.

"Yes."

That one word was all he needed. Reaching into the back pocket of his jeans, he fumbled for his wallet. Yanking out a condom, he tore open the package. He could sense her growing nervousness and tried to hurry.

"Everything will be all right, sugar," he hastened to reassure her as he sheathed his cock in latex. That done, he lifted her easily, his cock poised at her moist entrance.

The pounding on the door startled them both. Candy jerked backward, her eyes large and shocked as she slapped her hand over her mouth.

"Hey, are you in there?"

In that moment, he could cheerfully have throttled Katie. He closed his eyes and took a deep, cleansing breath, desperately trying to center himself and dispel his anger.

The pounding came again and this time the door handle jiggled. Candy's appalled gaze met his as Katie tried to shove open the door. Lucas lunged forward and leaned against it. "What do you want?"

There was a slight pause on the other side of the door. This time there was amusement in her voice. "Some of the guests are leaving and want to speak with you."

Candy scrambled to her feet, yanking down her skirt and grabbing her blouse. She kept glancing at the door as she hauled on her blouse and buttoned it. Not bothering with her bra, she stuffed it in her purse. Yanking on her jacket, she securely fastened the two buttons.

"Fuck!" Lucas scraped his hand through his hair. Obviously, the mood was shot to hell. "I'll be right there," he growled.

Not bothering to remove the condom, he carefully zipped and buttoned his jeans. He figured the condom would keep the front of his jeans from staining. Candy was standing quietly behind the door with her purse clasped tight to her chest. Frustration filled him as he grabbed his T-shirt off the floor, shook it out and slipped it over his head. He contemplated what to say as he tucked it into his jeans.

Sighing, he walked over to her and pulled her into his arms. At first she was stiff and unyielding, but gradually she softened toward him. "I'm sorry about that, Candy. I'll go and deal with this and then we can go to my place."

He knew he wasn't going to like what she had to say when she stepped out of his embrace. "I think it might be best if I just go." She licked her lips nervously as she ran her hand through her hair, trying to tame her wild curls.

"I'd like you to stay." Before she could say no again, he hurried to add, "Just think about it. Let's go and enjoy some food and just talk for a while."

She rewarded him with a hesitant smile. "Just talk."

"Yeah. I'll take what I can get." His wry grin made her smile widen just a tad. "Come on and I'll introduce you."

Hauling open the door, Lucas stepped out into the kitchen. The light momentarily blinded him and he blinked. It took him a second to realize that Candy wasn't paying any attention to him. In fact, the two women seemed to be staring at each other.

"Candace?" Katie seemed shocked to see the other woman.

"Katie?"

Lucas had a bad feeling about this. But like an impending car crash, there was nothing to do but hang on and hope for the best. Then what Katie had said finally sunk in. "I thought you said your name was Candy?"

She cleared her throat nervously. "It is, but I've been trying to go by Candace. For professional reasons," she added with a nod, turning back to Katie. "People don't always take a woman called Candy seriously."

"I can understand that." Katie glanced at him questioningly before turning her attention back to Candy. "But I hadn't realized that you'd finally met Lucas."

Candy froze, becoming a statue as all the pieces finally clicked into place for him. He groaned and fought the urge to go back into the storage closet and close the door behind him. Fate wouldn't be so cruel. But Lucas knew that not only could Fate be that cruel, she usually was.

"Lucas?" The ice thawed from her, quickly turning to fire as she glared at him. "You're Lucas Squires?"

Lucas nodded curtly. "And you must be Candace, or rather, Candy Logan." He couldn't believe the woman of his dreams was the same woman he'd been avoiding for weeks now. The woman whose number was continually on his call display, who'd been hounding him with emails begging, bribing, cajoling and all but demanding he do promotional work for that damned cookbook that Katie had talked him into doing. "We need to talk," he added gruffly.

The look she gave him would have daunted a weaker man, it was so filled with anger and disdain. He might have been more understanding, but his cock was still throbbing and his balls still ached. At this moment, it didn't matter who she was—he still wanted her with a need that bordered on acute pain.

"I think we've said all that needs to be said." Drawing herself up with the dignity befitting a queen, she turned away from him. The smile she gave Katie was strained. "I'm sorry for any discomfort this situation might have caused you. I hope it won't affect our friendship."

"Of course not," Katie hastened to assure her.

Candy nodded and headed for the kitchen door. Lucas realized that she was going to just walk away without another word to him. "We're not done yet." His blunt words made her stumble slightly, but she quickly regained her balance, hitched her purse higher on her shoulder and kept walking.

The door swung closed behind her and Katie walked over to him and placed her hand on his arm. "Lucas, what's going on?"

He shook her off as he headed to the still swinging door. "Not now, Katie."

Opening the door, he just caught one final glimpse of Candy as she disappeared through the front door with her coat flung over her arm. He hurried across the room, ignoring people as they attempted to speak to him. He could sense Katie hard on his heels. Yanking open the door, he sighed with relief when he saw her climbing into a taxi. He didn't want her driving when she was so obviously upset.

When the taxi disappeared around the corner, he closed the door and turned around to face Katie. "Tell me everything you know about Candy."

Chapter Five

℘

Candy stormed into her apartment and slammed the door shut behind her. She thought about opening it again, just so she could have the satisfaction of slamming it shut a second time, but she resisted the childish urge. Barely. She was desperately trying to hold on to her feelings of anger because, if she didn't, she feared she would break down and cry and that just wouldn't do.

Tossing her purse onto the table just inside the door, she bent over to unzip her boots. "Stupid things." She glared at the offending footwear as she hauled them off and tossed them aside. That's what she got for buying something on sale. The reason they'd probably been marked down was because they were so darned uncomfortable. The problem was they looked fantastic and made her legs look really good. She was vain enough to admit that she liked that about them, plus the extra four inches in height didn't hurt either. She just wished they didn't make her feet ache so much. At five-foot-four, she felt she needed the extra height advantage. People didn't always take a smaller woman seriously, especially with a name like hers.

Limping slightly, she made her way to the closet and hung up her coat. When that was done, she leaned back against the closet door and closed her eyes. She thumped her head repeatedly against the door. What had she done? Not only had she almost had sex with a stranger, that stranger had turned out to be the elusive client she'd been chasing for weeks now. "Way to make a professional impression, Candy," she muttered. "What were you thinking anyway? Okay, so actual thinking had very little to do with it. It's all Missy's fault anyway for putting the idea that I needed to get laid into my brain." Sighing, she realized there was no one to blame for this debacle but herself. Nobody had made her do anything and she was responsible for her own actions.

Finished berating herself for the moment, she opened her eyes, pushed away from the door and headed to the kitchen. After the day she'd put in, she deserved a glass of wine and a long, hot bath. She turned up the heater as she passed through the living room, rubbing her hands over her arms. It was cold, but she was always trying to save money, and that meant lowering the heat when she wasn't home. Still, she hated times like this when she felt so cold. Well, a hot bath and her flannel nightgown would warm her up in no time.

Opening the refrigerator door, she pulled out a bottle of white wine she'd opened last weekend when Missy had joined her for a girls' night of pizza and "chick flicks". There was just enough left in the bottle for her to have a glass. Perfect. Yanking open the cabinet door, she pulled down a wineglass, uncorked the wine and poured it all into the glass. Thumping the bottle onto the counter, she started to reach for the glass and then stopped.

"How dare he?" Practically quivering with anger, her hands fisted at her sides, she began to pace the tiny kitchen. Five steps one way, turn and five back in the other direction. Every step she took emphasized the fact that she wasn't wearing any underwear at all. He had her panties and her bra was in her purse. She could feel the sticky wetness between her thighs and her breasts still ached.

How dare he give her the best sexual experience of her life and then turn out to be her nemesis! Coming to a dead stop in the center of the room, she realized that was the crux of the problem.

For once in her life, she'd done something wild and crazy and it had come back to kick her in the teeth. How was she ever going to face the man again? How was she ever going to face her new friend, Katie? Candy bit her lip as she mulled over those questions, but right now she couldn't come up with any answers.

"I told Missy I was no good at this kind of thing," she muttered. As if in answer, the phone began to ring. Snagging her wineglass off the counter, she padded back into the living room and slumped down on the sofa, grabbing the phone. "Hello."

"Hey, little sugarplum."

The glass of wine slipped out of her nerveless fingers. It hit the edge of the coffee table on the way down, shattering and sending wine and shards of glass showering to the carpet. It was a voice she'd never thought she'd hear again. One she'd hoped she'd never hear again.

"You there, Sis?" The voice, low and deep, now held a hint of concern.

Candy swallowed hard. "Justin?" She hadn't heard her brother's voice in more than a decade. Two years her senior, he'd spent his younger years in and out of trouble, having minor brushes with the law and spending time in juvenile detention before finally disappearing just before his seventeenth birthday.

"Yeah, Candy. It's me." He paused. "I know it's been a long time."

"A long time?" she practically yelled into the receiver. "It's been years."

"Fifteen. It's been fifteen years," he quietly replied.

She thought she detected sadness in his voice, but she couldn't be sure. Nor was she willing to fall into the same pattern her mother had lived by for years. Candy's father had been a petty criminal, in and out of jail his entire life until he'd finally died there, caught in a prison riot and stabbed to death. Her mother had always taken her father back the moment he was released from prison, always believing his empty promises that "this time will be different". Candy was afraid that Justin had followed in their father's footsteps. "So where have you been? Prison?"

The silence on the other end was almost deafening. Then came a sharp bark of laughter. "I guess I deserve that."

Candy said nothing. She really didn't know what to say to the virtual stranger on the other end. He might be her brother, but she really didn't know him. He sighed deeply and she could practically picture him running his fingers though his shoulder-length hair. It was a habit he'd had, something he'd always done when he was frustrated.

"Look, Candy, I want to talk to you."

She couldn't think. As horrible as it sounded, she wasn't sure she wanted to see her older brother. "I'm not sure that's such a good idea."

"I've already talked to Mom."

"When?"

"A week ago."

Those three words made her stomach clench and she grabbed a pillow and held it tight to her belly. Her mother had talked to Justin and hadn't told her. Candy felt betrayed right to her very core. While her father had disappointed them and Justin had abandoned them, Candy was the one who had stood by her mother. It was Candy who'd taken extra years to finish college, not only because she had to pay her own way, but because she'd always given her mother money to help her get by. In fact, she still sent her mother money every month to help make things easier, skimping and doing without things herself. And this is what she got for it.

She felt sick to her stomach. "I have to go."

"Just think about it, okay? I'll call you again in a few days."

She closed her eyes to try to push back the tears that threatened. Part of her wanted to tell him to come over now just so she could see him. She'd loved her older brother. Desperately. The lonely child she'd been had soaked up all the casual care and concern he'd lavished on her when they'd been growing up. Justin had always slipped her extra lunch money, taken her places like the museum and the movies and always made sure she had something special for her birthday. His leaving had cut her to the core and the betrayal that she'd felt then was once again bubbling to the surface.

"I can't talk anymore." She pushed the words past her tight throat, barely swallowing back a sob.

She heard his whispered "I love you" as she hung up the phone.

Candy didn't know how long she just sat there staring at the phone, but gradually she became aware of the shivers racking her body. She was so cold. Dragging herself off the sofa, she jerked and cursed as she stepped on a shard of glass. She'd forgotten all about the shattered wineglass. She lifted her foot, grateful that the glass hadn't been driven in. Instead, she had a half-inch cut that was seeping blood.

Feeling much older than her thirty years, she got some paper towels from the kitchen and went back to clean up the mess. Gathering as many pieces as she could, she sopped up the wine and deposited the mess in the garbage. That was the best she could do for now. She'd vacuum and scrub the carpet tomorrow.

Stumbling toward the bathroom, she flicked on the taps and began to run a hot bath. Turning, she placed her hands on the vanity and stared at the wild-eyed woman in the mirror. The brown eyes staring back at her looked slightly bruised and haunted. Her hair was a tangled mess, reminding her of what had happened earlier in the evening.

She laughed, but it wasn't a pleasant sound. At least the phone call from her brother had accomplished one thing—it had certainly taken her mind off her problem with Lucas Squires. Staring at the woman in the mirror, she shook her head. "What the hell did you do? Walk under a ladder? Smash a mirror?" There had to be some reason for the cosmic bad luck she'd had today.

Her life had changed irrevocably since she'd awoken this morning. This morning, she had still been excited about her new project and optimistic that she could get her client's cooperation. She'd felt she'd had a good relationship with her mother—not stellar, but good. She and her mother didn't really understand each other, but at least they'd had something. Or so she'd thought. And her brother…well, sad to say, but she hadn't thought about him in a long time. Not really. He'd always been more of a passing thought, a memory that had faded over time.

Now look at her. She'd had the best sexual encounter of her life with a complete stranger and even though they'd never finished, she felt branded by his touch. His hands and mouth had been like magic on her body. She shivered at the thought and a deep, throbbing need began to pulse low in her belly.

Pushing away from the mirror, she yanked off her clothing and peeled off her stockings, letting them drop to the floor. Usually, she was careful with her belongings, but tonight she really couldn't bring herself to care. Stepping into the tub, she ignored the stinging in her foot as she sat down and let the hot water envelop her. When the tub was full, she turned off the taps and sat back, her mind still reeling.

Okay, so she'd had a sexual encounter with a stranger who just happened to be her new client. She was a professional—she'd deal with it. Starting tomorrow, she'd go and see him and set things back on the right course.

Picking up a facecloth, she soaked it in the water, wrung it out and draped it over her face. She'd have to deal with her mother too. She still couldn't believe her mother hadn't told her she'd heard from Justin. The betrayal sat like a lump in her stomach. But she could deal with that too.

As for Justin…well, she didn't know what she was going to do about that. Did she really want to see him? What did he want? *Probably money*, the cynical side of her nature replied. If he didn't want something, why did he wait all those years to contact her? On the other hand, could she live with herself if she didn't see him?

Her thoughts went 'round and 'round until the water in the tub cooled and she thought she would scream. Pulling the plug, she stood and stepped out of the tub. Grabbing a towel, she quickly dried herself, gathered her clothing and padded to the bedroom. Her stockings were ruined, so she tossed them into the trash before she hung her suit in the closet. Her blouse went into the clothes hamper. As she tossed it in, she caught a whiff of soap with a tinge of sandalwood.

Lucas.

Slamming down the lid of the hamper, she dug out a clean flannel nightgown and pulled it over her head. She knew she should clean and bandage her foot, but she just didn't have the energy. The soap and water would have to suffice for now. Crawling into bed, she hauled the covers up tight around her face. She glanced at the clock and was mildly shocked to realize that it wasn't quite eight o'clock.

She jerked when the phone rang, but made no move to answer it. Instead, she lay in bed and stared at the phone on her bedside table. She knew the answering machine in the living room would pick it up. When the message finished and the beep sounded, a familiar voice filled the room. "Pick up if you're there. It's me." There was a slight pause. "Candy, where are you, girl? I've been waiting to find out what happened. Did you crash the party and make contact with Mr. Squires? Call me."

Candy snorted. Missy had no idea just how successful she'd been at making contact with Lucas Squires. She almost took her friend's call, but she knew she couldn't talk without crying. Not yet. The lump in her throat was huge.

The phone rang again, its shrill sound seeming unusually loud. Once again, she stared and waited. This time the voice was male and deep. "Candy, it's Lucas. I was just calling to make sure you got home okay." He paused, but finally sighed and continued. "I want to see you tomorrow. We definitely need to talk." His tone lowered, becoming more intimate. "Sleep well and dream of me. I know I'll be dreaming of you."

With a click, he was gone and Candy was left staring at the phone. How could he? If she dreamed of him, it would be a nightmare. Suddenly the tears she'd been forcing back for the last two hours poured out. Burying her face in her pillow, she sobbed until her chest hurt and she thought she might throw up. Sitting up in bed, she grabbed a handful of tissues from a box on the bedside table and blew her nose before taking a deep breath.

She hadn't felt this bad in a long time. In fact, not since she'd accused her ex-boyfriend Gary of cheating on her and he'd stormed off, slamming her for not trusting him. She had absolutely no luck with men. Lucas was just another shining example of that.

Curling back up in bed, she punched her pillow until it was comfortable and then she yanked the covers over her head, willing herself to sleep. She'd get over Lucas and everything else. She'd do what she'd always done. She'd put her head down and work. Rolling over, she closed her eyes, shutting out the world.

Chapter Six

ფ

Lucas stared at the closed door in front of him. He contemplated turning around and just walking away. After all, he certainly didn't need the hassle. He'd been arguing with himself ever since he'd rolled out of bed. He glanced at his watch. That was over four hours ago. It was just past nine and he'd already put in three hours in the kitchen. But there was still time to walk away, go back home and get on with his life. He could pretend that yesterday had never happened.

Shifting the box he was holding, he tucked it carefully in the crook of his arm before raising his free hand to knock. It was too late to turn back now. The memory of Candy's face, one minute filled with sexual longing and pleasure, and then filled with disappointment and anger had kept him awake all night long. Without giving himself any more time to question himself, he gave two hard, sharp knocks.

"Come in."

As her voice drifted through the closed door, his cock stirred. He glanced down at the growing bulge in his jeans. It was ridiculous that a woman he'd just met could have such an effect on him. Shaking his head in disgust, he opened the door and stepped inside her office.

Her chair was turned away from the front of her desk, facing her computer, which sat at a right angle to her main workspace. She was currently absorbed in whatever was on her computer screen, staring at it intently. She held up one finger and then furiously continued to type. "Be right with you."

Lucas quietly closed the door and leaned back against it, content just to watch her work. Nope, she hadn't been just a figment of his imagination. She'd obviously made an attempt to subdue her curly hair, but several locks had escaped and were hanging down in front of her face. As he watched her, she absently swiped at one of the rogue locks, tucking it behind her ear before continuing her work. It was such an automatic gesture, he knew that she'd done it many, many times before.

He took the opportunity to survey her office. You could tell a lot about a person by their surroundings. The office was small but neat, painted a subtle shade of yellow. Two armchairs, covered in a dark green fabric, were strategically placed in front of her desk. Several prints hung on the wall and he was surprised but pleased to see one of Katie's smaller watercolors displayed prominently in a place where Candy could see it from her desk. A few fairly large plants were strategically scattered around the room. All in all, the effect was one of comfort and efficiency.

Her desk was another matter. There were stacks of files, magazines and papers. Pens, pencils, notepads and an appointment book were scattered across the top of her workspace, but right in the center of it all sat a large canary-yellow coffee mug that was half full. Candy obviously liked her coffee.

The furious tapping captured his attention again and he studied her carefully as she continued to work, taking in the curve of her cheek, the long line of her neck and the graceful way she held herself as she worked. She chewed on her lower lip and then typed one last line before hitting the save button. Obviously pleased, she sat back in her chair and swiveled it around to face the door. The greeting died on her lips as she realized it was him standing there. Not exactly the reaction he was hoping for. But at least she wasn't screaming at him to get out.

Lucas sauntered forward to stand in front of her desk. "Morning, Candy."

The color drained from her face only to be replaced a moment later by a dull shade of red that crept up her cheeks. Lucas eyed the open v-neck of her blouse, wondering if her blush continued on down to her chest. She was once again wearing a suit. This one was a deep chocolate brown and matched her eyes nicely. He couldn't really see much of it because she was sitting down, but he'd bet good money that it was just as shapeless as the one she'd worn yesterday and probably a size or two too big.

"What are you doing here?" Her hand went to her throat in a nervous gesture.

"I told you yesterday that we weren't finished." Sauntering around the side of her desk, he kept his gaze locked on hers.

Her eyes widened as she swiveled her chair to face him. "What do you want?" Her voice squeaked. He could see her struggling to maintain her composure and was surprised by how badly he wanted to soothe her.

"I brought you something." He laid the plain white bakery box on the top of her desk. Placing his hands firmly on the arms of her chair, he leaned down and kissed her. He kept it light and quick, and before she could even think to protest, he pulled back and smiled at her.

She cleared her throat and licked her lips nervously. "What did you bring?"

Lifting the white box, he opened it. "Close your eyes."

Her eyebrows came together as she frowned at him. "Why?"

"Because it's a surprise." He could see the indecision on her face before she finally heaved a huge sigh and closed her eyes.

"I'm too busy to play games," she muttered.

Lucas ignored her grumbles and waved the box in front of her face, allowing the scent to waft up in front of her. She sniffed cautiously and her eyes popped open. "No peeking," he admonished as he pulled the box away so she couldn't see what was inside.

Curiosity filled her face, but she closed her eyes again. He kept his eyes on her as he laid the box on the desk and drew out one of the treats he'd baked earlier this morning. "Open your mouth." His voice was husky as memories of his erotic fantasies filled his head. His erection was straining hard against the front of his jeans as he watched her tentatively open her mouth.

Swallowing back a groan, he placed the chocolate treat to her lips, all the while wishing it was his swollen cock that she was so eager for. When her tongue came out to lick the chocolate, he almost came. He was sweating beneath his leather jacket and T-shirt. His balls tightened painfully as she finally bit off a small piece and began to chew.

Moaning with pleasure, she rolled the offering around in her mouth before swallowing. Her eyes fluttered open as she stared first at him and then at the brownie he was still holding. "That's absolutely incredible." Her husky tone made the hair on the back of his neck stand on end.

"I'm glad you like it." He offered her another bite, which she quickly accepted. Lucas was surprised that she actually let him feed her. It was such an erotic experience to watch her devour the chocolate treat he'd baked especially for her.

As she took the last piece, her tongue flicked his finger and they both froze. He could see the recognition come to her face as she realized what she was doing. Pushing him away with one hand, her chair rolled a few inches away from him. "What am I doing?"

Although he knew it was a rhetorical question, he answered her anyway. "Enjoying a brownie."

Her gaze immediately sharpened as she reached over and snagged the box off the top of her desk. "These weren't in the cookbook." She sent him an accusatory stare. "Why weren't these in the cookbook?"

Lucas chuckled slightly. "I take it you liked it."

She stared down at the box in her hands, an almost reverent expression on her face. "These are phenomenal." There was a shy, almost hesitant look on her face when she gazed back at him. "You made these for me?"

He could tell the idea pleased her and he was glad he'd given in to the urge to make them. "Made them fresh this morning." He could see the question forming on her lips again. "And they're not in the cookbook because I didn't want them in there."

He saw no reason to tell her that the real reason his special brownie recipe wasn't in the cookbook was because he'd sold it to a giant food manufacturer. Katie's husband, Cain, had helped him with the negotiations. In fact, Cain had actually been the one to suggest the idea after he'd tasted some of them. The deal was very lucrative, not only giving Lucas money up front, but making sure he obtained a percentage of the profits as well. It was the main reason he'd been able to afford the new building he'd just bought.

"But they're fantastic. They should have been in the book." Her eyes darkened as she became more impassioned about the subject.

"Be thankful there was a cookbook. I didn't even want to do the damned thing." He ran his fingers through his hair in frustration, reminding himself again why he'd bothered to come all the way over here this morning.

"Then why did you do it?" she snapped back.

"Because Katie asked me to." The memory of how Katie had come to him after the deal was all but done, cajoling him to do it made him angry all over again. The only reason he'd even agreed to it was because she'd said it would be a good way to publicize her artwork. And she'd also reminded him that he owed her for selling her first painting without her permission. The little minx had him on that and she knew it. A smile tugged at the corner of his mouth at the memory. That action had been responsible for Katie and Cain meeting.

"I hadn't realized that you and Katie were *close*." The way she said the word *close* made his hackles rise. "I thought she was married."

"Katie is like a sister to me." As hard as he tried, he couldn't keep the anger from his voice. "And you obviously don't have a very high opinion of me." He paused. "Or Katie." This had obviously been a waste of time. Sighing, he turned away.

Candy scrambled out of her chair and grabbed his arm, stopping him cold. "I'm sorry, Lucas. That was uncalled for." He could hear the sincerity in her voice. "I had a really bad night last night and I'm taking it out on you. Please, let's start over."

He took a deep breath and nodded. "Okay."

"Sit down and tell me why you came here this morning."

He knew she expected him to go around the front of her desk and sit in one of the chairs. Instead, he propped himself against the edge of the desk, crossing his arms over his chest. "I came to make sure you were all right after last evening. You left so abruptly after we were interrupted."

"Yes, well," she began. She met his gaze squarely as she slowly sat back down in her chair. "I don't do things like that, Lucas."

"Like what?" He kept his tone even and unthreatening when all he wanted to do was pull her into his arms and hug her.

"Like what?" She stared at him as if he were nuts. She raked her hand through her hair, dislodging a few more locks from the barrette in the back. "Like practically getting naked with a man I don't even know."

"Candy." He leaned forward and hauled her chair over in front of him. With his hands locked around the arms of the chair, he effectively had her caged in. "For the record, I didn't think it was something that you usually did." Taking one hand off the chair, he carefully tucked a curl behind her ear. It sprang back immediately, making him grin slightly. Her hair was as unpredictable and untamed as she was. "And as long as we're on the subject, it's not something that I do either."

She cleared her throat. "Okay. As long as you know that and understand that there won't be a repeat performance."

That made him scowl. "Why not?"

"You're a client, Lucas." She laid her hand on his forearm and he wished he wasn't wearing his coat so he could feel her fingers brushing against his skin.

"You don't work for me and I don't work for you. There is no conflict. Besides which, that's what I'm here to talk about."

He could tell he'd aroused her interest, but she leaned back in her chair and eyed him coolly. "Oh?"

He'd give her credit—she didn't jump at the bait, but waited to see what he'd offer. He admired her for that. A lot of other people would have started demanding an explanation, but she obviously had patience. "You want me to do some promotion for the book."

"Yes. It's the reason I've been trying to track you down for the past few weeks." She tried to reach around him to snag her calendar off her desk, but gave up when she realized that he wasn't moving. He caught a haunting whiff of vanilla-scented lotion as she shifted closer to him.

Leaning forward, he cupped her chin in his hand. "I'll agree to do a select few promotional interviews. But," he continued before she got too excited, "only if you agree to have dinner with me."

"That's blackmail."

"The brownies were blackmail to get you to talk to me. Okay, technically they were more of a bribe than blackmail, but you ate one of them," he pointed out.

"That's different," she sputtered. "I didn't even know you had brownies. And this entire conversation is absurd."

"That may be, but the offer stands as is. You want me to do some promotions, then you'll have dinner with me." He rubbed his thumb across her bottom lip. It was lush and full and moist. "Besides." He angled closer to her, bringing his mouth nearer hers. "I'm not asking you to have sex with me. Just dinner." Giving in to temptation, he licked her bottom lip, tasting the chocolate from the brownie she'd eaten mingled with her own sweet flavor.

"Just dinner?" she whispered as she shifted forward until their lips were barely touching.

"Hmmm," he agreed as his lips skimmed across hers. "That doesn't mean I won't try to convince you to have sex with me, Candy. I want to finish what we started. We'd be so good together. You know it as well as I do." He slid his tongue past her lips and tasted the warmth of her mouth before retreating. "I want to fuck you until you scream with pleasure. I want to lick every inch of your body until you beg me to fuck you again." He slipped his tongue into her mouth again, mimicking the sexual act.

Both of them were breathing hard now. Candy's hands had moved at some point and were now gripping the sides of his neck as she pulled him closer. He forced himself to retreat once again. "Have dinner with me, sugar. You won't regret it."

She let out a whimper as he captured her mouth again. This time there was no holding back. What was it about this particular woman that made him lose all control? At his age, he thought his days of being led around by his dick were long over. But Candy made a mockery of his self-discipline. His entire body was clenched tight with need and he was so incredibly close to shoving everything off her desk, spreading her across the hard surface, flipping up her skirt and driving himself into her waiting warmth.

And she would be wet for him. He knew she would.

Without breaking their kiss, he hauled her out of the chair. Pulling her between his spread thighs, he cupped her ass in his hands and rubbed her mound over his erection. Tugging at the fabric of her skirt with his fingers, he yanked it upward until he could slip his hand beneath it. Once again, she was wearing thigh-high stockings. He promised himself that one day he'd fuck her while she was wearing nothing but a pair of those ridiculously high-heeled shoes that she seemed to favor and these fabulous stockings.

The image made his cock throb, so he yanked open his jeans, allowing his erection to spring forward. At the same time, he pushed her skirt upward in the front and pulled her closer so that his aching flesh was pressed tight against the heat of her silk panties. He almost yelled with pleasure as she rotated her hips, grinding her pussy against him. Clasping her silk-covered behind with his hands, he silently encouraged her.

Slanting his lips over hers, he devoured her mouth, fucking it with his tongue, claiming it as his. He pushed one of his hands lower over her ass, slipping it between her thighs. She widened her stance, letting him touch her, moaning her pleasure as his fingers slid over the slick, wet fabric. Skimming the edge of the fabric, he slipped his fingers beneath.

His breath was coming so hard now that he was afraid his chest might burst. She was hot and wet, just as he'd known she would be. Damn, she was so naturally sensual and giving, she drove him wild. He had to have her.

There was a loud knock at the door.

They pulled apart and stared at each other. Lucas swore as he gingerly removed his hand from inside her panties. Candy hurriedly pushed her skirt down and stared at his groin as he carefully zipped his jeans over his erection. Even though he was clenching his teeth against the pain, he almost grinned at the look on her face. Part hungry, part appalled, it made him feel better to know that she was in this just as deep as he was. "Sugar, you're not helping."

Her head jerked up and she gasped, her cheeks turning pink.

The person on the other side of the door knocked again. "Candy, are you busy?" The doorknob turned and a woman walked in. Lucas managed to seat Candy back in her chair and take a step away from her before the new arrival realized that there was someone else in the office. She looked startled but recovered quickly. "I'm sorry, I didn't know Ms. Logan was busy. I'll come back later."

"That okay. We're done...for now." He left those last two words hanging in the air. It was up to Candy now. She knew his terms. The last thing he wanted to do was leave her, but he forced himself to walk across the room. It was surprisingly difficult given the tightness of his pants. He saw the other woman's eyes widen in surprise, but thankfully she refrained from making any comment.

When he got to the door, he turned back. Candy was still sitting in her chair, looking slightly stunned. Her lips were swollen, her cheeks were rosy and her hair was a bit more mussed. But other than that, she appeared almost exactly as she had when he'd arrived. "Enjoy your brownies."

As he turned to walk out the door, he tossed one parting challenge over his shoulder. "I'll wait for your call."

Feeling much better in spite of his unrequited sexual desire, he sauntered toward the elevator, already planning what he'd make Candy for dessert.

Chapter Seven

Missy never took her eyes from Lucas as he strolled out of the office. She carefully closed the door and turned toward Candy. "Should I even ask?" Before she could respond, Missy was shaking her head. "Forget I said that. I *have* to know."

Seating herself comfortably in one of the chairs, Missy propped her elbows on the arms and steepled her fingers together in anticipation. She waited quietly for about thirty seconds before her curiosity finally got the better of her. "Girl, who is that hunk of man who just left here? I know I interrupted something. With the heat level in here, I'm surprised y'all didn't set off the sprinkler system."

Candy pushed a lock of hair out of her face and blew out a breath. "That, my dear, was Lucas Squires."

Missy's mouth dropped open and then abruptly clamped shut. "You're joking."

Her friend's reaction made her grin. It was rare that anything ever ruffled Missy's composure. "Nope." Ignoring the dampness between her thighs and the desire still flooding her body, she leaned forward and picked up the white box from her desk. She offered it to Missy. "Here, have one of these. You'll definitely feel better."

Missy plucked a brownie from the box and took a large bite. More slowly, Candy selected another of the chocolate treats, bit into it and allowed the flavors to explode on her tongue. She knew what to expect. Her friend, on the other hand, was in for a surprise.

First Missy frowned, then she began to chew more slowly and her eyes closed as she continued to eat. She swallowed and moaned with pleasure before opening her eyes and staring at the remaining piece of brownie in her hand.

Candy took another tiny bite while she waited. Missy eventually looked at her, then back at the brownie and then back to her again. "Please tell me he didn't make these?"

Nodding smugly, Candy chewed and swallowed, refusing to talk while she still had chocolate in her mouth. "He made them for me this morning."

"Omigod. If you don't want him, I'll take him."

A wave of jealousy washed through her at Missy's casual comment and her entire body stiffened. She'd always been insecure about her own looks and didn't want to think what might happen if Missy made a play for Lucas.

"I want him." As soon as the words left her mouth, she knew they were the absolute truth. She did want him. Badly. She wanted to have dinner with him and spend time getting to know him as they promoted his book. But most of all, she wanted to sleep with him.

She'd never reacted to any other man she'd ever met the way she did to Lucas. There was an earthiness about him that drew her. The man oozed bad boy sex appeal with his jeans, T-shirt and leather jacket. The explosiveness of their first two meetings guaranteed she'd be more than sexually satisfied if she decided to take him up on his offer. But why did she always seem to attract men who weren't good for her?

Candy wanted a stable man in her life. One who was responsible, dependable, made a decent living, worked hard and paid his taxes. Maybe that sounded boring, but after the examples of her father and brother, Candy wasn't willing to settle for anything less.

But that didn't mean that she couldn't have a fling with Lucas. The man never said he wanted a long-term relationship. He'd quite bluntly stated that he wanted to fuck her. She licked her suddenly dry lips, almost hearing him whisper the words as he kissed her.

"Mmm." Candy jerked up her head in time to watch Missy swallow the last of her brownie. "Okay, you can have him, but only if I get more of these." Sighing, she sat up straight and gave the box a baleful stare. "But enough of this. What happened at the party yesterday afternoon?"

Candy debated exactly how much to share with her friend, but in the end, she spilled it all. Okay, maybe not quite all the graphic details, but the gist of what had happened.

"So let me get this straight." Missy ticked each item off on her fingers as she listed them. "You didn't know who he was?" When Candy nodded, she continued. "But you ended up almost having sex with him in a storage room?" Again, she paused for confirmation. "Then he shows up with these amazing brownies for you this morning?" Missy's gaze wavered toward the white box before coming back to Candy. "He'll do the promotion, but only if you have dinner with him, which really means he wants to have hot monkey sex with you? Am I right?"

"I wouldn't call it hot monkey sex." Missy arched a perfectly plucked eyebrow at her. "Okay, maybe I would," Candy conceded. "But you can see the problem, right?"

"Are you nuts?" Missy sat forward in her chair, reached across the desk and grabbed Candy's hand. "This guy is hot for you. I swear I saw steam rising off the both of you when I walked into the room. All jokes aside, though, in all the years I've known you, I've never seen you react like this to any man. You owe it to yourself to take a chance."

She wanted so badly to believe her friend. "But what about conflict of interest?"

"Girl, you're not his lawyer, doctor or priest. You're his publicist. You'll work with him for a few weeks now and maybe a few weeks after the book is released and then you'll both go on to other things. You have other clients and he has a business to run. Who is going to care if you start a relationship?"

"That's what Lucas said." Candy could feel the tight ball of tension that had been in the pit of her stomach since yesterday evening loosen ever so slightly.

Missy nodded as she squeezed Candy's fingers. "See, he is a man of good sense. He had brains enough to see past your armor to the woman beneath."

"What do you mean by that?"

"Candy, honey, I love you like a sister, but look at yourself. You wear bland suits in the wrong size and send out *do not touch* vibes to every man you meet."

Missy's words appalled her. "I do not." She felt the absurd need to defend her sensible, if slightly dull, suits. "This suit is businesslike and appropriate. I don't want to pick up men at work. I don't want to pick men up at all." She startled herself with her last statement.

"I know you don't. Ever since you and Gary broke up, you've pulled into a shell. That was over a year ago, Candy. It's time to move on, or at least live a little and have some fun. Maybe Lucas isn't a forever kind of man, or maybe he is, but you'll never know if you don't try." Missy released her hand and stood. "I don't want to see you bury yourself any longer. There's more to life than just work. You're both consenting adults, so there's no problem if you want to have dinner." Missy offered her last few words with a sly, teasing smile and a wink. "Or hot monkey sex."

"I'll think about it." Her friend had certainly given her a lot to mull over.

"You do that, but you let me know the second you've set a date for dinner with Lucas."

"You're so sure that I'll agree to his terms." Candy picked up a pen and began to tap it nervously against the top of her desk.

"Yes. You're stubborn, not stupid. And we're going shopping for an outfit that will knock the man's socks off." Glancing at her watch, she sighed. "I was going to ask you if you wanted to go for an early coffee break, but we've pretty much used up the time."

Candy smiled at the other woman, already intrigued by the idea of shopping for something special to wear for her date. She was darned lucky to have as supportive and understanding a friend as Missy. "Here." She pushed the white bakery box closer. "Take one for the road."

Missy squealed with joy, snagged a brownie and was out the door in a flash, obviously not about to give Candy the chance to change her mind. Her "see you later" drifted through the door. The sound of her heels tapping quickly as she hurried back down the hall to her office faded in the distance.

Candy pulled out her file on Lucas' book and her calendar, opened them and tried to pick out the best ten promotional opportunities. She didn't think he'd agree to more than four or five, but she wanted to be prepared. Her eyes strayed to the phone, but she forced herself to look away. "Stay strong," she muttered as she snagged the last brownie from the box. Lucas had made her wait. Now it was his turn.

"Fuck!" Lucas swore as he bashed his thumb. Tossing the hammer to the floor in disgust, he glared at his throbbing hand.

"That's no way to treat good tools." The male voice was filled with amusement.

Lucas grimaced, his thumb throbbing, as he offered his friend a wry smile. T. S. MacNamara, general contractor and longtime friend, was leaning against the doorjamb, shaking his head. "Obviously, it's not safe to put a hammer in your hands today. What's up?"

Lucas hesitated. T. S. was his oldest friend and knew him better than anyone else, even Katie. He and T. S. had been in prison together when they were in their late teens and early twenties. Their very youth, and the fact that they weren't considered to be hardened criminals or high-risk inmates, had resulted in them both getting jobs in the kitchen. They'd banded together for safety's sake and had become close friends. They knew things about each other that no one else did. In fact, Lucas was sure that nobody else knew T. S.'s real name.

"Ah." His friend nodded sagely. "It's either money or women, and I know it's not money." Pushing away from the doorjamb, he sauntered into the room. "Or maybe it is money. I know for sure that this place is putting a dent in your pocketbook. Your contractor is a little pricey, but you get what you pay for." He flashed a roguish grin. "Should I worry about my next payment?"

Lucas laughed, something he rarely did. His friend had always been able to do that for him, even when they were in prison. T. S. showed an easygoing, humorous side to the world, but behind it, Lucas knew, lay a man who fought his own share of nightmares and demons.

They'd both made something out of their lives, though— Lucas with his coffee shop and T. S. with his carpentry skills. When Lucas had purchased the building, he knew there was only one man he'd trust to do the renovations. Yes, he was a little expensive, but the work was first-rate quality. And Lucas didn't have to worry about his contractor fleecing him or running out on him. That counted for a lot.

"What would you say if I told you it was money?"

This time it was T. S. who laughed. "Send my work crew to another job site and then roll up my sleeves and teach you how to use a hammer properly." Leaning over, he picked up the tool, examined it and laid it in the nearby toolbox. "Seriously though, is it money?"

"No, it's not money." Lucas rubbed a hand across the base of his neck, trying to loosen the stiff muscles. As every hour went by, the tension in his neck and shoulders got worse. It was midafternoon and Candy still hadn't called. He knew because he was carrying his cell phone in his pocket and checking the damned thing every half-hour or so to make sure it was still working.

T. S. ambled over to a cooler in the corner, lifted the cover and pulled out a couple of cans. He opened one and took a swig before heading back over to where Lucas was still standing and offering him the unopened beer. "If it's a woman, then you need this."

Taking the proffered can, Lucas opened it and took a swig, grateful to get the taste of dust out of his mouth. He'd thought that doing some work on his own building might help, but he hadn't been able to keep thoughts of Candy from intruding.

T. S. strolled over to the makeshift desk in the center of the room that consisted of two sawhorses with a piece of plywood laid on top and settled himself on one end. Lucas knew the man had the patience of a saint and would wait as long as it took for Lucas to start talking. The image made him smile.

The sinner and the saint, or the devil and the angel—that's what they'd been nicknamed in prison. Lucas with his blond hair and fair skin had been the angel and T. S. with his black hair and olive-tone complexion had been the devil. He shook his head at the memory. Together they watched each other's backs. In those days, you didn't mess with one without incurring the wrath of the other.

Sighing, he carried himself and his beer over to his friend. "Her name is Candy."

"Sweet." His friend saluted him with his can before taking another swallow.

Lucas laughed. "Yeah, she is that. But she's prickly too." Oddly enough, he liked that about her. "She wears these boxy suits two sizes too big, she's bossy and has the tenacity of a bulldog." He'd learned that over the past few weeks as she doggedly continued to try to track him down. Now that it was his turn, the little vixen was making him wait. Darned if he didn't admire her for that.

"And you really like her," his friend interjected.

"I do," he confessed. "She's not the usual kind of woman I date." He hesitated. "She'd mean something. Maybe too much."

T. S. nodded in understanding. Neither of them had ever settled into a serious relationship. They both had too much of a jaded past filled with too many horrific memories. "A woman like that is definitely trouble. Maybe you should just walk away."

"Too late for that." He'd already come to that conclusion as he waited for his phone to ring. There was something between them that neither one of them could deny.

"Then you, my friend, are seriously screwed." Finishing off his beer, T. S. plunked the empty can down on top of the piece of plywood.

"Maybe." He wasn't willing to admit that to himself. "We're both adults. Nothing wrong with having a good time for as long as it lasts."

"You keep telling yourself that." Pushing himself off the plywood, he slowly turned in a circle with his arms spread wide. "You finally decide what you want to do with this space?"

That was the great thing about having a friend who was as close as a brother. He knew when to back away and let things lie. The subject was closed for now, but Lucas knew that T. S. would bring it up again if he thought that Lucas needed to talk.

Standing, he fished a folded piece of paper out of his back pocket. Opening it, he laid it atop of the plywood. "I want to put in office space here. I figure the rental property will bring in a good secondary income."

"Plus, you won't have any neighbors." T. S. leaned over and stared at the paper that held a rough drawing.

Lucas fought back another grin. "There is that." His friend did know him well.

Hauling a pencil out of his shirt pocket, T. S. began to sketch on top of the plywood. "I see what you're going for, but this way would maximize your space." He continued to draw and within minutes the two men were immersed in construction plans.

Then his phone rang.

Candy tapped the toe of her shoe impatiently as she held the telephone receiver to her ear and listened to the shrill ring. She glanced at her watch, wincing slightly. She really hadn't meant to make him wait this long, but she'd gotten buried in her work and had lost track of time. She counted three rings and was getting nervous when the phone was finally answered.

"It's about damned time."

She smiled at the aggravation in his voice and couldn't help coming back with her own dig. "Now you know what it's like."

"I figured you'd make me wait." She could hear the humor in his voice and was relieved that he was taking it so well. It said a lot about the man.

She sat back in her chair and crossed her legs, just enjoying the sound of his voice. Low and slightly rough, it sent shivers down her spine. "I didn't really mean to make you wait quite this long." She figured she owed him that much honesty. "I got tied up with work."

"Doesn't matter. You're calling now." He paused. "Well?"

She didn't make him wait any longer. "I'd love to have dinner with you."

"Tomorrow night?"

Candy sucked in a deep breath and took the plunge. "Tomorrow night."

"About seven?"

"That would be good."

"I'll pick you up then." His voice lowered to almost a whisper. "And Candy, don't worry. Nothing will happen that you don't want to happen."

That's what she was afraid of, but she was no coward. She wanted this. "Okay."

He continued on, briskly now. "I'll see you at seven."

The line went dead before she could respond and she hung up her own phone. A man of few words was Lucas. Dialing her phone once again, she waited until Missy picked up on the other end. "Want to go shopping tonight?"

Chapter Eight

ෂ

Candy stared at herself in the mirror, not quite able to believe the transformation that she and Missy had wrought in just under twenty-four hours. She'd never realized just how ruthless her friend could be.

Her lips curved up in a smile as she relived last night's shopping trip. Missy had poked, prodded and threatened her until finally she'd shoved Candy in a dressing room and brought her outfit after outfit with orders to try them on. Like a general commanding a battle, she'd gone on the offensive, not giving Candy the opportunity to object or to run.

It had been so much fun to shop for something sexy rather than something work-appropriate. She hadn't done anything like this in far too long. They'd practically closed the stores last night, they were out shopping so late, but it had definitely been worth it.

Turning sideways, she viewed her image in the mirror. This dress was nothing short of spectacular. Falling to just above her knees, it was a deep burgundy in color, and its crushed velvet fabric felt luxurious and sensual. The sleeves were long, coming all the way to her wrists, and the neckline was high. There was a spectacular cutout in the front that showed off her cleavage to advantage. But that wasn't the best part of the dress.

Spinning around until her back was to the mirror, she glanced over her shoulder. The dress hooked at the neckline with five small fasteners. Other than that, her entire back was exposed. She'd never worn something quite so revealing before. It was cut so low in the back that several inches of flesh below her waistline was showing. She'd had to buy new underwear to wear under the dress.

The trip to the lingerie shop had been almost arousing. She'd felt decadent and scandalous trying on the skimpy garments, imagining Lucas' reaction when he saw them. And there was no doubt in her mind that he would definitely be seeing them. After much deliberation, she'd settled on a thong in a rich, creamy beige. It was part of a set and came with a pushup bra, and even though she couldn't wear a bra with this dress, she'd bought it anyway. In fact, she'd liked the set so much, she bought another one in black. She hoped she'd have another opportunity to wear them.

She'd never worn a thong before, but she'd wanted to be daring. The thin string had settled between the cheeks of her behind and the small patch of fabric on the front barely covered her pubic hair. She felt half naked in the underwear, but she felt sexy too. Laughing, she spun around and faced the mirror once again.

Thigh-high stockings and a new pair of black velvet four-inch heels completed the ensemble. She'd spent a small fortune on the entire outfit, even though they'd bought the dress and shoes at discount warehouses. But the results were worth it.

She hadn't been sure about the dress at first, but Missy's enthusiastic response to it had finally won her over. The fabric of the dress hugged her body, emphasizing her large breasts and hips, making her slightly uncomfortable, but her friend had assured her that she looked spectacular in it.

In the end, she hadn't been able to leave the dress behind for something more sensible and less showy. This was about having an adventure and she was determined to embrace every moment of it. She'd even run out on her lunch hour and had her hair trimmed and her nails done to match her dress. She had toyed with several hairstyles, but had ended up piling the curly mass on top of her head and anchoring it with a black rhinestone-studded hair clip. Rhinestone studs adorned her ears and were the only jewelry she wore. Now she was ready and getting more and more nervous by the moment.

Placing a hand over her stomach to quiet the butterflies dancing there, she took a deep breath. She was as ready as she'd ever be. Grabbing her purse off the bed—another purchase from the night before that Missy had convinced her she just *had to have*—she made her way into the living room to wait. Opening her bag, she checked the contents and closed it again. She had her keys, wallet, cell phone, tissues, lipstick and condoms—another purchase from last night. She assumed Lucas would have some, but she wasn't taking any chances. A smart woman took care of herself.

Glancing at the clock on the stereo, she went to the closet and pulled out her coat, slipping it on. She didn't want Lucas to see the dress until they arrived at the restaurant. She wanted to surprise him and, she admitted to herself, she wanted to make a dramatic entrance and gauge his reaction.

Truthfully, she wanted to knock his socks off.

She heard one hard, sharp knock on her front door and she jumped even though she'd been expecting it. Even though she knew it was Lucas, she checked the peephole. Unlocking the door, she opened it and promptly lost her breath. In jeans and a T-shirt, the man was gorgeous. In a suit and tie, he was devastating.

A black wool overcoat was open to reveal his suit. A tailored black jacket molded his upper body to perfection. She knew it had been made especially for him because there was no way with his muscular build he could buy something off the rack that would fit him so well. Underneath it, he wore a white shirt with a dark burgundy tie.

Candy knew she should say something, but she was honestly at a loss for words. The silence thickened the longer they stood there staring at each other. Finally, it was Lucas who broke it. "You look amazing."

Swallowing past the lump of nerves in her throat, she managed to croak out a "thank you". His eyes were glued to the cutout in the front of her dress as he spoke. Some of her nerves abated and confidence filled her as she realized that he was as enthralled with her as she was with him. She bit her lip to keep from laughing, wondering how he would react to her little surprise when she slipped off her coat. Suddenly, she was in a hurry to find out.

"I'm ready if you are." Remembering her manners, she quickly added, "Unless you'd like to come in for a moment."

Lucas shook his head and offered her his arm. "No, we've got reservations and I don't want us to be late."

Candy stepped out of her apartment, locking her door behind her before taking Lucas' arm. She could feel the muscles flex and ripple beneath her fingers. It was arousing to have all that leashed power just beneath her hand. As they walked to the elevator, Candy knew for sure that this night would change her forever. The next time she returned to her home, she would not be the same woman she was now. Ready to embrace the experience, she boldly stepped into the elevator with him and ignored the shiver that ran down her spine as the door closed.

The restaurant was elegant and Candy was very glad that she'd sprung for the new outfit. Any of her older dresses would have left her feeling uncomfortably underdressed. Lucas guided her to the coat check area and began helping her out of her coat. As the fabric slid down her arms, exposing her back, he froze behind her.

He sucked in a deep breath before he continued to remove her coat and handed it to the woman running the coat check. As he slid off his own overcoat and waited for their tickets, she tried to squelch the disappointment that he hadn't responded to her dress. She bit her bottom lip, turning away to compose herself.

A large, muscled arm slipped around her waist, pulling her back tight against a large, very aroused male body. She could feel Lucas' erection pressing into her behind as he lowered his head to whisper in her ear. It seemed to burn into her flesh through the barriers of their clothing.

"You look good enough to eat." He nipped her earlobe and she shuddered. "In fact, I think I'll have you for dessert."

She could feel herself creaming at his words and swallowed hard as she tried to concentrate on the here and now. They were in the foyer of a public restaurant, for God's sake. She'd thought he hadn't been affected by her dress, but obviously she'd been wrong. His reaction was everything she'd hoped for and more, but what she hadn't counted on was her own reaction to his reaction.

Keeping her slightly ahead of him, Lucas placed his hand on her back and led her toward the dining room. The maitre d' seemed to know Lucas on sight and assured him quickly that his table was ready. The walk across the room seemed to take forever and she felt as if every eye was on her, somehow knowing just how aroused she was. She wished she hadn't worn her hair piled on top of her head. Right now, she'd be grateful to have the extra hair covering at least a part of her back and exposed chest.

She was concentrating so hard on putting one foot in front of the other, Candy was surprised when Lucas caught her by the crook of her arm, halting her progress. The table they'd stopped in front of was in a quiet corner of the room. As Lucas seated her, he leaned down, brushing her temple with his lips. "Breathe, sugar."

Candy laughed and felt some of her earlier apprehension disappear. Now that she was seated at their table, she didn't feel like she was on display. While Lucas took his own seat, she surveyed the restaurant with interest. The hardwood gleamed beneath tables set with fine linen tablecloths that fell all the way to the floor, delicate china and heavy silverware. Thick, white candles sat in silver holders on every table, their glow creating a muted, romantic atmosphere. A low, jazzy music played in the background as potted plants, strategically placed, created an air of intimacy about the place.

"Do you like it?" Lucas' much bigger hand reached over and covered hers. She hadn't realized she was clutching her purse in a death grip and made herself loosen her hold.

"It's lovely." That was an understatement. She didn't think she'd ever been anywhere quite this nice before.

"Not as lovely as you are, but then, I don't think anything else could be." Clasping her hand in his, he slowly raised it to his lips and kissed each of her knuckles.

Candy was suddenly robbed of breath, not only by his compliment, but also by his actions. She couldn't take her eyes off her hand as he held it so gently in his. The contrast of his darker, much larger one clasping her smaller, more fragile one was spellbinding. And when he licked one of her fingers, she almost moaned with pleasure.

The sound of someone discreetly clearing his throat next to their table made her keenly aware once again of her surroundings. She tried to yank her hand away, but Lucas' closed firmly around her fingers. And although he wasn't hurting her, there was no way she could escape him. He placed one last kiss on her hand before slowly returning it to her lap. Then he turned to the waiter as if nothing had happened.

Their waiter, obviously a man of great self-possession and discretion, greeted them and offered Lucas the wine list. With both men treating the whole incident as if it were nothing, she relaxed and began to enjoy her evening. Once the wine was ordered and sampled, they debated what to order for dinner. In the end, she chose the salmon in dill sauce with baby potatoes and glazed carrots while Lucas chose the evening special, halibut in a cream sauce.

When the waiter was gone, Candy picked up her wineglass and took a sip of the rich red wine, rolling it around in her mouth before swallowing. "So," she began.

She could see the amusement in Lucas' eyes as he took a sip of his own wine. "So?" he returned her words to her.

"So tell me about yourself." She reminded herself that she was a publicist, for heaven's sake. She knew how to talk to people. The key was always asking the right questions.

"Not much to tell." His eyes warmed as he watched her. "I'd much rather talk about you."

"What about me?" Was it her, or was the restaurant suddenly very warm? Her dress felt confining suddenly as her breasts swelled under his appraisal. She could feel her nipples tightening and pushing against the fabric.

"What secret fantasies do you have?"

Candy could barely catch her breath. "I don't have any fantasies." Even as the words tumbled past her lips, she knew she was lying. Right now, she had a very detailed fantasy running through her head, one in which they were both naked and Lucas was fucking her senseless.

"Now that's a pity." He leaned closer to her, his eyes and words seducing her. "I, on the other hand, have many fantasies. Shall I share one?"

She nodded, unable to speak as heat flooded her veins.

"I have a fantasy of you sitting here having supper with me wearing no panties. In fact, I want you to take off your panties and give them to me. I want to see what you wore for me, smell your arousal and feel your heat." She couldn't believe what he was saying to her, but he wasn't anywhere near finished yet. "Then I want you to spread your legs wide so I can touch you and make sure you're ready for what I have planned later."

Lucas broke off suddenly and sat back in his chair as the waiter arrived at their table with their dinner. Candy couldn't even look at the man as he placed her plate in front of her, but she did manage to nod her thanks. The images that Lucas conjured up were almost more than she could handle. Her body felt as if it were on fire.

As the waiter walked away, Lucas leaned forward again, his eyes intent. "Will you give me my fantasy, Candy?"

She didn't recognize the sultry voice that answered him. "Yes."

The desire in his eyes flared higher, but he said nothing as he sat back in his chair, picked up his wineglass and took a swallow. When she hesitated, he arched an eyebrow at her as if daring her to chicken out.

More determined than ever, she grabbed her own glass and took a large gulp, needing the warmth of the wine in her stomach. Plunking the glass back down, she reached beneath the table. Taking care to make sure the linen tablecloth was covering her lap, she eased the fabric of her dress over her thighs.

She kept her eyes on Lucas as she pushed her hands higher, grasped the thin strings on the side of her hips and tugged. His face looked as if it had been carved from stone, and as she watched, she could see a muscle in the side of his jaw twitch. Mr. Squires wasn't as unaffected as he pretended to be.

That knowledge gave her the courage to lift herself as discreetly as she could and pull. Slipping her panties over her legs, she pushed them over her knees, letting them fall to her ankles. Carefully, she unhooked the garment from one foot before leaning down slightly so she could reach them with one hand. Quickly she pulled them off her other ankle and sat up straight once again.

"Give them to me." His voice was almost a guttural snarl as he held out his hand. Candy hesitated briefly before pressing the small wad of fabric into his palm. His fingers closed over it immediately.

As she watched, he raised his closed fist to his nose and sniffed before lowering it to his lap. "You smell delicious."

She felt her cheeks flush with heat. Trying to act nonchalant, she picked up her fork and took a bite of her salmon. After all, her dress and the tablecloth covered her completely so no one could see her. But that didn't seem to matter—she still felt totally exposed. It was embarrassing and arousing at the same time.

Lucas lowered his hand back to his lap and slowly opened it, rubbing his thumb across the silky material. Candy almost choked on her food, the action was so erotic. Finally, he slipped her panties into his jacket pocket and began to eat his own meal.

She'd just swallowed another mouthful when he casually leaned over and pushed the tablecloth away from her lap. "Are you wet for me?"

It was all she could do not to whimper aloud. "Yes." She could feel the cream seeping from her slit.

"Hmmm." He nodded as he eased his hand into her lap, sliding it under the fabric of her dress. His fingers sifted through her pubic hair and straight between her swollen labia. He didn't stop, slipping his finger into her core and pushing it deep.

Candy gasped and grabbed the edge of the table, her gaze sweeping around the room. Surely people knew what they were doing. But the tables around them were filled with people chatting and eating. Nobody was paying them the least amount of attention. It was instinct that made her try to close her legs, but Lucas pressed his thumb against her clit and rubbed it. "Keep your legs open, sugar. I want you soaked in your own juices by the time I take you back to my place for dessert."

The man was diabolical. Casually, he picked up his own fork and enjoyed a few mouthfuls of his meal. At the same time, with his other hand, he pushed another finger inside her to join the first, stretching her even more. "Lucas," she gasped, almost panting for breath. "Please." At this point she wasn't sure if she was asking him to stop or to give her more.

His eyes smoldered and the smile that turned up the edges of his mouth was wicked. "Oh, I aim to please you, Candy. And I will, over and over, all night long." But he withdrew his fingers, stroking over her sensitive skin one final time before resuming eating.

Candy focused on just trying to breathe. All around them people were laughing, talking and enjoying themselves. Lucas made casual conversation as he enjoyed his dinner. She managed to respond to several of his questions with what she hoped were intelligent responses, but for the most part she just nodded when appropriate. She could feel Lucas' eyes on her, watching her intently as she picked at the food on her plate.

Candy no longer had an appetite, at least not for food. Her needs were much more primal and basic. She couldn't stand the waiting. Placing her fork across her plate, she finally met his gaze. "I don't want to be here anymore."

Lucas frowned and glanced at her plate. She shuddered when he reached under the table and smoothed the skirt of her dress back over her legs. His frown deepened as he skimmed his thumb across her full bottom lip. "You hardly ate anything. I didn't mean to make you so uncomfortable you couldn't eat. This is all about pleasure and it seems I've made you feel anything but that." Leaning forward, he kissed her lips ever so gently. Her insides clenched tight. "I'm sorry, sugar."

Not feel any pleasure! Was the man insane? If she felt any more pleasure, she was going to have an orgasm right in the middle of the restaurant.

"I'll take you home." He raised his hand to signal to the waiter that he wanted the check.

She was stunned. Take her home? Reaching over, she grabbed his hand. His concerned gaze flew back to her. "I don't want to go home. I want dessert."

The frown on his face faded, replaced by a look of such fierce desire that Candy almost cried out. No man had ever looked at her with such naked need in his eyes. Her heart pounded in her chest as he nodded. "I want that too."

The waiter arrived with the bill and Lucas quickly took care of it, collected their coats and hustled her out of the restaurant and into the cold winter's night.

Chapter Nine

∞

The apartment door closed with a solid *thunk*. Although she wanted this to happen, Candy was nervous. The ride back to Lucas' place hadn't helped any, as both of them were quiet, wrapped up in their own thoughts. She jumped slightly when his hands clasped her shoulders.

"Relax, sugar. All I want to do is take your coat."

Now she felt like a complete idiot. Really, she had to get a hold of herself. She unbuttoned her long coat and allowed him to slip it off her shoulders. While he was hanging up her coat and removing his own, she looked around his home, interested to see what kind of a place he lived in. She knew it was a new apartment, built at the same time the store was being renovated two stories below, but she still hoped to learn more about the man beside her by his surroundings.

He'd flicked on the dim light in the foyer as soon as he'd opened the front door. She was surprised to see that it opened directly into a large room, which was shrouded in shadows.

"Would you like a tour?"

"I'd love one." She was undeniably curious about him and wasn't about to turn down the opportunity to see his home.

With his hand on the small of her back, he led her into the room. He stopped by a large support beam and touched a few switches. The room came alive, bathed in soft, muted lighting. Her breath caught in her throat as she stepped away from him, slowly turning in a circle as she tried to take in the magnificence of the room all at once. "This is gorgeous."

"Thank you." She could hear the pride in his voice. *No wonder*, she thought as she drank it all in.

The living area was painted a pale yellow, making it feel warm and inviting. The furniture was large and masculine. The sofa and two loveseats, covered in a rich chocolate brown fabric and grouped into an intimate seating area, looked incredibly comfortable. She could all too easily imagine the two of them curled up on a cold winter's evening. A huge oak cabinet with doors dominated the wall across from the sofa and she'd bet good money that his electronic equipment was housed there. A large, patterned area rug completed the sitting area.

"It really is lovely, Lucas."

"There's more." He wrapped his arm around her shoulders as they walked across the floor. Her shoes sounded loud against the hardwood. Floor-to-ceiling drapes in a chocolate brown that matched the sofa practically covered the far wall. Lucas left her standing in front of them and then tugged them open. The view was breathtaking.

"Oh, Lucas." She really didn't know what else to say. The lights of the city gleamed in the darkened skyline, making both the moment and the view seem magical and beautiful.

"Yeah, I know." He stood behind her, slipping his forearm around her waist and pulling her back against his hard body. "I put in a stairway that leads to the roof and I plan to put in a rooftop patio this summer so I can sit out on hot summer nights and enjoy it."

Candy just nodded. She could picture it in her mind, filled with plants and comfortable furniture and maybe even a barbecue. But she was surprised by just how sad it made her feel. By the time summer arrived, their business association would have ended, and she was realistic enough to know that the likelihood of her ever seeing the rooftop patio was remote at best.

She'd gone into this relationship with her eyes wide open and she didn't expect it to last. But that didn't mean she wouldn't enjoy every single moment that they had together.

Shaking off her melancholy, she turned in his arms and smiled at him. "Show me more."

His lips grazed the sensitive outer shell of her ear as he nuzzled her neck. "It gets better."

She didn't know how that was possible, but he turned her toward the dining area. A large wood trestle table sat in splendor atop a sumptuous area rug. Two huge wooden chairs dominated the ends while long, high-backed benches flanked the sides of the table. It looked very old and very solid, and Candy loved it on sight. She didn't realize she'd slipped out of Lucas' grasp and hurried forward to stroke her hands over the backs of the benches before reaching out to tentatively touch the table until he laughed. Like a guilty child, she pulled her hands away and tucked them behind her back.

"No, don't stop. Go ahead and touch it." Picking up her hands with his, he laid them back on the table, covering them with his own. "I did the exact same thing the first time I saw it. I knew it had to be mine."

She could certainly understand that feeling. She'd love to own something like this. It spoke of history and permanence and felt almost alive beneath her fingers. In the quiet of the room, she'd almost swear she could hear the sounds of people who'd sat at it over the past several hundred years. "It's amazing, Lucas." A large antique sideboard dominated another wall, its construction simple but the quality obvious.

"But there's still more."

She was loath to leave the table behind, but allowed him to lead her to the kitchen. A three-foot-wide granite countertop jutted out at a right angle from the wall separating the kitchen and dining area. About eight feet long, the countertop was actually at two different levels. The lower section had two comfortable stools pushed up next to it on the dining room side, making it a cozy breakfast nook. The slate floor was almost too beautiful to walk on and the appliances were obviously high quality and gleamed even though the light was dim. The amount of counter space was incredible, but it was surprisingly uncluttered, everything tucked neatly away in the vast expanse of oak cabinets that filled the area.

"Wow." She didn't know what else to say. Her own apartment had a postage stamp-sized kitchenette and she didn't cook very much, but this looked like a cook's dream straight out of a fancy decorating magazine.

Lucas chuckled as he tugged her into the kitchen behind him. Turning her, he backed her up against the lower section of the counter. His hands were warm as they stroked down the length of her bare back before coming to rest at her waist. Wrapping his fingers around her, he lifted her and perched her on the edge of the counter.

Candy licked her lips in anticipation as he leaned toward her. When their mouths met, she sighed deeply. This was what she wanted. What she needed. His hands came up to frame the sides of her face and she could feel the roughness of his fingers against her cheeks. The contrast was highly arousing. There was no doubt that Lucas was strong and tough, but his touch was always gentle, always restrained, as if he were well aware of his strength and didn't want to hurt her. It made her feel special and cherished, but it also made her want to strip away his control and have him be as wild for her as she was for him.

His tongue stroked along the seam of her lips and she parted them eagerly. But instead of plunging inside, he barely flicked the inside of her mouth before withdrawing again. Her hands gripped his shoulders for support, digging into the muscled expanse beneath his suit. Over and over, he tasted the inside of her lips but went no farther into her mouth. It was intoxicating and it was maddening.

Finally, unable to take it any longer, she sifted her fingers through his short hair, gripped his skull in her hands and pulled him tighter. Plunging her tongue into his mouth, she took what she wanted. She stroked his tongue with hers, reveling in his deep groan of pleasure as he responded to her. His tongue played with hers before he tilted her head for a better angle and began to plunder her mouth.

Heat rushed over her skin. Her clothing felt tight and confining and when his hands left her face to spread her thighs wide open, she eagerly complied, almost whimpering when he shoved the skirt of her dress high on her thighs and pushed his way between them. His hands slid over her hips, pulling her close, angling her so she could feel the outline of his erection pressing against her slit. She could feel his cock pulsing through the fabric of his pants and her sex throbbing heavily in response.

Lucas tore his mouth away from hers, gasping for breath. "Dessert. I promised you dessert." Stepping away, he removed his suit jacket and tossed it over the end of the counter. His tie quickly followed.

"Dessert." Her mind was muddled with desire. She wanted him now. No more waiting.

He smiled at her as he unbuttoned his shirt and tossed it aside. The large expanse of male flesh distracted her. She hadn't gotten a good look at it that day in the storage room. It had been too dark to see much. She knew his chest was impressive by feel alone, but that was nothing compared to actually seeing it. His shoulders looked about a yard wide and his chest was thick with muscle as it tapered down to his waist. She'd never seen an abdomen like his before outside a magazine. His abs were clearly defined and rock-hard.

Reaching out, she laid her hand on him. The muscles beneath her fingers jumped before hardening to steel and the heavy thump of his heart beat against her palm. Placing her other hand on his stomach, she slid it upward, enjoying the feel of the crisp line of hair that ran from the center of his chest downward and disappeared into his pants. The hair was blond but slightly darker than the hair on his head.

He captured her hands in his and kissed them before stepping back. "Much more of that and you won't get dessert." His voice was deep and husky with desire and she shifted uncomfortably as her body clenched with need.

Turning from her, he lit the candle under a small fondue pot that was set up on the upper part of the counter before he went to the refrigerator and pulled out several containers. While he was rummaging around the cupboards, setting up a few more things, she took the opportunity to study him further. The man was as fine from behind as he was from the front. The muscles in his back and arms rippled as he moved about the kitchen, and his butt was tight enough to make any woman drool.

But it was the tattoo that captured her interest the most. It wrapped around his entire upper left arm and seemed to be barbed wire, if she wasn't mistaken. It definitely enhanced his bad-boy image. "Was it painful to get?"

He placed a plate on the counter next to her. "Was what painful?"

"This." She traced her finger over the design.

"Not really. I was young and brave and stupid." He laughed, but the laughter didn't reach his eyes. Reaching over, he plucked something off the plate and held it to her lips. "Taste."

Candy was smart enough to know when someone wanted to change the subject, so she didn't mention the stylized Celtic knot tattoo on his left shoulder. Maybe he was embarrassed by it. After all, lots of people did things when they were younger that they wished they hadn't. She dismissed it from her mind as something smooth and cool touched her mouth.

Flicking her tongue out, she tasted chocolate and strawberry. Taking a bite, she savored it. Licking her lips, she opened her mouth for more and he obliged, feeding her the entire treat. "That was delicious."

Twisting around, she looked with keen interest at the plate he'd laid there. A cream-filled, bite-sized pastry sat next to what looked like another one of those amazing brownies. There was another chocolate-covered strawberry as well, but this one seemed to be dark chocolate on one side and white chocolate on the other. Candy moaned in anticipation.

Lucas chuckled as he picked up the pastry. It looked ridiculously tiny in his large fingers, but he held it firmly yet carefully as he raised it to her mouth. "Open." She automatically parted her lips and he popped it inside.

It occurred to her then that she trusted Lucas. Not just in a superficial way, but deep down all the way to her core. The way he handled the food said so much about him. He'd touch her the same way—firmly but gently, making sure she found satisfaction before he did. After all, up until now, she was the one who'd had all the pleasure. He was the one who'd been left unfulfilled. But not once had he mentioned it or complained. He seemed to get great enjoyment out of pleasing her and that made him a very unique man in her eyes.

Too many men were in it for their own pleasure without any thought of their partner. A quick wham, bam, thank you, ma'am. She'd been lucky not to have that experience often, but it had happened to her while she was in college. Not all men were as giving, caring if their partners found pleasure. As long as they came, they didn't care. She'd heard that complaint more than once from her few female friends, and the women's magazines were filled with letters griping about just that thing.

Theirs might not be a forever kind of relationship, but it would certainly be a mutually pleasurable one. And she'd never realized just how erotic it was to have a man feed her. The pastry practically melted in her mouth. The soft cream filling was slightly sweet and there was a touch of peppermint that made her mouth tingle.

Lucas bent forward and licked her lips. The single stroke made her nipples tighten as she imagined his rough tongue tasting them, touching them. As if he could read her mind, he cupped one of her breasts in his hand and stroked her distended nipple through the fabric. This time she moaned aloud, unable to swallow back the sound of her pleasure.

She almost cried out at the loss when his hand slid upward, cupping the back of her neck. His other hand joined the first and he slowly, methodically began to unhook her dress. When he was done, he lowered the bodice, exposing her breasts to his view.

"Now for the real dessert."

Lucas could feel his mouth water as he lowered the top of Candy's dress. Her breasts were large and full, tipped with pale pink nipples that were puckered into tight nubs. Nothing would stop him from having her this time. He had the entire night to discover all her secrets, to touch every inch of her velvety skin, to taste her and to savor her.

His cock, which was already rock-hard, pressed against the zipper in his pants, straining to be released. He'd take her, and soon. But first, he had to taste her.

His fingers looked large and rough against her creamy skin as he cradled her breasts. He plumped the soft mounds with his hands as he leaned forward and traced around the edge of one of her nipples with his tongue. Her fingers dug into his shoulders and he knew her short nails would leave a mark. Nuzzling his way to her other breast, he repeated his action.

He smiled when she gripped his short hair and tugged his mouth to the tip of her swollen nipple. He knew what she wanted and was more than willing to oblige. Stroking the hard nub of one breast with his thumb, he rasped his tongue across the other before capturing it with his mouth and sucking hard.

Candy moaned and arched her hips toward him, trying to get closer. With his free hand, he pushed beneath the skirt of her dress, shoving it high, until his fingers found her sex. Damn, she was so hot and wet it took all his control not to come in his pants. He found it incredibly exciting that she held nothing back, but gave herself completely.

His fingers traced the swollen, slick lips of her labia before slipping past her tight entrance and deep into her core. Using his thumb to stroke her clit, he thrust his fingers in and out of her cunt, her inner muscles clenching tight around them.

Candy was panting hard now as she hooked her legs around his waist and pumped her hips against him. He knew she was close by the desperate way she gripped his head, holding him to her. A bead of sweat rolled down his back as he continued to pleasure her. Capturing her nipple carefully between his teeth, he flicked the bud with his tongue. A high, keening noise escaped her lips as she tightened herself around him. He pushed his fingers as deep as they would go. Then she came.

He could feel the gush of liquid from her core, coating his hand. She cried out again, the sound music to his ears as he kept his fingers in motion to bring her the maximum pleasure. "Enough," she finally groaned. "I can't take any more." She seemed to melt in his arms, almost becoming boneless against him.

Carefully, he withdrew his fingers from her as he raised his head from her breast. She gave him a sleepy, sated smile as her eyes drifted shut. Lucas captured the lobe of her ear between his teeth, giving it a slight nip. Candy moaned, her neck arching to give him better access. "Now it's my turn," he whispered.

Chapter Ten

&

All remnants of sleepiness fled as Lucas growled in her ear. He sounded hungry for her, and even though moments before she'd been totally sated, she could feel her body already beginning to respond to him again. The hunger, so recently appeased, was returning. Once again, Lucas had given her pleasure. Now, she wanted to give it to him.

"Lift me off the counter." The sultry command sounded strange coming from her lips, but she knew what she wanted to do. Wrapping his hands around her waist, he lifted her down, holding her steady until she found her balance.

Placing her hands on his shoulders, she pushed him back a step and was surprised at how easily he moved. His chest and torso gleamed with a light sheen of sweat. He was so large and strong, there was no way for her to make him move if he didn't want to. His hands hung by his sides, his fingers clenched into fists. But she felt no fear, only anticipation.

Her dress hung around her hips, leaving her naked from the waist up, but Candy didn't feel embarrassed at all. Instead, she felt womanly and powerful. Lucas' eyes were like blue fire as he watched her, heating her skin until it was almost burning.

Giving her hips a quick shimmy, she loosened her dress, letting it drop around her ankles before stepping out of the folds. She stood there clad only in her thigh-high stockings and high-heeled shoes. With her hair still piled on top of her head, there was nothing to hinder his view of her.

"You are so beautiful." His words washed over her like a physical caress. Usually, she felt self-conscious about her ample curves, but not with Lucas. He made her feel sexy.

One step brought her directly in front of him and she placed her hands on his chest, kneading the muscles beneath her fingers. Leaning forward, she flicked his flat nipple with her tongue and smiled when his hand tangled in her hair, pulling her closer. Taking her time, she nibbled and licked her way down his washboard abdomen. He sucked in his stomach as she worked her way lower.

Standing straight again, she smiled at him and then lowered herself gracefully to her knees. "Candy," he groaned as she positioned herself in front of him, using her dress to cushion her knees. She made quick work of his button and zipper and his cock thrust out in front of him. The man did like to go commando!

Wrapping her hand around his length, she stroked him from base to tip. He was a big man in all ways and his erection was no exception. The head was like a large plum and as she watched, liquid seeped from the tip. Leaning forward, she licked at it with her tongue. She savored his taste—salty and warm.

"Take me in your mouth, sugar." His low command sent a shaft of desire pulsing through her core. She wanted to do everything with him. Anything he wanted.

Opening her mouth as wide as she could, she slid the head of his cock past her lips. She swirled her tongue around the tip before taking him deeper. As she learned his size and shape with her mouth and tongue, she kept her hands busy. She cupped and stroked his swollen testicles with one hand while continuing to stroke the base of his cock with the other.

"That's it, baby," he moaned. "Try to relax. You can take more." He flexed his hips forward and she found that she could indeed take him deeper.

His movements got jerkier as his hips pumped faster. She could feel his scrotum getting tighter to his body as his cock throbbed harder. He tangled his fingers in her hair, holding her steady as he thrust his cock deeper into her mouth. "I'm coming." He started to pull away, but she wouldn't let him. She wanted all of him, everything he had to give her.

He came hard and fast, his cum shooting down her throat. She gagged reflexively, but recovered quickly and swallowed. She kept sliding her hand up and down his length as he emptied himself. When he was done, she gave the head of his cock one final swipe with her tongue before sitting back on her heels. She felt as satisfied as a cat that had just eaten a bowl of cream.

Lucas reached out his hands and grasped the counter for support as he struggled for breath. While she was waiting for him to recover, she admired the view. He really was an exceptionally good-looking man. He was so hard everywhere, it gave her shivers just thinking about it.

Finally, he hitched his pants back up and zipped them closed. His eyes were unreadable as he stared down at her. "Thank you."

For the first time, she realized how vulnerable she was just sitting naked at his feet. "You're welcome." She struggled to stand and he was right there, practically lifting her back to her feet.

"Are you ready to continue dessert now that we've taken the edge off?" There was a glint in his eye that told her he was up to something, but she'd come too far to stop now.

Trying to seem sophisticated and nonchalant about standing around in the kitchen in the nude, she nodded. "Sure."

Before she could blink, he had her sitting back on the wide, low counter as he turned away and fiddled with the fondue pot he'd set up earlier. She supported herself with her hands as her legs dangled over the edge.

"Lie back."

She blinked at him, uncertain she'd heard him correctly. "Lie back?"

He didn't ask again. Reaching out, he gripped her by the shoulders and lowered her until her back was touching the wide countertop. It felt cold against her back and she arched upward. Lucas tweaked her nipple with her fingers, making it pucker even tighter. "Perfect."

He reached out and took the small pot off the flame, holding it carefully by the handle. "Chocolate is an aphrodisiac." Grabbing a small brush off the counter, he dipped it into the melted chocolate and began to paint around the edges of her nipples.

Candy sucked in her breath as the chocolate touched her skin. It wasn't hot enough to burn, but it was incredibly warm. The soft bristles of the brush stroking her flesh, combined with the heavenly smell, was incredibly arousing as Lucas continued to paint her breasts with the chocolate, leaving her nipples bare. "Lucas," she moaned as the side of his hand "accidentally" brushed her nipple as he worked.

"Shhh," he admonished. "I'm an artist at work. I put in this lower counter so I could sit if I was doing any intricate decorating work on cakes and such. But I can see now that it has many other possible functions." He stood back and admired her breasts before beginning to paint around her bellybutton. "Baking and decorating are art forms much like painting or sculpting, you know."

No, she didn't know. How could he expect her to think, let alone try to follow a conversation with that brush tickling her sensitive skin? But he didn't seem to expect her to answer as he kept on working. He set the fondue pot back of the counter before carefully placing a candied cherry in her navel.

Leaning over her, he licked both tips of her nipples until they were wet before dusting them with sugar. She looked down at herself unable to believe what he was doing. Her breasts were dark with the chocolate rimming her nipples while the tips themselves shimmered white in their sugar coating. She could just see the cherry peeking out of her navel.

"Almost done." Her eyes flew to his. "Then I get to eat." Her head went back to the counter with a *thunk* and she closed her eyes. Surely, he didn't mean what she thought he did.

Warm liquid oozed between her thighs and she forced her eyes open again. Lucas was holding a bottle of honey, letting a slow trickle of the golden substance dribble between her thighs. "Lucas!" she wailed as she tried to close her legs, but with him standing between them, it was impossible.

He placed the bottle back on the counter and leaned forward. "I've been dreaming of this dessert for days." Candy cried out as he took one of her sugared nipples into his mouth and sucked hard. He slowly and methodically ate his way outward, licking and sucking all the chocolate from around her breast. Then he did the same to the other one.

Candy writhed and moaned, feeling her cream seep from her core and slip between the globes of her behind. It mixed with the warm honey and the smell of both permeated the air.

He worked his way down her stomach, kissing and licking a path to her navel. She sucked in her stomach as he plucked the cherry out with his teeth. Holding it securely, he surged upward and kissed her, slipping the cherry past her lips before retreating once again.

The cherry was sweet and sticky in her mouth. She managed to chew it up and swallow it just before Lucas' mouth moved between her thighs. His tongue swiped up one side of her labia and down the other. She thumped her feet against the cupboards as she arched her hips toward him.

"Delicious," he murmured as he sucked her swollen lips. "Your essence adds the perfect flavor to the honey." Candy could only shiver as he sucked the hard nub of flesh at the apex of her sex.

She felt so empty and desperately wanted to feel him inside her. "Lucas," she wailed as he continued to taste her. "I want you. Now," she added forcefully, tugging at his hair.

His hair was standing up in small spikes and his lips glistened from the combination of honey and her cream as he straightened. A smear of chocolate covered his cheek. Reaching into his back pocket, he yanked out a condom. He had his pants open, his erection sheathed and was poised at her entrance before she could even blink.

He wrapped his hands around her upper thighs, holding them wide open as his cock probed at her opening. He inserted the blunt tip, stretching her. He was so big and it had been such a long time for her. But she wanted him, all of him. "More." She was unable to reach him with her hands, so she tilted her hips upward, trying to drive him deeper.

Lucas didn't hesitate. Holding her legs wide open, he thrust himself forward one inch at a time until his cock was buried to the hilt. Her inner muscles flexed and relaxed, accommodating his girth and length. It was almost uncomfortable, but it felt so good. But it wasn't enough. "Move, Lucas."

He pulled back until just the head was still inside her, then he surged forward. "Harder," she moaned.

"Tell me what you want," he ordered as he pulled back once again and held himself still, poised at her entrance.

She knew what he wanted. She wanted it too. "Fuck me, Lucas. Hard." She'd never said those words before, but found it surprisingly liberating.

It was if a dam broke within him, shattering his reserve. This time he plunged hard and deep. Over and over, he hammered into her. It was fierce and wild and elemental and she loved it. She'd never felt anything like it in her life.

He shifted, leaning over her and wrapping his arms beneath her, his hands cupping her shoulders as he held her steady for each thrust. She locked her ankles at the base of his spine, pushing him against her with every thrust. It was too much. It would never be enough.

Her fingers dug into his arms as she tilted back her head and screamed her release. Her body convulsed as he shoved his cock to the hilt one final time. She could feel him heaving over her, heard him shout as her own body tightened around him. She sucked air into her starving lungs, gasping for breath as she continued to spasm around him.

She managed to unlock her ankles and let her legs slide down his flanks as her arms fell back to the counter beside her. Lucas buried his head between her breasts and she could feel his lungs heaving against her as he struggled to catch his breath.

When he started to pull away, his face stuck to her for a moment before he managed to pull himself upright. The motion pushed him deeper inside her and her cunt pulsed again, making her moan as he carefully withdrew. She turned her head and watched him, her eyes mere slits as he removed the condom, dumped it in the garbage and grabbed a napkin to clean himself up. That done, he hitched up his pants again, yanking the zipper up but not bothering to button it.

It was only then that she realized just how sweaty and sticky she felt. "I need a shower." She tried to sit up, but it was too much trouble. She'd try again in a minute.

Lucas smiled at her. It was the first time she'd ever seen him *really* smile. It changed his whole face, making him look younger and more carefree. She felt absurdly pleased that she was the cause of it.

"You're a mess," he laughed as he eased her into a seated position.

Grumbling, she halfheartedly pushed him away. "You're no better."

He swept her into his arms, carrying her across the living room and toward a hallway. "I know. That's why we're both getting a shower."

Chapter Eleven

ဆာ

Almost two weeks later, Candy still blushed every time she remembered the night of their first "official" date. She still had a hard time looking at his kitchen counter without being swamped by the memories of what had happened there.

And the shower afterward! She waved her hand in front of her face to cool herself off. She'd never showered with a man before and the experience had been earthmoving, to say the least. Lucas had made sure to soap every inch of her body. "Just to make sure that all the chocolate and honey is gone," he'd assured her with a wicked gleam in his eye. Well, she'd gotten back at him for that, returning the favor.

They'd ended up tumbling, soaking wet, into his bed where he'd made love to her again. Honestly, the man was insatiable, but where he was concerned, so was she. They'd spent much of their free time together since then, as well as some work time. True to his word, Lucas had agreed to do some of the promotional events she wanted him to.

She'd set the first one up to coincide with the grand opening of the new Coffee Breaks. Lucas had been surprisingly charming to the reporter, answering her questions patiently. Candy had been pleased that the book would get a big write-up for the "Arts" section of the Sunday edition of paper, but she'd also been uncomfortably jealous of the easy way he'd interacted with the reporter.

At least she had been until Lucas dragged her back into the kitchen with him. There he'd pinned her up against the wall, kissed her senseless and in a growl reminiscent of a cranky bear had told her that he was only putting up with this publicity nonsense because of her and that she darn well owed him for it. She'd been thrilled to her toes and had eagerly *shown* her thanks later that night.

It had become a game between them from that moment onward and for every promotional event he did for the book, he teasingly told her that he expected something from her in return. Candy twirled in her chair and laughed as she remembered what had happened after he'd given an in-depth interview to a local interest magazine. They'd barely made it through his front door before he'd taken her up against the wall. It had been hard and fast and incredibly erotic.

She licked her lips in anticipation over what might happen after his appearance on a local cable talk show tomorrow afternoon. Her pussy contracted and her nipples tightened, making her groan. The man was turning her into a sex fiend. She shook her head and turned her chair back to face her desk. But it was more than that. Much more.

They'd spent a lot of time together over the past few weeks and the more time she spent with Lucas, the more she liked him. Liked him! Who was she kidding—she was in love with the man. Groaning, she lowered her head to her desk. She hadn't meant for it to happen. Hadn't even known that it could happen so fast. But it had and she had to deal with it.

Raising her head, she rubbed her temples and sighed. The man was playing havoc with her emotional well-being. Like someone on a roller coaster, her emotions kept swinging back and forth from happy to sad to frustrated. But she was an adult and had gone into this affair with her eyes wide open. She couldn't cry foul and change the rules now just because she had to go and get all emotional.

But it was Lucas' fault. Beneath that gruff, hard exterior lurked a man with a large heart. She saw it in the way he interacted with his employees, whom he treated more like an extended family than people he paid to work for him. She saw it in the obvious affection and caring he had for Katie and her husband.

The first time she'd seen Katie again after the storage closet incident had been initially somewhat awkward. They'd run into each other at the official opening of Coffee Breaks and it had taken all Candy's determination not to slink away from the other woman. But Katie had smiled and simply asked, "Should I call you Candace or Candy?"

That had made her laugh. "Since nobody I know will call me Candace, I've given up on the idea. So, call me Candy."

Katie had made no mention of finding them alone in the storage closet or about what they'd obviously been doing in there. But she had issued a subtle warning, telling Candy how special Lucas was and how those who knew him wouldn't like to see him get hurt.

She pressed her hand over her stomach, trying to settle her jumbled nerves. As if she would hurt him. She was more likely to be the one to bear the scars from this relationship, as she was in far over her head. It had happened so quickly, she hadn't had time to stop it.

But she wasn't sure she would have stopped it even if she could have. Spending time with Lucas was soothing her ravaged ego. She hadn't been truly aware of just how badly it had been damaged by her breakup with Gary. Lucas made her feel sexy and womanly and very beautiful.

But it was much more than that. He filled empty spaces within her that she hadn't even realized were there. To their mutual delight, they'd discovered that they had a lot more in common then either one of them had anticipated.

They were both homebodies and loved to curl up in the evenings and watch movies. Lucas had taken to cooking them dinner almost every evening and she loved to work alongside him in the kitchen, helping him prepare their meal. They shared long discussions about everything from politics to books to views on life in general. She not only found him fascinating, but also loved the intent way that he always listened to what she had to say and treated her opinions with respect, even if he didn't always agree with her.

It was a new experience for her. In previous relationships, she'd been guilty of hiding her true thoughts, not wanting to rock the boat or make trouble, but with Lucas she didn't feel that restraint. Because she knew this wasn't a forever kind of relationship going into it, she hadn't held back at all. In fact, with Lucas, she was more herself than she'd ever been with any other man in her entire life. It was liberating and really brought home to her just what had been wrong in earlier relationships.

Drawing herself up straighter in her chair, she renewed her determination to enjoy her time with Lucas no matter how long it lasted. She wouldn't allow her unrealistic expectations and her emotions ruin it. She would tuck her love away in her heart and in years to come she would always have the memories of this special time together. Her heart ached in her chest, but she ignored it. Yes, it was easier said than done, but she was determined.

Sexually, there was no doubt that they were compatible. Lucas seemed to know just how to touch her to bring her the most satisfaction. He'd spent hours stroking her skin, leisurely pleasuring her. At times he could be as playful as a large cat, tumbling her around his huge bed or hauling her onto the dining room table for a quickie. But other times, he would be serious and intense as he brought her to peak after peak of pleasure until she couldn't bear it anymore.

He challenged her to try new things, encouraged her to take what she wanted and to not be afraid of her sexuality. But it was the times after sex that had changed her the most.

She'd had a live-in lover before, but sleeping with Gary had been nothing like sleeping with Lucas. Always before, she turned away, needing her own space. But Lucas had never allowed it. His favorite position seemed to be spooning up behind her with her bottom snuggled against his groin and her head tucked under his chin. With his forearm locked just under her breasts, he kept her close with him throughout the night. Either that or she'd wake up and find herself sprawled across him, using him for a mattress. Both of them liked that position, as Lucas always woke hard and ready for her. She'd almost been late to work twice this week because of an early morning quickie.

Her breath was coming faster and her nipples were puckered against her bra, making them ache. She straightened her jacket and moaned as the fabric rubbed against her breasts. Her whole body clenched and she gritted her teeth in frustration. She had to stop thinking about Lucas. Deliberately, she changed her thoughts, but all these musings about relationships brought her mother to mind.

Tapping her fingers on her desk, she stared at her phone. She'd been avoiding her mother for quite some time now — ever since the night she'd gotten the unexpected phone call from Justin. Her mother had left several messages on her machine, but for once in her life, Candy had ignored them. She'd needed the time to get over her feelings of betrayal.

But it had gotten to the point where she was just being childish and petty and she didn't like that image of herself. The time had come to talk to her mother. Grabbing her phone, she dialed her mother's number before she could talk herself out of it. She held her breath, half hoping her mother wasn't home and she could just leave a message.

"Hello." Candy slowly released her pent-up breath when she heard her mother's voice on the other end of the line.

"Hi, Mom." Leaning forward, she propped her elbows on her desk and eyed her empty coffee cup longingly. She should have gotten herself some coffee first.

"Candy!" There was no mistaking the delight in her mother's voice, which made her feel all the worse. "Are you all right, dear? I've been trying to reach you for days."

She squashed the feelings of guilt that welled up inside her, telling herself she'd had every right to take some time to think before calling her mother. But it didn't quite work. "I know, Mom. I'm sorry, but I've been busy."

"As long as there's nothing wrong."

Taking the opening, she plunged onward. "But there is something wrong. Justin called me."

There was silence on the other end and then her mother sighed. "Oh?"

Anger stirred inside her as she realized her mother wasn't going to say anything else. "He told me he was talking to you first. Why didn't you tell me you'd heard from him?"

"That's the reason, Candy. Listen to yourself. You're so angry with him instead of just being glad to hear from him."

"See, that's what I don't understand, Mom." Righteous indignation filled her. "It's just like with Dad. He'd disappear for days, weeks or months and you'd just forgive him and take him back. Now it's the same thing with Justin, but he's been gone years, not months. Years!" Her temples started to throb as the beginnings of a tension headache descended on her.

"What I did with your father is my business," her mother snapped back.

"But it was my life too," she retorted. "How do you think it felt to have a convicted felon as a father? That was bad enough, but you kept taking him back every time he got out of prison."

"Right or wrong, it was my choice, Candy. And I did my best to be a good mother."

Usually she dropped the subject, feeling guilty whenever she questioned her mother, but not this time. "Yes, you did your best, but it was still hard on your kids and that's something you've never acknowledged. I think that's why it was so easy for Justin to fall into the same pattern."

"I'm not responsible for Justin's actions." Her mother's voice was getting shriller and more defensive with every word she spoke.

Candy rubbed her temples, realizing this was futile. Her mother was who she was, and as she said, had made her own choices. She'd done the best she could, but like all humans, she had her shortcomings. It was a slight revelation to Candy to realize that her anger stemmed from the fact that she'd wished her mother had been perfect and more of the kind of mother she'd wanted growing up.

They'd never agree on some issues, Justin and her father being two of them, but it was time for Candy to let them go and move on. A weight lifted off her shoulders as she dropped her burden of guilt. She'd done her best, just as her mother had done, so maybe it was time to forge a new relationship, based on the here and now instead of the past.

"What did Justin have to say?" She was curious to see if he'd said more to their mother than to her.

"Just that he wanted to see me and to see you, of course."

"You've seen him?" She knew the answer even before she'd asked the question. Candy could tell from the tone of her mother's voice that she'd seen him.

"Yes. He's been over for supper several times."

Candy swallowed the lump of emotion that welled up from deep within her. "How—" She broke off, cleared her throat and tried again. "How does he look?"

"He looks good. The years haven't been easy ones, but he looks good." Her mother paused. "He looks a lot like your father."

She rubbed her throbbing temples and scrunched her eyes tight to hold back the tears. "Yeah, well, Dad always was a good-looking son of a—"

"Candy!"

"I was going to say, gun, Mom." That was the one thing that James Logan had had going for him. He'd definitely been a handsome and charming devil. "Did Justin say anything else, like how long he was staying or what he's been doing?"

"Not really. He mostly asked about me and my life." She paused. "And you, honey. He asked a lot of questions about you. I wish you'd agree to see him. I know it would mean a lot to him."

"Did he ask you to plead his case?" That was definitely something her father would have done.

"No. He actually did the opposite and asked me not to say anything at all to you." She could hear her mother's growing impatience. "But I still think you should see him, Candy. At least once."

"I'm still thinking about it, Mom."

"I didn't think you'd be that cold and unforgiving to your brother."

The criticism hit Candy hard. "Well, he didn't seem to care how I felt all these years he's been away. Why should I care about his feelings now? He's a stranger to me."

"He's your brother." Those three simple words broke Candy's heart because although she knew they were true, she felt as if she'd lost her brother years ago. He hadn't died, but it was as if he had, because in all the ways that truly counted, he had been dead to her all these years. But what had hurt the most was that he could have been dead in truth and she might never have known.

"I said I was thinking about it and that's the best I can do right now." It was time to change the subject. "Did you get the money I deposited in your account last week?"

"Yes, I did. You know I really appreciate it, Candy, but you don't have to give me money anymore. I'm getting more hours over at the market."

But Candy could hear the weariness in her mother's voice. For more than thirty years, her mother had worked mostly minimum-wage jobs. Married and pregnant young, she'd barely finished high school and had no other training. Her mother was a hard worker and never complained, but she'd made sure that Candy had stayed in school. They hadn't had much while she'd been growing up, but they'd always had food and a roof over their heads. And for that alone, she figured she owed her mother.

"I don't mind, Mom. I just wish it could be more."

"It's more than enough, Candy."

In spite of their many differences, Candy didn't doubt that her mother loved her. In the end, that was what mattered the most. They might never have a really close relationship, but they'd always have that between them.

"Talk to your brother, Candy, just in case you never get the opportunity to do it again." She softened her voice. "You don't want to have to live with regrets." Back to her brisk self again, she hurried on. "I have to go or I'll be late for my shift at the market."

"Bye, Mom." She barely heard her mother tell her goodbye before the line went dead. It was the buzzing in her ear that finally broke her out of her thoughts and she slowly hung up her phone.

Regrets. That's what it all boiled down to, and Candy finally began to understand why her mother had taken her father back all those times. She hadn't wanted to live with the regrets she might have had if she didn't. Candy didn't necessarily agree with her mother, but she felt she did understand her a little better.

After all, she didn't want to have regrets either. That's why she was willing to let her relationship with Lucas run its course. But, unlike her father, Lucas wasn't lying to her and pretending to be something he wasn't. And therein lay the big difference for Candy. It was the lies her father had told over the years, always promising that things would be different and that he wasn't really a criminal which had hurt the most. She much preferred Lucas' bluntness to pretty lies. Lucas wanted her sexually, plus he respected her and genuinely liked her. And that was good enough for her.

As for Justin, well, she'd just have to think about that a little longer. She went back to work, but her mother's words kept ringing in her ears.

The phone rang again and she pushed her personal problems to the back of her mind. "Good morning, Candy Logan's office."

"Good morning, sugar."

His low voice slid over her like hot caramel over an ice cream sundae and just like that, she felt better, happier. "And what can I do for you, Mr. Squires?"

He laughed, the sensual sound skittering across her skin, making goose bumps rise on her arms. "I can think of several things at the moment."

"Lucas." His name came out as part admonishment, part moan as several fantasies of her own flitted through her brain.

"You shouldn't ask me such provocative questions if you don't want me to answer them." She could hear voices in the background and knew he was calling from work. "But that's not why I called."

Candy squirmed in her seat, trying to ignore her growing arousal. "Why did you call?"

"Two things. First, are you coming over for dinner tonight?"

"Do you want me to?" She wondered if he wasn't beginning to get tired of having her around every single evening.

"I wouldn't have asked if I didn't," his rough voice growled over the phone.

"I'd love to come over for dinner. Should I bring anything?"

"Just yourself, sugar."

"Okay." She glanced at her watch, knowing she had to cut this short. "What was the second thing?"

"Check your purse. I slipped a little something inside this morning before you left." She heard someone calling him in the distance. "I've gotta run, but I'll see you tonight." The phone clicked in her ear and she pulled it back and looked at it. What was it with people hanging up on her this morning?

Curious now, she opened her bottom desk drawer and dragged out her large leather handbag. She hadn't really looked in it this morning, she'd been in such a hurry when she'd left his place to get home and change in time to get to work. Thankfully, Lucas was always up at the crack of dawn, but still, she'd barely had enough time. She didn't know how much longer she could keep that up, but for now, she was managing. And the payoff of spending all night snuggled up in bed with Lucas was reward enough for any minor inconveniences.

Unzipping her purse, she rummaged around inside and found the small plastic container that had worked its way to the bottom. Prying off the lid, she peered inside. Nestled on a napkin was a masterpiece of layers of light, fluffy pastry separated by a cream and chocolate filling. A light drizzle of chocolate decorated the top layer.

Candy groaned even as she carefully plucked the treat from the container and laid it on the lid. If she wasn't careful, she was going to put on a ton of weight. Lucas did seem to enjoy feeding her. Now she definitely needed coffee.

Glancing at her closed office door, she decided she wasn't taking any chances. Stowing her purse back in the bottom drawer, she yanked open the top one and shoved some papers aside. When she had enough room, she placed the pastry and the container inside and pushed the drawer closed.

She sniffed the air carefully and decided it was probably safe. Ever since word of the brownies had gotten out, many of Candy's coworkers had started stopping by unannounced to check and see if she'd gotten any more of them. Unfortunately, Missy had been quite vocal in her praise of them and some of the other women in the office were jealous that they hadn't gotten any.

But Candy only had one pastry and she wasn't sharing.

The phone rang again just as she reached for her mug. Casting a longing stare at her empty mug, she sighed as she picked up the receiver. "Candy Logan's office."

"Ms. Logan, this is Barbara Bates from Jasper Publishing in New York."

Candy straightened in her chair. "Yes, Ms. Bates. What can I do for you?" Her curiosity was piqued. It wasn't every day she got a call from a big New York City publisher. Okay, so she'd never had one before. This was her first.

The other woman laughed. "Maybe we can help each other. As you may or may not know, we recently signed a former writer of TK Publishing, Karissa Fields."

"That's wonderful. I always knew that Karissa would make it big."

"Well, Karissa speaks very highly of you as well. In fact, according to Karissa, you're very good at what you do, Ms. Logan." The other woman paused briefly before continuing. "We have a position opening up in our publicity department and would like to interview you if you're interested."

Candy had to close her mouth, which had dropped open. "Uh, this is quite a surprise."

Ms. Bates laughed again. "I'm sure it must be. But we'd really like you to think about it. I've chatted with other authors you've worked with and they all speak very highly of you. I know that you were officially the assistant on these earlier jobs, but according to everyone I talked to, there was really no doubt in anyone's mind who was really doing the work."

"I'm very flattered by your offer," Candy began, not really sure how to respond. On one hand, it was a fantastic offer. But, on the other, it meant packing up and moving away from her friends and family and a job that she was comfortable in. It also meant leaving Lucas.

"You don't have to say yes or no right now. I realize this is very sudden and you probably want to think about it," Ms.

Bates continued briskly. "Why don't I give you my number? Take a week and think about it, then give me a call."

Candy yanked a notepad in front of her and jotted down the phone number. Her mouth dropped open again when the other woman listed the beginning salary. "I'll definitely give your offer some thought." She tossed her pen down on top of her desk. "And thank you, Ms. Bates, for the offer. It really is quite generous."

"I hope to hear from you soon, Ms. Logan."

Candy was sure she said goodbye to the other woman, but she wasn't exactly sure what else she might have said. Her mind was spinning with the possibilities. New York City, a big publishing company and more money than she had ever made in her life.

She pulled open her desk drawer to look for her calendar and came face-to-face with the exquisite pastry that Lucas had made for her. She couldn't believe she'd actually forgotten about it.

Coffee and sustenance first. Then she'd think about the job offer.

Picking up her mug, she walked to the door, but glanced back at her desk. She thought about taking the pastry with her, but didn't want to risk anyone smelling the chocolate or cream. Easing her door open, she slipped out, closing it behind her. She was smiling as she hurried to the break room for a refill.

Chapter Twelve

೮ი

Lucas didn't want to be here. For a man who valued his privacy, this promotional stuff was taking its toll on his good humor. He had no idea why people wanted to know about his private life. It was called private for a reason. So far, with the print interviews he'd been able to steer the conversation back to the book, focusing on Coffee Breaks, the recipes themselves and Katie's artwork.

He wasn't looking forward to this afternoon at all. Yes, it was only a local cable show, but it was still television and it was taped in front of a live audience. He'd only agreed to do it when the host of the show, Angela Murray, had consented to keep her questions confined to the upcoming release of the book and the recent reopening of Coffee Breaks. It was only a short seven-minute segment, and Lucas was her first guest of the day, so he was hoping it would be over quickly.

Much like yanking off a bandage fast to avoid pain, Lucas wanted this over and done with. He doubted Candy would be pleased by the analogy, but he didn't care. He was only doing this because it made her happy. He couldn't care less about publicity for the book. As far as he was concerned, he'd done his part just in helping Katie write the damned thing.

He stepped back out of the way as a man carrying what looked like a large microphone of some kind hurried past him. Leaning back against the wall, he amused himself by watching Candy work. The woman loved her job, no doubt about it, and she was incredibly good at it. She'd obviously had dealings with the people here at the television station before and called many people by name.

She'd even swooped by Coffee Breaks first and bought several large boxloads of goodies to bring along for the staff and the audience. Lucas was still ticked off that she'd insisted on paying for it. When he protested, she'd just laughed and said it came out of her promotional budget. It was good business to take along samples for people to taste. He still wasn't thrilled with the idea of her paying, but he'd satisfied himself by adding extras to the boxes when she wasn't looking.

He watched her as she talked with the host of the show. *Afternoon with Angela* was a popular local production, and it was plain to see that Angela liked to be in charge of every detail. She blithely ordered people around, unmindful and uncaring of the fact that everyone was already busy. He'd seen her yelling at her makeup artist earlier when she'd thought there was no one else around. He wasn't impressed.

She was such a contrast standing next to Candy. Angela was polished from head to foot in a red power suit that hugged her tall, lithe body. Her short black hair was perfectly styled and her makeup impeccable. Candy, on the other hand, was wearing another one of her bland, beige suits that was about two sizes to big. Several strands of hair had already escaped from the big silver clip that anchored it in an intricate twist. And whatever lipstick she'd put on earlier, she'd long since chewed off. Lucas wanted to get her to himself for a few minutes and muss her up even more.

As soon as this was over, he was going to take her back to his place for the rest of the afternoon. Maybe cook her something special for supper. He enjoyed cooking for Candy. She took such pleasure in whatever he fed her, enjoying every single bite. His body tightened painfully. Watching her eat was as good as watching most women in the throes of an orgasm. The way she delicately closed her mouth around the fork and slid the food into her mouth gave a man ideas. And then she'd close her eyes as she chewed, making little mewling noises of enjoyment as she savored it.

Lucas shook himself. God, he was getting turned on just thinking about her eating. He had it bad. He'd been right when he'd told T. S. that Candy was trouble. Once again, Angela turned away from Candy as she was trying to talk to the show's host. Lucas barely resisted the urge to go over and grab Candy's hand and drag her out of here. It was hard to watch the other woman treat her with such a visible lack of respect.

But Candy had class and tenacity and waited patiently, bringing Angela's attention back to her time and again until she'd finished whatever it was she was saying to her. Finally, Angela nodded briskly, said a few words and then walked away as her producer informed her it was almost time to begin.

Candy turned and made her way back toward him, being careful to step over all the cables running across the floor. Once again, she was wearing a pair of those impractical high heels, but they did make her legs look fantastic. He shifted as his cock began to stir again.

By the time she reached him, she was smiling. "Everything is settled. You'll be first and we can leave as soon as your segment is taped."

"Good."

She placed her hand on the arm. He'd refused to wear a suit, thinking he'd have a fight on his hands. But once again, she'd surprised him, laughing and telling him to wear whatever he was comfortable in. He'd opted for jeans, boots and a white shirt. "I know you didn't want to do this, but it will be over before you know it."

"You owe me for this," he reminded her, loving the way her eyes darkened with desire.

"Hmm, what do you have in mind?" She squeezed his arm gently. Anyone looking at them would just see a publicist calming her client. Only he could see the fire in her eyes, feel the subtle tension in her body.

"We go back to my place as soon as we're finished here."

"I'd planned to go back to work." She paused and coyly peeked up at him from under her long, brown eyelashes. "But I could probably be persuaded."

"Time, people!" The shout startled them both and Candy dropped her hand and took a step back. He missed the contact immediately.

A harried-looking man with a clipboard came running up to them. "Okay," he whispered. "We're starting now and I'll let you know when to walk on. You'll shake hands, sit, and before you know it, you'll be done."

Lucas nodded as a cheerful voice came over the loudspeaker welcoming everyone to another taping of *Afternoon with Angela*. A short musical ditty followed as Angela walked out on stage, looking poised and confident as she waved at the studio audience before making her way to sit behind her desk.

"Good afternoon, everyone, and welcome to the show. We've got an exciting lineup today. Margaret Baxter will be here later to talk about an upcoming local hospital fundraiser and we'll also be speaking with Jason Diamond, the president of a local environmental group that is concerned about the City Council rezoning law that was just passed."

She smiled and sat forward in her chair. "But first, I've got a treat for you. Lucas Squires, the owner of Coffee Breaks, a popular local coffee shop, has recently written a brand-new cookbook that is due to launch in two weeks. And he's here today to talk to us. Please help me welcome my first guest today, Lucas Squires."

The audience began to applaud and the man with the clipboard motioned him forward. Lucas glanced at Candy and she smiled at him, giving him a quick thumbs-up. Taking a deep breath, he forced himself to walk across the stage, reminding himself that he'd done much harder things in his life.

He shook Angela's hand and waited until she was seated before taking his own seat next to her desk. He nodded at the audience as he tried to relax.

"Welcome to the show, Lucas." He nodded at her and she continued on when it became apparent he wasn't going to add anything to her opening gambit. "Tell us about the book. What made you decide to write a cookbook?"

"I didn't." He took another breath, knowing he had to do some talking or these seven minutes were going to last forever. "It was actually Katie's idea. She's the artist whose work is featured in the book." He was warming to the topic now. It was easy to talk about Katie.

"That would be Katie Benjamin," Angela prompted.

Lucas chuckled. "Sorry about that. I tend to think everybody knows Katie." The audience laughed along with him and he relaxed slightly. "She's an amazing artist and her work for the book is among her best to date. Many of the original paintings used in the book are available for sale at the Stacey Stoner Gallery. I even bought a couple of them for Coffee Breaks. I figured I better buy them while I could still afford them." Once again, the audience laughed.

"Obviously, you're a big fan of her work." He caught an edge to Angela's voice and turned toward her. "But how did a man like yourself come to create such wonderful recipes?"

Lucas shrugged. "Years of baking and trying different things in the coffee shop. I'd experiment with recipes, changing ingredients, and eventually created quite a few original ones."

"That's not quite what I meant." Her eyes glittered in the harsh studio lights and Lucas felt his guts twist. Whatever was coming wasn't going to be good. "I meant," she paused and leaned toward him. "How do you go from convicted felon to cookie baker?" A huge gasp rose from the audience.

Stunned by the unexpected attack, Lucas sat there and stared at Angela as she smiled triumphantly. "After all, you did go to prison for assaulting a man." She turned to the audience. "His own father, in fact." The audience was murmuring loudly now. "Tell us, Lucas, how does a man with such a violent and criminal history come to write a cookbook?"

Lucas slowly came to his feet. Angela shrank back dramatically as if expecting him to become violent. He shook his head at her theatrics, turned and walked off the stage. The audience's chatter became louder, the noise casting him back in time to that courtroom years ago, it was so similar. He almost expected to hear the wooden pounding of the judge's gavel as he demanded order in the court.

He could hear Angela talking in the background, but he paid no attention to what she was saying. Right now all he wanted to do was grab Candy and leave. He looked neither right nor left but forged a direct path toward her.

Her face was deathly pale as she stared up at him, her beautiful brown eyes filled with horror. One of her hands covered her mouth and the other one had a death grip on her purse. He wanted to wrap his arms around her and hug her tight, but first he had to get them out of there so they could talk. "Come on. Let's go."

He put out his hand, but she shrank away from him. Lucas felt as if someone had plunged a dagger in his heart. "Is it true?" Her voice shook so hard that he could barely understand it.

"We'll talk when we get home." He had to get out of here. His gut was telling him to grab her and run from this place.

"Is it true?" Her voice was stronger now.

The betrayal Lucas felt was so great he felt something inside him dying. If Candy cared anything at all for him, she'd be furious about this unexpected attack and want to talk to him. Hell, he'd even hoped she'd wrap her arms around him and tell him it didn't matter. That might be unrealistic, but at this point he didn't care. He was hurting and it didn't seem to matter a damn to her. He was the same man he was this morning. The same man she'd slept with and shared herself with the past few weeks. But that didn't seem to count for much of anything at this moment.

He felt a numbness in the pit of his stomach, growing with each second that he stared at her until it enveloped him completely.

"Yes." He offered no other explanation, but turned and walked away, his heart growing colder with every step.

Candy couldn't believe Lucas was just walking away from her. The sound of that one stark word, "Yes", was still ringing in her ears. She wanted to run after him, to yell at him not to walk away and leave her here alone. She wanted him to haul her into his arms and tell her it was all a lie. But she did neither as she absorbed the impact of that one word. *Yes*.

The man she loved was an ex-con. Oh, God. The irony was almost too much to bear and she jammed her hand over her mouth to keep in the hysterical laughter that threatened. Obviously, she wasn't as different from her mother as she had thought.

The producer was tugging on her arm, pulling her back to reality. Lucas might have walked out, but his reputation and her career were still at stake. That reality sent her plummeting back to earth in a hurry. Candy felt a calm professionalism settle over her, burying her emotions beneath it.

It was her turn to attack.

The atmosphere was surreal. The world continued to function as if nothing extraordinary had taken place. They'd hurriedly announced the next guest and Angela was sitting at her desk, acting as if nothing had even happened. Everything around Candy came into sharper focus as she used her anger to anchor herself.

Going on the offensive, she narrowed her eyes at the man. "If you air one minute of that segment, my company will sue you. I've got a written document, signed by your host, agreeing to the topics to be discussed and I can guarantee you that that topic wasn't on the list." Right now, she was thankful and grateful that Lucas had been adamant about getting it in writing. It gave her a heck of a bargaining chip.

The producer was sweating heavily now, and he swiped his hand across his forehead. "But Angela…"

Candy held up her hand, cutting him off. "Ms. Murray's signature is on that document, so I suggest you go remind her of that fact during the next break. I also advise you to tell her that, unless she wants to find herself in court, she will immediately tell the audience she was mistaken and issue a formal public apology. Then I might consider not suing her and the station. I'll have to talk to Mr. Squires first and see what his thoughts on this matter are."

Several other executives had gathered around and heard the tail end of her tirade. The tension was palpable and they descended upon Angela during the break. She spoke in low, angry tones at first, but she quickly paled and glanced over toward where Candy was standing. Candy crossed her arms and glared back at her. Good, they'd warned Angela she was in danger of being sued, and Candy hoped she was also smart enough to realize that the station would drop her like a hot rock if she became a liability.

It was a much more subdued Angela Murray who took the stage to tape the final segment of her show. But in typical Angela form, she apologized in one breath and in the next was blaming her research department for giving her information that wasn't necessarily factual. But it was enough for now. Candy had no idea how much damage this might have done to Lucas' reputation, but she'd done her best to repair it.

Gathering her belongings, she left the station, telling the manager she'd be in touch. It would do them good to worry for a few days. The big metal door slammed shut behind her. There was a definite finality to the sound that made her shiver.

She stood there in the cold with the wind whipping around her, not really knowing where to go. She couldn't go back and face work and Lucas' apartment was no longer an option. Feeling alone and lost, she stumbled her way down the street. The bright lights of a bookstore beckoned her and she hurried toward its warmth.

Chapter Thirteen

ଛ୬

Candy wrapped her hands around the paper cup filled with coffee. She'd bought it more for the warmth than anything else. It gave her a legitimate excuse to sit here in the quiet corner of the bookstore café and stare out the window. Her fingers flexed around the cup as her mind tried to assimilate everything that had just happened.

Letting go of her coffee, she buried her face in her hands and took a deep breath as emotion threatened to overwhelm her.

"Candy?"

The voice was a familiar one, but one that she hadn't heard in more than a year. Lifting her head, she stared into the face of her ex-boyfriend, Gary Baker. Could this day get any worse?

"Are you okay?"

He frowned and she could see the obvious concern on his face. It almost made her laugh. Too bad he hadn't been as concerned about her when they'd been going together. Maybe then he wouldn't have cheated on her. What was it about her and men? She seemed to have some innate talent that made her pick ones that were all wrong for her.

She realized that he was really starting to look worried, so she pulled herself together. "Yeah, I'm fine." She resisted the urge to just leave her coffee and beat a retreat for the exit. She took the opportunity to really examine Gary. He was still as handsome as ever with his wavy brown hair and light brown eyes. Tall and well built, he turned women's heads wherever he went.

And that, she remembered vividly, had been part of the problem. But strangely enough, she no longer felt anything when she looked at him. He was more of a vague memory from the past. It occurred to her in a moment of great clarity that she really hadn't loved him. Not in the way she should have. Not in the way that she loved Lucas.

Suddenly she wanted to ask him the question that had been burning in her gut for more than a year. "It's probably pretty late for me to even ask you this, but I guess I have to know. Why did you cheat on me, Gary?"

She caught a fleeting glimpse of pain cross his face before it disappeared. "May I?" He motioned to the chair and waited until she nodded. Pulling out the seat, he settled himself into it and laid his coffee cup on the table in front of him. He rubbed his hand along his jaw as he stared at her. As if coming to some internal decision, he reached out and took her hand in his. "I never cheated on you."

His words stunned her. "Of course you did," she muttered. "All those late nights you said you were working, but you weren't there when I called your office. Then there was the fact that you were so secretive." She tried to tug her hand away, but he stubbornly held on. "Of course you were cheating," she reiterated more strongly this time. "What else could it have been?"

"Ah." He smiled gently as he rubbed his thumb across the top of her hand. "Now that's the real question, and the one you should have asked back then." Releasing her hand, he sighed. "But you didn't trust me. In fact, I always felt from the very moment we started dating that you were waiting for me to mess up somehow, to disappoint you. I thought you'd get over it with time." He shook his head. "But obviously I was mistaken."

"I don't think that wanting a partner to be faithful is asking too much." She wasn't the bad guy in their relationship. But his words cause a huge lump in the pit of her stomach.

"No, it's not," he agreed. "But neither is wanting a partner who trusts you. And you didn't trust me. The ironic part of the situation was that I wasn't cheating on you."

"Of course you were." The words were automatic as the lump in her stomach grew.

"I was working, Candy. I had taken a second job." He paused and let that fact sink in before he continued. "And of course I was being secretive. I'd just saved enough money to buy a huge diamond ring so that I could propose to you. Imagine my surprise when you accused me of cheating on you." He shook his head and took another deep breath. "No discussion about what might be wrong, no trust on your part. You accused me on the flimsiest of evidence." There was pain in his eyes when he finally looked at her again.

Candy was stunned. He'd been planning to propose. He'd been working an extra job to buy her a ring. "But..." She really was at a loss.

"Yeah." He sat up straighter in his chair and took another mouthful of coffee, giving himself time to compose himself. "It hurt. Maybe I should have tried harder to make you understand." He sighed. "In fact, I know I should have explained myself instead of just getting angry."

"I'm sorry." She really didn't know what else to say.

"Me too, Candy. You had issues with trust, but I had my own problems too, especially when it came to cheating. My parents cheated on each other constantly and it was the one thing I vowed never to do in a relationship. When you accused me of doing just that, I lost it."

It was quite a revelation to see their relationship from his perspective. "I didn't realize that about your parents, Gary."

"No reason you would know." He rolled the paper cup in his hands. "We didn't really talk. Not about the things we should have."

"That's not true." The accusation stung. "We always talked."

"Not about things that really mattered. Like I said. Not about the things we should have." Raising his cup to his mouth, he studied her as he took a sip. His examination made her uncomfortable and she resisted the impulse to squirm in her seat.

"I really don't want to rehash old news. What's past is past. I've got more important things on my mind right now." Like the way Lucas had looked when he'd left the television studio.

"You're still doing it." He sat back, shaking his head.

"Doing what?" As if he had any right to be critical of her.

"Avoiding the problem. Not wanting to talk about things." He held up his hand to stop her from speaking. "I'm not criticizing you, Candy. It's just that I recognize the signs. Up until recently, I kept doing the same thing myself." He smiled ruefully. "Then I met someone—someone very special. It was only then I understood that, unless I changed the way I acted, this relationship would probably end up like ours did." He laughed and his eyes twinkled with humor. "I still fall back into old patterns sometimes, but she's good about kicking my butt when I need it."

"I'm glad for you." And she really was. He was right about one thing—she hadn't loved him in the way he'd deserved.

"Thanks. But the real reason I came over was because I though we both needed some kind of closure so we could move on with our lives. You're a wonderful, warm, giving woman, Candy, but you do have unrealistic expectations of people. You want people to be perfect, but you always expect them to disappoint you. No one can live up to your standards. I just don't want you to keep on hurting yourself that way." Gary pushed away from the table, leaned down and brushed a kiss across her cheek. "I'm sorry about what happened to us. Sorry if I ever hurt you. I never wanted that."

Candy saw the sincerity in his eyes. "Me too." Reaching out, she squeezed his arm. Their relationship hadn't worked out, but they were both still good people. Gary was right. They just hadn't been able to talk honestly to each other and with the baggage they'd both brought with them, they hadn't been able to survive the first big crisis.

"Take care of yourself." Picking up his coffee cup, he turned and walked away, not once looking back.

"You too," she whispered. A sense of closure washed over her. Candy watched him disappear, still reeling from his revelations. He'd painted a pretty honest picture of their relationship and of her. Her coffee grew cold as she sat there pondering his words.

The minutes ticked by as she replayed memories from her past. Did she have unrealistic expectations for her mother, her father, her brother, and most of all, for Lucas? Did she really have unrealistic expectations of people? Did she really expect people to disappoint her?

"Yes." The whispered word fell from her lips. Just look at her relationship with her mother. She'd expected her mother to be what she wanted, rather than what she was. But the truth of the matter was that her mother had done the best she'd been able to do. Candy was no longer a needy child and it was time to get past that hurt.

Then there was her relationship with her brother. She hadn't even been willing to give Justin a chance to explain what had happened. Just as she'd done with Gary. She swallowed the lump growing in her throat. And it was just what she'd done with Lucas.

It wasn't pleasant to revisit her life and realize that she held a large amount of responsibility for her own disappointments. Everyone made mistakes and everyone had things in their life that they weren't proud of, herself included. Who was she to expect people to live up to her impossible standards?

She could picture the look of disappointment on Lucas' face just before he'd walked away from her. She'd been so caught up in her own disappointment and anger that she hadn't stopped to view it from his perspective. She hadn't supported him when he'd needed her most.

Her head was pounding now and the ache in her stomach was a solid ball of misery. No matter what Lucas had done in his past, she knew who he was now. He was nothing like her father. Lucas would never lie to her. In fact, he'd immediately admitted that he'd been in jail when she asked.

But beyond that, Lucas was a man to be trusted. His word was his bond. Hadn't she learned that in the past few weeks? If he said he'd do something, it was as good as done. Besides which, he owned a thriving business and worked hard.

What had she done?

Had she thrown away the best thing that had ever happened to her because of her own prejudices and insecurities? Candy swallowed back the tears that threatened. It wasn't pleasant to see yourself in an unflattering light, but for once she felt like she was seeing herself the way she truly was. Stiff, unbending and unforgiving.

But that was about to change. Pushing out of her chair, she left her cold coffee behind on the table as she zipped up her coat and plunged back outside into the freezing cold. Darkness had descended upon the city, making it seem even colder. She hurried down the sidewalk, a woman on a mission.

She had no idea if Lucas would even talk to her, but she had to try. If nothing else, she owed him an apology and an explanation. She didn't want to think about the fact that he might not forgive her. A year ago, she wouldn't have forgiven him if their positions were reversed.

She pushed the fact that this was only supposed to be a temporary relationship out of her head. Maybe it had started that way, but Candy knew that she'd been lying to herself from the beginning in an attempt to protect herself from hurt.

But it hadn't worked. She'd loved Lucas almost from the very first and if there was even a chance that he might feel that way about her, then she was going to fight for their relationship.

She only hoped that it wasn't already too late.

Lucas stormed into his apartment, ripping off his coat as he went. Who in the hell did that woman think she was? It was a tossup as to which woman he was talking about—Angela Murray or Candy Logan. But whereas Angela had only pissed him off, Candy had sliced him right to his very core.

He tossed his coat over the coat rack just inside the door and then stood there with his hands on his hips and his head bowed as he struggled for control. Who was Candy to judge him? She hadn't lived his life, walked in his shoes. Besides which, he hadn't asked her into his life—she'd barged in. *But you didn't let her go*, a small voice whispered in his head.

No, he hadn't let her go. And just look what he'd gotten for his trouble. His past was going to be exposed on some stupid cable television talk show and his heart, which he'd always managed to guard, had been ripped out of his chest. God, how he wished that Katie had never come up with the idea for that damned cookbook!

Striding into the kitchen, he opened the refrigerator and hauled out a beer. Opening it, he took a long pull on the bottle. The brew tasted bitter going down, but he took another swallow. His immediate concern was how this was going to affect his business. He'd worked too damn long and hard to lose what he'd built from his own blood and sweat. He prowled around his apartment, feeling confined by the four walls.

A thump came on the door just before it was thrust open. Lucas spun around, ready to deal with whoever had invaded his privacy. For a split second, his heart jumped and he wondered if Candy had chased him home to apologize to him.

"Oh, it's you." Walking over to his sofa, he slumped down on the leather cushions.

"Is that any way to greet your best friend?" T. S. shook his head in mock sorrow as he sauntered across the apartment and into the kitchen. He opened the refrigerator and helped himself to a beer before strolling back to the living room and joining his friend on the sofa. "Hard day?"

Lucas snorted. "If you call having my past dragged up on a talk show and having Candy look at me like I'm some hardened criminal that might taint her by even being in the same room with her, then yeah, I'm having a hard day."

T. S. let out a soundless whistle. "I told you she'd be nothing but trouble."

"Yeah, you did." He sipped his beer. "But who cares, right? It was only temporary anyway. It was a good time, but it's over now."

"Uh-huh." T. S. raised his eyebrow but made no further comment.

"I mean, we both know that she's way out of my league. A classy lady like Candy and an ex-con." He gave another bark of humorless laughter. "What a joke."

"It's her loss." T. S. turned to Lucas, his face deadly serious. "You're the best person I know. I wouldn't have survived prison without you. I was skinny and so damned green, they'd have eaten me alive in there if it hadn't been for you. So screw her if she thinks you're not good enough. *She's* not good enough."

Lucas inhaled deeply. He appreciated what T. S. was saying, but it didn't ease the pain or the pressure in his chest. "Thanks, man." They sat in silence for a while. "It's just as well it ended now before it got any more serious. We both know it couldn't be permanent. I wouldn't take that chance."

"Man, I wish you'd get over that crap." T. S. scowled as he took a pull on his beer. "You are nothing like your old man.

If anything, you're the exact opposite. You're so controlled all the time. It's scary."

"Yeah, I can tell you're terrified." Lucas sprawled back against the cushions and stared up at the ceiling.

T. S. laughed. "I'm shaking in my boots. I meant that other people are afraid of you."

They sat in companionable silence for a long time. That was the great thing about a friend like T. S.—he knew when to shut up and just let things be. Lucas finally stirred. The beer in his hand had gone warm, so he leaned forward and plunked the almost-empty bottle on the coffee table. "She was special." He swallowed hard.

"I know."

"I'm going to go work out for a bit." Lucas forced himself up off the sofa. He needed to work off some of this pent-up anger before he exploded.

T. S. stood next to him and deposited his empty bottle on the table as he nodded. "Okay. I'm going to go and finish up some work. If you want to talk or go out to eat or just hang, let me know." He turned to leave, but stopped and swore under his breath. Swiveling back around, he hauled Lucas into a quick bear hug. "I'm real sorry, man." Releasing him, T. S. hurried out of the apartment, slamming the door behind him.

Lucas swallowed hard. "Me too." His whispered words seemed to mock him as he headed to his bedroom to change into his workout gear.

Chapter Fourteen

ဆ

Lucas swore, his hands gripping the heavy iron bar tight as he lowered it carefully back into the cradle. Lying on the weight bench, he waited to see if whoever it was would knock again. He'd only been working out for about twenty minutes, barely enough time to work up a sweat. Who the hell could be banging on the front door?

The knock came again, this time louder. It wasn't T. S.— he wouldn't bother to knock but just invite himself in. Maybe it was Katie? Closing his eyes, he took a few calming breaths before heaving himself up off the leather bench. He wanted to ignore the knocking, but he knew he couldn't. It was possible that there was something down in the coffee shop that needed his attention.

Hitching his drawstring pants up around his waist, he grabbed a towel and wrapped it around his neck, rubbing his face with one end as he padded on bare feet to the front door. He didn't bother to turn on any lamps, as the streetlights shining in through the living room window shed enough light to allow him to see. He yanked the door open and the terse greeting died on his lips. She was the last person he'd expected to see.

Candy stared up at him, her brown eyes looking huge and her features fragile. Her cheeks and nose were red from the cold and she was breathing heavily, as if she had run all the way here. Lucas snorted inwardly. Yeah, like she'd rushed all the way over here to apologize to him.

"Can...can I come in?" She chewed on her lush bottom lip as he watched her.

Pulling open the door, he stood back and waited for her to enter. He could sense her nervousness as he shut the door and she gave a startled jump when he locked it. "Are you sure it's safe to be alone in a dark room with an ex-con?" He knew it was childish, but he couldn't resist the small dig.

Her dark eyebrows came together in a scowl as she unzipped her coat. "I'm perfectly safe with you, Lucas, and we both know it." Hanging up her coat and purse, she strode into the living room, leaving him to trail behind her.

She stopped so unexpectedly, he almost plowed into her from behind. She spun around to face him and opened her mouth to speak, but nothing came out. He noticed that her eyes were glued to his chest. Obviously, she still wanted him sexually, even if she didn't think he was good enough for her in other ways. The cynical part of his nature prodded him to take advantage of that fact. If she wanted his body, then he should take what he wanted. Have one fuck for the road. Give her something to remember him by.

His cock responded immediately to her interest, lengthening and thickening against the front of his workout pants. Doing nothing to hide his arousal, he casually swiped at a bead of sweat that trickled down his forehead. "What do you want, Candy? I'm busy."

She flinched at his harsh words, but he resisted the urge to soften toward her. That's what had gotten him in trouble to begin with. Dropping the edge of the towel, he crossed his arms across his chest and waited.

She swallowed audibly, but then seemed to gather herself together, standing tall. "You'll be happy to know that your segment of the show won't air and that Angela Murray issued an apology to her audience, telling them that the information was false."

"Thanks." He owed Candy that much. "But I don't think it will do much good. Somebody will get nosy and poke around. I'm sure it will be out in the papers before long."

"What happened, Lucas?"

"That's none of your damn business, sugar." A few hours ago, he would have gladly shared with her. Now, he didn't want to talk to her at all. He tried to ignore the impulse that was screaming at him to wrap her in his arms and never let her go. Their relationship had proven to be nothing more than an illusion.

She flinched but held her ground. He ruthlessly squashed the feelings of pride and admiration that welled up within him. "I guess I had that coming."

His muscles strained with the effort it was taking for him not to grab her in his arms. His cock was throbbing with the need to bury itself in Candy's welcoming warmth. He wanted to lose himself in the comfort and security of her body.

She placed her hand on his arm. It looked so small and pale against the bulk of his muscles. "It doesn't really matter."

"No?" His jaw was clenched so tight, he could barely get the word out. Any tighter and he was sure it would shatter.

"No." She shook her head, her eyes luminous in the muted light.

"Prove it."

His harsh words and the cold, unyielding expression on his face almost sent her running from the room. This was not the Lucas that she was used to. This man wasn't the playful, passionate lover and companion that she'd spent most of the past few weeks with. This was the face of a man who'd had the kind of past that she couldn't even begin to imagine. A man who'd spent time in prison. A man that she'd hurt deeply with her lack of faith and trust.

But beneath that implacable façade, the man she loved was still there. She had to believe that, to trust in him. Taking a deep breath, she took the biggest gamble of her entire life. "Prove it how?"

His pale blue eyes, usually so warm and inviting, were as cold as ice as he stared down at her. He slowly moved his gaze over her body, lingering on her breasts and at the juncture of her thighs before moving all the way to her feet and then all the way back up again.

Even though she was fully dressed, she felt stripped naked beneath his detached stare. Her body responded immediately to his visual caress. Her nipples hardened into tight nubs, pushing against her bra. Between her thighs cream began to flow as her inner muscles clenched in anticipation.

"Take off your clothes."

"What?" Surely she hadn't heard him correctly.

"Strip for me, sugar." He circled her slowly, assessing her. "If it doesn't matter, then strip for me. I want to fuck you. Right here. Right now."

His cold, emotionless words made her stomach clench. Her legs began to shake and she had to lock her knees to keep from crumpling to the floor. She'd wounded him deeply earlier today and this was his way of making her pay. "Is that what it will take for you to believe me?"

Lucas shrugged, his massive shoulders moving negligently. But she wasn't fooled. She could see the tension in every muscle of his body. "We won't know unless we try, now will we?" he taunted softly.

Candy was no coward and she'd already made her decision to fight for her relationship with Lucas. She trusted him not to hurt her, at least physically. If that's what it took to convince him that she still cared for him and trusted him, then so be it.

Decision made, her hands crept to the buttons on her blouse. She could hear Lucas' deep intake of breath as he came to stand in front of her. Her fingers shook as she slipped each button from the opening, but finally it was wide open. Pulling the tails out from her skirt, she slipped the fabric from her upper body and let it fall to the floor.

Lucas gripped the ends of the towel in his hands, his knuckles turning white from the pressure. Good. He wasn't as unaffected as he was trying to project. That gave Candy a much-needed boost of courage as she reached behind and unhooked her bra. It was one of the new ones that she'd bought with Lucas in mind, but never had she imagined removing it under such circumstances. Bending forward, she allowed the straps to fall down her arms, and then the bra joined her blouse on the floor.

"Pretty." Reaching out, he rubbed one of the swollen tips with his thumb before withdrawing it. "Offer me your breasts. Cup them in your hands and give them to me."

The hair at the nape of her neck stood on end and she suddenly wished that her hair was down instead of up in its usual twist. Maybe then she wouldn't feel quite so exposed. She'd never done anything like this before in her life. It scared her, but it was also incredibly arousing.

Lucas stood waiting for her to decide what she was going to do. She knew instinctively that if she refused, all would be lost. Her own anger threatened to boil to the surface, but she swallowed it. They'd talk later. For now, her beast was very angry and it was up to her to soothe him. Cupping the weight of her breasts in her hands, she pushed them high.

He nodded, as if pleased by her compliance. "Your nipples aren't hard enough yet. Play with them."

She hesitated only the slightest of moments before catching each tip between her thumbs and forefingers and rolling them gently. A low moan of pleasure escaped her lips and he pursed his lips together, making him look almost cruel in the dim light.

"Harder, Candy. I want your nipples to be as hard as pebbles."

Her hips began to rock as she pinched them tighter, the pleasure shooting straight down to her pussy. She could feel herself creaming her panties.

"Now your skirt." His voice was heavy with desire.

She gave her nipples one final tug before sliding her hands over her belly and around to the back of her skirt. The button was quickly undone and the zipper pulled down. Giving her hips a shimmy, she allowed the skirt to slide down her hips and legs to pool around her ankles.

"The panties."

His low, guttural tone was incredible arousing to her and she could feel the liquid arousal slipping from her core. She hooked her fingers in the waistband of her panties. Her breasts felt incredible heavy as she leaned forward, inching the lace band of her underwear lower over her hips and thighs and down across her legs. Standing straight, she stepped out of the mound of fabric, kicking it to one side.

His eyes practically burned her flesh as they swept over her body. She could see his erection straining against the front of his pants. She reached down to unzip her boots.

"Leave them."

Slowly, she straightened once again. Clad only in her thigh-high stockings and high-heeled boots, she stood proudly in front of him.

"On your knees, sugar." His blunt request caught her off guard and she began to realize just how deeply she had wounded him. He might think he was punishing her, but in fact, he was giving her the opportunity to show him her love.

Taking a step toward him, she sank to her knees in front of him. She licked her lips as she tugged on the drawstring and loosened his pants. As she shoved them down his legs, his cock sprang forward, ready and eager. But she wanted him naked. Pushing the pants down around his ankles, she waited as he lifted one foot at a time, tugging the fabric away.

Sitting back on her heels, she stared up at Lucas. He was breathtakingly handsome and she loved him with all her being. Wrapping her hands around each ankle, she slid them over his strong calves and across his rock-hard thighs, reveling in the way the muscles flexed and rippled beneath her fingers.

Coming up on her knees again, she cupped his heavy testicles with her hands, gently rolling them, caressing them. Lucas groaned as she teased him. She loved the feeling of the crisp hair of his groin against her fingers as she traced his sac and rubbed the sensitive skin just behind it.

Sensing his growing restlessness, she wrapped her fingers around the base of his erection and slid them up to the top. The skin was as soft as velvet, but what was beneath was pure steel. His cock throbbed against her palms and she could feel an answering pulse begin deep within her own core.

The head of his cock was broad and dark, and as she leaned forward, she could see a bead of liquid seep from the tip. She lapped at it with her tongue, circling the entire crown before licking a path down his length and back up again. His fingers tangled in her hair. He swore and plucked at the two decorative pins holding her hair up. She heard them drop to the floor as her hair cascaded down around her shoulders.

This time, his fingers sifted though her hair as he guided her mouth back to the top of his erection. Opening her mouth wide, she took him as deep as she was able. But still she wanted more. Moving closer for a better angle, she began to slide her mouth up and down his length.

"That's it, sugar. Suck it hard." He thrust his hips back and forth, driving his cock deeper down her throat with every thrust. "I want to fuck your mouth until I come."

His words made her moan and the vibrations made him shudder as he began to thrust harder now. Wrapping one hand around the base of his erection, she pumped up and down his length. She reached her other hand around him, digging her fingers into his hard butt and pulling him tighter with every thrust of his hips. She wanted to give him this pleasure. Wanted to bring him to orgasm with just her mouth.

She could feel his muscles squeeze tight, and then his entire body jerked as he came. His semen jetted down the back of her throat, but she continued to suck hard as she swallowed. Even when he was finished and his cock began to soften, she was reluctant to release him.

Finally, he tugged gently at her hair and she allowed his cock to slip from her mouth. His hands cupped her head, holding her against his hard thigh. Candy resisted the urge to squirm. She was so aroused, her skin felt as if it were too tight. She raised her head to look up at him and his hands slipped free of her hair. She immediately missed the contact and felt the loss of the connection to him.

His eyes were soft and, for the briefest of seconds, he was her Lucas again. Then his expression hardened and he took a step away from her. Something nudged her face and she jerked back, shocked to see his erection growing once again.

"We've only just begun."

His words sent shivers down her spine, raising goose bumps on her arms and thighs. He held out his hand to her and she placed her hand in his. His fingers closed around hers as he helped her to her feet. She almost cried out when he released his hold on her, but she stiffened her spine, ready for whatever came next.

"Go over to the window, bend over and place your hands on the sill." There was a note of challenge in his tone, as if he expected her to be too cowardly to rise to the dare.

Although her legs were shaking, she turned and sauntered over to the window, swaying her hips as she walked. She consoled herself with the fact that the room was so dark that no one would see her standing there naked. At least she hoped they couldn't. Leaning forward, she placed both palms on the smooth wood of the windowsill, curving her fingers around it for support.

"Spread your legs wider." His voice came from directly behind her, making her jump. She hadn't heard him crossing the room behind her. His bare feet had made no sound against the floor. Candy felt like she was being stalked by a massive, sleek predator intent on playing with his victim before he devoured her whole.

The action would leave her ass and her sex totally exposed to him. She was well and truly at his mercy. Her stomach clenched with a mixture of fear, arousal and need. God, she wanted his cock inside her, plunging deep into her core as they both came. Gripping tighter to the edge of the window, she slid her legs apart.

"Wider." He tapped the inside of her ankle with his foot and she opened her legs as far as they could go, stretching her legs almost to the point of discomfort. "Perfect," he purred behind her. "Now, don't move."

Chapter Fifteen

೫෨

Lucas stood back and admired the erotic picture that Candy made, spread wide in front of him. The high-heeled boots she wore brought her to the perfect height and angle for him to take her this way. Her thighs were smooth and the curve of her ass was enticing as she bent forward. His gaze swept the long, supple line of her spine, all the way to the nape of her neck.

He couldn't see her breasts, but he knew they would be hanging heavy from her body. The weight of them would be incredibly arousing for her. His cock jerked in reaction to his thoughts, reminding him of his own arousal. Her hair hung down around her face, hiding it from his view, and he wished he hadn't removed the hairpins, wanting to see her every reaction.

In truth, he was shocked she was still here. He'd been purposely crude and demanding, trying to drive her away. But she'd met his every demand and then some. She was everything he'd ever dreamed of and more. Too bad it wasn't real. But right now, he didn't want to think about what had happened earlier, or what would come later. Candy was spread before him, a feast for a starving man, and he wasn't foolish enough to turn away from it.

He could smell her arousal as he knelt behind her—a heady combination of musk and sweetness that was pure Candy. He'd never had a sweet tooth in his life until he'd met her. Now, he had a definite taste for Candy.

His fingers felt rough against the soft, silky skin of her inner thighs as he traced a path toward her core. He could feel her trembling beneath his touch, and it both humbled and aroused him that she would leave herself so open and vulnerable to him.

A cocktail of anger, lust and longing all swirled in his blood, making it hard for him to think straight. But right now all he wanted was to feel Candy come apart in his arms as he brought her to a screaming climax. Even now, all he wanted was her pleasure.

Satisfaction filled him, body and soul, as he slowly slid his fingers along the slick folds of her labia. She was so wet and hot, coating his fingers in her cream. She shifted her weight, rocking her hips slightly to bring him closer to her core. He dipped one finger deep, swirling it around before withdrawing it again. Her moan of pleasure was sweet to his ears.

Stroking backward, he circled the tight, puckered bud of her ass with his finger, using her own moisture to ease his way as he inserted the tip of his finger. She cried out and he froze, but she didn't tell him to stop. He could hear her labored breathing in the quiet of the apartment building. His own breath was none too steady as he pushed his finger deeper into her behind. A car horn sounded in the distance, but neither of them paid any attention to it. The world outside didn't exist for them. All of their attention was focused on each other.

Her inner muscles clenched tight around his finger as he carefully pushed it deeper. "No one has ever touched you here before, have they?"

Candy shook her head. "No." He could barely hear her whispered reply, but it filled him with a savage satisfaction that he was the first to touch her in this way.

With his free hand, he stroked her swollen sex, circling her slit. He could feel the tension growing within her as he feathered his touch over her clitoris, barely caressing the sensitive bud. He growled with pleasure as she began to thrust her hips back and forth, taking his finger deeper within her ass. He slowly withdrew it until only the tip was still inside and then carefully surged back into her again.

Her cries were becoming more frantic now as he continued to finger-fuck her behind as well as tease her hot pussy. "Lucas." Her voice was filled with desperation and need.

"Tell me what you want." He needed the words from her.

"I want you, Lucas." Her hips were pumping frantically now.

"Want me to what?" Leaning forward, he nipped at the plump flesh of her lush ass.

"I want you inside me." The last word was more of a long, drawn-out moan.

"Not yet." He wanted her hotter and wetter and begging him to fuck her. He slipped two fingers into her core, thrusting them deep as he continued to work his finger in and out of the tight hole of her behind. "Come for me."

"Lucas." She screamed his name as she convulsed around his fingers. The gush of liquid between her thighs, the clenching of her muscles and the shaking of her body…he registered every single smell, sight and sound.

When her knees bent and she sagged against the window, he eased his fingers out of her and surged upward to stand behind her. Wrapping his forearm around her waist to keep her upright, he leaned over to whisper in her ear. "We're not done yet, sugar."

Candy shivered as he nipped at the side of her neck, nuzzling her hair out of the way so he could place love bites on her nape. Lucas' cock was hard and eager once again and he slipped it between her thighs, allowing it to skim across her swollen flesh. She sucked in a breath even as she tried to slide her sex across it. He laughed, pleased that he could arouse her again so easily. He'd never had another woman who suited him as well as she did.

Sliding his hands over her supple torso, he cupped her breasts. They were large and full, tipped with tight nipples. As he continued to slide his erection back and forth over her sex, he played with her lush breasts, circling the tips with his thumbs. She moved in tandem with him, pushing her breasts against his hands, while her hips moved sinuously back and forth, pleasuring herself with his erection.

Lucas nipped and licked her neck and shoulders, savoring every moment of the exquisite pain as his cock throbbed for release. His balls were heavy and every muscle of his body was clenched in anticipation of claiming her. The savage part of him, the part that demanded restitution for the earlier pain she'd given him, wanted her to plead him to take her, needed her to beg.

"What do you want?" He rolled her tight nipples between his thumbs and forefingers as he nipped her earlobe and whispered in her ear.

"You." She rolled her hips seductively, almost pushing him over the edge.

He gritted his teeth and tried to control the need pounding in his body and brain. "Not good enough. If you want it, sugar, you've got to ask for it." He gently pinched her nipples as his tongue swirled around the shell of her ear. "I won't give it to you until you tell me what you want."

He felt the change in her then, the release of control, the giving of herself to him completely. Triumph filled him as she gasped, "I want you inside me."

"More," he demanded.

"Fuck me," she cried. "Lucas," Candy pleaded. "Please fuck me."

He pulled back until the head of his cock slipped just inside her slit. Without warning, he plunged inward, slamming his balls against her as he buried himself in her heat. He could feel the sensitive muscles stretching to accommodate him as she cried out, her back bowing against him. "Relax, sugar, you can take all of me." He needed her to take all of him, to want every inch of him inside her. She felt so damned good wrapped around him, so soft and so wet. Perfect.

Too perfect. Sanity reared its head and he realized that for the first time in his life, he wasn't wearing a condom. Part of him didn't want to wear one, wanted her to take him as he was, wanted to spend himself inside her, marking her as his for all time. The sane part screamed caution.

He could feel her quivering in his arms, could feel her heart pounding in her chest as his hands cupped her breasts. Like him, she was poised on the edge, so close to coming. He held them both still, not moving an inch.

"Please." Her whispered plea broke his control and he began to thrust.

"Yes," he groaned. All thought, all restraint fled as he pumped in and out of her body. He held her tight, wrapping one arm around her waist and bracing the other against the windowsill as he slammed his cock into her over and over. Her feet left the floor with each plunge. He wanted to get so far inside her that she'd never be free of him again.

His balls drew up tight as his cock throbbed. Blood pounded in his brain, pushing him harder, demanding he claim her. He was so damned close. Candy was crying and thrashing in his arms. They were almost there. She screamed his name as her orgasm took her. He could hear her cries and feel her body spasm as he plunged again and again.

At the very last second, sanity surfaced enough for him to pull out of her. He pushed his cock hard against her back, grinding his length against her as he came, emptying himself against her soft skin.

His knees buckled and he lowered them both to the floor. Burying his face in her shoulder, he gulped air into his lungs, desperately trying to breathe. He'd never felt anything like this in his life. A fine sheen of perspiration covered them both and the smell of sex permeated the air around them.

Lucas didn't know how long they sat there on the floor when he realized Candy was shaking. Carefully, he lifted her, turning her in his arms. Brushing back her hair from her face, he froze. She was crying. Tears seeped out from the corners of her eyes, trailing down her cheeks. "Candy?" At the sound of her name, she burst into tears.

He wrapped his arms around her and held her tight. Oh, God, what had he done? In his need to assuage his anger and hurt, he'd taken her in a frenzy, pounding out his frustration into her body. He was no better than a damned animal. His arms tightened around her and he forced himself to loosen his grip. He couldn't hold on to something that wasn't his to begin with.

She was right. He wasn't good enough for her. What kind of a man would hurt the woman he loved? *A man like his father*, the voice in his head whispered.

And he did love her. Somehow, she'd snuck past his well-guarded heart and wrapped herself around it, claimed it as her own. And what had he done? He'd taken her without caring, like some animal in heat, pounding into her just to appease the demons within him. With the return of control came memory. He'd driven into her so hard that her feet had left the ground. He was so much larger and stronger than she was.

Burying his face in her hair, he inhaled her unique scent as he rocked her in his arms. Because he loved her, he knew he had to let her go. There was too much of his father in him and he would not risk her safety any longer. Rising to his feet, he carried her back to the sofa and sat. He reached out and snagged the towel from where it had landed on the floor and used it to wipe the sticky residue of his cum from her back before swiping it over his arm and belly.

He tilted back her head and dried her tears with his thumb, absorbing every sensation, knowing this was probably the last time he'd touch her precious face. She stared up at him, her eyes luminous and slightly swollen. She opened her mouth to speak, but he placed his hand gently over it, stopping her.

"I'm sorry, Candy." He plucked her blouse off the floor and helped her put it on, buttoning it carefully. "We both know that this was only a temporary thing, and I think, after all that's happened today, it's time for it to end."

She froze in his embrace, but he stood with her still in his arms. Reluctantly, he let her feet slide to the floor, making sure she was steady before he grabbed her skirt and helped her back into it. "Lucas." She laid her hand on his arm and he flinched away. He didn't deserve her compassion after what he'd just done.

Picking up her bra and panties, he thrust them into her hand as he ushered her to the doorway. He wrapped her in her coat, zipping it tight. She looked absolutely shattered standing there in the dim light. And no wonder. She'd come to talk and he'd taken her crudely and without consideration. He figured that the only reason she hadn't run screaming was that she was still in shock.

"I'm going to call you a cab to take you home." He wiped all emotion from his face and his voice. He had to get her out of here quick before he did something stupid, like falling on his knees and begging her not to ever leave him. He had to be strong, for her, but he knew he couldn't hold out much longer.

"We need to talk, Lucas." Her voice shook, but it was filled with determination as she shoved her underwear into her purse.

The sound of footsteps outside the door was like a light in the darkness. He recognized the heavy tread of boots. Yanking open the door, he put his hand on the small of Candy's back and all but pushed her out into the hallway. T. S. froze in place, his eyes going from Lucas to Candy and back to Lucas again.

"Take her home for me. Please." He slammed the door shut and locked it, knowing that T. S. would make sure that she made it home okay.

The murmur of voices drifted through the door and then the sound of footsteps moving down the hallway, gradually fading away. Lucas stood there naked, aching in a way that he hadn't done since he was kid. His chest actually hurt and he rubbed his hand over it. Swearing, he whirled around and slammed his fist into the wall. Plaster cracked and crumbled. He jerked it back and just stared at his closed fist, ignoring the pain.

Going to his knees, he buried his face in his hands and cursed the man who'd fathered him, a man who had shared his blood and genes with him. A lone tear slipped down his cheek as he slowly stood and stumbled down the hall toward his workout room.

Candy stood in the glaring light of the hallway, not quite sure how she'd gotten here. She felt shell-shocked. What had just happened? One moment she been having the most erotic experience of her life with the man she loved, and the next he was apologizing and all but throwing her out of his home.

The finality of the lock being engaged from inside the apartment was like a smack in the face. Just like that, they were finished. Their affair was over even as aftershocks of her last orgasm still lingered.

"Hey, you okay?"

She jumped at the sound of the male voice, so close to her. What was his name again? She remembered meeting him on the opening day of Coffee Breaks. She nodded, not sure she could even speak if she wanted to. Right now she needed to get home. Locking her shaky knees, she walked down the hallway toward the stairs.

"Hey." She pulled away when his hand touched her arm, practically bouncing off the wall in her haste to get away from him. He held up his hands in mock surrender. "I'm not going to hurt you, but Lucas wants me to take you home."

"I don't care what Lucas wants." Her voice was rough, her throat raw from the unshed tears she swallowed back.

"Your kind never does."

His easy dismissal of her fired her already frayed temper. "What the hell is that supposed to mean?"

T. S. sneered at her. "Couldn't wait to be rid of him when you found out he'd been in prison, could you? You didn't even want to know the facts."

"No," she replied honestly. "I didn't, not at first. But I came to talk with him and now he's the one throwing me out." She turned away and brushed at the tears that slipped down her cheeks. Why was she even bothering to try to justify her actions to someone she didn't even know? Turning, she started to walk away again, weaving slightly as the physical and emotional turmoil of the day took a toll on her.

T. S. MacNamara, that was his name, she thought as she valiantly headed toward the stairs. She sensed him watching her. Then he swore and she heard the sound of heavy work boots hurrying after her. Practically running now, she started down the stairs. In her haste, she missed one and started to plunge forward. She screamed and held out her hands as a strong arm wrapped itself around her upper body, plucking her to safety.

"What the hell are you trying to do, kill yourself?" His voice was gruff, but he was gentle as he stood her back on the stairs.

"I just want to go home." The tears were coming faster now and she swiped them away, despising herself for shedding them. *I don't usually cry and definitely not in front of a complete stranger.*

"I'm sure you don't." She hadn't realized she'd said the words out loud until he commented on them. "Look." He swiped a hand through his hair, his agitation plain. "I don't know what just went on between you two, but I know that you hurt Lucas. Even with that, he wants me to see you home safely. You can either go by yourself and I'll follow you or you can let me take you. It's your choice. But either way, I'm seeing you home."

"Do you want to know what just went on?" Candy was a woman who'd been pushed to the limits of her emotional and physical well-being and lashed out to protect herself against further hurt. "I just had the most amazing sexual experience of my life with the man I love and then he threw me out. So if I hurt him today, then we can call it even."

Reaching out blindly for support, she grabbed the railing and stumbled down the stairs. Once again, a powerful male arm stopped her. Candy was getting sick and tired of being manhandled by large men. "Let me go!"

"Not until you talk to me."

"There is nothing to say." She pulled out of his grasp and kept on going down the stairs, but he was hot on her heels.

"You said you loved him." His voice was insistent.

She refused to answer him. Her only goal was getting to the door and hailing a cab to take her home.

"What did he say when you told him?"

Candy rounded the corner and kept moving steadily downward. She was almost there.

"Will you stop!" He surged in front of her and blocked the staircase. She stumbled to a halt as he spread his arms wide, placing a palm on either wall.

"I didn't get a chance to say anything. He didn't want to talk. He only wanted to fuck, and once that was done, he couldn't wait to get rid of me. I've had enough humiliation for one day. Now move!" She all but screamed the last two words at him. If he didn't move, she was going to kick him where it would hurt him most. Standing a few steps above him, she had the perfect angle to do some damage.

T. S. looked shocked as he slowly lowered his arms and stood to one side. She cautiously skittered past him, keeping her eyes on him as she passed. "You mean too much to him. That's why he sent you away."

Candy flinched as his words hit her like stones. Her harsh laugh held no pleasure. "He sure has a funny way of showing it."

"You're both too much alike. Both of you trying to protect yourselves and all you end up doing is hurting yourselves more." He fell into step behind her as she pushed open the side door and stepped out into the cold, dark night. "Give him a few days, but if you really do care, if you really do love him, don't give up on him."

She gave no indication that she heard anything he said. She'd think about what he said. Later. When she was safe at home. Rushing out to the road, she waved at a passing taxi, almost reduced to tears again when he just drove by without stopping.

"Let me take you home." His voice was softer now and tinged with pity. Candy scrunched her shoulders up around her ears to try to stay warm. She didn't want anyone's pity. "Please." He was closer now. "Lucas won't rest tonight unless I come back and tell him that you made it home okay."

He wrapped his arm around her waist and guided her to his truck that was parked just up the road from the building. Unlocking the door, he took one look at her boots and her skirt and scooped her up, depositing her on the seat. He made sure she was tucked in safely before he closed the door and hurried around to the driver's side. The ride home was made in complete silence after she'd given him her address. He said nothing when he parked in front of her building, but once again hurried to her side of the truck and lifted her down. Like a large watchdog, he followed her up the stairs and all the way to her apartment door, waiting patiently while she dug though her purse for her keys.

Just as she was about to close her door, he finally spoke. "Don't give up on him, Candy. He deserves to have some happiness. You both do."

"Thank you for the ride home." She closed the door gently and engaged all the locks. It was only after the sound of footsteps faded in the distance that she finally allowed the tears to flow unchecked.

Stumbling to her bedroom, she hauled off her clothing and tumbled into bed, pulling the covers tight around her. The sound of her sobs were raw and painful as she cried for what she'd lost in her past, but most of all, for what she'd lost today. She cried so hard, she made herself sick, barely stumbling to the bathroom in time. Eventually, there were no more tears left to shed and with a cool cloth over her swollen eyes, Candy crawled back in bed and fell into a fitful sleep.

Chapter Sixteen

൭

The next few days were the hardest that she'd ever been through in her entire life. For the first time ever, she couldn't lose herself in her work. It no longer interested her. She did manage to lay the groundwork for several upcoming projects, but avoided anything that had to do with Lucas. In fairness to the cookbook, she did schedule Katie for several interviews, playing up the local artist angle.

Physically, she ached for several days from the unusual sexual activity. Each twinge was a reminder of the mind-blowing sexual experience she'd shared with Lucas. Every night, she soaked in a tub of hot water, trying to rid herself of each muscle ache and the memory that went with it. Eventually the physical discomfort disappeared, but she feared that the memories never would.

Candy knew that she looked a wreck. She wasn't sleeping and food didn't interest her at all. Mostly, she concentrated on just getting through each day with the hope that tomorrow would be easier. She jumped every time the phone rang, her heart pounding hopefully in her chest. But Lucas never called her.

For the first time since she received the phone call from Barbara Bates, she was seriously considering interviewing for the job in New York City. Maybe she really did need to admit that whatever relationship she had been building with Lucas was over and it was time to move on.

She knew that Missy was worried about her, but Candy wasn't ready to talk about what had happened with Lucas. She'd probably never be ready for that. She'd just told Missy that it was over between her and Lucas and thankfully her friend had let it go for now.

Today was day four, but it wasn't getting any easier. Her experience with Lucas had changed her forever. There was no going back to the woman she'd been before she'd met him. That cold, unforgiving, work-driven woman had disappeared forever. In her place was a woman who understood what it was to love deeply and lose. A woman who understood that people weren't perfect and that sometimes you wished you could change your past.

The phone rang and this time there was no surge of hope or expectation. At least she was making progress, she thought as she reached for her phone. "Candy Logan's office."

"Hi, Candy."

Candy closed her eyes and placed a hand on her jittery stomach. This was something else she'd been avoiding, but the time had obviously come to deal with this as well. Taking a calming breath, she cleared her voice. "Hi, Justin."

"I won't keep you long." He paused before continuing. "I know you're busy at work, but I wondered if you'd given any more thought to meeting with me."

The woman she'd been several weeks ago had refused him, but today…today everything was different. Today, she knew she had to see him, if only for one last time. "Where and when would you like to meet?"

She heard his swift intake of breath and knew she'd surprised him. "How about lunch today? I can be at the diner just down from your office in half an hour."

Obviously he didn't want to give her time to change her mind. She glanced at her watch and decided she could take an early lunch. "That sounds great. I'll see you then." She gently hung up the phone, feeling good about her decision. For better or worse, Justin was her brother and she owed it to him and to herself to talk to him. Turning back to her computer, she felt a new surge of energy. She had time to finish answering her emails before she had to go and meet her brother.

"Famous last words," she muttered as she yanked the door of the diner open and hurried inside, leaving the cold, bitter wind and sleet behind her. She'd gotten so wrapped up in her work that she was ten minutes late. She only hoped that Justin hadn't left yet.

The door closed behind her and she was enveloped in the homey warmth of the place. The smells of coffee and spices filled the air, making her stomach growl. She glanced around the room, suddenly unsure. She hadn't seen Justin in years. Would she even recognize him?

A man rose slowly from a booth in the far corner. Tall and broad, his straight hair hung down to his shoulders, giving him the appearance of a shaggy lion. Her legs moved of their own volition, bringing her closer to him. His nose had a bump in the center and she wondered when he'd broken it. The crooked half-smile was endearingly familiar, as was the warmth in his chocolate brown eyes.

"Justin?" Her voice was little more than a whisper, but the stranger opened his arms to her and she walked straight into them. They closed tight around her, holding her almost desperately to him. She could hear the pounding of his heart through his soft T-shirt and suddenly he was a stranger no more. Candy couldn't begin to count how many times he'd held her like this when were children, and the lost years suddenly dissolved and ceased to matter.

She threw her arms around him, hugging him for all the years she'd been unable to do so. When he finally pulled away, it was she who didn't want to let go and she gripped the front of his shirt tight in her fingers as if to keep him from disappearing again. His rough hands cupped her face as he studied her. "God, you're beautiful, Candy."

She could feel the blush stealing up her cheeks and ducked her head. "Thank you." She forced herself to release the death grip she had on his shirt and step back. "You're still as handsome as ever." And he was, in a rough way. Not classically beautiful, but he'd certainly catch any woman's eye.

Justin laughed and ushered her into her seat before sliding into the one across from her. "Thanks for seeing me. I know this wasn't easy for you."

"No, it wasn't, but it should have been." Taking her time, she unzipped her coat and slid it off, laying it across the back of her chair. She tucked her purse down by her side and straightened her suit jacket before facing him again. "You don't need to tell me where you've been or what you've done. Just tell me what you plan to do."

Justin studied her for a long moment. He opened his mouth to speak, but the waitress interrupted them. They hurriedly gave their orders for the soup and sandwich special as the waitress poured them each a cup of coffee. When she was gone, Justin picked up where he'd left off. "What happened, Candy? You seem different from the first time I talked to you."

Candy fiddled with her napkin and sighed. "I am different. I was just angry with you when you first called. Then I did a lot of thinking and faced a lot of things about myself. And it wasn't pretty." She tried to smile as she met her brother's worried gaze. "I guess you can say I finally grew up and stopped blaming everyone for not being perfect."

Her brother reached across the table and caught her hand in his. "I don't blame you for being angry. You wouldn't be human if you weren't hurt by what happened. You didn't have an easy life and I didn't make it any easier." The sorrow in his eyes was replaced by admiration as he continued. "But you've grown into a heck of a woman. Mom told me a lot about your job and also about all you've done for her. You should be proud of yourself."

His honest, straightforward praise helped undo the knot in her stomach and made her sit up a little straighter. "Thank you, Justin." She gave his fingers a squeeze. "Now tell me about yourself. Whatever you want. You don't have to tell me about your past unless you want to."

Justin released her hand and took a sip of coffee. When he put the mug back on the table, he kept his large hands wrapped around it. "I was in prison, but it's not exactly what you think."

Her stomach clenched but she forced herself to relax. "Tell me."

He seemed uncomfortable, his gaze always scanning the room as if he were looking for something. Watching. Whatever he'd done and wherever he'd been, his life obviously hadn't been easy. For the first time, she felt no resentment toward her brother. Maybe because, for the first time, she wasn't thinking only about how his actions affected her. For once, she was thinking about him.

"I ran with a wild crowd back then, but you know that."

Candy nodded, silently encouraging him to continue.

"Let's just say that I got caught one night in the wrong place at the wrong time. It wasn't the cops that caught me, but another government agency. An agency without a name, that doesn't really officially exist. I can't tell you about it, so please don't ask." Justin shook his head and sighed. "They offered me a deal and I did what I had to do."

Candy was stunned. This was not what she'd expected to hear. "But how could something like this happen to you? This is America."

"I wasn't here, Candy. I was down in South America at the time. It was either do what they wanted or spend the rest of my life rotting in a prison down there—that is, if they didn't just execute me first." There was so much pain in her brother's eyes that she wanted to cry.

"But you were just a teenager." She still couldn't wrap her head around what he was telling her.

"I was old enough and stupid enough. I've got no one to blame but myself. The lure of easy money was too great, but you know what they say. 'If it looks too good to be true, then it probably is.' And that *easy money* cost me the next fifteen years of my life."

"But what happened? It's been so long."

"I can't really talk about it." He gave a humorless laugh. "Let's just say that I've retired."

"That's incredible." Candy shook her head.

"Yeah, almost unbelievable. I wouldn't blame you if you didn't believe me, Candy. I lived it and I almost don't believe it."

She could see the pain etched in the corners of his eyes and in the tight way he grimaced. His eyes were ever watchful, scanning his surroundings, and she realized that he didn't feel safe. He sat so still in his seat, not shifting or shuffling, but ever vigilant. The sleeves of his shirt had been pushed back and she could see the faint lines of scars on one of his arms. What other scars did his clothing hide? As bad as they might be, she thought that his emotional scars were probably worse.

Whatever else her brother might have been, he'd never been a liar. "I believe you." Her simple acceptance brought tears to his eyes.

Justin closed his eyes and pinched the bridge of his nose, bringing his emotions quickly back under control. "Thank you." His simple words belied the deep emotion behind them. "It was thoughts of you that saved me, that got me through the long, dark years. You were the best thing in my life and I cursed the day I ever left home and left you behind. But I never gave up hope and I fought for what I wanted. And after fifteen long years," his voice trembled slightly, "I'm finally home."

Now it was her turn to cry. His blunt, honest words moved her deeply. The awkwardness that she'd expected between them didn't exist. This was the brother she remembered, the one she'd looked up to and loved. "Welcome home."

The waitress bustled over to their table, deposited their lunch and hurried away again. The first tentative seeds had been sown, and deep down inside, Candy knew that she finally had her brother back in her life for good.

Sensing his unease with talking about his past, she sought to lighten the mood between them. "Do you have a wife or a girlfriend?" She was suddenly eager to know as much as possible about his life now.

"No, honey." If it was possible, his eyes looked even sadder as he shook his head. "My work didn't encourage close relationships."

There was something in his words, in the hesitant way he spoke them that made her ask, "But there was someone, wasn't there?"

Justin laid down his spoon and rubbed his hand across the back of his neck. "It was a long time ago, Candy. She died."

"Oh, Justin. I'm so very sorry." Although she wanted to know what had happened, she knew she would never ask him. If he wanted her to know, he would tell her.

"Yeah," he sighed. "Me too." He picked up his coffee and took a sip, his eyes scanning the room. "What about you?"

"Me?"

The corner of his mouth tilted up slightly. It wasn't quite a smile, but it was close. "Yeah, you? Did you ever get married? Is there someone special in your life? I didn't ask Mom about your love life." He stopped and the glimmer of a smile was wiped off his face. "You don't have to tell me if you don't want to."

"No," she assured him. "I don't mind. It's no secret or anything. I never got married. Never really came close." She thought about Gary's revelation and knew that she'd gotten closer than she'd ever thought. "I was seeing someone, but, well…" she stumbled. "It didn't work out."

"I'm sorry, Candy. It's his loss." He reached over and took her hand.

She shook her head. "No, it was as much my fault as his. Probably even more of my fault. I didn't trust him when he needed it. I hurt him badly."

Justin wrapped his fingers tight around hers, giving her an encouraging squeeze. "Then don't give up on him. Some things are worth fighting for." He released her hand and resumed eating his soup. He had a few mouthfuls and paused. "Sometimes hope is all we have."

His words reverberated in her head. He'd never given up hope and he'd faced long, hard years. T. S. had told her not to give up on Lucas. If she really loved him, she owed it to herself and to Lucas not to give up on them. If nothing else, they needed to talk. She'd needed to apologize to him for not wanting to listen to him at first. They'd both hurt the other one with their lack of trust and understanding. But Candy wasn't willing to let go of what they had without fighting for it.

The rest of lunch was fairly quiet, as if the emotion of the first few minutes was more then enough for them both to deal with. Talk turned to more mundane things. She told him about her work and he told her that he'd rented an apartment not far from hers. He walked her back to work and they made plans to have supper early next week.

Back at her desk, Candy picked up her pen, tapping it against the top of her desk. Lunch with her brother had certainly given her a lot to think about. And while she was willing to fight for her and Lucas' relationship, she was also realistic enough to know that wanting something to happen didn't guarantee success. There might be no way to repair the damage that had been done to their relationship. If that happened, she knew she'd want a change.

Picking up the phone, she reached out and snagged the phone number that Ms. Bates had given her and dialed quickly before she changed her mind. It was answered almost immediately on the other end. Candy took a deep breath. "This is Candy Logan. If the job is still open, I'd like to interview for it and find out more about the position."

By the time the conversation was over, she had an appointment for the next day. She already knew it would be no problem for her to take a personal day and fly to New York City. She could go and check out this job and be home again by tomorrow night.

Then she'd make her final attempt with Lucas. She had a plan. She reached for the phone again, filled with renewed determination. Dialing the number, she waited as the phone began to ring.

Chapter Seventeen

∞

Lucas threw himself into his work. He wasn't sleeping and spent all his time either working out or baking. In fact, his shop had never been so well stocked and running so efficiently. He even had all of his paperwork up-to-date. Thankfully, T. S. had let him know that he'd seen Candy home safe and sound—otherwise he would have gone out of his mind with worry.

Awake, he tormented himself with the images of their last night together. His crude demands and rough treatment replayed like a never-ending loop in his brain, torturing him. Several times a day, he picked up the phone to call her just to ask if she was all right. But each time he did, he hung up again. He didn't deserve to know.

And asleep…that was worse than when he was awake. Every night, he dreamed of Candy. Long, hot, erotic dreams filled with her loving him in every way imaginable. Last night's had been the worst, or the best, depending on how he felt at any given moment. Naked and glistening in the moonlight, she'd climbed on top of him and taken him inside her. Then she'd ridden him slowly at first, gradually moving faster and faster until they'd both come.

Lucas shuddered. He hadn't had a wet dream since he was a teenager, but he'd had one last night. But what was worse was the empty sense of longing he'd had when he'd awoken and found his arms and his bed empty. But it was for the best, he reminded himself. He loved her too much not to protect her, even if that meant he lost her.

He'd taken off after work and gone for a long walk. He'd wandered the city streets for hours, ignoring the bite of the winter air as it whipped past him. He'd hoped to clear his head, but it hadn't helped. If anything, his thoughts were even more jumbled than before.

Unlocking the side door of the building, he let himself in and locked the door behind him. T. S.'s van was still parked outside even though quitting time had been several hours ago.

Climbing the stairs, he wondered if T. S. wanted to split a pizza and a few beers. He could use the distraction. As he rounded the corner and headed up the next flight, he heard the clunk of work boots coming toward him. His friend bound down the stairs, obviously on his way home.

"Hey, man. About time you got home."

Lucas paused on the stairs. "I went out for a walk." He shrugged and stuffed his hands in the pockets of his leather coat. "I thought it might help."

"Did it?" T. S. came to a halt a few steps above him, his expression concerned.

Once again, he shrugged. "Not really." Sighing, he dragged his hands back out of his pockets and shoved one hand through his hair. "You want to go get a pizza or something?"

"Or something," he muttered. Shaking his head, T. S. continued on down the stairs until he was even with Lucas. "I've got to go. Just remember that no matter what, I've only done what I thought was best for you."

That sounded ominous. "What have you done?" His brow furrowed as he stared at his friend, trying to read his expression. But T. S. was very good at hiding his emotions.

"Only what I had to do. Hopefully, once you get over being mad, you'll thank me." He glanced down at his watch. "I gotta go. I'll talk to you tomorrow." He left Lucas standing there and hurried down the stairs. The door slammed shut behind him as he left the building.

Shaking his head, Lucas continued up the stairs to his apartment. He supposed he'd find out what that was all about eventually. Mentally, he ran through the contents of his refrigerator. There wasn't much there. Perhaps he'd order a pizza for himself.

Unlocking the door to his apartment, he let himself into the dark interior. Removing his leather coat, he hung it up on a hook just inside the door before he bent over and yanked off his boots. The walk and the cold wind had tired him, and he reached his arms above his head and stretched. He stood there debating between a long, hot shower and ordering some supper for himself.

A slight shuffling sound caught his attention and he froze. Someone was in his apartment. The snap of a lamp being turned on was unnaturally loud and the brightness from the overhead light momentarily blinded him. He froze as his vision returned, unable to believe his eyes.

"Hello, Lucas." Candy was curled up on his sofa, waiting for him. A soft smile lit her beautiful face.

"What are you doing here?" Her smile faded at his harsh tone, but there was nothing he could do about that. He had to get her out of here fast before he gave in to temptation, tossed her over his shoulder, dragged her to his bedroom and fucked her all night long. He'd kill T. S. for this, because there was no doubt in his mind that it was his friend who'd let her in. He was the only other person with keys.

Uncurling her legs, she stood. Only her thin stockings covered her feet and her toes curled against the area rug. Lucas wanted to pluck her into his arms and carry her so her feet wouldn't be cold. Propping his hands on his waist, he glared at her as she padded across the floor toward him.

She didn't stop until she was standing right in front of him, her toes touching his. It hit him just how much smaller than him she really was. Her personality was so huge and the high heels that she favored made her seem much larger than she truly was. In truth, she was a tiny bundle of curves. He almost smiled as he pictured how she'd bristle if he said such a thing to her.

The urge to smile left him when she placed her hand on his chest. "I came to talk to you."

"There's nothing to talk about." It was ridiculous that a woman about eight inches shorter and about eighty pounds lighter could hold him in place with just the touch of one hand. But it was true. Lucas didn't think he could force himself to move away from her touch if his life depended on it. "It was a great time, but it's over." He stared at a spot over her shoulder, refusing to look at her.

"What are you so afraid of, Lucas?" Her soft question struck him like a physical blow. How could she even ask him that after what had happened the last time they were together?

The scowl on his face had been known to make grown men flinch with fear. Lucas slowly lowered his gaze to hers, but instead of being frightened, she looked almost serene. For some reason, that fired his temper all the more. "What am I afraid of?" His voice was mocking. "What am I afraid of?" His voice was louder now. "What the hell do you think I'm afraid of?" The last question was half shouted as he gripped her by the shoulders and shifted her away from him. The temptation to shake some sense into her was almost overwhelming. Didn't she have any concept of self-preservation?

"Yourself? Me?" She stepped closer to him again. "Both?"

"You have no right to be in my apartment." Lucas stepped back out of her reach as he searched for her coat. The quicker he got her out of here, the better.

"I know." She followed him as he turned and walked away from her. "I know I hurt you the other day and I'm sorry for that. It was a knee-jerk reaction because of my own past." Like a terrier, she nipped at heels. He couldn't shake her or her words. "My own father spent most of his life in prison, and my brother's been there as well. I know what that did to my mother and to me. It was the last thing I wanted for myself."

Lucas halted so suddenly that Candy slammed into his back. He whirled around and caught her before she tripped and fell. No wonder she'd reacted to the news like she had. He didn't blame her for not wanting a man with such a dark past in her life. But she wasn't finished.

Grabbing onto the front of his T-shirt, she kept talking. "But it didn't take me long to realize that you're not like my father at all. He was always making promises he couldn't keep and blaming other people for everything that went wrong in his life. But you…" She gripped his shirt even tighter. "You're a man of integrity. You work hard and if you say you're going to do something, it's as good as done. No matter what's happened in your past, it doesn't matter. I know you had your reasons."

The pain almost brought him to his knees. These were the words he'd longed to hear. And maybe if he'd heard them before he'd manhandled her the other night, they would have made a difference. But the other night had been a reminder of the tainted blood flowing through his veins. He had a temper and a history of violence that he'd tried to leave behind him. But it always lurked, just under the surface. He knew what he was capable of doing. And it scared him.

She looked so earnest staring up at him. Her chocolate brown eyes were huge and luminous with unshed tears. Once again, he was hurting her even though it was the very last thing he wanted to do. He cupped her face in his hands. "Thank you for that, Candy. But it's still over between us."

"Why?" She covered his hands with her own, trapping them against the softness of her cheeks. "Why is it over?"

He decided that honesty was the only way out. Once he told her the truth, she'd understand why she had to leave. "Because I'll only hurt you in the long run."

"I don't understand."

He gently pulled his hands away and paused to push a lock of hair back behind her ear. "I know." He didn't want to see the look of disgust on her face and the fear that was sure to come, but he knew he no longer had a choice. "My father beat me and my mother."

No longer able to look at Candy, he turned and walked across the room and stared blindly out the window. "He was angry all the time. Anything and everything set him off." Lucas tried to block out the memories that threatened. "I'd come home from working at the market and had fallen into bed. I'd been saving my money and was planning to move out in less than a month. It was the screams that woke me."

The world outside the window faded as the past replayed in his mind. "I don't know why that night was different from any other. It just was. My mother was bleeding when I got to the living room and I challenged the old man, told him to leave her alone." He shook his head at his own stupidity. "I was tall but scrawny back then, and my father was a huge man. But I was so angry. It was as if a red haze enveloped me and I wanted to kill him. Next thing I knew, he was lying on the floor unconscious and my mother was telling me to run before the cops got there. The neighbors always called the cops. But it was too late."

The glass was cool against his fingers when he laid his hand against it. "I was arrested, sent to trial and found guilty. Didn't seem to matter what the old man had done." Lowering his hand, he turned around, surprised to find Candy right behind him. He hadn't heard her approach.

"What happened to your mother?"

Lucas closed his eyes against the pain, the memory as sharp as it had been all those years ago. "He beat her to death not long after I went to prison."

"Oh, Lucas." Her arms wrapped around him, her grip surprisingly strong as she hugged him. "I'm so sorry." He could hear the tears in her voice as she sniffed and buried her face against his chest.

This was the first time he'd ever shared his sorrow over his mother's death with anyone else. No one had ever hugged him and told him they were sorry or shed tears for him. T. S. knew what had happened, and so did Katie, but both of them had always respected his right to bear it alone. But not Candy.

His arms slid around her waist, pulling her tight to him. He lowered his head, nuzzling his face against the softness of the curve of her neck, reveling in her caring as she reached up and stroked her hand through his hair. But reality finally intruded and he made himself step away from her once again. "Now you see why it's over between us."

Her eyebrows came together as she frowned at him. "I'm so sorry for what happened to you and your mother. But I don't understand what that has to do with us."

Lucas' already frayed temper began to heat up again. "Because I'm like my father, Candy. His blood runs through my veins. I look in the mirror every single day and see his face staring back at me. I'm capable of beating a man almost to death." Swearing, he stalked away, prowling around the room. "Then there's the other night."

"What about the other night?" He could hear the caution in her voice.

"I took you without care or control the other night. I was no better than an animal, lashing out at you in anger. I hurt you, Candy." He was in agony now, just wanting her to leave so he could lick his wounds in private. He'd never felt so emotionally exposed in his entire life. "I won't risk your safety."

"That is the biggest load of bull I've ever heard."

He whirled around and she was right behind him. Anger raced through him. How dare she make light of this! He'd just laid himself emotionally bare before her and she was mocking him. "It's not bull."

She poked her index finger at his chest. "Yes. It. Is." She spaced each word carefully as if he wouldn't understand her any other way. "You're a coward."

A fury unlike anything he'd ever experience enveloped him. How dare she accuse him of being a coward? "Don't push me, sugar. You won't like what happens."

"Oh, yeah?" She got right in his face, practically boring a hole in his chest with her finger. "What are you going to do?" she demanded. "Hit me?"

It was as if all the blood drained from his body. "God, no. I would never hit you, sugar." He felt himself sway on his feet.

"Exactly." She wrapped her hands around his neck and forced his head downward until he was staring right at her, their noses practically touching. "You would never hurt me physically."

"But the other night—"

She interrupted him. "Was the most erotic experience of my life."

He could see the sincerity in her eyes. But most of all, he could see the love. A weight seemed to fall away from him as the significance of what had just happened finally seemed to seep into him. Yes, he had come from violence and was capable of violence, but never against her or anyone he truly loved.

"Lucas, your past has made you the man you are. You're so controlled and self-contained it's almost scary. Yes, we'll probably fight and yell at each other." She laughed. "We're both such strong-willed people, I don't think we can avoid that. But." She stroked her hand over his face and smiled at him. "You'll never hit me. You're not capable of harming a woman."

Her belief in him humbled him. And her hand on his face and the closeness of her body was arousing him unbearably. His earlier anger had transmuted itself into lust. He wanted Candy. No, he needed her. He needed to claim her as his, once and for all.

"Be sure, sugar. Because once I take you, there's no going back." His cock was rock-hard beneath his jeans and the urge to fuck her was all-consuming.

In answer, she whipped her blouse over her head and dropped it to the floor. "I certainly hope not." Her smile was wicked and filled with erotic promise as she turned and sauntered toward the bedroom, her lush hips swaying gently from side to side.

The pure, unadulterated happiness that filled him was only superseded by the lust for this woman that pounded through his body. She was his and once he claimed her, he would never let her go.

Swooping down on her, he caught her up in his arms and tossed her over his shoulder. She laughed and reached down and squeezed his butt in response. He swatted her bottom playfully as she did it again. And her shrieks of delight mixed with his own low laughter as he carried her into the bedroom and kicked the door shut behind him.

Chapter Eighteen

ɕͻ

One minute Candy was hanging over Lucas' shoulder and the next she was flying through the air. She bounced once on the mattress before sinking back against its softness.

He followed her down onto the bed, his expression intense as he framed her face in his hands. "Although there's been nothing in the papers about what happened at the talk show taping, there's still a chance it will get out. If not now, then someday. My past will always be there, sugar. I'm a rough man with a violent past. That will never change."

She stared up into the face of the man she loved and knew deep in her heart that his past no longer mattered to her. "What you are is a good man, Lucas. The best I've ever known." She covered his hands with her own. "I'm sorry for your past because it hurt you, and I'm sorry for the death of your mother. But I'm glad that I found you."

He closed his eyes and nodded. When he reopened them, they were blazing with undisguised lust. But beyond that, she could see the deep, abiding love, and it filled her with hope for the future. This was a man a woman could depend on, now and forever. And he was all hers!

One question nagged at her. She hated to ask, afraid of ruining the mood, but she had to know. "What happened to your father?"

Lucas sat back on his heels, reached his hands behind his back, grabbed a handful of fabric and yanked his T-shirt off over his head. He flung it aside as he leaned over and found the opening of her skirt. "He died in prison." Making quick work of the zipper, he tugged her skirt down her legs, tossing it behind him.

She knew that Lucas didn't want to talk about it any longer and that was fine with her. She knew what she needed to know. While she still had many questions to ask him, they could wait. Right now, she needed him to make love to her. Needed to join her body to his and give him the comfort and release from his torment that sex could provide.

Smiling at him, she stroked her hands up her belly and cupped her lace-covered breasts. She was wearing a new strawberry-colored lacy bra and matching panties. "Do you like my new lingerie?" She batted her eyelashes, flirting shamelessly with him.

He laughed and the sound was like music to her ears. "You look good enough to eat." His voice was low and gruff and sent shivers down her spine. He licked his lips as he leaned down. "And I plan to taste every sweet inch of you."

His tongue traced the edge of the lace, sweeping across the top of her breast. A fire was burning low in her belly and she knew that only he could appease it. What was it about this particular man that ignited such passion and desire in her? He raised his head and the sensual gleam in his eyes curled her toes. And when his mouth covered her nipple, sucking at it through the thin lace covering, thought fled and was replaced by physical need.

The fabric of his jeans was rough against her skin as he settled between her legs. The action spread her legs wide, draping them over his hard thighs. His fingers trailed up her arms, raising goose bumps in their wake. He hooked his thumbs beneath the strap of her bra and slowly lowered it over her arms, dragging the lace cups from her breasts.

"Beautiful," he whispered reverently as he skimmed the tips of her breasts with his fingers. The light touch seemed to reach every nerve ending in her body, making her tingle from head to toe.

He stroked his tongue across one swollen peak before taking it deep into his mouth and sucking hard. Candy gasped and arched her hips. She felt so empty inside. "Lucas," she moaned as she clutched at his shoulders, digging her nails deep.

He growled, the sound low in his throat, as he left her breasts and kissed a heated path down her torso to her bellybutton. Dipping his tongue inside, he swirled it around. Her fingers tugged at his hair, trying to push him lower. He laughed and nipped at her hipbones, which were exposed by the low cut of her panties.

She could feel the dampness between her thighs and knew he could smell and feel her desire for him as he dragged his tongue over the lacy fabric.

Lucas sat back on his heels and traced the lace band at the top of her thigh-high stockings. "You're so fucking sexy in these and those ridiculous high heels you usually wear. But right now, I don't want anything between us."

She almost took offense at his disparaging remark about her footwear. Almost. But when he edged his fingers beneath the band of the stocking and began to slowly roll it down her leg, she promptly forgot everything but the feel of his hand against her skin. As he lowered the stocking down her leg, he kissed and licked every inch of flesh he exposed. By the time he got to her foot, she was sweating.

He whisked the stocking off and kissed the top of each of her toes as he dug his thumbs into her arch. "Oh, God," she moaned as his fingers continued their magic on her foot. He stroked the sides of her foot and the bottom, paying particular attention to her arch and the ball. It was heaven.

Just when she was a mass of jelly on the bed, he placed a kiss on the arch of her foot before lowering it back to the bed. Then he reached for the top of the stocking on her other leg and began all over again.

Candy scrunched her fingers into the sheets as she rolled her head from side to side. His lips and tongue were hot against her leg as he stripped her stocking away from her.

Then he proceeded to treat her other foot to the same amazing foot rub. It was incredible.

By the time he placed a kiss on the arch of her foot and lowered it back to the bed, Candy was purring with contentment. She curled her toes against the sheets, feeling strangely relaxed and aroused at the same time.

Lucas rolled off the bed and peeled off his jeans. Luckily for her, he seemed to dislike wearing underwear and he was naked in a matter of seconds. Her blood thickened as she stared at him.

His shoulders were impossibly wide and his arms were thick with muscles. His chest had a smattering of dark blond hair between his nipples and a thin, narrow line down the center. His torso tapered down to a trim but muscular waist. But it was what was below his waist that held her attention at the moment. His cock was long and thick as it jutted out from the nest of hair at his groin. She'd never met a man as physically impressive as Lucas. And he was all hers.

"Roll over."

Anticipation flooded her body as she languidly rolled over onto her stomach. Her panties rubbed against her sex, making her moan. He laughed as he stroked his finger along the thin band of fabric between her bottom. "You want it bad, don't you sugar?" His thumb grazed the puckered opening of her behind, making her squirm.

"I like the thong you're wearing." His hands squeezed the globes of exposed flesh. "You've got a great ass." Candy pushed up on her knees slightly, thrusting her behind more firmly into his hands. Bending down, he stroked his tongue down the line of her panties before nipping at her bottom with his teeth. The love bites drove her wild as he left no area untouched.

Coming up on his hands and knees, he covered her with his body. She could feel his breath on her nape as he pushed aside the mass of her hair, exposing her neck to him. He started at the top and worked his way down to the base of her spine, licking, sucking and kissing her. The man really was trying to taste every inch of her.

He rubbed his erection against the cleft of her behind and she opened her legs wider to try to get more pressure where she needed it most.

"Lucas," she cried, shoving her hips back toward him. "I want you." Rubbing her slit against his cock, she pushed hard. "Now."

She felt his large body shudder with need and then, finally, his hands skimmed the waistband of her panties. But he didn't pull them off. Grabbing the lace in his hands, he tugged. The fabric shredded instantly, no match for his strength or the force of his need. He shoved the remainder of her panties down her leg. The air was cool against her heated flesh and she gasped at the erotic sensation.

Lucas leaned to one side and she heard a drawer open and close, followed by the familiar crinkle of a condom being opened. "What do you want? Tell me, Candy. Do you want my cock in your ass or your pussy? Do you want it hard and fast or slow and easy?"

"Yes," she cried as his words ignited a fire deep in her soul. She never thought she'd want to do those all things with a man, but with Lucas she wanted everything.

"What, sugar? Tell me!" His hands were almost rough as he gripped her hips. "Show me?"

Candy came up on her hands and knees, spreading her thighs wide. "I want it all, Lucas." She pushed her ass higher. "I want everything."

His fingers dug in deep, as if needing something to anchor himself. Candy curled her fingers, grabbing fistfuls of the sheets. She could hear him take a deep breath before he slid one of his hands between her legs and stroked it across her sex. It was exciting and arousing to be at the mercy of Lucas' sexual whims, to open herself up to him, offering him whatever he needed. Her breathing was shallow and her body taut as she waited to see what he would do.

His temples pounded because of the blood rushing to his head. Need unlike anything he'd ever experienced threatened to overwhelm him. Candy was his. She knew everything about him, yet she had made herself vulnerable to him, offering him everything and anything he wanted. She was his for the taking. If there was anything more arousing, he didn't know what it could possibly be.

He could smell the heat of her arousal, feel it as his fingers were coated in her cream. She was on her hands and knees in front of him with her legs spread, eager to take him in whatever way he chose. "Open your legs wider."

He almost howled in triumph when her knees slid across the sheets. He'd never seen a more beautiful sight than Candy with her lush ass and wet, pink cunt totally exposed to him. His cock throbbed as he rolled on the condom and coated it in lubricant, demanding he take her and mark her as no other man ever had.

Coating his fingers with her juices, he rubbed them along the dark cleft of her behind, tracing the tight opening before pushing the tip of his finger inside. She was tight, but he forged inward until his finger was buried as far as it could go. With his other hand, he teased the slick folds of her sex, occasionally dipping inside her slit.

Candy slowly undulated her hips as he removed his finger from her tight bottom. Grabbing the tube of lubricant that he'd already opened, he coated his fingers with the cool, slick gel. He pushed one finger past the taut band of muscles at her opening and then carefully began to insert a second one inside her ass.

"You're so tight, sugar." Lucas could feel a bead of sweat roll down his back as the muscles of her behind clamped down on his fingers. He didn't want to hurt her.

"I know," she moaned. "It hurts, but it feels so good too."

He stroked his thumb over her swollen clitoris as he pushed two fingers into her pussy. She was so aroused, so close to coming. He could feel it in the way her muscles rhythmically tightened and released. It was now or never.

He removed his fingers from her behind and carefully inserted the tip of his cock. It was a tight squeeze, but the gel he'd spread over the condom helped. Lucas' chest was heaving as he struggled to control himself. He didn't want to come until Candy did.

The hand teasing her pussy was soaked with her juices as he continued to stroke his fingers in and out of her depths. She was crying out now and when she pushed her ass back against him, he slid deeper into her. His cock was only about halfway into her, but he didn't think she could take any more. Not now.

And it was enough that she wanted to take him this way. Had taken him. Her cries were frantic now as she bucked against him, seeking release. He pushed harder with his fingers, stroking her clit, driving deep into her core. Shoving a third finger inside her, he felt the change. Her entire body spasmed, clamping down on his fingers and his cock.

Lucas gritted his teeth and hung on, trying not to come yet. But his balls drew up tight to his body and his cock began to pulse. It was too late. The muscle in his jaw throbbed as he forced himself to keep his body steady. The need to shove his cock deep was overwhelming, but the need to never hurt Candy was greater. So, as he held his body rigid, his cock jerked as he came.

As their bodies shivered and shook with their release, Lucas closed his eyes and absorbed every feeling. It was incredible. It was only when Candy began to slip back down to the mattress that he carefully removed his fingers from her pussy. Bracing his hand on the bed to keep from slumping down on top of her, he groaned as he eased his cock from her behind.

Using what energy he had left, he rolled to the side of the bed and removed the condom, dumping it in the bedside garbage container. Candy hadn't moved from where she'd slumped back against the mattress. Lucas tugged the sheets out from under her and crawled in next to her, pulling the covers over them both. He eased her into his arms and she snuggled, settling herself against his chest. Her breath feathered across his skin as she slept easily in his arms. He tightened his arms around her as he drifted off to sleep.

Candy awoke feeling better than she had in days. The feel of a large, male body tucked so closely around her own assured her that it hadn't been just a dream. They were both lying on their sides facing each other and she could feel the steady rhythm of his heart beneath her palm. A calm descended upon her. This was where she belonged.

Her eyes snapped open as she felt his cock growing, pushing against her stomach. His pale blue eyes twinkled and his lips were turned up in a wicked grin. "I guess you're awake," she teased.

"I guess I am." As he stretched one hand over his head, she thought he resembled nothing more than a sleepy, satisfied bear.

"Is it morning yet?" She stifled a yawn.

"No." He brushed a lock of hair out of her face and smoothed it over her shoulder. "It's still night."

She tangled her fingers in his chest hair before flicking one of his nipples. "So, where do we go from here?" Part of her knew that this conversation should wait until morning, but the other part of her needed to know where she stood.

He froze next to her. She could feel every muscles tighten beneath her hand. "Where do you want to go?"

Candy was beginning to wish that she'd kept her mouth shut until morning when she was thinking more clearly. She shrugged, stared at his chest and tried to figure out what to say. She didn't want to say anything to disturb their newfound closeness, but she wanted him to know everything. "I got a job offer." She hesitated when she felt him tense next to her. "In New York City."

"I see." He sat up in bed and she was left staring at his back. "Is it a good job?"

She wished she could see his face. It might give her a clue as to how he felt about this. "Yes, it's a great job with a huge publishing company. The salary and benefits are much better than I have now."

"That's good."

"I haven't decided to take it." She sat up, tugging the covers around her as she reached out and placed her hand on his back. He flinched when she touched him, but didn't move away.

"If it's the best thing for you, then maybe you should."

She froze. "Didn't tonight mean anything to you?"

"Sugar." He turned and slipped a finger under her chin, tilting it up until she was looking into his face. "Tonight meant everything to me. I love you." His face was solemn as he stroked her jaw with his thumb. "I want you in my life. Now and forever." He paused and his smile was tinged with sadness. "I know you might not be ready for that right now, and maybe you might never be ready. But I'll take whatever you want to give me. If we have to have a long-distance relationship, then I'm willing to try. I can't leave my new location right away, but I can come to New York on weekends and you can come back here. We can make it work."

The sheer depth of emotion in his voice mesmerized Candy. He loved her. He had said the words, but more than that, his every action proclaimed it. She knew he'd held back when they'd made love. His care for her humbled her, while at the same time, it made her heart sing.

He'd been brave—she could do no less. "I love you too." She stroked her thumb across his bottom lip. "I want to be with you. Now and forever. I never really wanted to move, but I knew I couldn't stay here if things didn't work out between us. Too many memories."

"Are you sure, sugar? I don't want you to regret not taking that job at some point in the future." His brows furrowed. "Your career is important." He nipped at her thumb, teasing the pad between his straight white teeth.

And he thought he was too rough and uncaring. Candy was moved by his concern for her. "I'm sure." She reached out and stroked her fingers over his brow, smoothing away his frown. "I'm happy where I am. And I don't want to leave my life here."

"You'll move in with me?"

"You asking me or telling me?" His quick change of subject left her breathless. He certainly was moving fast.

Lucas laughed. "Asking, sugar. Like I said, I'll take what I can get."

"Yes." Candy wanted to love Lucas again. This time, she didn't want him to have to hold anything back.

"Marry me, sugar?" The words tumbled from his mouth in a rush. "Damn, I didn't mean to ask yet. I wanted to buy a ring and cook you supper. Set the scene and do it right. Forget I said that."

"No."

Lucas closed his eyes and hung his head. "That's okay, sugar. I understand." He raised his head and tried to smile. "Like I said, I'll take what I can get."

"I didn't mean no, I won't marry you. I meant no, I can't forget you asked."

Lucas froze. "What does that mean exactly?"

Joy spilled through her veins as she launched herself at him, knocking him onto his back as she climbed on top of him. "Yes. Oh, yes." She covered his beloved face in kisses. "I'll marry you, Lucas."

Her lips covered his and their kiss deepened. Lucas wrapped his hand around the back of her neck and pulled her tight as he devoured her mouth, claiming it for his own. His cock nudged against the inside of her thigh and she reached behind her to stroke it with her hand.

Lucas tore his mouth from hers. "Take me inside you, Candy."

She didn't hesitate. Raising herself up on her knees, she slowly lowered herself onto him. This time there was no barrier between them, and the feeling was exquisite. Placing her hands on his chest for support, she wiggled around until she was comfortable.

Lucas laughed. "You're killing me, sugar." He gripped her hips in his hands and held her steady. "As good as this feels, I need to get a condom."

She smiled at him as she began to move, slowly lifting herself up and then coming back down. "I'm on the Pill. I've also got a clean bill of health."

"I've never made love without protection, except for the other night with you, so I'm clean." His hips bucked beneath her. "You're sure?" he gritted out between clenched teeth.

"Oh, yes," she moaned.

"Thank God," he gasped as she raised herself again. This time she came back down harder. "This feels so fucking good. As good as I dreamed it would."

"And have you dreamed of me?" Riding him like this made her feel powerful and wicked.

"You have no idea," he groaned as she continued to tease him, riding him harder and harder.

It was much later when Lucas finally came back to his senses again. Candy was draped across his body and his semi-erect cock was still inside her. Just as she had in his dreams, she'd ridden him until he'd exploded. But the reality was far better then the dream could ever be.

He loved the weight of her body covering him and held her tight when she shifted as if to move away from him. She yawned against his chest. "We still have so much to talk about."

"We'll talk tomorrow and the day after that and the day after that," he assured her.

"I want you to meet my brother." Her voice slurred slightly.

"I'd like that, sugar." He stroked her back with his hand, soothing her. "There are some things I need to tell you too."

"Okay." Her easy acceptance made his heart swell with love.

"It's about those brownies you love so well." He needed to tell her about the money that he'd made selling the recipe.

"Yum," she whispered. "You'll make me brownies."

His arms tightened around her. "I'll make you brownies."

"Love you." He knew the moment she finally gave up the fight and drifted off to sleep.

"I love you too, Candy." He was still awake when dawn broke across the horizon, but for the first time in years, he was looking forward to the future.

Also by N.J. Walters

∞

Amethyst Moon

Annabelle Lee

Anastasia's Style

Awakening Desires 1: Katie's Art of Seduction

Awakening Desires 2: Erin's Fancy

Dalakis Passion 1: Harker's Journey

Dalakis Passion 2: Lucian's Delight

Dalakis Passion 3: Stefan's Salvation

Dalakis Passion 4: Eternal Brothers

Drakon's Treasure

Ellora's Cavemen: Dreams of the Oasis IV (*anthology*)

Ellora's Cavemen: Legendary Tails IV (*anthology*)

Ellora's Cavemen: Seasons of Seduction III (*anthology*)

Heat Wave

Jessamyn's Christmas Gift

Tapestries 1: Christina's Tapestry

Tapestries 2: Bakra Bride

Tapestries 3: Woven Dreams

Three Swords, One Heart

Unmasking Kelly

About the Author

☙

N.J. Walters worked at a bookstore for several years and one day had the idea that she would like to quit her job, sell everything she owned, leave her hometown and write romance novels in a place where no one knew her. And she did. Two years later, she went back to the same bookstore and settled in for another seven years.

Although she was still fairly young, that was when the mid-life crisis set in. Happily married to the love of her life, with his encouragement (more like, "For God's sake, quit the job and just write!") she gave notice at her job on a Friday morning. On Sunday afternoon, she received a tentative acceptance for her first erotic romance novel, Annabelle Lee, and life would never be the same.

N.J. has always been a voracious reader of romance novels, and now she spends her days writing novels of her own. Vampires, dragons, time-travelers, seductive handymen and next-door neighbors with smoldering good looks all vie for her attention. And she doesn't mind a bit. It's a tough life, but someone's got to live it.

N.J. Walters welcomes comments from readers. You can find her website and email address on her author bio page at www.ellorascave.com.

Tell Us What You Think

We appreciate hearing reader opinions about our books. You can email us at Comments@EllorasCave.com.

Why an electronic book?

We live in the Information Age—an exciting time in the history of human civilization, in which technology rules supreme and continues to progress in leaps and bounds every minute of every day. For a multitude of reasons, more and more avid literary fans are opting to purchase e-books instead of paper books. The question from those not yet initiated into the world of electronic reading is simply: *Why?*

1. *Price.* An electronic title at Ellora's Cave Publishing and Cerridwen Press runs anywhere from 40% to 75% less than the cover price of the exact same title in paperback format. Why? Basic mathematics and cost. It is less expensive to publish an e-book (no paper and printing, no warehousing and shipping) than it is to publish a paperback, so the savings are passed along to the consumer.

2. *Space.* Running out of room in your house for your books? That is one worry you will never have with electronic books. For a low one-time cost, you can purchase a handheld device specifically designed for e-reading. Many e-readers have large, convenient screens for viewing. Better yet, hundreds of titles can be stored within your new library—on a single microchip. There are a variety of e-readers from different manufacturers. You can also read e-books on your PC or laptop computer. (Please note that Ellora's Cave does not endorse any specific brands.

You can check our websites at www.ellorascave.com or www.cerridwenpress.com for information we make available to new consumers.)

3. *Mobility.* Because your new e-library consists of only a microchip within a small, easily transportable e-reader, your entire cache of books can be taken with you wherever you go.

4. *Personal Viewing Preferences.* Are the words you are currently reading too small? Too large? Too... ANNOYING? Paperback books cannot be modified according to personal preferences, but e-books can.

5. *Instant Gratification.* Is it the middle of the night and all the bookstores near you are closed? Are you tired of waiting days, sometimes weeks, for bookstores to ship the novels you bought? Ellora's Cave Publishing sells instantaneous downloads twenty-four hours a day, seven days a week, every day of the year. Our webstore is never closed. Our e-book delivery system is 100% automated, meaning your order is filled as soon as you pay for it.

Those are a few of the top reasons why electronic books are replacing paperbacks for many avid readers.

As always, Ellora's Cave and Cerridwen Press welcome your questions and comments. We invite you to email us at Comments@ellorascave.com or write to us directly at Ellora's Cave Publishing Inc., 1056 Home Avenue, Akron, OH 44310-3502.

Discover for yourself why readers can't get enough of the multiple award-winning publisher Ellora's Cave.

Whether you prefer e-books or paperbacks,

be sure to visit EC on the web at www.ellorascave.com

for an erotic reading experience that will leave you breathless.